THE O'HARA AFFAIR

Kate Thompson is an award-winning former actress. She is happily married with one daughter, and divides her time between Dublin and the West of Ireland, where she swims off some of the most beautiful beaches in the world.

For more information about Kate, please go to www.kate-thompson.com.

By the same author:
The Kinsella Sisters

KATE THOMPSON

The O'Hara Affair

AVON

AVON

A division of HarperCollins*Publishers*
77–85 Fulham Palace Road,
London W6 8JB

www.harpercollins.co.uk

A Paperback Original 2010
1

A catalogue record for this book is
available from the British Library

ISBN-13: 978-1-84756-100-8

Set in Minion by Palimpsest Book Production Limited,
Grangemouth, Stirlingshire

Printed and bound in Great Britain by
Clays Ltd, St Ives plc

A thousand heartfelt thanks go to the following: Maxine Hitchcock for her editorial vision; the team at Avon for their dedication and support – especially Keshini Naidoo, Sammia Rafique and Caroline Ridding; Charlotte Webb for her *nonpareil* copy-editing skills; Moira Reilly for her PR nous and pizzazz, and Claire Power for making my presence felt ☺; my friend Joan Bergin for consenting to be Fleur's real life pal; Cathy Kelly, Marian Keyes, Fiona O'Brien and Hilary Reynolds for their *beyond* invaluable sorority and for reading early drafts – and double thanks to Marian for allowing me to quote from her brilliant novel 'This Charming Man'. Thanks must also go to all those people I met on Second Life – especially burly Dave for the LOLs!

Finally, not enough thanks can go to my best and most beloved friends of all: my husband Malcolm; my daughter Clara.

In loving memory of my *belle-mère*, Hazel

'There comes a time in every woman's life when the only thing that helps is a glass of champagne.'
Bette Davis

Chapter One

Fleur O'Farrell felt foolish. She was standing in front of the wardrobe in her bedroom, regarding her reflection in the mirror. Fleur normally took real pride in her appearance – but this afternoon she was wearing a floral print skirt over flouncy petticoats, a cherry-red cummerbund, and a low-cut blouse. Her feet were bare, a silk shawl was slung around her shoulders, and great gilt hoops dangled from her earlobes. The crowning glory was the wig – an Esmeralda-style confection of synthetic black curls. She looked like a chorus member from a second-rate production of *Carmen*.

Her friend, Río Kinsella, had talked her in to playing the fortune-teller at the annual Lissamore village festival. Río usually took on the role herself, but this summer she was up to her tonsils in work, and had not a moment to spare. So Río had furnished Fleur with the gypsy costume, as well as a crystal ball, a chenille tablecloth and a manual called *Six Lessons in Crystal Gazing*. The flyleaf told Fleur that these words of wisdom had been published in 1928.

Turning away from the mirror, Fleur reached for the dog-eared booklet. The cover featured a bug-eyed gal transfixed by a crystal ball, and the blurb went: 'Are you lacking in self-confidence, unemployed or discouraged? Are you prepared

1

for the future, or blindly groping in the darkness? Do you wish for health, happiness and success?'

Evidently not a lot had changed in the world since 1928. People were still asking the same questions, and still entertaining the same hopes and ambitions. Nowadays, however, instead of using crystal gazing as a means of self-help, people were unrolling yoga mats and sticking Hopi candles in their ears to assist them in their navel gazing. Much the same thing, Fleur supposed. *Plus ça change, plus c'est la même chose . . .*

A blast of hip hop drew her to the open window. A youth was lazily patrolling the main street of the village, posing behind the steering wheel of his soft-top and checking out the talent. Being high season, there was a lot on display. Girls decked out in Roxy, Miss Sixty, and Diesel promenaded the pavements and lounged against the sea wall, hooked up to their iPods, gossiping on their phones or browsing on their BlackBerries. Beautiful girls with gym-toned figures and sprayed-on tans and GHD hair, sporting must-have designer eyewear and designer bags to match. High-maintenance girls, whose daddies footed the department-store bills and whose mummies stole their style. Girls who did not know what the word 'recession' meant.

Lissamore was not usually host to such quantities of de luxe *jeunesse dorée*. The village was, rather, a playground for their parents, a place where those jaded denizens of Dublin 4 came to unwind for a month in the summer and a week at Christmas. Once the yearned-for eighteenth birthdays arrived, the princelings and princesses tended to migrate to hipper locations in Europe or America.

But this summer, because a major motion picture was being made in the countryside surrounding Lissamore, the village had become a must-visit zone. Wannabe film stars had descended in their droves after an article in a national newspaper had mentioned that extras were being recruited for *The O'Hara Affair* – a movie based on the back story of Gerard O'Hara, father to Scarlett of *Gone with the Wind*. An additional allure was the fact that the movie starred Shane Byrne, a local hero and Ireland's answer to Johnny Depp.

The film was good news for the village during such a time of blanket economic gloom. Locals who had been made redundant since the collapse of the construction industry were being employed as carpenters and sparks and painters, hitherto jobless youngsters had been taken on as runners, and an ailing catering company had been given a new lease of life. Fleur's shop had been honoured with several visits by the film's leading lady, Río had charmed herself into being offered a gig as a set-dresser, and even Fleur's lover, Corban, was involved – albeit it at a remove. He was an executive producer on *The O'Hara Affair*, and, while his artistic contribution to the film was negligible, his money talked. Because he had part financed the production, he, too, was due a credit.

'Did he text back yet?' It was a girl's voice – a typical princess, to judge by the accent.

'No,' came the morose reply.

Craning her neck a little, Fleur looked down to see two girls sitting on the windowsill of her shop, Fleurissima, below. The girl with the D4 drawl she recognized – she had been in and out of the shop half a dozen times in the past fortnight, helping herself to pricey little wisps of silk and tulle paid for by Daddy's gold Amex.

'Did you put a question mark at the end of your last message?'

'Yes.'

'Shit. That means you can't text him again, Emily. Like, the ball's in his court now.'

3

'I know. I should never have put the stupid question mark. He's ignoring me, the bastard.'

'How many Xs did you put?'

'Three. But two of them were lower case.'

'Ow. Three's a bit heavy. I'd only put two lower case ones next time.'

'If there *is* a next time. There was a comment from that Australian girl on his Facebook this morning.'

'Uh-oh . . .'

Fleur felt like leaning out of the window and calling down: 'Just pick up the phone and *talk* to him!' But she knew that the rules laid down by mobile phone etiquette meant that picking up a phone was not an option. Fleur couldn't understand how kids nowadays coped with the uncertainty, the insecurity, the emotional turbulence generated by the text messaging phenomenon. It must be a kind of enforced purgatory, sending texts toing and froing through the ether – like playing ping-pong in slow motion.

But Fleur was as in thrall to her phone as the girls on the street below, she realized, because when her text alert sounded she automatically reached for her nifty little Nokia. Accessing the message, she saw that it was from her niece, Daisy. The text read: **Hey, Flirty! On my way now with cake & wine** ☺ **XXX**

Because Fleur's middle initial was T for Thérèse, Daisy had come up with the nickname 'Flirty' for her. Fleur loved it: it sounded so much more youthful and fun than 'Aunt Fleur', which was what her nephew called her.

Cake & wine sounds good, she texted back, adding ♥ for good measure.

Cake and wine *did* sound good. Especially wine. It had been busy in the shop today: Fleur's jaw was aching from all the smiling she'd been doing, and her feet were killing

4

her. Her boutique specialized in non-mainstream labels sourced from all over Europe: from evening chic to skinny jeans, from beachwear to accessories, all Fleur's stock was hand-picked and exclusive to her – and none of it was cheap. From October, when the tourist trade dropped off and the summer residences were boarded up, Fleur hibernated, opening the shop only at weekends. After today, when two overdue deliveries had arrived at the same time, Fleur was looking forward to hibernating already. She reached up a hand to pull off her gypsy wig, then decided against it. It would give Daisy something to laugh at, and she loved to hear her niece laugh.

Tossing her shawl on the bed, Fleur negotiated the spiral staircase that led down to her living area. Since the demise of her little dog Babette, Fleur had taken the brave step of redecorating. She had painted the walls in Farrow & Ball Wimborne White, had the floorboards sanded and lime washed, and her furniture reupholstered in pale damask. Cobwebby lace was draped around the windows, a pair of alabaster angels stood sentinel on either side of the fireplace, and a chandelier scintillated overhead. All eight of her dining chairs were overlaid with nubbly linen slip covers, and her chaise longue was piled with tasselled white cushions. Fleur's room was all white for a reason. She had sworn that she would never get another dog, because the pain she felt when Babette had died had been so unendurable she never wanted to go through anything like it again. And what better way to resist the allure of that puppy in the pet shop window or the sad eyes of a rescue dog in an ISPCA ad than by creating a pristine environment – one that would not welcome muddy paws or moulting hairs.

The only splashes of colour in the living space were courtesy of the artwork on the walls – much of which was by

Río. Most of Río's paintings were seascapes in vibrant oils, but the one that stood out was a portrait that had been painted some twenty years earlier. It depicted Fleur sitting back in her chair at the end of her long dining table, a glass of Bordeaux in front of her, a Gauloise between elegant fingers (she had stopped smoking two years later, and still missed it sometimes). Her hair was twisted into a loose chignon, and she was toying idly with a tendril that had escaped. Her attention was focused on someone to her right, someone with whom she was clearly rather coquettishly engaged. In truth, the painting depicted Fleur in full-on flirtatious mode, one eyebrow raised like a circumflex, mouth in a provocative pout, eyes agleam with intention. Fleur loved it.

Moving into the kitchen – where the aroma of last night's ragout still lingered – Fleur set a tray with plates, napkins, glasses and a wine cooler. She was just about to carry it through to the deck, when the door bell rang. 'Come on up, Daisy-Belle,' she purred into the intercom. 'I'm on the deck.'

Fleur's deck overlooked the Lissamore marina, and was perfect for spying on the comings and goings of boats and boatmen. Corban had a pleasure craft berthed there, but so far this summer he'd had few opportunities to use it, as he'd been stuck in Dublin on business. When Río had asked Fleur to describe her lover, Fleur had laughingly called him her very own Mr Big.

Corban was the latest in a fairly long line of *amours*: Fleur was most certainly not the marrying kind. She'd tried it once when, aged nineteen, she had fallen in love with a beautiful Irish boy who was studying at the Sorbonne in Paris. Fleur remembered that epoch only dimly, as one might remember scenes from an art house movie viewed long ago through rose-tinted glasses: picnic lunches by the Seine, reading the poems of Emily Dickinson and Sylvia Plath in translation; strolls through the narrow winding streets of the Latin Quarter; rough wine and rougher cigarettes in cheap café bars; stolen hours in his bed when the concierge was napping; visit after visit to museums and galleries, and hour after hour of gazing into each other's eyes, slack with desire and limp with adoration. And when Tom asked her to come with him to Ireland, she had said – breathless as Molly Bloom – 'Yes, yes! I will, yes!'

They had married in the registry office in Dublin, and for a year she was pleased to receive letters as Mrs Thomas O'Farrell. Thereafter, following her separation and subsequent divorce, she trashed any correspondence addressed to 'Mrs Thomas', 'Mrs Tom' or 'Mrs T. O'Farrell'. She would never be 'Mrs Tom, Dick or Harry' for any man. She was Fleur – Fleur Thérèse Odette O'Farrell (she'd retained the 'O'Farrell' because no one in Ireland could pronounce her real surname, which was de Saint-Euverte). And Tom? Tom had gone off to Canada with a Mountie. She hadn't seen him since.

'He*llo*! What in God's name are you wearing?' Fleur turned to see Daisy framed in the French windows, regarding her with a curious expression.

'It's my outfit for the village festival. Ta-ra!' Fleur held her skirts out and attempted a Flamenco-style twirl. 'I am the fortune-teller. What do you think? Smoking, ain't it?'

'Mystic Meg, eat your heart out,' replied Daisy, strolling across to the table and dumping a carrier bag on it. 'Let me take a photograph.' Holding up her iPhone, she adopted the exaggerated stance of a pro photographer, and segued into the usual clichéd directive: *Lovely! Chin a little higher! Drop your shoulder!*

Click, click, click went Daisy's camera, while Fleur twirled some more and hummed a little Bizet, and then Daisy slid her phone back into her bag and kissed her aunt on both cheeks. 'How did you get roped into being the fortune-teller?' she asked. 'I thought that was normally Río's gig.'

'I'll tell you later. I want to hear all your news first. Sit down and give me the wine and the cake.' Daisy took a bottle of wine and a cake-box from the carrier bag, and Fleur reached for the corkscrew. 'Have you seen sense and ditched that bad boy?' she asked, stripping foil from the neck of the bottle.

'Yes. You'll be glad to know the bad boy's ancient history, Flirty. But I've got some even better news.'

'Oh? What's that?'

'Guess.'

'You have landed a new contract?'

'No.'

'You've been asked to be a judge on *Ireland's Next Top Model*?'

'Yes, I have actually. But that's not the good news.'

'You have a photo-shoot with Testino.'

'In my dreams.'

Fleur poured wine into the glasses and handed one to Daisy. 'A *Vogue* cover?'

'Get real!'

'OK. I give up,' said Fleur.

'That's it! That's *exactly* what I've done!'

'What are you talking about?'

'I've given up modelling.'

Fleur set her glass down. 'I am guessing this isn't a joke.'

'No joke. This is real, I promise.'

'But why, Daisy?'

'I've fallen out of love with it. It's that simple. I'm going to Africa to do voluntary work.'

Fleur took a sip of wine, and gave her niece a look of assessment. It was clear from Daisy's expression that she was resolute. Daisy was a Capricorn, and once a Capricorn decides upon a course of action, Fleur knew, there was no turning back.

'Well. Good for you. Was it a tough decision?'

Daisy shook her head. 'No. My agent asked if I needed twenty-four hours to think about it, and I said "Yes . . ." and then "*No!*" practically simultaneously. I really didn't need to think twice. I've been miserable in this job for a long time.'

'You've only been modelling for two years,' Fleur pointed out.

'Well, I've been miserable for a whole year of those two, and that's a long time to be miserable. I was never cut out to be a model.'

'You are a brave girl.'

'No, I'm not. I'm just doing what I've always wanted to do, and that's make a difference. You've no idea what it's like to be surrounded by size zero girlies moaning about putting on half a kilo when there are people all over the world starving.'

'Won't you miss your celebrity status, beauty?'

'Nope. I'd rather be famous for having a real talent like singing or writing or painting. Being famous for being a model is just embarrassing.' Daisy cut two slabs of chocolate sponge and plonked them on to plates. 'Ha! Bye bye, stupid diet. Bring on the calories.'

'What made you decide on Africa?' asked Fleur.

'A friend who's over there told me I had to come out. She's recruited a whole bunch of people via Facebook.'

'How resourceful!'

'Yep. I've been in touch with everyone else who's going, and they're all really sound. Facebook's brilliant for networking. Have you joined up yet, Flirty?'

'I keep meaning to, but I've been so busy lately. Perhaps I will get around to it in the winter, when things have calmed down.'

'Things will be hotting up for me this winter. I'll be working in a township in Kwazulu-Natal, building a school.'

'Actually physically building?'

'Yeah. My mate says that she's completely knackered at the end of every day, but that she's never felt better in her life.'

'Well. I am full of admiration – and not a little jealous. I would have loved to have had an opportunity to do something like that when I was your age. When are you off?'

'Next week.'

'No! So soon?'

'Someone dropped out, so I got in like Flynn. If I hadn't got a place on this trip, I'd be waiting another six months.'

'Well, *bon voyage!*' Fleur raised her glass in a toast. 'Here's to Africa!'

'And here's to you, Mystic Meg!' Daisy took a sip of wine, then gave Fleur a look of appraisal. 'One question. How are you going to do it?'

'The fortune-telling?'

'Yeah.'

'Río lent me a crystal ball.'

Daisy raised a cynical eyebrow. 'A crystal ball? Does it work?'

'But of course! I looked into it earlier and it told me that at half-past seven this evening I would be drinking Sancerre and feasting on gâteaux with my niece. And presto! How uncanny is that? It is now seven-thirty and that is exactly what I'm doing.'

'So presumably you're just going to gaze into the ball and come out with mumbo-jumbo stuff about travelling over water and meeting tall dark strangers?'

'I guess so. I haven't really thought about it. Río gave me an instruction manual, but it's pretty useless.'

'How does Río usually do it?'

'She improvises – she's brilliant at it. She has such intuitive flair.'

'I hate to say this, Flirty, but you're not very good at improvising.'

Fleur shrugged. 'I'll just have to try. Río says she raised nearly four hundred euros last year, and Corban has agreed to double the sum I take in. And all the money raised is going to the Hospice Foundation.'

'But if word gets out that you're rubbish, no one will want to know.'

Fleur looked put out. 'It's only five euros a go, Daisy. And it's for charity.'

'Flirty – if you're not worth it, people are going to spend their five euros on the tombola instead. If you want to double your money, you're going to have to dream up some way of impressing the punters.'

'But I can't be expected to read people's fortunes, Daisy! That is madness!'

'Of course it's madness. But . . .' Daisy narrowed her eyes and gave Fleur the benefit of her best sphinx-like smile '. . . but I'm having quite a good idea. Where's your crystal ball?'

'Upstairs.'

'Show me.'

'OK.' Fleur got to her feet and eased into a stretch. 'Ow. I'll get out of this costume while I'm up there. If I don't take off the cummerbund I'll have no room for your cake.'

'Why did you lace it so tight?'

'Vanity, of course, *chérie*.'

Upstairs, Fleur doffed her fancy dress and got into lounging pyjamas. On reflection, she decided she was glad that Daisy had decided to quit her modelling career. She knew that her elder brother, François, was uncomfortable with the notion of his daughter being caught up in such a superficial milieu. Being the father of an only daughter, François was a staunch protector of his pride and joy, and had reared her quite strictly, as is the manner of French fathers. Fleur remembered how François had been sent by her own father to rescue her when she had run off to Dublin. The ironic thing was that her brother, too, had fallen in love with Ireland – more specifically, with a Galway girl – and both siblings had stayed, building businesses on the west coast. Fleur had her boutique in Lissamore, and François had his – a fishing tackle shop – in nearby Galway. Fleur was glad she had family so close: although she and her brother were chalk and cheese (François was into hunting, shooting and fishing in a big way), she was mad about her beautiful niece, whom she treated as her surrogate daughter.

Her phone alerted her to a message: Daisy had forwarded the picture she had taken earlier. Ooh la la – it was quite fun! Her gypsy skirts were all a-twirl around her thighs, the cinched-in waist enhanced her curves, and she was smiling directly to camera. She'd forward it to Corban, for a joke. She composed the caption: Gypsy Rose Lee will tell your fortune for a modest remuneration, then pressed Send. By the time she'd got back downstairs with the crystal ball and *Six Lessons in Crystal Gazing*, Daisy was checking something out on her iPhone.

'My idea is *inspired*, Flirty. Have a look at this.'

'What is it?'

'It's my Facebook profile.'

'Wow. You have so many friends,' said Fleur, looking over Daisy's shoulder. 'But what has this to do with your inspired idea?'

'Aha! Behold.'

Aiming the cursor at 'Status' on the top of her profile page, Daisy typed in, 'Anyone in the Coolnamara region this weekend? Check out the fortune-teller at the festival in Lissamore. She rocks!'

Fleur gave her niece a sceptical look. 'Daisy – that's just *inviting* disaster!'

'No, it's not. Because this is what you are going to do. Watch this.'

Daisy clicked on a name, and another profile appeared on the screen. The person in question was a pretty girl called Sofia. As Daisy scrolled down, Fleur learned that Sofia's birthday was on the second of October: she was a Libra. Her relationship status was single, she was interested in men. A click told Fleur that Sofia's favourite movies included *Mamma Mia* and Disney's *Beauty and the Beast*, her favourite book was *The Boy in the Striped Pyjamas*, she had a brown belt in karate, and she made excellent pasta because her mother was Italian. Her photo album included shots of herself standing against a variety of landmarks: the Sydney Opera House, the Eiffel Tower, the Colosseum. Remarks that had been posted on her wall read: 'See you when you get back from Coolnamara – Club M, Friday week?' 'Hmm . . . I hear you met a cutie in Paris!' 'You saw Cheryl Cole in Top Shop? Awesome!'

'This is most illuminating, my dear,' said Fleur. 'But why should you want to share with me the information that one of your friends met a cutie in Paris and has a brown belt in karate?'

'I know for a fact that she's in Lissamore this weekend.'

'So?'

'So, picture this. She's messing about on Facebook. She learns that there's a shit-hot fortune-teller at the festival, and decides to investigate. Put yourself in her shoes.'

13

'What do you mean?'

'Pretend you're Sofia.'

Fleur gave Daisy a bemused look, then shrugged and said: 'OK. I'm Sofia.'

'Welcome, Sofia!' said Daisy, doing a kind of salaam and adopting a mysterious expression. Gazing into the crystal ball that Fleur had set on the table, she added in a dodgy Eastern European accent: 'I think you might be a Libra, Sofia, yes? Hmm. What else can I tell you about yourself? I see – I think I see you in a suit of trousers – white trousers, with bare feet. You are dancing – no, no! You are kicking! I guess perhaps you might have a talent for karate, Sofia? And there is more – you have travelled, travelled far and wide. I see many foreign countries in the crystal – Sydney, Paris, Rome . . . And what is this? You are in a club, now, and this time you *are* dancing. But dancing in the future. Next Friday, perhaps? Next Friday I think you are going dancing with a friend, to a place called the – could it be Club N?'

'No,' said Fleur with a smile, as the penny dropped. 'It's Club M.'

'There!' Daisy flopped back in her seat with a triumphant smile. 'You see! It's ingenious! Word spreads like lightning through the Facebook community, and anybody who's spending the bank holiday weekend in Coolnamara will come flocking to see – what's your fortune-teller name?'

'Haven't an idea.'

'Tsk-tsk. How about Tiresia?'

'From Thérèse?'

'No. Tiresias was a famous soothsayer in ancient Greece.'

Fleur sighed in admiration. 'My niece has brains as well as beauty!'

'Sounds good, doesn't it? The famous Madame Tiresia, who knows all!'

14

'Daisy – how exactly do you propose that I do this?'

'Simple! You check out profiles on your iPhone, which you will have cunningly concealed under the table.'

'But I don't do Facebook.'

'Aha! But you log on as me – popular minor celebrity and model, Daisy de Saint-Euverte. You saw how many friends I have. And those friends have friends, and I have influence. Sometimes being a C-lister can be useful.'

'You've clearly had too much wine. This can't possibly work.'

'Don't be so negative, Flirty!' Daisy reached for *Six Lessons in Crystal Gazing* and started leafing through it. 'Just think of all the moolah you can raise for the Hospice Foundation.'

'But we have got to anticipate the worst. Lots and lots of things could go wrong. What if Mister Norman No-Friends from Nenagh enters the booth. What do I say to him?'

'You tell Norman that there is no hope of telling his fortune because . . . because he doesn't have one!'

'I couldn't say that! Poor Norman will think he's going to die.'

'Um. OK. Tell him you can't see his aura. Listen to this: "It is quite possible for the gazer to be able to see things in the crystal at one time and not at another. In fact, many of the best crystal gazers have lost the power for weeks together. This being so, you should not be discouraged if such images fail to appear at your command." There's your disclaimer. Print it out and display it by the entrance to your booth.' Daisy checked out the cover of the booklet. 'It's by Dr R A Mayne. There you go! Your spiritual mentor has impressive credentials.'

'But that book was published in 1928.'

'Your punters don't need to know that. Come on – let's have another go. This time you can tell my fortune. My name

15

is . . . Jana.' Daisy's fingers twinkled over her iPhone, then she handed it to Fleur.

'Jana!' said Fleur, peering at the display as if she were reading Ancient Egyptian. 'Um, welcome.'

'Pretend to be gazing into the ball,' instructed Daisy.

'I can't look at the ball and Jana's profile at the same time!'

'Then we'll get you a veil. Try this.' Daisy unwound the chiffon scarf she was wearing and dropped it over her aunt's head. 'Perfect! Go again.'

'Jana,' repeated Fleur. 'I think you might be a Pisces, yes? I see – um – a book with the title *The Time Traveler's Wife* and I see Meryl Streep wearing dungarees – holy moly, is *Mamma Mia every*one's favourite film on Facebook?'

'Tut-tut! You're stepping out of character, Madame Tiresia. Here, have some more wine.'

'Thank you, Jana. Now – where were we? I see you singing – singing in front of Simon Cowell. Perhaps you have auditioned for the *X Factor*?'

Some forty minutes later, Fleur had told half-a-dozen more fortunes, and was really beginning to have fun.

'Not bad for a Facebook virgin,' remarked Daisy, upending the wine bottle. 'You'll get hooked, Flirty, mark my words. Now, let's do one more. This time I'm going to be Paris Hilton.'

'Paris Hilton is one of your Facebook friends?'

'No, she's not. But we all know everything there is to know about Paris. You should have no problem uncovering *her* secrets.'

'Welcome!' enthused Fleur, waving her hands over the crystal ball. But just as she was deliberating over questions for Paris, the phone in the kitchen sounded. Reaching for her wineglass, she excused herself and shimmied inside to pick up. It was Corban.

16

'Hello, *chéri!*' she crooned into the mouthpiece. When Fleur had a little too much to drink, or when she was enraged – which was seldom – her French accent became marginally more pronounced.

'I just got your message,' he told her, 'and I have to say, you look pretty damned hot as Gypsy Rose Lee. But you made a mistake.'

'I did?'

'Yeah. Gypsy Rose Lee was a burlesque artist, not a fortune-teller.'

'Oops.'

'And she was a *very* sexy lady. The original Dita Von Teese.'

'What are you getting at, Mister O'Hara?' Fleur started toying with a strand of hair. She couldn't help flirting with Corban, even on the telephone.

'You know I said I'd double your take, Fleur? I'm prepared to quadruple it. On one condition.'

'Name it.'

'When I call in to you on Friday evening, I want to see you wearing those gypsy threads.'

Fleur's mouth curved in a provocative smile. 'So that you can take them off?'

'No. So that *you* can take them off. While I watch.'

Fleur's smile grew even more provocative. She pretended to buy time while taking a sip from her wineglass. Then she laughed out loud. 'Done deal,' she said.

Chapter Two

Dervla Vaughan (née Kinsella) stepped through the front door of her new home and set her bags down on the hall floor. The sun filtering through the mosaic glass of the fanlight cast a jewel-like pattern onto the stone flags, and when she slipped off her sandals the patch of spangled sunlight warmed the soles of her feet. The air was redolent of fresh paint, with here and there a trace of linseed oil. If you added base notes of baking bread, then bottled it, the scent could rival any room candle dreamed up by Jo Malone. It was perfectly quiet in the house: the only sound that of birdsong, and the distant baaing of sheep from the fields beyond the garden.

Her dream house! Moving into the centre of the hall, Dervla executed a slow turn, taking in each and every one of the three hundred and sixty delectable degrees that surrounded her. Off the hallway, to left and to right were two spacious, high-ceilinged reception rooms. In her mind's eye they were washed in soothing shades of buttery yellow and eau-de-nil, furnished with understated antiques and carpeted in faded Aubusson; but right now the rooms were works in progress, with tools of the decorator's trade heaped in a corner and undercoat spattered on dust sheets.

Her eyes followed the graceful line of the cantilevered

staircase. On the floor above her, bedrooms and bathrooms had unparalleled views over the countryside, with sea shimmering and mountains slumbering on the horizon. The views were as yet unframed by curtains, but Dervla had improvised with yards of unbleached muslin in the master bedroom, to soften the magisterial appearance of the high casements. More muslin was draped from the tester over the king-sized bed, each side of which was flanked by a pale rug: not the Aubusson carpets of Dervla's fantasy, but pretty in their own way. A chest at the foot of the bed contained bed linen, but aside from that, and the cushions piled on the window seat, the room was unfurnished.

Only one room in the house had been finished – finished to pretty high spec, at that. Christian – Dervla's husband of less than a year – had surprised her one day by taking her hand and leading her up the staircase that accessed the turret room at the very top of the house. Unlocking the door, he'd thrown it open to reveal a dedicated office space with units to house computer, printer and scanner. There was an ergonomic chair cushioned in leather, and shelves just waiting to be filled with books and stationery. 'This is where you'll finish that book!' he'd announced. 'What do you think? Isn't this a dream space for a writer?'

It *was* a dream space for a writer – her very own ivory tower. The only snag was that Dervla wasn't a writer: she was – like thousands of other professionals recently made redundant – an *aspiring* writer. Having been a successful auctioneer in a former life and in a former economy, Dervla had been commissioned to write a beginner's guide to selling property. She knew she had lucked out: other estate agents had sunk without trace since recession had struck. But even though she had a publishing deal and a deadline to work to, Dervla felt like a complete fraud every time she sat down in front of her keyboard and opened the file entitled *How to Sell Your House – What Every First-Timer Needs to Know*. Her contract specified eighty thousand words, and as the deadline inched closer, Dervla was feeling less and less confident that she'd be able to deliver.

It wasn't entirely her fault – for the past few months she'd been inundated with the kind of stress that might floor a less resilient individual. Closing down her business, putting her Galway penthouse on the rental market and moving into the Old Rectory had all taken its toll on her energy, and she'd had little spare time in which to get any writing done. But now that she had a room of her own – a room with a view and an ergonomic chair, to boot – perhaps inspiration would come to her.

Crossing back to the front door where she'd dumped her bags, Dervla picked up her computer case, then made for the staircase that curved up to the first floor. A narrower spiral staircase took her to the turret room. Switching on her computer, she strolled over to one of the three double-glazed windows while she waited for the screen to shimmer into life.

When they'd bought the Old Rectory, the turret had been windowless – blocked up since the introduction of the window tax in the eighteenth century. Dervla and Christian had gleefully reinstated windows to east, west and south, thereby ensuring that the room was filled with light. From this vantage point the steeple of the little church on the outskirts of Lissamore village was just discernible, and you could hear the bells chime, too, when the wind was coming from the right direction. Sheep baaing! Birdsong! Church bells chiming! The kind of pastorale that accompanied Thomas Hardy adaptations on television, now made up the soundtrack to her life.

Chimes of another kind were coming from her bag. On honeymoon in Mexico, Dervla had fallen in love with the sound of the wind chimes on the veranda where she and Christian had slept. She'd made a recording to use as her phone tone, and every time her phone rang now, she picked it up with a pang of nostalgia.

Her sister's name was lit up on the display.

'Hey, Dervla,' said Río, breezily. 'Have you moved in yet?'

'Yes. I'm in my turret.'

'Wow! Like a princess in a fairy tale. Any sign of your prince?'

'He's on his way from the airport.'

'With the wicked stepmother?'

'She's not my stepmother, Río. She's my mother-in-law.'

'Mother-in-law! The scariest words in the world.'

'According to Fleur, the French call them *belles-mères* – beautiful mothers.'

Over the phone, Dervla heard her sister suppress a snort. 'What are you going to call her? I mean, call her to her face? "Daphne", or "Mrs Vaughan"?'

'According to the carer it depends on what kind of a mood she's in. If she's in a snit she insists on being called Mrs Vaughan, but when she's in good form she doesn't mind Daphne.'

'You could always call her Daffy.'

'That would be very politically incorrect, Río.'

Dervla moved to the window that overlooked the stable yard. It had been spread with golden gravel, and terracotta planters had been arranged around the water feature – a raised pond complete with underlighting. A gleaming new thatch roofed the outbuildings that had been converted into a cottage-style dwelling for her mother-in-law, and – to complete the rustic look – shutters painted duck-egg blue flanked a half-door crafted by a local carpenter. The exterior was deceptive: inside, the cottage had been modernized, and now boasted a state-of-the-art kitchen, a big, comfortable sitting room with an HD plasma screen and a tropical fish tank, and underfloor heating. There was also adjoining accommodation for Mrs Vaughan's carer, Nemia.

'Are you all set for her arrival?' Río asked.

'Yep. There's a shepherd's pie ready to go, and a bottle of vintage Moët in the fridge.'

'Posh!'

'One of the pluses of being married to a wine importer. We got a case from Christian's partner as a wedding present.'

'Is Mrs Vaughan senior allowed a drink?'

'What do you mean?'

'Well, I don't imagine a person with her complaint would have much tolerance for alcohol.'

'Oh. I see what you mean. Yikes. I never thought of that.'

Christian's eighty-four-year-old mother suffered from dementia. Because she had been born and reared near Lissamore, it was Christian's wish that she should spend her final days in the place she still called home. She and her carer had left London earlier that day on what was to be Daphne's final journey to her native Coolnamara.

'You could always just pour her a glass of fizzy water and pass it off as champagne,' suggested Río.

'I don't think she's *that* confused.'

'When did you last talk to her?'

'A couple of days ago. She hadn't a clue who I was, of course, but Christian thought it was a good idea to give her a gentle reminder of my voice from time to time, to get her used to it.'

'Does she even know who *he* is?'

'He claims she does. But then, he constantly refers to

himself as "Christian, your son", when he talks to her on the phone.'

'Jesus. It's a bitch of a disease, isn't it?'

'Yes. It is.' Dervla realized that she didn't want to talk about her mother-in-law any more. She sat down at her desk and started to doodle squares on a Post-It pad. The shapes evolved into a house like one a child might draw, with four windows and a door. 'So what's new, Río?'

'I'm bored.'

'You're on the set of a blockbuster movie surrounded by Hollywood luminaries and you're *bored*?'

'Well, I guess I'm more pissed off than bored. One of the actors complained today that his snuffbox was too gay, and that horrible little child star has a million riders written into her contract.'

'There's a child star in the movie?'

'Well, she's twenty-something, but she behaves like a child. Her name is Nasty – short for Anastasia – Harris.'

'Oh – I've heard about her. Didn't she get married recently, to some film star old enough to be her daddy?'

'Yeah. She married Jay David.'

'Of course! Hollywood royalty.'

'And she's living up to it. She's every bit her sugar daddy's little princess.'

'Have you met him?'

'No. He can't take time off his schedule to visit Ireland. Rumour has it he'll be flying in on his Gulfstream for the wrap party, though.'

'Is she any good as an actress?'

'According to her husband – who is, of course, completely non-partisan – Nasty is the new Julia Roberts. Her talent will blaze forth into the world like a supernova. And boy, does she believe it. The problem with princesses like her is

24

that the more their demands are met, the more outrageous they become.'

'Like J. Lo insisting on her coffee being stirred counter-clockwise?'

'You got it. Nasty insists on having rose petals scattered in the loo bowl—'

'No!'

'Yes. And the bed sheets in her trailer – Egyptian cotton, of course – have to be changed every day. And this morning she decided that her character should have a parasol, even though parasols were unheard of in nineteenth-century Coolnamara.'

'Shouldn't that be wardrobe's problem? I thought your job was strictly set-dressing?'

'The line between the two gets blurred, sometimes. I spotted a lovely découpage screen in the transport van this morning, by the way. I thought I'd nab it for you as a house-warming present when we're wrapped.'

'You're not going to steal it?'

'No – I'll get it at cost. And it's genuine Victorian, not repro.'

'Thanks. That's sweet of you.'

'Hang on two seconds, Dervla.' There came the mumbling of a man's voice in the background, and Río said: 'No, no, you great lummox – not you, Dervla – a dudeen is a clay pipe. Yeah – and be *careful* – they break easily.'

A Victorian screen would look great in the drawing room, Dervla decided, as she doodled a chimney on to her house. They could set it in front of the door of a winter's evening to stop draughts – although of course, with double-glazed windows and underfloor heating and a blazing turf fire, there wouldn't *be* any draughts. Scribbling a plume of smoke puffing from her chimneypot, Dervla pictured herself and her husband sitting on either side of the fireplace reading their books in companionable silence, Christian's trusty Dalmatian at his feet. She'd definitely start reading Dickens – preferably in leather-bound editions. Or maybe she'd take up knitting? Knitting had a certain cachet: all the actresses on *The O'Hara Affair* were busy with five-ply Guernsey wool and number twelve needles, according to Río.

'Sorry about that.' Río was back on the phone. 'The feckin' eejit hadn't a clue what a dudeen was. Probably thought it meant a hot girl. So. Tell me more of your news. How's your gaff shaping up?'

'Well, the bathroom's nearly finished, and the kitchen.'

'Utility, too?'

'Yes. But we're just glorified campers at the moment. The only real piece of furniture we have is the bed.'

'Sure, isn't that all you loved-up pair need?'

Dervla smiled. 'I have to confess I miss my fix of Corrie.'

'You mean you don't have a TV?'

'No. They delivered the big screen we ordered for Daphne, but forgot ours. Oops. That reminds me –I'd better run down and set up the channels before she arrives. And double oops – I forgot to turn her heating on.'

'But it's not cold.'

'She's a fragile little old lady, Río. She feels the cold, especially in the evenings.'

'Be off with you, so. Call me tomorrow and let me know how the welcome committee went, won't you?'

'Will do. Bye, Río.'

Dervla put the phone down, added a tail to the spotty dog sitting on the doorstep of her two-dimensional house, then scampered downstairs, the sound of her feet on the bare boards echoing around the empty space.

In the hallway, she retrieved her shoes, and made for the

back door. As she crossed the stable yard, the crunching of gravel startled a cat that had been snoozing in a patch of sun. As it skedaddled, Dervla wondered if she should try and encourage it by leaving food out, but then realized that the Old Rectory would be no place for a cat once Kitty the Dalmatian moved in.

In Daphne's cottage, Dervla's feet made no sound. Footsteps here were muffled by the pure wool deep-pile carpet that had been laid just days ago. The colour matched the curtains, made to measure in a rose-coloured brocade, which was echoed in the loose covers on sofas and armchairs. Much of Daphne's furniture had been shipped from her house in London, so that her new surroundings would have a reassuring familiarity to them. The furniture included a very elegant walnut escritoire, a Regency rosewood bookcase, and a nineteenth-century beech day bed; her exquisite collection of japonaiserie was displayed in a bevelled glass case that ran the length of an entire wall. Christian had told her that a pair of porcelain vases dating from the K'ang-hsi period (whenever that was) were worth in the region of 20,000 euros, and Dervla thanked Christ that she would not be responsible for dusting them.

She flicked the main switch that controlled the heat, then wandered through Daphne's new home to make final checks. The conversion of the old outbuildings had cost Christian a lot of money – more than had been spent so far on the refurbishment of the Old Rectory. But they had looked upon it as an investment. Once the old lady died or had to be moved into proper residential care, the cottage could still generate income as an up-market artist's retreat. Dervla had already worded the ad that she'd place in such select publications as *The Author* magazine:

27

Coolnamara, West of Ireland. Comfortable, well-equipped, single-storey house, sympathetically converted from period mews buildings adjoining eighteenth-century manor. Lissamore village with shops, pubs and seafood restaurant just 10 mins; fabulous beach and mountain walks nearby. Perfectly lovely, undisturbed surroundings: ideal for writer/artist.

Dervla didn't much like herself for contemplating the death of Christian's mother, but she was a pragmatist, and – like all estate agents – was unsentimental when property was involved. Naturally, it behoved Christian to take care of Daphne in her declining years, and Dervla respected his decision to bring her home to Coolnamara. While her mother-in-law lived here, Dervla would do all she could to make her welcome and comfortable. She'd spent all weekend getting the place ready, with the help of a local girl, Bronagh. Between them, they had arranged Daphne's furniture and displayed her paintings and photographs to advantage; they'd filled vases with flowers (Christian had specified that yellow lilies were her favourite on account of the vibrancy of the colour and the headiness of their scent) and made beds and stocked fridge and freezer. Dervla had even unpacked her mother-in-law's clothes, marvelling at the vintage labels on many of the garments as she'd hung them in the wardrobe: Balenciaga, Givenchy, Lanvin. Daphne Vaughan had been a classy dame. A model, Christian had told her, whose career could have taken her to Paris if she hadn't decided to get married.

The wedding of Daphne to the honourable Jeremy Vaughan had been recorded in all the society pages as *the* event of the year 1945. Christian had showed her the cuttings in the scrapbooks that had arrived, along with all his mother's other effects. They showed the couple on their wedding day, on honeymoon, and at the christening of their first child, Josephine. There were articles on what Daphne had worn to Cheltenham; to the Proms and to Henley, and a picture of them smiling lovingly at each other at the Queen's garden party. Daphne was described as a model wife and hostess, and doting mother. When Jeremy died – leaving her very comfortably off with a trust fund and investment portfolio – the widow had been inconsolable. The photograph of the funeral – cut from the *Daily Telegraph* – showed her standing at the graveside swathed in Blackglama fur, holding the hands of her two young children. Christian had been just twelve.

Moving back into the sitting room, Dervla activated the digital box. While waiting for it to boot up, she wandered over to the glass-fronted bookcase. Since Bronagh had unpacked the books, she was curious to inspect Daphne's library. What might her taste in literature be? Eclectic, by the look of it. On the shelves, volumes of poetry sat next to obscurely-titled novels, many of them French. There were books on gardening, books on history, and books on art and artists. As well as being sophisticated, Christian's mother was clearly cultured. There were lots of complete works, too, many of which were beautifully bound in leather, and Dervla was delighted to see that a set of Dickens was displayed. Nice! She could realize her dream of sitting by the fire, turning the pages of *Little Dorrit* or *Great Expectations*! Reaching for a volume, Dervla realized too late that the 'book' was actually a box with a hinged lid. The lid fell open as she slid it off the shelf, and a second volume, bound in vellum, fell to the floor. Dervla stooped to pick it up. It was a diary, and on the cover, in black italics, were the words *Daphne Beaufoy Vaughan, 1968*.

She wouldn't open it. She *shouldn't* open it. But of course, Dervla couldn't help herself.

The pages of the journal were covered in sprawling, energetic writing – as if the hand of the author could not keep up with the torrent of thoughts splashed over the creamy paper. Dervla's eyes scanned the script, lighting randomly on a paragraph here, a sentence there. 'The most far-fetched vow I ever made,' she read, 'was when, as a child, I swore that if I ever had children I would love them unreservedly: a promise I have been utterly powerless to keep.' 'As well as being non-conformist, I happen to be very proud, and that, of course, makes one aloof.' 'We have been married for over two decades now, and still have nothing to say to one another.' 'Spent the weekend with L. in the Royal Albion in Brighton. We fought like tigers, as usual.' 'Have decided to send C. & J. to boarding school. Children are not conducive to conducting an *amour*.' 'R. presented me with a diamond so paltry I promptly hurled it into the lavatory. Much to my amusement, he retrieved it.'

Dervla sank to her knees on Daphne's thick-pile carpet. It took her a scant ten minutes of riffling through the journal to learn that Daphne had had a string of lovers; that she despised the wives of those lovers, and that she especially despised her husband. On the last page, she declared that she was going to relate the story of her life so far in the form of a novel.

Oh. Oh God! Was there more? Again, Dervla couldn't stop herself from reaching for another of the faux volumes. Inside was an identical vellum-bound journal with the owner's name writ large in her distinctive script. The date was 1969. Systematically, Dervla worked her way through the hollow *Collected Works of Charles Dickens*. There were thirteen volumes, and each contained a journal. By Dervla's calculations, the diaries spanned the years 1960 to 1973. The final volume contained a splenetic attack on the literary agents who had repeatedly declined to represent Mrs Vaughan on the basis that her novel appeared, in fact, to be a work of thinly disguised autobiography too slanderous ever to find a publishing house.

Dervla sat motionless on the floor, gazing at script so jagged it looked as if it had been penned by a razor dipped in ink. Did Christian know about these diaries? Did his sister, Josephine? Dervla knew that Christian had attended boarding school from a young age, but he had told her it was the Vaughan family policy: his father had attended Eton, and his grandfather before him. Dervla privately thought it shocking that children be shunted off to boarding school on account of some antediluvian tradition: now that she knew that the real reason was to facilitate his mother's *amours*, she found it infinitely more shocking. Her quandary now was: should she tell Christian about the diaries? She thought not. Sleeping dogs were best left to lie, and Dervla knew what power past secrets had to inflict damage.

The sound of wheels on gravel made her turn. Through the window, she could see Christian's car rounding the corner of the big house into the courtyard. Quickly, Dervla shoved the last journal into its leather-bound casing, noticing ruefully that the title of the volume in question was – ironically – *Hard Times*. How hard would it be to defer to her mother-in-law, knowing what she now knew?

She watched as the Saab pulled up outside the front door of the cottage. Christian got out, rounded the bonnet and opened the passenger door, leaning in to offer his mother support as she struggled to her feet. Meanwhile, a pretty, almond-eyed girl emerged from the rear and started hefting bags out of the boot.

'We're here now, Mum!' Dervla heard Christian say.

'Where, exactly, are we?'

'We're at your new home.'

'I've never been here before in my life,' came the auto-cratic reply.

'I know that, Mum. It's your *new* home.'

Daphne was wearing a navy blue trouser suit with a turquoise silk blouse. A string of pearls was looped around her neck, a Kelly bag dangled from the crook of her right arm, and on her feet were blue canvas pixie boots. She looked around, and as she did, her gaze travelled to the open window in which Dervla stood framed. Mother and daughter-in-law locked eyes, and then: 'There's someone in there,' pronounced Daphne. 'You said this was *my* house.'

Dervla moved out into the hall, took a deep breath and shook back her hair. Then she counted to three and opened the door, estate agent's smile perfectly in place.

'Hello, all!' she called brightly. 'Welcome!'

'Hello, love,' said Christian. 'Come and say hello to Mum, and Nemia!'

Dervla stepped onto the gravel and advanced, willing her smile not to falter as she reached out and took Daphne's free hand in both her of own. 'Did you have a good journey, Daphne?'

'What kind of a stupid question's that?' said Daphne, with-drawing her hand.

'This is Dervla, Mum,' said Christian. 'Remember her? She's my wife.'

'I've never seen her before in my life.'

'Well, it's been some time since you met. Let's go inside, shall we, and have a cup of tea? And if we're lucky, there might be biccies.'

'There *are* biccies,' said Dervla. 'Choccie biccies.'

'Choccie biccies! Yum yum,' said Christian.

He offered Daphne his arm as they began to move towards

the cottage, then looked back at Dervla and gave her a tired smile. Her heart went out to her husband. He didn't need tea and biccies as much as a huge Scotch. Dervla remembered the champagne that she'd stashed in the fridge, and, as she saw Daphne stumble over the threshold, decided against producing it.

'Hello. I'm Nemia,' came a voice from behind her, and Dervla turned.

'Oh – I *am* sorry! How rude of me not to have introduced myself. I'm Dervla.'

'Nice to meet you, Dervla.'

'Likewise. Hey. Let me help you with those.'

'Thanks,' said Nemia. 'There's nothing very heavy.'

Dervla swung a carrier bag out of the boot, noticing that it bore the logo of a pharmacy in Galway.

'Did you have to stop off somewhere on your way here?'

'Yes. We just needed to stock up on some basics.'

'How was your journey?'

'Fairly uneventful. There were no delays, which helped.' Nemia reached into the boot, and produced another carrier. 'Oh, crap. There's a split in this bag. Can I just transfer the breakable stuff to yours?'

'Sure.'

Nemia delved into the bag, then handed over a couple of distinctive Côté Bastide bottles. Sliding them into her bulky carrier, Dervla was about to observe that Côté Bastide just happened to make her favourite bath oil – but the words never made it out of her mouth. Instead, as she took in the contents of the bag, a single word emerged from between her lips.

'Nappies?'

Nemia turned to her and smiled. 'Just in case,' she said.

Chapter Three

Sliding an arm out from under the duvet, Fleur reached for her watch. Eight-thirty. Corban had left an hour ago. She'd smiled as he'd kissed her goodbye, her eyelids fluttering open briefly before she'd tumbled back into dreamland. She'd hoped to have a leisurely breakfast *à deux* this morning, with freshly juiced oranges and croissants on the deck, but Corban had had other plans. He'd scheduled an early meeting with the director of *The O'Hara Affair*.

As she set her watch back on the bedside table, Fleur's eyes fell on the flamboyant gypsy threads that she'd discarded the previous night with Corban's help. Undressing her – or watching her undress – was one of Corban's peccadilloes, and because it made him happy, she was glad to oblige. Fleur indulged her lovers – to a point. Once they showed signs of complacency, or became overfamiliar, she showed her displeasure. By saying 'no', by being unavailable, by being a little less free with her favours, she kept her men on their toes. It was a highly skilled game, and one at which she was very good.

Or had been, until she met Corban. Corban was proving a lot less malleable than the lovers she'd had to date – all of whom had been considerably younger than she. Río had used to joke about Fleur's penchant for toyboys, declaring that her love life would make a great biopic. But since Corban had taken centre stage, she wasn't sure whether the story of her life was a rom com or a melodrama. Aspects of it fitted both categories, she supposed, but whichever genre it belonged to, it was certainly X-rated.

Sinking back against her pile of goosedown pillows, Fleur allowed her mind to meander back to the first time she and Corban had met, six months ago. It could make a stand-out scene in a movie . . .

INT. UPMARKET HOTEL.

BALLROOM. NIGHT.

A charity ball in Dublin. The theme: the Tudors. The ballroom billowing with society dames dolled up as Elizabeth, bejewelled frocks and coppery-coloured curls everywhere. The men all emulating Jonathan Rhys Meyers as Henry (or trying to); everyone in masks.

Fleur had struck lucky with her frock. Joan Bergin, the costume designer of the *Tudors* TV series was a friend, and Joan had wangled a divine outfit for Fleur. It included an elaborate wig, a gold mask, and a magnificent gown, the bodice of which was embroidered with droplets of lapis lazuli and tiny seed pearls. The mask, too, was trimmed with pearls. It concealed most of Fleur's face, but stopped short at the jaw line, leaving mouth and chin exposed. Exposed, too, was most of her bosom: her breasts pushed so high by the boned corset that she felt practically naked. The effect was one of rather sexy regality, of come-on combined with 'look, but don't touch'. The get-up, however, was bloody uncomfortable, and after a couple of hours of small talk in the crowded ballroom (during which much champagne was poured by overzealous waiters, and baroque music was played to deaf ears), Fleur yearned to escape.

'Ladies and gentlemen—'

Oh, no! The speeches were about to begin. She *had* to get out of there. Murmuring excuses, she threaded her way through the throng of Walter Raleighs and Mary Stuarts, troubadours and serving wenches.

French windows took her onto a terrace. Here it was balmy, the air sweet with night-scented stock. The sound of the string quartet came faintly, and she could hear a fountain splashing at the far end. As she moved towards it, the silk lining of her underskirt moved against Fleur's legs like a caress. She longed to dance, but because no one was versed in the arcane steps of the gavotte, no one was dancing this evening; and now everyone would be sitting listening to speeches for the next hour.

Dipping a hand into the bubbling water, Fleur laid the palm first on her forehead, then her breasts. The coolness was so sensual that it made her want to slip off her shoes, gather up her skirts and get wet, like Anita Ekberg in *La Dolce Vita*. As she went to lean over the pool again, she became aware of a man lounging against a pillar, watching her. He was unmasked. A predatory half-smile curved his mouth, and he was eyeing her cleavage as if he wanted to dive straight in.

The insolence! Fleur dismissed him with a toss of her head and a curl of her lip; but her hauteur was wasted. He responded with a low laugh, peeled himself away from the pillar and sauntered towards her. The next thing she knew, her arms were pinioned and she was being kissed more forcefully than she'd ever been kissed in her life.

Her initial impulse was to pull away, but the greater her resistance, the more insistent the kiss, until Fleur's champagne-muzzy mind thought *Pourquoi pas? Who cares?* His kiss was so expert, so masterful, so goddamned *sexy*, that it would have been too selfless an act not to kiss him back. As he pulled her harder against him she was aware of his erection, aware of the subtle scent of spice, the subtler one of sweat, aware of his breath on her cheek as he released her mouth and trailed a kiss along the line of her jaw.

'I think you'd better stop now,' she managed finally, sounding as if she'd been inhaling helium.

'Really? I think the lady doth protest too much.' His voice in her ear contrived to sound both sceptical and amused. A finger skimmed the curve of her throat, pausing briefly to trace the scoop made by her collarbone, and then the stranger allowed his hand to travel further, sliding it beneath her bodice and cupping her breast. 'Something tells me you don't want me to stop. Something tells me you're more trollop than sovereign, Rachel. Perhaps you should have thought about attending the ball as the whore Boleyn, rather than the virgin Queen.'

Rachel? *Rachel!* Oh, horror, *horror*! This was clearly an egregious case of mistaken identity. What to do? What to say? Fleur knew she should disabuse him at once, but the sensations being triggered in her by the touch of this man were so unexpectedly, so *wickedly* erotic that she didn't want to come clean, didn't want to explain that she wasn't who he thought she was, didn't want him to back off with an awkward apology. She heard her breath coming faster, felt her nipple rise under his fingers, and – as he thrust a knee between her legs – recognized the surge of lust that made her want to grind herself against him . . . Oh! She *was* shameless! She *wanted* to be a whore, a hussy, a harlot!

'Slow down, sweetheart,' he murmured, disengaging his hand, dislodging his knee, and leaving her weak as water. 'Let me go check if there's a room available.'

And the tall, dark stranger – who, before the night was out would be a stranger no longer – had bestowed a smile upon her before dropping a brusque kiss on her mouth and strolling back into the ballroom . . .

The strains of Edith Piaf's *La Vie en Rose* interrupted Fleur's sentimental journey. Corban's name was displayed on the screen of her iPhone.

'Hello! I was just thinking about you,' she told him with a smile.

'I'm glad to hear it. What were you thinking, exactly?'

'I was thinking about the first time we met.'

'Soppy girl.'

'It would make a great short story.'

'Or a Mills & Boon.'

'Now there's a thought! I read somewhere that sales of romantic fiction have gone through the roof recently. Everyone's trying to escape into fantasy land.'

'Might be too raunchy for Mills & Boon. You'd have to shut the door on the bedroom activity.'

'*Au contraire.* They publish really sexy stuff these days.' Fleur stretched languorously. 'Let's see – how would our story go? "'I'm not who you think I am,' confessed our heroine, as the masterful stranger took her hand. 'I don't care who you are, any more than you care who I am,' he growled, leading her into the bedroom of the magnificent, luxury penthouse."'

'It wasn't a penthouse,' Corban corrected her.

'In my Mills & Boon version it is. "She set her champagne flute down on the marble-topped bedside table and turned to him. His gaze was fierce. 'I must have you,' he told her. Her bosom heaving, she sank upon the four-poster, looking up at him through the slits of her golden mask. 'Now?' she breathed. 'Now!' he insisted. Without further ado, he reached for his manhood. She gasped when she saw—"'

'OK. Enough's enough. Time to shut the door. Incidentally, did I really growl, and did you really gasp?' asked Corban.

'Of course. Gasping was mandatory. It was the raunchiest thing I've ever done. Until last night, that is. It's a pity I'll have to give Río back her gypsy costume.'

'I'm sure we can think of some other suitably titillating attire. I rather fancy you as a schoolgirl.'

'No! Schoolgirl's too pervy, Corban. And I'm far too old. French maid is more my line, don't you think? *Il y a quelque chose d'autre que je peux faire pour Monsieur?*'

'Translate.'

'Is there anything else I can do for you, sir?'

'Well, yes, actually, there is. I scribbled a number on yesterday's *Financial Times*, and forgot to enter it into my phone. Could you text it to me?'

'Sure.' Fleur swung her legs out of bed, and reached for her peignoir. 'Whose phone number is it?' she asked, as she padded downstairs.

'Shane Byrne's. I want to arrange lunch with him.'

'Lucky you. Where are you taking him?'

'There's a new place that's opened not far from where they're shooting today. I thought I'd try that.'

'What's it called?'

'Chez Jules.'

'Oh! How brave of Jules to open when all around him restaurants are closing. I hope it works out for him.'

The *Financial Times* was on the breakfast bar, open at some arcane article on investments. A number was scrawled in the margin, with the initials S. B. beside it. How many people in the world had access to Shane Byrne's private phone number? Fleur wondered. Maybe she should auction it at the charity gig this afternoon, to raise more money for the hospice. Reaching for her mobile with her free hand, she started texting Corban. 'Shall we eat out tonight?' she asked, as she keyed the numbers in.

'No. I'll pick something up on the way back. Fillet or sirloin?'

Fleur's heart sank a little. Corban adored red meat, while she favoured chicken or fish. However, since she didn't have many opportunities to cook for her man, she might as well serve up what he was partial to. 'Why not bring me some good quality braising steak, and I'll do Carbonade de Boeuf?'

'Excellent. I'll get us a Bordeaux to go with it.' There came a blip over the line. 'Ah – incoming call. I gotta go, lover. Did you find that number?'

'Yes.' Fleur pressed 'Send'. 'It's on its way to you now. *A plus tard, chéri.*'

Setting the phone down, Fleur tied the sash on her robe, broke off a hunk of baguette, spread it with butter and thick comb honey and moseyed out onto her deck. The first time she'd appeared on the deck in her peignoir, the village had been mildly scandalized; now, no one turned a hair.

It was a shame that she'd be breakfasting alone, she thought. It was a perfect morning for perusing the papers over *café au lait* and shooting the breeze with her lover. They managed so seldom to spend quality time together, as demands on Corban to spend precious weekends in his Dublin office were ever more pressing. Even though he had a boat moored in the marina, *Lolita* spent most of her life at anchor. There had only been one excursion so far this summer, and the curtains of Corban's holiday apartment on the harbour were constantly drawn. No wonder really – any time Corban O'Hara could afford to spend in Lissamore was spent *chez* Fleur.

'Hey, gorgeous!'

Looking down, Fleur saw Seamus Moynihan unwinding the hawser of his boat from a bollard.

'Hello, Seamus! Off to inspect your lobster pots?'

'I am. But sure I don't know why I'm bothering. There's no demand for lobster since that outcry on the radio.'

'What do you mean?'

'Some gobshite complained on a talk show about lobsters being killed inhumanely, and the politically-correct brigade have decided to boycott them.'

Fleur felt a pang of guilt. She should have talked Corban into going for lobster this evening, in O'Toole's seafood bar, with Guinness instead of Bordeaux. It made sense to support the local community now that times were hard. She knew well that the only reason her shop was doing such brisk business was because word had got out on the street that Elena Sweetman, the star of *The O'Hara Affair*, had taken to dropping in to Fleurissima. Once the movie was wrapped she – and all the workers employed on the film – would be back to leaner times.

'Maybe you'll have luck tonight,' she told Seamus. 'There'll be lots of people looking for restaurant tables now that the festival's in full swing. And I'm sure they are not all politically correct.'

Seamus shrugged. 'Even the festival's down-sized this year. There's no fun fair, and no ceilidh. And I heard that Río's too busy on the film to do her fortune-telling gig.'

'Oh – but she's enlisted a replacement.'

'Who might that be?'

Fleur bit her lip. 'I don't know,' she lied. She didn't want to confess that she would be ensconced in the fortune-telling

42

booth today. If word got around, people might not bother forking out money to see the local boutique owner do a bad imitation of Río, who always bluffed a blinder. 'But I hear she's very good,' she added, lamely.

'Maybe I should pay her a visit, so,' remarked Seamus. 'She might see something in my future to give me a glimmer of hope. Nets brimming with fish, for instance.' Raising a hand to shield his eyes from the sun, he squinted at the horizon. 'God be with the good old days when you actually caught something out there.'

Fleur gave him a sympathetic smile. 'Well, *bonne chance* today!'

'*Bonne chance*?'

'It means "good luck", darling!'

'I'll need it.' Seamus pulled at the throttle of his outboard and chugged away from his mooring. 'If I do have *bonne chance*,' he threw back over his shoulder, 'I'll drop a couple of mackerel in to you later.'

'Thank you, Seamus! *Salut!*'

Resting her forearms on the railing, Fleur watched as the boat made its way out of the marina, foam churning in its wake. Gulls looped the loop lazily in the sky blue above, and a tern plummeted headlong into the marine blue below, breaking the surface with barely a splash. She could see the submerged shape of a seal over by the breakwater; and a couple of beat-up-looking cats on the sea wall were laughing at Seamus's lurcher, who was lolloping along the pier in pursuit of the post mistress's Airedale.

There was a shrine to Fleur's little doggie, Babette, on the deck. It comprised a photograph of Babette that Daisy had taken, and had framed as a present for Fleur. Fleur had surrounded the photograph with flowers and candles and some of Babette's toys. She had buried her best friend six months ago, on the beach at Díseart, where the dog had loved to romp. Fleur still missed the Bichon Frisé with the laughing eyes and the perma-smile.

From the hill above, the church bell chimed nine. Fleur had promised Río that she'd be in the fortune-telling booth ready to go at midday. For the past week, she had practised her crystal ball skills every evening, using Daisy's password to gain entry to her Facebook page for research purposes. Some of the comments on Daisy's wall had expressed a genuine interest in going to see Madame Tiresia. 'If she got your future sorted, Daisy-Belle, then I'm deffo gonna go!' one girl had written. 'She might make me lucky 2 ☺'

Fleur had felt a twinge of guilt when she'd read that one. She guessed that some people really *did* believe in tarot and horoscopes and all that jazz: you just had to look at the number of fortune-tellers advertising in the back pages of gossip magazines, who charged rip-off rates for their services. But then, Fleur wasn't ripping anybody off. All the money she took today was going to charity – and then some. Corban had been true to his word. After she'd donned her gypsy outfit for him last night, he'd made out a cheque to the Irish Hospice Foundation, signed it, and left the amount blank.

'You've just quadrupled your donation,' he told her. And then he'd taken her by the hand and led her upstairs to her bedroom.

It was funny, Fleur thought, that dressing up for Corban didn't embarrass her. If any of her former lovers had suggested that she dress up to have sex, she'd have told them where to get off. But then, in all her previous relationships, Fleur had been the more experienced partner: her lovers had deferred to her. In her current relationship, Corban called the shots; and it hadn't taken long for Fleur to find what a relief – and what a turn-on! – it was to be told what to do rather than doing the telling.

The mini Mills & Boon scenario she'd dreamed up earlier had rehashed much of what had actually happened on the night she and Corban had first met. Having gone off to book a hotel room, her tall dark stranger had returned to find Fleur sitting on the edge of the fountain in an attitude of bewilderment. 'What's wrong?' he'd asked. 'I'm not who you think I am,' she'd told him. And his response – as per the stupefying response of her Mills & Boon hero – had been: 'I don't care who you are, any more than you care who I am.' And then Corban had escorted her upstairs to the room and – with a passion that compensated for the deficiency of ceremony – had *baisé*'d her.

Smiling, Fleur leaned her chin on her forearms. Why was there no equivalent word for the sex act in English? 'Fuck' was too rough. 'Shag' too casual. 'Making love' was far too fey. The only verb that accurately conveyed the delicious-ness, the pleasure, the sheer *je ne sais quoi* of coitus was the French one: *baiser*.

She remembered how, afterwards, he'd unmasked her and laughed and said: 'You're Fleur O'Farrell!'

He'd seen her in Lissamore, he'd told her, going about her business, and thought how quintessentially French she was, and how very lovely. He'd Googled her and viewed her website, but he had never found an opportunity to woo her. And now that he had her in his bed, he told her, he didn't intend to let her go.

'What about Rachel?' she'd asked.

'Ancient history,' came the response. 'Let's not talk about her.'

So they'd talked about him for a while instead. Over a

glass of champagne, Fleur learned that Corban O'Hara was a successful entrepreneur who had taken to financing films. *The O'Hara Affair* was his most ambitious project to date. He was divorced, he told her, *sans* children. A pleasure craft, recently acquired, was moored in the marina at Lissamore, where he owned a holiday apartment – also recently acquired. He supported numerous charities, including her favourite, the Hospice Foundation. And when he let a hint drop as to his age, Fleur realized that – at nearly a decade older than her – he was the most grown-up lover she'd ever had. It made her feel deliciously, absurdly youthful.

And then they'd had some more champagne, and she'd told him a little about herself, and they'd discovered that they each had a penchant for Paris and piquet and the Monsieur Hulot films, and they'd laughed and larked a little and then *baisé*'d some more.

But Rachel – whoever she might be – preyed on Fleur's mind. Corban had booked the room for Rachel, and the champagne and the flowers that had been brought to that room had been intended for Rachel, not for her. Fleur felt bad about the fact that she'd muscled in on another woman's man, and it unsettled her to know that Corban had cheated on this Rachel with such insouciance. But any time she questioned him about her, he just said those two words: 'Ancient history'. So finally, she made herself stop thinking about Rachel altogether.

'Flirty! Good morning! Isn't it a gorgeous day?'

Daisy was hailing her from the sea wall that skirted the main street of the village. She was wearing frayed cut-offs that revealed an astonishing length of golden leg, and a man's hoodie. Despite the dressed-down ensemble, she still looked as if she'd stepped out of the pages of *Vogue*. Fleur felt a great surge of love for her niece. She was so beautiful, so full of *joie de vivre*, so *young*!

'Good morning, Daisy-Belle!'

'But bad, bad Flirty, to be lazing in the sun when she should be hard at work!' Daisy scolded her. 'Why aren't you doing your homework?'

'Homework?'

'*Livre de visage!*'

Oh. Facebook. Daisy was right. Fleur should be practising her fortune-telling skills, not lounging around on her deck, coasting on a nostalgia trip.

'OK, OK. Do you fancy joining me for coffee?'

'No, thank you kindly. I'm off for a swim. Catch you later!' And Daisy swung a leg over the pillion of the motorcycle that was waiting for her, a helmeted youth revving the engine. He handed her a lid, and they were off, buzzing up the village street like a hornet.

Fleur wandered back into her kitchen and booted up her laptop before fixing herself coffee. Sitting down, she entered Daisy's password, and perused the new postings on her wall. A lot of messages that meant nothing to Fleur, some photographs, a couple of links to YouTube videos.

Fleur now knew how engrossing Facebook could be. Over the past few days she had been distracted from her 'homework' on numerous occasions: once you got sucked in to YouTube it was difficult to pull yourself away. She found herself checking out all the silly Bichon Frisé footage, and even contemplated putting up some of the sequences she'd compiled of Babette. And, of course, it was impossible to resist all the clips from old movies – Rita Hayworth singing 'Put the Blame on Mame', Marilyn crooning 'I Wanna be Loved by You', Ava Gardner rhapsodizing over her man in *Showboat*.

She had also followed links to numerous blogs, many of which made her want to weep for the young people out there who seemed so lonely, despite the myriad methods of communication available to them:

I've finally hit triple digits with Facebook friends – altho the females outnumber the males. Why? Now, topping out at a hundred, I have more Facebook friends than real life ones. Sad, or what?

It's scary to see pictures and details of former friends/enemies. Revisiting the past is no fun. Some 'friendships' should never be resurrected, not even in a virtual sense.

I say to myself, aww fuck. Even tho I hate this person, I guess I'd better add them as my friend . . . I'll take ANYONE now.

Have you noticed the weird thing is that girls seem to be way more flirtatious on Facebook than in real life. Why is that?

Scrolling through Daisy's Facebook friends, Fleur found crazy girls, dreamy girls, beauty queens, nymphs. Princesses, preppie girls, Barbie dolls, tramps. Wannabes and It girls, Latinas and Goths. Goddesses and nerdy girls and cheer-leaders and vamps. Girls with names like Tinkerbell, L'il Monkeypaws and Puss. Or plain Emily and Martha and Jennifer and Luce. The pages of Facebook were adorned with girls galore.

'Hi, Miriam,' Fleur murmured, clicking on a link. 'Welcome.

You had a birthday recently, didn't you? . . . Come on in, Rosa. Don't be sad about your boy breaking up with you. You have a holiday to look forward to . . . Hi, there, Nelly. You've got to get those red shoes you've been hankering after. If you shimmy down to Fleurissima this afternoon, maybe you'll find they've been reduced by fifteen per cent . . . Hi, Kitten; hi, Angel; hi, Naomi; hi, Paige . . .'

Glancing at the time, Fleur saw that it was nearly half-past ten. Time to jump into a shower, pull on her disguise, and get her ass down to the community centre. But a new notification on Daisy's wall made her click one last time.

Oh! Bethany had the most candid eyes she had ever seen. Her birth date told Fleur she was eighteen, but she looked younger. She had the other-worldly appearance of one of Cicely Mary Barker's flower fairies – tousled hair, delicate bone structure, translucent skin. She was Pisces, a Friday's child, an incurable dreamer. She loved cats and cuddles and jacaranda-scented candles. She played piano, loved to paint, and was no good at games. She adored Harry Potter and the music of A Camp and Muse. She haunted art galleries. She was partial to Dolly Mixtures. She hated polystyrene cups. She was going to be in Lissamore this weekend. She was looking forward to visiting Madame Tiresia.

And Madame Tiresia was looking forward to meeting her.

Chapter Four

'It is quite possible for the gazer to be able to see things in the crystal at one time and not at another. This being so, you should not be discouraged if such images fail to appear at the gazer's command.' Dr R A Mayne

If Madame Tiresia fails to detect your aura, there will be no charge for your consultation.

Bethany regarded the disclaimer on the placard outside the fortune-teller's booth. It was a bit like that terms-and-conditions-apply-share-prices-may-go-down-as-well-as-up stuff that voice-overs rattled off at the end of bank ads on the radio. In other words: let the buyer beware. Still, it was worth a try. Her horoscope had told her to heed the advice of a wise woman this week, and since Daisy de Saint-Euverte had been raving about Madame Tiresia on Facebook, Bethany had to assume that this was the wise woman in question. Bethany believed in horoscopes, even though she pretended to be cynical about them.

Although they had never met in real life, she had been thrilled when Daisy had accepted her as a friend on Facebook. It didn't matter that Daisy had thousands of friends, it still felt kinda cool. Bethany's friends numbered just over a hundred now, but she had to admit that she was a bit indiscriminate about the friendships she'd acquired. What must it be like to be as popular as Daisy de Saint-Euverte? Bethany had never been popular at school: she hadn't been bullied as such – just ignored. She had been in awe of those girls who seemed so effortlessly confident, whose hair swished like something out of a shampoo commercial, and who spoke in loud D4 accents. She'd never been part of a crowd that screamed and hugged whenever they met, and who threw pink pyjama parties where they necked vodkatinis and watched the singalong version of *Mamma Mia* while texting their boyfriends. She'd been invited to one of those dos by a cousin, and she had screamed and giggled and sung along on cue, but she had felt like a complete impostor. She had been glad the next day to return to the fantasy realms that lay beyond the portal of her Xbox.

The other reason for Bethany's low self-esteem was the fact that she had never had a boyfriend. She reckoned it was because her boobs were too small. She'd been going to ask her parents if she could have a boob job for her eighteenth birthday, but she knew they would have pooh-poohed the idea. They'd tell her not to be so stupid, that she was beautiful as she was. They didn't understand what it was like to be a teenager. They didn't know that it was horrible.

A gang of girls was coming along the promenade now, a phalanx of linked arms and GHD hair and blinging teeth. Bethany knew that if they saw her vacillating outside the fortune-teller's, she'd be subjected to their derision. And there was nothing more lacerating than the derision of teenage girls. She'd never forgotten the snorts of mirth that had erupted in the classroom when the careers guidance teacher had announced that Bethany wanted to be an actress ('Sure after all, girls,' the teacher had chortled, fanning the flames of her peers' ridicule, 'isn't Bethany O'Brien a fine name for a thespian? With a grand alliterative name like that, you wouldn't be after needing any talent at all, so you wouldn't.') At least today she had somewhere to hide: there'd been nowhere to hide in the classroom that day. Pulling aside the curtain, she ducked into the booth.

It took a moment or two for her eyes to adjust to the gloom. The tented space was lit by a single, crimson-shaded lamp. At a table covered in a star-spangled chenille cloth, a veiled woman was sitting gazing into a crystal ball in which Bethany could see herself reflected in miniature.

'Erm, hello, Madame Tiresia,' she said, feeling awkward. 'My name—'

'Sit down, Bethany,' said the woman.

'Oh! How did—'

'I know your name? I saw it in the crystal. I've been waiting for you.'

Well, so far, so impressive. What clever trick had Madame used to get her name right? She'd try to work it out later, the way she and her parents did after watching Derren Brown on the telly. Moving towards the table, she sat down opposite Madame Tiresia.

'Before we start, I must ask you to cross my palm with five euros.'

'Oh – of course.' Bethany pulled out her purse and handed over a five euro note, which Madam Tiresia slid into a manila envelope. The envelope was bulging: business must have been brisk. Bethany wondered how many of Daisy's Facebook friends had taken her advice and sought a consultation with the fortune-teller. She'd check Facebook out later, and see what the consensus was.

'Let me see what else the crystal has to show,' said Madame Tiresia. 'You sat exams recently, Bethany. You think you did quite well, but you're scared that you may not have done well enough.'

'You're right.'

Hmm. Bethany guessed that that could apply to virtually every girl her age who came into the booth, since most teenagers this summer would have taken exams, and most would be feeling insecure about results.

'What else do I see in the crystal?' continued Madame Tiresia. 'I see . . . a fish. Two fishes. What does that signify?'

'Um. I don't know. Maybe my mum's going to do some kind of fish for supper.'

Madame Tiresia gave a low laugh. 'No. The crystal is telling me that you were born under the sign of Pisces. Is that so?'

'Yes.'

'You are a talented young lady, Bethany. Artistic.'

Bethany shrugged. 'I – I suppose I am.'

'I see a keyboard. Do you play the piano?'

'Yes. I do.'

'And you love to act. It is your dream career. Have you applied to theatre school?'

'Not yet.'

'Isn't it about time you did?'

'I guess so. They've actually extended the deadline to the school I want to go to, but I keep putting it off.'

'I see. You're putting it off because you're scared of rejection?'

Bethany nodded.

'The crystal ball is telling me that you shouldn't procrastinate any longer,' said Madame Tiresia. 'If you want this thing badly enough, you must take action now.'

'Oh.' Bethany looked dubious. 'OK.'

'The ball is telling me too that you've had a reason to be

unhappy lately. What is the reason for your unhappiness, Bethany?'

'I – I guess it's just . . . I'm eighteen and I've never had a boyfriend.' Oh! What was she doing, blurting out personal stuff like that! It was a fortune-teller she was talking to, not an agony aunt!

'You badly want a boyfriend?'

'Yeah. I know it's stupid, but I feel like a loser without one.'

'But you are a special girl, Bethany.'

Bethany shook her head. 'No way! I'm not special!'

'You are a special girl, Bethany,' repeated Madame Tiresia. 'And special girls have to be particular about the kind of boy they allow into their lives. You must not settle for just any Tom, Dick or Harry.'

Bethany drooped. 'It's just that nearly all the other girls I know have boyfriends.'

'Ah – but they probably *have* settled for any Tom, Dick *and* Harry. They think that by surrounding themselves with friends, it proves to the world how popular they are. But they're indiscriminate. You, Bethany, being special, must wait for that special boy. He is out there somewhere, waiting for you. But you must be patient.'

Funny. That's what her mother always said to her. Bethany had always pretended to her mum that she didn't care that she didn't have a boyfriend, that she was perfectly happy without some punk hanging around, cramping her style. But the real reason she told her mum this was to reassure her, because she didn't want her to know how badly she was hurting. She'd never told anyone how badly she was hurting. Until now . . .

'I know it's hard, Bethany,' continued Madame Tiresia. 'It's hard to be different. And it's even harder when you're beautiful, because beautiful girls are expected to be carefree and fun-loving. You do know that you are beautiful, don't you?'

'Me? Are you—' Bethany had been about to say, 'Are you mad?' but, realizing how rude it would sound, stopped herself and changed it to, 'Are you serious?' Nobody apart from her parents had ever told her that she was beautiful. At school, she felt so ordinary next to the glossy girls who spent a fortune on their appearance. Plus, she was always being asked for her ID.

'You're beautiful, Bethany. You're a natural beauty. Trust me.'

'But everybody picks on me and calls me pleb and loser!'

'You're neither of those things, Bethany.'

'Oh – I've been a pleb and a loser for as long as I can remember.' Bethany gave a little laugh, as if she didn't care that people called her names – even though in reality it hurt like hell. 'I remember when all the girls in my class were getting confirmed and boasting about the frocks they were going to wear, and I pretended that I had a frock with lace petticoats and pearls sewn on and in fact there wasn't a frock at all because I wasn't getting confirmed. My parents are atheists, you see and have no truck with religion. And when the other kids found out I was lying they gave me such a hard time.'

'I can imagine. Children can be very cruel.'

'They're even worse when they grow up. I've had so much grief since people found out that I want to be an actress.'

'But haven't you always wanted to be an actress?'

'Yes – since I was a little girl. But I never told anyone. I just used to act out scenes all by myself in my bedroom.'

'So you've never acted in public?'

'No. I used to help out with the drama group at school, but I didn't have the nerve to audition. I just used to fetch

56

and carry for the stage manager, and sit on the book in the prompt corner during shows. And then when people found out that I had – well, aspirations – they decided I'd got too big for my boots. They started sniggering and saying things like, "Got yourself an agent yet?" and, "When's DiCaprio coming to find you?" And I'd have to laugh and pretend I can take a joke. I've got pretty good at pretending. Maybe that's why I identify so much with Laura in *The Glass Menagerie*. They're doing it in November, in the Gaiety School. I'd give anything to play Laura. In my dreams!'

'Dream building is a good starting point. Tell me this. Assuming your application is successful, how are you going to put yourself through school? Will your parents finance you?'

'I'll live with them, because I can't afford to rent anywhere. But I'm going to have to get some kind of a part-time job.' Bethany gave a mirthless laugh. 'That'll be a challenge, the way things are in the employment market.'

'So you'll be looking for work when you go back to Dublin?'

'Yeah. I'd much rather stay here, though, until term starts. I love it here.'

'Why don't you try and get a job in Lissamore, then?'

'I've tried. There's nothing going.'

'You're wrong. There are jobs going. Did you look for work on *The O'Hara Affair*?'

'As an actress? Are you – serious? I wouldn't have the nerve.'

'Not as an actress, no. As an extra.'

'I'd have loved that, but somebody told me there was no point. Apparently hundreds of wannabes like me applied. Oh – that's an awful word, isn't it! Wannabe.'

'No. There's nothing wrong with wanting something.

Wanting something is proactive. Apathy is far, far worse. That's why your classmates made jokes at your expense. They don't have the courage to dream.'

'What do you mean?'

'You said an interesting thing earlier. You said that people decided you'd got too big for your boots. That's because you have a dream, Bethany, and maybe they don't. And because they're jealous of your dream, they want to destroy it. Seeing you fail will make them feel better about themselves. Think about it.'

Bethany thought about it, and as she did, she felt a creeping sense of relief that what she'd always suspected to be true had been put into words by someone so much older and wiser than her. Was that the reason she was confiding all her secrets in Madame Tiresia? 'That's horrible, isn't it?'

'It's human nature. But a much easier way of feeling better about yourself is to have a positive mantra. You lost your phone recently, didn't you?'

'Yes. How did you – oh. The crystal, of course.'

'Of course,' echoed Madame. Was Bethany imagining it, or was there a smile in her voice? 'And when you lost your phone, what did you say to yourself?'

'I told myself that I was an idiot.'

'You see? *You* told *yourself*.' Madame shook her head. 'If *you* are telling yourself that you're an idiot, Bethany, you are simply giving other people a license to do the same. If your self-esteem is rock bottom, you can hardly expect other people to respect you. So next time you lose your phone, don't tell yourself you're an idiot. Say, instead: "Oh! I have lost my phone – but hey, that happens to everyone from time to time. Losing my phone doesn't mean I am an idiot. In fact, I think I'm pretty damned special."'

Bethany wrinkled her nose. 'But isn't that kind of arrogant?'

'Not at all. I have never understood why people think it is an insult when someone makes the observation, "You think you're so great." Tell me – how would you respond if someone said that to you?'

'I'd tell them no way – I *don't* think I'm great.'

'You see! How negative is that? The correct response is, "That's because I *am* great!"'

'I'd never dream of saying that!' protested Bethany.

'You don't actually have to articulate it. Say it to yourself. Say it now, Bethany. Say, "I think I'm great".'

'No. I can't.'

'Say it!'

'I think I'm . . . great,' said Bethany, without conviction.

'There you are! Say it to yourself every time you want to call yourself an idiot. Say it over and over. "I think I'm great, I think I'm great, I think I'm *great!*" Let it be your mantra. Picture that little girl who pretended she had a confirmation dress with petticoats, the little girl who could only act a role in the privacy of her bedroom. She's afraid – she needs reassurance. Get to know her, make her your friend. Give her the respect she deserves, and I can guarantee that people will start to respect you, too.'

Bethany's mind's eye saw herself as a child, standing in a circle of little girls all comparing notes on their confirmation dresses. They'd been insecure, too, of course, with their bragging about how much their dress had cost and where it had been purchased. As for those girls she'd seen earlier – the ones with the swingy hair and orthodontic smiles – maybe they too sought help from internet sites or cried hot tears while updating their blogs? Maybe even Daisy de Saint-Euverte suffered from the blues, or the mean reds, like Holly Golightly in *Breakfast at Tiffany's*.

'The crystal tells me you should try for work on the film.' Madame Tiresia's tone was authoritative.

'What?'

'The crystal is certain that if you try, you will succeed. Go home now, and send off an email application for work as an extra. You'll find it on *The O'Hara Affair* website.'

'You really think I should?'

'I do. Nothing ventured, nothing gained.'

Bethany smiled. 'That's what my mum always says.'

'Mums can be pretty wise women.' Madame Tiresia passed her hands over the crystal, setting her bangles jingling. 'Alas, Bethany, your time is up. The crystal's gone cloudy.'

'Oh. Well – thank you for your advice, Madame. I'll send off an application right away. I'll send off two! One to the movie people, and one to the Gaiety School! My horoscope said I should heed the advice of a wise woman.'

'Do you believe in horoscopes?'

'No,' she lied. 'But I believe in you.'

'That's the spirit, beautiful girl. Shoo.'

Bethany rose to her feet. But before she lifted the flap of the booth she turned back to Madame. 'D'you know something? I kinda feel more like I've been talking to a counsellor or a shrink or something rather than a fortune-teller. You should be an agony aunt – no offence!' she added hastily. 'You're a really good fortune-teller as well.'

'I know I am,' said Madame Tiresia. 'Give your cat Poppet a cuddle from me when you get home.'

'Wow!' said Bethany. 'How did you—?'

'How do you think?'

Utterly mystified, Bethany shook her head, gave a little smile, then left the booth. Outside, the gaggle of girls was sitting on the sea wall, swinging their legs.

'I think I'm great,' she murmured to herself as she plugged herself into her iPod. 'I think I'm great. I think I'm *great!*'

She smiled as the Sugababes told her how sweet life could be, how it could change. *Nothing ventured, nothing gained* – that's what Madame had told her, that's what her mother told her, and really, the old clichés were the ones that always made the most sense. She could change her life around, and she was going to do it today because, after all, she was *great* – wasn't she?

It was lucky for Bethany that the strains of the Sugababes drowned out the small arms fire of snide remarks that came her way from the sea wall as she headed for the narrow road that would take her home to Díseart.

As soon as Bethany left the booth, Fleur scribbled a 'Back in five minutes' sign and stuck it on the tent flap. Then she phoned Corban. 'Lover?' she said. 'Can you do me a favour?'

'That depends. Run it by me.'

'There's a girl who'd love to work as an extra on the film. Do you think you could organize it for her?'

'That's not my department, Fleur.'

'I know. But I told her that it would happen.'

'You mean, Madame Tiresia told her it would happen?'

'Same difference. Surely you have some influence in the casting?'

'I had some say in casting the leads, yes. Extras are a whole different ball game.'

'Please, Corban. I really like this girl.'

'What makes her so special?'

'She's vulnerable. She's desperate to be an actress, but she's not going to make it without a leg-up and some kind of experience.'

'What age is she?'

'Eighteen. But she looks younger. She could easily pass for a child. And didn't you say that most of the extras were too well-fed-looking to be famine victims? This girl's a skinny little thing. Very pretty, though, in a – um . . . What's that word you use for "growing into"?'

'Nascent?'

'Nascent! That's it. You can tell that she's uncomfortable with the way she looks. I remember going through that stage when I was her age. It's horrible – really horrible. You don't realize that you're turning into a swan. You think you're going to be the ugly duckling for ever.'

'What's her name?'

'Bethany O'Brien.'

'Easy to remember. OK. Leave it with me. I'll have a word with the casting assistant and ask her to look out for your Bethany.'

'Thank you, darling. She'll be sending through an email application this afternoon. How did your meeting go?'

'Not great. We're over budget. It looks as if this is going to be the most expensive movie ever made in Ireland.'

'Oh. Then what can I say but – enjoy your lunch.'

'Thanks. How's your fortune-telling lark going?'

'It's fun.'

'Maybe you should take it up full time. Predicting the future could be a lucrative way to earn a living in these uncertain times.'

'Only if you get it right. I hope people don't come looking for their money back.'

'Well, it's unlikely that your Bethany will.'

'What do you mean?'

'The casting assistant's just come in. I'll pull some strings and get your girl a job, starting asap.'

'You star! Oops! I'd better go. Someone's put their head

around the tent flap. Time to have my palm crossed with more euros.'

Fleur stuck her phone in her bag. It wasn't seemly for a fortune-teller to be caught chatting on a mobile. And as for the device under the tablecloth? Well, nobody need ever know about that. She called to the next girl to come in, then started to scroll through Daisy's very useful list of Facebook friends.

'Hello, Madame. I'm Gina.'

'Gina. Sit down. Might your surname be Lombard?'

'That's amazing! How do you—'

'I don't know. But the crystal does,' said Fleur, with a smile.

Chapter Five

It was Daphne's eighty-fifth birthday and as a treat, Christian had booked a table for lunch at a newly opened restaurant, for which he was sourcing the wine. Nemia had dressed Daphne in a shirtwaister with a pie-crust collar, American Tan tights, and faux-suede shoes with elasticated sides. Her hair was coiffed in a bouffant, and she'd been sprayed with her favourite scent, *Je Reviens*. She sat in the passenger seat of Christian's Saab, singing random snatches of old musical numbers and reapplying her lipstick, while Dervla zoned out in the back, mulling over the events of the past few days.

Getting her mother-in-law settled into the cottage had been rather a fraught affair, and Dervla wasn't sure how well she'd handled things. On their first evening, Nemia had opted out of joining them for dinner, claiming that she'd prefer to cook for herself in the cottage and – since Nemia was a vegetarian – this made sense. Dervla had gone to some trouble, setting the kitchen table in the Old Rectory with flowers and candles, and putting Des O'Connor on the iPlayer. She'd downloaded it specially for Daphne, hoping that familiar music from a bygone era might help to make her feel at home. She'd also shifted the table across to the window, so that Daphne would have something to look at. Her eyesight was failing, but she could still make out motion and colour, and the wisteria growing around the window frame was spec-tacular – a pelmet of purple.

'Why are we eating in the kitchen?' Daphne demanded, on being shown into the room.

'Because we have no dining room yet.' Setting the serving dish on the table, Dervla started spooning out portions.

'What do you mean, you have no dining room?'

'It's being decorated.'

'Oh. What's that noise?'

'It's Des O'Connor.'

'Des O'Connor! Turn him up.'

Dervla did as she was told.

'Grub's up, Mum!' said Christian, rubbing his hands together with exaggerated enthusiasm.

'What are we having?' asked Daphne, lowering herself into the chair that Christian was holding out for her.

'Looks like shepherd's pie to me,' said Christian.

'That's exactly what it is!' enthused Dervla. 'Shepherd's pie! Made by my own fair hands! Except it's not strictly speaking shepherd's pie, because it's made with beef, not lamb. I suppose it should be called cowman's pie instead.'

'Isn't it known as cottage pie?' Christian supplied.

'Oh, yes! I think you're right.'

Dervla felt as if she were doing a bad audition for a job as a children's television presenter. Her smile had never felt more fake. Having finished serving, she was about to sit down when Daphne lowered her head and said: 'For what we are about to receive . . .'

Yikes! Grace? Dervla gave Christian a look of enquiry. He responded with a nod, and Dervla took her place at the table, murmuring, 'May the Lord make us truly thankful.'

'Amen.' Daphne peered at her plate. 'What is it?'

'It's shepherd's pie, Daphne,' Dervla reminded her.

'Oh, good. I love shepherd's pie.'

'We all love shepherd's pie.' Christian took up his fork and tried a mouthful. 'Mmm. It is delicious.'

'I'm going to eat this now,' announced Daphne. 'Shall I eat it?'

'Yes. Do.'

Dipping her fork into the shepherd's pie, Daphne scooped some up. But as she brought the food to her mouth, a lump of mashed potato dropped onto her lap.

'Oops!' said Dervla. 'I'll get a cloth.'

Daphne gave her a cross look. 'I don't have a napkin! I should have a napkin.'

'I'll get you one now.' Dervla helped herself to a cloth, and tore some sheets off a roll of kitchen towel. Then she wiped the mashed potato off Daphne's lap, and distributed the makeshift napkins. 'Nappies for everyone!' she carolled.

'Dear God,' remarked Christian. 'I hope not.'

Dervla widened her eyes at him, and he winked. Resuming her seat, she tried hard not to laugh, but it was proving impossible, and then, to make matters worse, Christian started to laugh too.

'What's so funny?' asked Daphne.

'Nothing,' he told her. 'I just remembered a joke.'

Daphne looked put out. 'Well, if it's so side-splittingly funny, I think you might have the manners to share it.'

'Um. OK. A grasshopper walks into a bar. The barman looks astonished. "Hey – whaddaya know?" he says. "We have a cock-tail named after you." The grasshopper gives the bartender a bemused look and says: "You have a cocktail called Steve?"'

Dervla started to laugh again. It was one of those awful fits of spasmodic laughter that happens when you are painfully aware that laughing is completely out of order, like laughing in church, or in the doctor's waiting room.

Daphne gave Dervla a frosty look. 'I think that is not a joke at all. Or if it is, it's a very silly joke. You should be ashamed of yourself, Christian, for telling such silly jokes. What age are you now?'

'I'm forty-five, Mum.'

'You're never forty-five!' exclaimed Daphne.

'I sure am. And feeling every day of it.'

'But are you my son?'

'Yes.'

'Then what age am I?'

'You're well over eighty, Mum.'

'But I don't want to be that old! That's dreadful!'

'Yes. But, sure – you're as young as you feel.'

There was a pregnant pause as Daphne digested the news that she was eighty-something and Des O'Connor crooned over the speakers about Spanish eyes. 'I'm carrying on the tradition of my family,' she pronounced finally. 'Living to a funny old age. My parents are still alive, you know. Aren't they?'

Christian set down his fork. 'What do you think, Mum?'

'No.' Daphne drooped a little. 'It's terrible when your memory deserts you.'

'That's what happens when you reach your age,' Christian reassured her. 'It's OK. It's not your fault.'

Dervla and Christian exchanged glances. A sudden sobriety had fallen on the dinner table. They continued to eat in silence for a while. Then Daphne looked curiously at Christian and said: 'Did you marry someone?'

'Yes. I married Dervla.'

'Dervla?' she said, turning to regard her. 'Is that you?'

'Yes, Daphne,' said Dervla. 'Christian, could you pass me the salt, please?'

'Certainly,' said Christian. 'There you are.'

'Thank you.'

'You're welcome.'

Oh, this was awful, awful! Dervla felt as if she were spouting dialogue from a bad play. She couldn't be spontaneous. She couldn't just reach for the salt herself in case it looked unmannerly. She couldn't burp and then go 'Oops!' She couldn't say, 'Look at that queer-shaped cloud.' She couldn't say, 'I'm knackered.' She couldn't say, 'How are you getting on with the new Patricia Cornwell?' Because if she said any of those things, she'd have to explain to Daphne what she had said. She'd have to say, 'There's a funny-shaped cloud in the sky, Daphne. I was just pointing it out to Christian.' She'd have to say, 'I was just saying to Christian that I'm very tired.' She'd have to say, 'Christian is reading a book by an author called Patricia Cornwell, and I was wondering if he was enjoying it.' And then Daphne would be bound to come out with something like, 'Christian is *not* reading a book. He is eating his dinner.' And then . . . And *then*?

Hell. She couldn't allow this to happen to her. 'Look at that queer-shaped cloud, Christian,' she said, in a low voice.

'Wow! It looks like the UFO from *Close Encounters*.'

'That's just what I was thinking!'

'Why are you whispering?' shouted Daphne. 'You don't want me to hear!'

'We're not whispering, Mum,' said Christian.

'Then stop giving each other private looks. It's rude.'

'But we're married. We're allowed to look at each other.' He smiled at Dervla, and added in an undertone, 'And do rude things.'

'What do you mean, you're married?'

'Dervla and I were married last year.'

'What? Why did nobody *tell* me? I don't *believe* that the pair of you are married! *Congratulations and jubilations!*'

Christian started to sing along, then stopped abruptly, and slid Dervla an apologetic look.

'It's OK,' she told him. 'It really is.' And, taking a deep breath, she joined in the song she had never been able to bring herself to sing before in her life because it was so damned naff.

'There's a bird!' exclaimed Daphne, interrupting the sing-along. 'That was a bird, you know. I saw it land on the windowsill. And then it took off. It was a bird.'

There was another pause, then Dervla rose and started to clear away her plate. She wasn't hungry any more. And then she tensed, waiting for Daphne to say it was rude to clear away before everyone had finished. But thankfully, Daphne hadn't seemed to notice. 'Would you like a bowl of ice cream for pudding, Daphne?' she asked, in her children's television presenter's voice.

'No. I would not like a great big *bowl*. I would like a *dish* of ice cream for pudding. Thank you.'

'You're welcome.'

'Well, that was a lovely dinner, wasn't it?' said Christian, putting his knife and fork together.

'What did we have, again?'

'Shepherd's pie.'

Oh, God help us, Dervla thought, as she scraped leftover pie into the bin and went to fetch bowls – *dishes* – from the cupboard. Behind her, she could hear Daphne blowing her nose. When she went back to the table, a sheet of scrunched-up kitchen towel was sitting on her place mat.

That had been the first day. And now, sitting in the back of the car listening to Daphne singing about putting on her top hat and white tie and dancing in her tails, she thought the same thought again. God help us.

In the car park of Chez Jules Christian pulled up outside

the door, and came around to the passenger side to assist his mother out of the car. There was nothing much Dervla could do to help: she stood there watching as Daphne was shoe-horned out of the passenger seat and hoisted to her feet.

'I'll take over now,' said Dervla, taking hold of her mother-in-law's arm. 'You go and park.'

Daphne staggered a little as she redistributed her weight and clutched onto Dervla for support. Her bouffed-up hair had subsided, her American Tan tights were wrinkled round the ankles, and the lipstick that she'd put on in the car was lopsided, lending her the look of a badly made-up clown. Dervla suddenly felt a flash of pity for the old woman. To think that she had once modelled Balenciaga, conducted illicit affairs, and chucked diamonds down the loo! Had she ever imagined, as she'd stalked down the catwalk, that she'd end up like this?

A small boy was toddling across the car park, holding on to his mother's hand. He stopped when he saw Daphne, and stared at her, mouth agape. 'Old hag, Mammy!' he said. 'Look, Mammy – old hag!'

'Shh, Jamie!' said the woman in a terse undertone. 'Mind your manners!'

But it was true. Despite Nemia's attempts to style her hair and dress her up, Daphne did look like the kind of old hag you'd see in a storybook – beauty had turned into a beast.

As Dervla manoeuvred Daphne through the door of the restaurant, the maître d' came forward, concern on his face.

'Mr Vaughan's party,' said Dervla. 'He reserved a table for three.'

The maître d' smiled, and consulted his reservations book. 'Ah, yes! Follow me, please.'

As he led the way towards a table in an alcove on the far

side of the room, Dervla could see diners exchanging glances that said, quite clearly, *Oh my God, I hope they're not going to be seated at the table next to us . . .* The table was set for four, and Dervla knew damned well that the table plan had been deftly rejigged, to ensure that the Vaughan party would be seated in the most inconspicuous part of the restaurant. The maître d' drew out a chair for Daphne, and she fell into it with an 'Oof!' of relief.

At a nearby table, two yummy mummies were looking sideways at them, and talking in undertones. At another table, a middle-aged couple was sending Dervla sympathetic smiles. Was this inevitable when you got old? Dervla wondered. Did hitting a certain level of decrepitude mean that every time you emerged into public you were gawped at like something out of a freak show? She imagined the entrances that Daphne might once have made into restaurants, in her modelling days, when maîtres d' would bow and scrape, and diners gaze in admiration.

Although – she saw now – one person was regarding her with an engaging smile. It was a man she realized she knew. As Shane Byrne rose from his table and strolled over to her, diners did indeed gaze in admiration, for this was Hollywood royalty incarnate.

'Dervla! How lovely to see you. It's been a while.'

'Shane!' Dervla stood up and presented her face for a kiss. 'Río told me you were in town. You look great. How does it feel to be coming back as a hotshot movie star?'

'Not half bad. Apart from the camera phones. I can't go anywhere without someone sticking a phone in my face.'

'Remember your manners,' came the magisterial tones of her mother-in-law, 'and introduce me.'

'I beg your pardon. Shane, this is my mother-in-law, Daphne Vaughan. Daphne, this is Shane Byrne.'

Shane took Daphne's hand and raised it to his lips. '*Enchanté*,' he said, smiling directly into her eyes. 'I am delighted to make your acquaintance. And I hope you won't think it forward of me if I compliment you on the exquisite perfume you are wearing, madame.'

'Thank you. It's *Je Reviens*, you know. That means "I will return". I've worn it since I was a girl.'

'Not so long ago, then,' remarked Shane.

Daphne gave him a coquettish look. 'Ha! I can tell you are a Casanova.'

'Only around beautiful women,' said Shane.

'It's Daphne's birthday today, Shane,' Dervla told him.

'Twenty-one again?'

Daphne gave a tinkling laugh. 'You *are* a Casanova! Would you care to join us for a glass of champagne?'

'There's nothing I would enjoy more. I am, alas, otherwise engaged. It was a pleasure to have met you, Madame Vaughan. And may I wish you all the compliments of the day.'

Shane turned back to Dervla, who was regarding him with admiration. What an awesome performance! And then she remembered how adroitly he'd charmed her when they were little more than teenagers, and her sister after her, and – if the tabloids were to be believed – a bevy of beauties in Tinseltown.

'So you're playing the lead in *The O'Hara Affair*?' Dervla said. 'That would be Scarlett's father?'

'I am not playing Scarlett's father,' replied Shane, with some indignation. 'Gerald O'Hara is short and bow-legged. I'm playing the wicked landlord who practises droit du seigneur and gets to tup all the local totty.'

'Nice work.'

'I can't complain. How's your line of business, Dervla?'

'I've given up auctioneering. Or rather, it gave me up. And I'm writing a book.'

'You're writing a book!' said Daphne. 'What nonsense.'

Shane raised an eyebrow at Dervla, and she shrugged. 'What can I tell you?' she said. 'Life's a little rough around the edges these days. And I *am* writing a book, actually. On how to sell your house.'

'Hey! Congratulations.'

Dervla gave a rueful smile. 'Unlikely to be a bestseller, but it's keeping me busy.'

'Congratulations!' said Daphne. 'And celebrations. We're celebrating something, aren't we? What, exactly, are we celebrating?'

'We're celebrating your birthday,' Dervla told her.

'I'll let you get on with it,' said Shane. 'Good to see you, Dervla.'

'Likewise.'

Dervla resumed her seat, and watched Shane move back to his table, where a handsome, rather saturnine man was studying the wine list. She hoped it would impress – Christian had taken such care compiling it. Picking up a menu, she felt her stomach somersault when she saw the prices. She hadn't been exaggerating when she'd told Shane that life was a little rough around the edges. The proposed expansion of Christian's wine importing business had coincided with the recession: people weren't buying much fine wine these days. He'd taken to stocking more downmarket stuff to supply those customers who'd taken to drinking at home instead of the pub, where a couple of glasses of wine could cost nearly as much as a full bottle from the off-licence. Sales of accessories like electric corkscrews and wine coolers and silver champagne stoppers had plummeted, and sommelier kits remained on the shelf, gathering dust. Christian's efforts to get night classes in wine appreciation up and running in the community centre had met with a dismally poor response.

Luckily, there was income from the renting out of Dervla's apartment in Galway, and from the cottage – Christian's sister had insisted that if Daphne was to live with the newly-weds, it was only fair that they receive rent in return from the income that Daphne's investments brought in. It wasn't a whole lot, but it kept things ticking over – just.

Dervla remembered how things had been at the height of the property boom, when she could have afforded to eat out every night if she'd felt like it. She remembered how she'd fantasized about sitting with Christian on the bench by the door of the Old Rectory, sipping chilled Sancerre and sharing with him her dreams of planting fruit trees and keeping chickens and maybe – if they were lucky – having babies. She'd pictured herself drifting around the garden in a wifty-wafty frock, carrying a trug full of vege-tables she had grown herself, vegetables that she would whizz up into a delicious purée, to be served later with roast rack of lamb at the dining table around which a dozen friends would have congregated, all laughing and swapping gossip and repartee. The women would be dressed in Cath Kidston florals, the men in Armani casuals. Kitty the Dalmatian would sport a fringed suede collar, and there'd be Mozart on the sound system.

How ironic, she thought, that now she'd made the defin-ite decision to grow her own fruit and veg, it wasn't for trendy ecological reasons: it was because it was cheaper. Ironic that – now she was actually installed in her dream house – she couldn't afford to furnish it. Ironic that the only Cath Kidston florals within her current budgetary remit would come second-hand from eBay. But it was terribly,

terribly sad that, instead of Mozart, the accompanying sound-track to her life was Des O'Connor.

'What does that funny-looking person think he's doing?' Daphne was glowering at the maître d'.

'He's showing Christian to our table,' Dervla told her. 'Now. What'll we have to eat?'

'What is there?'

'I'll read the menu to you. Potted crab—'

'Potted what?'

Oh, God. Dervla resisted the temptation to sling the menu on the table and leg it out of the restaurant. Instead, she smiled at Christian as he joined them.

'Hi, darling,' she said.

He gave her a brief kiss on the cheek before dropping into his chair. 'Is that Shane Byrne I see over there?' he asked.

'That's him. I felt very chuffed to be seen hobnobbing with him: he came over to say hello.'

'This place must be good if it's frequented by film stars. He's a bit older in real life than he looks on the screen, isn't he?'

'Stop gawking at him. He says he can't go anywhere these days without someone sticking a phone in his face.'

'What an idea!' said Daphne. 'Why should anyone want to stick a phone in his face?'

'Shane's famous,' explained Dervla. 'He's a movie actor.'

'That doesn't explain why anyone should want to stick a *phone* in his face.'

'Phones can take photographs now, Mum,' said Christian.

'What a lot of nonsense you talk,' said Daphne.

Christian sighed, then opened the menu. 'Hmm. Potted crab sounds good.'

Daphne regarded him with interest. 'Potted what?' she said.

*   *   *

The excruciating lunch dragged on over ninety long minutes. Daphne kept making remarks about the other diners in quite stentorian tones, and every time she did, Dervla died a little death. And she had constantly to remind her mother-in-law that the drink in the tumbler to her right was elderflower pressé, and the food on the plate in front of her was fish pie, and Daphne insisted that she'd ordered meatballs like Christian, not fish pie, and her nose dripped constantly and she chewed on her cuticles, and Dervla found herself chewing on *her* cuticles – something she hadn't done since her stressed-out estate agent days.

At one stage, Christian made his excuses: he wanted to combine business with pleasure by having a chat with the owner about some alterations to the wine list. So he upped and left Daphne and Dervla together. After a couple of polite enquiries – would Daphne like some more water? Would she care for a cup of coffee? – Dervla gave up making desultory conversation, and people-watched instead. A woman's three-seasons-ago Vuitton bag was showing signs of wear and tear, and her roots were an inch long. A man was studying the bill with a furrowed brow, clearly hoping there was some mistake. A young couple had opted for two starters rather than main courses. At least Dervla wasn't the only person in Coolnamara who was feeling the pinch.

Things were different at Shane's table, on the other side of the room. There, lobster thermidor and an excellent bottle of Meursault had been served (Christian had recognized the label). Holy moly! It was far from lobster and swanky vintage wine that Shane Byrne had been reared! But, Dervla noticed now, he wasn't the one footing the bill. His lunch companion was dealing with it, while Shane signed autographs for a couple of awestruck teenage girls. As Shane chatted to his fan club, clearly charming them as much as he'd charmed Daphne earlier, Dervla saw his host finish the business with the chip and pin, smile at the waitress, and produce a business card. The pretty girl accepted it, smiled back, and nodded.

Hmm. What was going on there? Like all estate agents, Dervla was an excellent reader of body language: she'd learned over the course of two decades spent showing houses to know instantly whether or not a potential buyer was interested, whether or not they could afford the property in question, and whether or not they were bluffing. Sitting side-on to the table, this man's demeanour was relaxed: legs apart – one crooked, one stretched forward; left arm draped across the back of his chair; hair skimming his collar. His tie was loosened, his topmost shirt button undone, his Hugo Boss jacket worn with the casualness another man might wear a chain-store anorak. His watch was a discreet Rolex, and he exuded the easy authority of a Machiavellian prince. 'Behold!' both his dress and his body language were saying, 'Here presides an alpha male.' Dervla had sparred with many alpha males in the course of her career, and had more often than not emerged victorious. She had enjoyed the cut and thrust, the deploying of guerrilla tactics, the element of espionage. She wondered what kind of an opponent this guy would make, what his fatal flaw might be – if he had one. He certainly had an aura of invincibility.

'What is that man doing over there?' demanded Daphne.

Dervla thought at first that her mother-in-law was referring to Rolex man, but then realized that her gaze was trained on Shane, who had finished signing autographs with a flourish.

'That's Shane Byrne. He's signing autographs.'

'What for?'

'He's a film star.'

'Oh! How exciting. I'd like to meet him.'

There was no point in telling Daphne that she'd met him already. Dervla waved at Shane, and he took his leave of the lovely girls and came over immediately.

Giving him an apologetic look, Dervla launched into introductions once again. Thankfully, Shane copped on immediately, and Groundhog Day began anew. After he had told Daphne how *enchanté* he was, and complimented her for the second time on her perfume, Dervla managed to fish for the information she wanted.

'Who's your lunch partner?' she asked, lowering her voice a little and hoping that Daphne wouldn't command her to speak up.

'He's one of the executive producers on the film.'

'Executive! I've never really understood that word. What do "executive" producers do, exactly?'

'Nothing much, except inject capital. It's a vanity credit, really.'

'So it's all about ego?'

Shane shrugged. 'In this case, there's extra kudos in the fact that Corban's name is in the film's title. I suppose having a film named after you is a bit like having a ship named after you, and Mr O'Hara's a major player on board this one.'

Wow. So Rolex man was Corban O'Hara, Fleur's current squeeze! 'What's he like?' she asked.

'He seems nice enough for a rich bloke.'

'Pot, kettle, Shane Byrne.'

Shane gave her an 'as if' look. 'O'Hara is *seriously* rich, Dervla. If he decided to withdraw funding, the film would capsize.'

'Does he have any creative contribution at all?'

'He can make a few suggestions; do a little hiring and firing. Being an executive producer is all to do with power. The movie set is his principality.'

'So it's like playing at being king?'

This was Daphne's cue to start humming 'My Lord and Master' from *The King and I*.

'That's exactly what it's like,' Shane told her.

Dervla looked again at Corban O'Hara, who was eyeing the two autograph hunters. They were now strolling along the terrace of the restaurant, giggling and texting, probably sending word of their close encounter with the film star to every girl they knew.

Dervla narrowed her eyes in speculation. 'If the movie set is his principality,' she said, 'could he practise droit du seigneur? Or has the casting couch become extinct in post-feminist la-la land?'

'I don't think la-la land is ready for *feminism* yet, Dervla, let alone post-feminism. Over there, you'd be known as that quaint contradiction in terms that is "a career girl".'

'I had a career once, you know,' announced Daphne. 'I was a model.'

'Well, I'll be doggone! You should think about taking it up again,' said Shane, and Daphne gave him a playful slap on the arm.

'I know all about men like you!' she scolded.

'What made you give it up?' Dervla asked her mother-in-law, genuinely curious to know.

'What made me give it up? My parents, I think. Yes. My parents wanted me to get married to someone.'

'And who was the lucky man?' asked Shane.

'He was called . . . lucky. He was much older than I. He was a businessman. We lived in . . . Belgravia.'

'Ritzy!' remarked Shane.

'Yes. It was ritzy. But it wasn't what I wanted. I wanted to marry Jack. But Jack died.'

'How sad,' said Dervla. 'Was Jack your boyfriend?'

'Yes. It was very, very sad. He died in a fire. He was a dancer. He was the love of my life.' Daphne spoke with such emphasis that Dervla sensed she had total recall of this event. She'd read somewhere that people suffering from dementia had stronger memories of yesteryear than yesterday. 'It was very, very sad,' she said again. 'It was tragic.'

Shane and Dervla exchanged glances. Then Shane sat down on Christian's seat, and took Mrs Vaughan's hand. There were tears in the old lady's eyes.

'I know what it's like to lose the love of your life,' Shane said. 'I lost mine.'

'Oh. Did she die?'

'No. But she wouldn't marry me.'

'Stupid girl! She should be ashamed of herself. What was her name?'

'Her name is Río.'

Dervla looked at Shane in amazement. 'Río, Shane? After all this time?'

'It's always been her.'

'Your bird of paradise,' she said with a smile.

'What are you two talking about now?' demanded Daphne. 'Are you having an affair?'

'No, Daphne,' Dervla told her. 'We're just reminiscing about something that happened when we were very, very young.'

'"The Young Ones". That's a song by Cliff Richard, you know.'

Dervla knew what was coming, and sure enough, Daphne turned back to Shane and started to serenade him with 'The Young Ones'. Dervla was impressed by Shane's acting prowess. He managed to look as if sitting in a restaurant having a love song sung to him by a superannuated diner was the highlight of his day. And in fact, now that she listened to the song, Dervla realized that the words were peculiarly poignant: she didn't think she'd ever heard them properly before. No matter about Daphne's short-term memory, it was highly possible that her recall of greatest hits of the sixties could get her a gig on *Mastermind*. The lyrics were all about how important it was to live in the present because the transient nature of youth meant that you might never have another chance to find love.

Is that why Daphne had conducted all those affairs after she married? To try to find the love that had been so cruelly snatched from her first time around? Christian had mentioned that his father had been much older than his beautiful wife – that he had, in fact, been a friend of his grandfather – but he appeared as reluctant to talk about his family history as Dervla was to talk about hers. Oh, God! She hoped that the ghosts of Daphne's amours would never come spilling skeleton-like out of the closet. It was just as well, for Christian's sake, that the 'novel' his mother had been planning to write had never found a publisher.

'Mum! What are you doing, singing to a film star?' Christian had returned from his business chat, and was smiling down at his mother.

'Is this person a film star?' asked Daphne. 'Do I know him?'

'He certainly is a film star.' Christian extended a hand. 'Hi. I'm Christian Vaughan, Dervla's husband. Nice to meet you.'

'Likewise. You're the wine importer, yeah?'

'That's right.'

And as Christian and Shane got to know each other, Dervla returned her attention to Corban O'Hara, who was still checking out the two teens texting on the terrace. He was distracted from the vision of loveliness by the BlackBerry on the table in front of him. Picking it up, he checked the display. Then he smiled, and looked directly at the cuter of the two girls. She was smiling right back at him.

Frowning, Dervla looked away.

Chapter Six

On the top of the double-decker bus that had been converted into a mobile canteen, the extras were on a tea break. Most of them were locals who had been working on *The O'Hara Affair* for the past three weeks, and most of them were playing starving peasants. The obesity rate in Coolnamara had plummeted, because as soon as word had got out that *The O'Hara Affair* was going to be shooting near Lissamore, half the population had gone on diets and taken up exercise classes in the community hall. The downside of playing a starving peasant was the costumes: they were filthy, raggedy old things. Bethany had been lucky: she was meant to be a lady's maid in the Big House, so she got to wear something rather more stylish: an ankle-length black dress with button boots, starched white pinafore and matching lace-trimmed cap.

On this, her first day, Bethany had been hanging out with a girl called Tara, who had also been cast as a lady's maid. There was a lot of hanging about on a film set, Bethany had discovered. In fact, she had come to the conclusion that extra work was deadly dull. She hadn't had a glimpse of a single star so far: all the principals were sequestered in their trailers. Not only that, extras were treated like cattle, with assistant directors herding them about and shouting at them: ADs were the most irritable people she'd ever come across. And a lot of the extras weren't the pleasantest bunch to work with, either. Because she and Tara had nicer costumes than the other girls, the pair of them were subjected to a lot of resentful looks, like the girls who won the challenge in *America's Next Top Model*.

But Bethany didn't care. She remembered what Madame Tiresia had said about the girls at school – the ones who'd been jealous of her because they hadn't the courage to dream. And now that she had plucked up the courage to chase that dream, here she was on her way to living it, even though it was proving to be boring.

Tara was a seasoned extra, having worked on the film for a couple of weeks now. She had learned about hitting marks, she had learned not to touch the lasagne at lunchtime, and she had learned to stave off the boredom with the help of her laptop. She had shared all of this arcane information with Bethany earlier that day, and now they were messing around on YouTube, looking at video clips of craziest cats.

'What's Shane Byrne like?' Bethany asked, as Tara clicked on 'Kittens Dancing to Jingle Bell Rock'.

'Shane Byrne,' Tara told her, 'is a sweetie. He's real friendly – a gentleman. You might see him later – he sometimes joins us for coffee on the bus.'

'On the *bus*? You're kidding!'

'It's true. He's not up himself, like the other stars, who wouldn't be caught dead talking to a mere extra.'

'He's from around here originally, isn't he?'

'Galway. He had a fling years ago with the woman who's doing the set-dressing, Río Kinsella. They had a son together.'

'I remember reading about that in some online fanzine. It said something about a "love child" and a "tempestuous" affair. You can tell just by looking at him that he's a bad boy, a bit like Johnny Depp, except that Johnny Depp—'

'Shh!' Tara stiffened suddenly. 'Let's change the subject.'

'What's – oh.' Following the direction of Tara's gaze, Bethany saw that Shane Byrne had just dropped into the seat behind her. He was accompanied by a man who was fingering a BlackBerry.

'Hey! I'm bored with YouTube,' said Tara, niftily changing tack. 'Let's have a wander around Second Life.'

'What?'

'Second Life. It's another great way of passing the time when you're hanging around waiting to be called.'

'Is that the game where you pretend to be somebody else?'

'Yeah. Except it's not really a game. It's more of a virtual world where you can interact with real people who are online at the same time.'

'How does it work?'

'You create an avatar who represents you – mine's called Mitzy.' Tara clicked on the Second Life icon, and waited for the site to download.

'Wasn't there something in the papers about a UK couple who divorced in real life after their avatars were unfaithful to each other on Second Life?'

'Yes.'

'Weird!'

'That's how seriously some people take it. That couple got married in Second Life before getting married in *real* life. And then, when she suspected him of having virtual sex with a Second Life lap dancer, she actually hired a virtual private detective to set up a honey trap. The funniest thing was that their avatars bore absolutely no resemblance to the way they looked in real life. In Second Life he was a six-foot-four love god, and she was a six-foot sex siren. Look – here's Mitzy – isn't she pretty?'

Bethany peered at the image that shimmered onto the

screen of Tara's notebook. A 3-D beauty with golden Rapunzel locks was standing poised on the step of a pagoda. She was wearing a fairy-tale ball gown, a glittering tiara, and ruby slippers.

'Wow,' said Bethany. 'How did you make her?'

'I chose a generic avatar, then customized her by changing her body shape and skin tone and hair, and shopping for outfits in the virtual mall. Look.'

Tara clicked a few times, and suddenly Mitzy was in a shopping mall, surrounded by other shoppers. These avatars ranged from the everyday – dressed in jeans and T-shirts – to the outlandish, in preposterous fancy dress. By pressing ←↑→ and ↓ on the keyboard, Tara was able to move Mitzy in different directions. She promptly sent her off window-shopping.

'Can you really buy this stuff?' asked Bethany.

'Yes – with virtual money called Linden dollars. You can buy anything you like here, be anyone you want to be.'

It was true. Those virtual Linden dollars could transform Mitzy into a cheer leader, a geisha or a trollop. She could be Scheherazade, Cleopatra, Pocahontas or Pink. The place was a virtual shopaholic's dream.

'It's amazing!' said Bethany. 'Look – you can even get tattoos!'

'And hair extensions. And nail art, if you could be arsed.'

'Hey – look at that dude! The one with the floppy hair who looks like Johnny Depp.'

'You really are into Johnny Depp?' Tara asked her, with a wicked smile.

Bethany smiled back. 'Big time.'

'I'm more an Orlando Bloom gal myself.'

Tara walked Mitzy up to the avatar, whose nametag read 'Silvius'. 'Do you want to talk to him?'

'How do you talk?' asked Bethany.

'You can use voice chat,' Tara told her. 'But I prefer instant messaging. Watch this': **Hello Silvius**, she typed. **I love your coat. Where did you get it?** She pressed Return, and the words appeared on the screen.

Silvius seemed to hesitate, and then, perhaps impressed by Mitzy's beauty and ruby slippers, the reply came back. **Hello Mitzy. Ty. I got it in Kings Plaza**

Thanks, said Mitzy/Tara. **I'll go there straight away.**

A couple more clicks, and suddenly the golden-haired avatar was standing in a department store where glam menswear and even more glamorous womenswear was on display.

'I don't understand,' said Bethany. 'Who creates these places?'

'Members of the Second Life community. I find it a great way to chill. Loads of people say they'd rather get a real life than go on Second Life, but I've met some really cool people on here. Wait till you see this.'

Within seconds, Mitzy was standing in front of a Tudor building, courtesy of Teleport.

'Where are we?'

'It's the Globe Theatre.'

'Like – Shakespeare's Globe Theatre?'

'Yep. We're on Shakespeare Island.'

'I love it!' said Bethany.

'You can teleport to loads of places. You can even visit an Irish pub in Temple Bar.'

Abruptly, a real voice dragged them away from their virtual world. One of the ADs was standing at the top of the stairs. 'There's been a hitch, boys and girls,' he announced, 'and we've had to rejig. The interior's been rescheduled for tomorrow. We're moving on to the exterior.'

'Bummer.'

Bethany and Tara drooped. The interior scene involved the staff of the Big House – including the ladies' maids – while the exterior was all starving peasants begging the evil landlord for food. Since their scene was postponed they could have gone home, but they had no transport, and Lissamore was a six-mile walk away. They'd have to stay on until all the other extras had finished for the day so that they could board the coach together. More bloody hanging around.

The AD made his way past them to where Shane Byrne was sitting with his companion. 'Mr Byrne, apologies for the inconvenience. I'll call you as soon as we're set up. May I get someone to bring you more coffee?'

'Please,' said Shane Byrne. Then he turned to his neighbour. 'I'm afraid I won't be congenial company for the foreseeable. I'm gonna have to go over my script.'

'No worries,' said the dark-haired man. 'I have some business I can get out of the way.' He reached for his BlackBerry as Shane reached for his script. 'Some day soon, you'll be learning your lines on screen,' he observed.

'Nah,' said Shane. 'I'll stick to hard copy. I always auction scripts off when I'm finished with them, and send the proceeds to Cancer Research.'

'Good idea.'

Behind them, Bethany and Tara were still slumped in their seats. The time on the screen of Tara's laptop read 3.15. They could be stuck here for another three hours. On the screen, Mitzy sighed and yawned.

'How did you make her do that?' asked Bethany.

'Easy,' Tara told her, 'I went to the gestures menu and selected "bored". I can get her to do all kinds of things.'

'Can I have a go?'

'Sure.'

Tara passed over her laptop, and Bethany started playing around with the keys, selecting Page Up to propel Tara's avatar towards a sign that read SLSC Academy of Performing Arts.

'What's SLSC?' she asked.

'Second Life Shakespeare Company. They put on plays apparently, but any time I visit there's hardly anyone here.'

Bethany propelled Mitzy through a door.

'Hey – look – we're in some kind of a gallery! This is amazing!' Around the walls were pictures of Shakespeare's characters from *Hamlet*. Bethany guided the avatar past portraits of Hamlet and Ophelia, Gertrude, Claudius and the Player King, before finding herself in the playhouse. She manoeuvred Mitzy up onto the stage, and stood looking around. There was something marvellously out-of-body about this.

'Where else can we go?' she asked Tara.

'How about a beach?'

'Yes!'

In the shake of a lamb's tail, Mitzy was standing on a deserted beach. It was night in Second Life, and dark waves were crashing onto the silver sand. Above her, stars pinpricked the sky, and seagulls called.

'I came here once,' Tara told Bethany, 'and there was an avatar of a girl in a bikini, waiting for her boyfriend. She told me she was living in Florida, and he was in the UK, and they used to meet up on the same beach at a prearranged time to go swimming together.'

'How sweet!' said Bethany.

'Hey – how about we set you up an account?'

'An account?'

'On Second Life. We may as well do something creative if we're going to be stuck here for the next couple of hours.'

'Cool!' said Bethany. 'I'd love that.'

Tara reclaimed her laptop. 'We'll have to fill in a form. The usual crap. And you'll need a password. Never divulge your password to anyone you meet on Second Life, by the way, because if you do they can steal your avatar and impersonate you. And there are some dodgy areas you'll want to stay clear of.'

'Like what?'

'Porn, of course. Sometimes you stumble across some pretty icky stuff. Let's go.'

The next few minutes were spent choosing a generic avatar for Bethany. They hit upon a pretty girl whom they decided to call Poppet, after Bethany's cat. Then Bethany dictated her email address and her date of birth to Tara, and supplied her with a password.

'You're in!' sang Tara, checking out Bethany's in-box, and clicking to activate her account. 'Welcome to Second Life, Poppet! Let's go and make some friends!'

She passed her laptop back to Bethany, who took her first stumbling steps into Second Life in the guise of pretty little Poppet in a pink-and-white polka-dot frock. Someone called Arabella flounced past her. Someone called Rambo bumped into her. Someone called Samuel invited her to sit beside him. By the end of the afternoon Poppet had learned how to fly, how to shop, and how to blow kisses. She'd visited a pub, a club, and Trinity College Dublin. She had made friends with a girl from Toulouse and a boy from upstate New York. She'd laughed and joked and stuck her tongue out at a clown who'd tried to dance with her. Bethany wasn't shy here! She had none of the hang-ups that stymied her socially in real life. And just as she was about to approach a haughty-looking diva and ask where she'd got her hair, Tara's laptop ran out of juice.

'We'll meet up tonight, yeah?' suggested Tara. 'Mitzy and Poppet could go virtual clubbing together.'

'Cool! What time?'

'Ten o'clock on Welcome Island?'

'It's a date.'

Tara shut the lid of her notebook and yawned. Then: 'Sheesh,' she said in a low voice. 'I got so caught up in that that I didn't even see him go.'

'Who?'

'Shane Byrne.'

Bethany glanced over her shoulder. The place where Shane Byrne had been was empty, his coffee cup abandoned. But his dark-haired companion was still working away diligently on his BlackBerry.

Later that day, Fleur accessed Bethany O'Brien's Facebook page. She'd changed her status to 'Tiresia rocks!'

Tiresia rocks? A bogus fortune-teller with an imperfect understanding of amateur psychology? Fleur gave a mental shrug. Whatever. Maybe she *had* made a difference to Bethany's self-esteem, and to the self-esteem of the dozens of other girls who had come to her for consultations. Her mumbo jumbo certainly hadn't done any harm. She reckoned that, on the whole, she'd provided reasonably good entertainment and had been value for money.

Scrolling down Bethany's update, Fleur smiled when she read the following: 'Got myself a job on *The O'Hara Affair*! Positive thinking works, *mes amis*!'

Bethany had, Fleur noticed, acquired some new friends today, on Facebook. Lola, Kitten, Carrie and Tara had all sent her messages, thanking her for the add. Hmm. Maybe it was time for her to add another one. Clicking on her web browser, Fleur typed 'sign up Facebook'. Then she entered the following into the relevant boxes.

First name? Flirty.

Last name? O'Farrell.

Password? Tiresia.

Gender? Female.

Birthday? Here Fleur hesitated. If she put her real birthday, would Bethany bother responding? Probably not. Why would an eighteen-year-old want to befriend a forty-something, after all? She reread Bethany's post. *Positive thinking works, mes amis!* The girl was upbeat, happy. What if she started posting updates like the ones Fleur had read when she was researching her role as Madame Tiresia? She remembered the desperation, the fear, the loneliness in those posts:

... topping out at a hundred, I have more Facebook friends than real life ones. Sad, or what? ...

some 'friendships' should never be resurrected, not even in a virtual sense ...

Even tho I hate this person, I guess I'd better add them as my friend. I'll take ANYONE now ...

Fleur had helped Bethany recover a little of her self-esteem. She didn't want to see that self-esteem plummet. Until Bethany was ready to take wing, Fleur would be there for her. She returned her attention to her Facebook application, typed 23/7/88 into the box marked 'Birthday', and pressed Save.

Flirty O'Farrell was just twenty-one, and she was going to make a new friend.

Poppet was flying over Shakespeare Island, wishing that somebody interesting would come out and play. Mitzy hadn't turned up this evening in their usual meeting place, and when she'd texted Tara, the word back was that her broad-band was malfunctioning.

Bethany had been visiting Second Life for a week now. Working on the movie kept her busy every day, and in the evening, living vicariously in front of her laptop was proving to be a good way of winding down.

Although 'busy' might be a bit of a misnomer. Hanging around the film set was as dull as ever. It was lucky that she was fed by the caterers, because come seven o'clock when she arrived home to Díseart, the last thing she felt like doing was feeding herself. Her parents had gone back to Dublin, her mother exhorting her not to hold any wild parties in their cottage. As if! Who would she invite?

It was the first time she had stayed in the cottage on her own. She had thought it might feel spooky, but tucked up in bed as she was now with the full moon shining through the window and the wash of waves within yards of the garden gate, she felt peculiarly tranquil. The lullaby lapping of waves had always had this effect on her. She remembered falling asleep to the sound when, on holiday as a child, her mother had finished telling her her bedtime story, before backing out of the room with a 'Night, night, sleep tight.' And Bethany had gone to sleep dreaming of princesses and dragons and unicorns and wizards. It was funny that now, in another century, the princesses and dragons and unicorns and wizards still existed for her, not in the fairy stories of her imagination, but in the virtual world on the screen in front of her.

Bethany had always had a vivid imagination. Shortly after her sixth birthday she had terrified her mother by readying herself to jump off an upstairs windowsill because she believed she could fly like Peter Pan. She'd queued with her father outside book shops at midnight, waiting for the new

Harry Potter, which she would devour in a single sitting. She'd discovered a computer game called Final Fantasy, in which, for her, the characters lived and breathed. She supposed that her imagination, her facility for transforming herself into different people and transporting herself to different worlds, was responsible for her all-consuming desire to become an actress. But as an extra on *The O'Hara Affair*, so far the only emotion she'd been required to register had been one of resigned stoicism.

But then, acting – proper acting – bore no relation to extra work, where you were just a piece of furniture, really. A mobile prop. Acting allowed your imagination to soar: an actress could be starry-eyed Juliet one day, tragic Ophelia the next. If she was in belligerent mode, she could be Katherina the shrew; if she was in good form, she could be vivacious Beatrice. All those fabulous heroines who had trodden the boards of the real live Globe Theatre, four hundred years ago! Rosalind, Viola, Portia, Cleopatra . . .

What would Shakespeare have made of this virtual world, where the theatre in which his plays had been performed was now displayed digitally, on an LCD screen? Would he applaud it, be excited by it? Or would he—

Oh! A green dot told her that someone else had arrived onto the island via Teleport. With a click of the mouse, Bethany sent Poppet off in search of the new arrival.

A youth was standing on a street corner, looking lost. He had floppy hair and Johnny Depp eyes. He was wearing something vaguely piratical: a bandanna, leather jerkin and boots. His name was Hero, and he was a cutie. Poppet moved over to him.

Hi, she said.

Hi, Hero said back. **This place is a bit empty.**

I know. Shakespeare Island's always empty. Nobody seems to know about it. Is this your first time here?

Yes.

Bethany decided to be proactive. **Shall I show you around?** she asked.

I'd like that, he told her.

I'll show you the Blackfriars Theatre if you like? she said. **It's this way. Or the Globe?**

I'd like to see the Globe. I've been there in real life.

Cool! she said.

Bethany felt a little fizz of excitement in her tummy. None of the other avatars she'd engaged with on Second Life had ever displayed an interest in anything to do with theatre. It was all gross-out movies and soap opera and sex.

I saw a production of *Romeo and Juliet* there in April, Hero told her. **It was awesome.**

The one with Ellie Kendrick?

Yes.

Wow. She *was* impressed.

Bethany walked Poppet around the corner and along a street constructed of Tudor-style, half-timbered buildings, pointing things out and chatting as she went. The entrance to the Globe was across a bridge.

This is awesome, said Hero. **They've done a great job. It looks just like the real thing.**

Wanna sit down? Poppet suggested.

Sure.

The pair of avatars sat themselves down on a wooden bench, and there was a slightly awkward pause as they looked at each other. In Bethany's experience, conversations on Second Life tended to peter out and residents would often disappear without warning. On numerous occasions Bethany had felt tempted to teleport in the middle of a conversation that was less than riveting, but her good manners always got the better of her.

Have you been a Second Life resident for long? she asked Hero, then cursed herself for sounding so formal.

No. I'm a newbie.

Me too. Met anyone interesting?

Not really. You're the first person I've had a proper conversation with. There are some real weirdos on here.

I know. And some real weird places too. I got stuck in a horrible building last week and had to teleport my way out of it.

What was it like?

Bethany didn't want to tell Hero that the building had been a gallery, the walls of which had been lined with pornographic photographs. She'd tried to escape, flying past image after disturbing image, urgently searching for a way out, but she had just kept banging into walls. It had unsettled her deeply, and she'd been wary about the locations she visited since.

It was just a spooky old house, she lied.

Were you scared?

A bit.

You should take care of yourself on here.

Don't worry. I'm a grown-up.

Over eighteen?

Yes. You?

I'm legal.

Hero stood up, and started to move around the theatre. As he explored, Bethany checked on his profile. Hero had created his avatar just two days after Bethany had created Poppet. He was interested in film and theatre, and his favourite actor was Johnny Depp. He lived in Dublin!

Hey, said Poppet. **You're Irish! So am I!**

No shit! What part?

Dublin. But I'm in the west right now, in Coolnamara. My parents have a cottage here.

I know Coolnamara. Aren't they making a film there?

Yes. *The O'Hara Affair*. **I'm actually in it!**

Hey! Are you an actress?

Sadly, no, she confessed. **Just an extra. But acting's what I'd love to do more than anything. I've applied to the Gaiety School.**

I hear that's a great course. I have a friend who's a casting director. She says the Gaiety students get the most work.

He had contacts! This was amazing!

You have a friend in casting? she asked.

Yeah. I even help out sometimes.

How?

She has a small baby. That means she can't get to all the shows she needs to see. I go on her behalf, and make recommendations.

What a cool job! Being paid to go to the theatre!

Bethany was so excited that she was typing too fast.

Beats being on the dole, observed Hero.

Maybe you'll get to see me in something some day! Let me know.

How?

A box opened on the top right-hand corner of her screen.

Hero is offering friendship, Bethany read.

Accept me as a friend, Hero continued. **Then we'll know any time we're online simultaneously. We can meet up here and talk. Maybe we'll meet other actors. That's why I came to Shakespeare Island**

in the first place. I thought it would be full of actors all wanting to chat about things thespian.

Me too! You'd better not tell them that you work in casting! Then they'll all be after you to try and get a job!

Good point. You won't mention it to anyone, will you?

Not if you don't want me to.

It's bad enough having to cope with wannabe actors in real life. I don't want to have to do it in Second Life too!

LOL!

A silence fell. But Hero didn't look twitchy. He didn't tap his foot, or look away, or scratch his head, as if thinking of something banal to say. Bethany knew he was only an avatar, but she could swear that there was something meaningful about the way he was looking at Poppet.

I have to go now, he said, finally. **When are you likely to be here again?**

I come most evenings. Yikes! Bethany hoped she didn't sound like too much of a loser. **There's nothing else to do in Lissamore**, she added hastily.

Why don't you come back to Dublin?

Because of _The O'Hara Affair_. I would have gone back with Mum & Dad, but I want to get as much work as I can before I'm a full-time student and broke again.

Do you live with your parents in Dublin?

Yes. It's great to have the place here to myself. There's no one to nag me about the state of the bathroom.

LOL. Aren't you lonely in Lissamore?

No. Not with Second Life. I usually hang out with my mate Mitzy here.

There was another pause, then:

Well, Poppet, here's to many more conversations,
said Hero.

**Yeah. *Slainte*! Hey – there's an Irish pub here
you know.**

Cool! Maybe we should visit it together next time?

I'd like that!

It's a date. Bye for now.

Bye.

Take care.

I will.

Bethany watched as Hero disappeared. She wondered
where he was off to next. Back to real life? Or maybe he'd
teleported to somewhere more interesting in Second Life.
Maybe he'd found her boring, and had just made up an
excuse to leave. Maybe he wouldn't contact her again. But
he was special – she knew he was! He had been the first
person to offer her friendship on Second Life, and it had
been the first time Bethany had had a half decent conversation with anyone apart from Tara. And he loved theatre!
The only way to find out that he was genuine, she
supposed, would be to come back tomorrow and see if
he showed up.

Moving Poppet towards the stage, she wondered what
it would be like to have someone watch her from the
balcony. If she used her microphone rather than instant
messenger, she could perform a soliloquy for her spec-
tator, do a virtual audition! She could recite her favourite
speech of Juliet's:

> Come, gentle night, come, loving, black-brow'd night,
> Give me my Romeo; and, when I shall die,
> Take him and cut him out in little stars . . .

Little stars. For some reason the words of the fortune-teller she'd visited last week came back to her. *That special boy is out there somewhere, Bethany, waiting for you. But you must be patient . . .* That special boy. Her Romeo! Her Hero!

Oh – don't be so stupid! she scolded herself. Don't be such a dreamer! One offer of friendship on Second Life hardly constituted a romance. But if – just *if* – she and Hero met up again and got on – well, why shouldn't things develop further? She'd heard loads of stories about people meeting up in cyberspace and then afterwards in real life: she'd even read a magazine article recently that had related the stories of three couples who'd met online and gone on to get married. She'd heard the horror stories, too, of course, about the paedophiles who preyed on young kids and groomed them over the internet, but she was a grown-up. She was, as Hero had said earlier, 'legal'. And she wasn't stupid.

Moving her cursor, Bethany selected an action, and Poppet started to dance. She lay back against her pillows, watching her avatar through half-closed eyelids. She'd seen couples dancing together on Second Life, locked in a tender embrace. It would be nice to think that one day she and Hero might dance together like that . . .

Ten minutes later, a cloud had obscured the face of the moon, the stars were washed out, the waves had worked their lullaby, and Bethany was fast asleep. But Poppet was still in motion, swaying all by herself on the stage of the timber-framed, cavernous theatre on Second Life's Shakespeare Island.

Chapter Seven

**Decluttering must be your number one priority.
When it comes to decluttering, be ruthless.
Declutter, declutter – then declutter some more.**

Hell. This was useless. Dervla was bored by her own book, and if *she* was bored by it, it stood to reason that the reader would be bored by it too. She'd looked at the word 'declutter' for so long that it no longer made sense. Was it even a word? Should there be a hyphen between the 'de' and the 'c'? Should she put 'unclutter' instead? She was utterly clutterly clueless. She wished she hadn't accepted the commission to write the damned thing. But the contract was signed and the advance spent, and she could hardly back out now.

She stood up from her desk and moved over to the window, easing herself into a stretch and trying to think positively. Fleur was a great one for positive thinking. Dervla remembered how, way back when she and Fleur had first met, Fleur had shrugged off the break-up of her marriage with the words: 'What can I say? The Mountie always gets his man. In this case, it just happened to be my husband.' It had been a fantastic icebreaker, and Dervla and Fleur had kept in touch ever since. Now that Dervla had moved back to Lissamore, she was glad to have Fleur to turn to if she needed guidance. Río couldn't be relied upon for objective advice, because Río was family.

So. What were Dervla's alternatives – *faute de mieux*, as Fleur would say? If Dervla hadn't accepted the commission, what would she be doing with her life instead? Everybody knew that writing was a solitary occupation, but she'd be even more solitary, rattling around in the Old Rectory with nothing to keep her busy. Christian was at work most of the day, so she had no company apart from the dog, and there was only so much dog-walking a gal could do. The decorators were finished, so there was no home-decorating to be done, and – because there was so little furniture – there wasn't even much housework to contend with. Because Dervla's passion for property had been so all-consuming in her auctioneering days, she had few hobbies or pastimes. Her gardening knowledge was rudimentary, and she didn't enjoy cooking much – Christian had more culinary nous than she. How could she – a woman in her prime – be such a waste of space?

Hel*lo*? Wasn't she supposed to be thinking positively? Maybe she should put in a call to Fleur – Ms Positivity Personified – or better still, meet up with her friend face to face.

Moving back to her desk, she was just about to reach for her phone, when it rang.

'Christian!' she said, into the receiver. 'Thank God! I'm having a horrible day, and I need someone lovely to talk to!'

'I'm afraid this won't be a lovey-dovey call, sweetheart. I need to ask you a favour.'

'What might that be?'

'Can you come and take over in the shop for an hour or so? Something's come up that I need to take care of, and I can't man the till.'

'Isn't Lisa there to do that?'

'Business was slack, so I gave her the afternoon off.'

'Sure I'll do it. I'd be delighted to have an excuse to skive off. But you do know that my wine savvy doesn't extend much beyond *The Bluffer's Guide*.'

'No worries. You'll be lucky to shift a bottle of house plonk the way things are going today.'

'So. What's come up?'

'Julian's broken his pelvis, and won't be able to do the tasting tour.' Julian was Christian's partner, who ran the Dublin branch of the business.

'Oh, shit! How did that happen?'

'He was in a prang with an SUV.'

'Oh, how horrible! Poor Julian. I've *always* said those things should be banned. I'm going to write to the Minister for Transport.'

'Atta girl!'

'How long'll he be out of commission?'

'Fucking forever. There's no way he'll be accompanying our oenophile friends to France next month.'

'Oh, Christian – what a bummer.'

'I'm going to have to spend the afternoon confirming reservations. If enough people haven't confirmed, we can refund those who have already paid, and cancel.'

'But isn't that wine-tasting tour one of your biggest earners?'

'Sadly, yes. And we're going to lose a lot of goodwill as well as money.'

'Hey – hang on. What's there to stop you going instead of Julian?'

'Have you forgotten what else is happening at the end of next month, Dervla?'

'What?'

105

'Nemia's on two weeks' leave.'

'Oh, Christ. I *had* forgotten.'

'I'm kicking myself now that I didn't take Josephine up on her offer.'

Josephine – Christian's sister – had volunteered to come over from Australia to help out while Nemia was away, but Christian had assured her that it wasn't necessary, that they'd be bound to find someone to cover. However, their efforts to find a replacement carer had been unsuccessful. The local girl who stood in for Nemia on her weekends off was employed elsewhere during the week, and so far only one person had responded to the ad they'd put up in the local shop. Christian and Dervla had agreed that it would not be appropriate to have a twenty-something youth in a Radiohead T-shirt looking after his mother, and had decided to do the caring themselves, with Christian taking time off work and allowing his assistant Lisa to run the shop.

'Look – don't worry about it, Christian,' Dervla told him. 'We'll work something out. I'll do some homework on the internet – we can always get professionals in for a couple of weeks. Or . . .' She allowed a silence to fall.

Christian picked up on his cue. 'I know what you're going to say, love. You're going to say that we could put Mum in a home.'

'Christian – it's just for two weeks!'

'I couldn't do it to her, Dervla. I just couldn't.'

'They say some of them are really nice now—'

'Dervla. This is my *mother* we're talking about.'

'Oh, Christian, please let's not row about this. Please let's just have a look.'

On the other end of the phone, she heard him sigh. 'OK. Have a look online and if we can't find someone to move in we'll pay a couple of them a visit.'

'I'll do that. What time do you want me down there?'

'Around four o'clock?'

'Four o'clock's fine. I might head into Lissamore after-wards and persuade Fleur to go for a drink.'

'Or a walk. It's a beautiful day.'

'Good idea. A walk, then a drink. I'll see you at four, love.'

'Thanks, Dervla.'

Dervla felt a little shaky as she put the phone down. Maybe she should ask Nemia if she could postpone her holiday? But she had booked a fortnight in Malta with a crowd of girl-friends, and it wouldn't be fair to ask. And as for cancelling the wine-tasting tour? That would be disastrous. Christian was right: aside from the monetary loss, it would mean that people might decide to take their custom elsewhere. Bacchante Wines had a loyal clientele, many of whom looked on the annual French tour as a kind of pilgrimage. They'd be deeply disappointed if it were cancelled. And, anyway, what if—

Aiiee! Here she was, painting a worst-case scenario. Positive, positive – be positive! Emulate Fleur! They'd be bound to find somebody to take care of Daphne. Dervla took a couple of deep breaths to steady herself. Accessing her internet browser, she typed 'professional care workers for elderly' into the Google search bar.

The first few sites she visited extolled the virtues of their care givers, but were coy about their rates. There were, instead, lots of references to 'dignity', 'individuals', and 'community'. Finally Dervla found an agency that boasted a tariff page. Sweet Jesus! Twenty-four/seven care *started* at €1250 per week (dementia and Alzheimer's sufferers extra: to be negotiated on assessment). Nemia – at €650 – cost just under half that. Oh – this was barking. There had to be a cheaper alternative.

Maybe a home would be cheaper? If so, then surely

Christian couldn't object to his mother spending just two weeks in residential care. Rather than trawl through the internet, Dervla decided that the *Golden Pages* might be easier to pinpoint the likely-looking ones. She reached for the directory, and went to Nursing Homes.

There were hundreds listed. Some could have been holiday resorts, to go by the descriptions, with 'Cuisine of High Standard', 'En Suite Luxury', 'Dedicated Activities Co-ordinators', 'Breathtaking Views', 'Hair Salons', 'Bespoke Furniture', 'Ayurvedic Massage', 'Hydrotherapy Pools' and 'Sun Lounges'. Dervla wouldn't mind taking time off somewhere like that! But again, when she visited the relevant websites, price was an issue.

Money, money, money! How expensive it was to grow old. How scary, how stressful, how – Oh! – she couldn't hack this right now. What she really wanted was a walk by the river, a blast of ozone-enriched air, a bucketload of endorphins, and someone to talk to. She ran down the stairs and called for Kitty.

The Dalmatian came lolloping from the kitchen, knocking into the umbrella stand. For such an ostensibly elegant dog, Kitty was incredibly clumsy. Dervla often wished that she had a videocam handy, so that she could send footage off to *You've Been Framed* – she had once seen the dog bang into a plate-glass window and apologize to her own reflection.

'Come, Kit!' she said now. 'We're off for a walk.'

They set off down the driveway of the Old Rectory, Kitty running ahead, checking to see that there was nothing sinister around the next bend, then coming back to report that all was well. And all *was* well – Christian had been right when he'd made the observation earlier that it was a beautiful day. How lucky was Dervla to be alive and well and living in the most beautiful corner of the west of Ireland! She should count her blessings! And yet, and yet . . .

'The thing is, Kit,' she told the dog, 'that I love your master very, very much, but I don't love my life right now. And of course I wouldn't want to go back to my estate-agent days – even though I was a bloody good estate agent – because I'm not the person I used to be. But I'm not the person I thought I might become, living a Cath Kidston lifestyle in the Old Rectory, because let's face it, nobody lives like that except in catalogues. And I've never had money worries before, and I'm frightened. And I wonder if everybody is frightened, or if – oh! Oh my God – Daphne, what are you doing?'

Daphne was sitting on the edge of the lawn, under a rhodo-dendron bush. She had taken off her cardigan and blouse, and her vest was ruched up around her neck.

'I was too hot,' she told Dervla. 'So I'm taking off my vest. Help me, will you?'

'Oh – of course.' Dervla went over to Daphne, and helped her pull her vest over her head, as if it were the most normal thing in the world to be doing on a sunny June afternoon, with a skylark singing madly overhead, and sheep baaing in the field next door. 'It's a beautiful day, isn't it?' she remarked conversationally.

'Yes,' said Daphne, from under her vest. 'And I shouldn't be wearing a vest on a day like this. I wonder what made me put it on? What a silly old fool I am.'

Dervla tugged, and the vest came free. She rolled it up, and handed Daphne her blouse.

'Would you mind helping me on with this?' Daphne asked. 'I seem to be all fingers and thumbs today.'

Dervla took Daphne's left hand and slid it into the cerise silk sleeve. 'What a beautiful blouse,' she said, feeling like Alice in Wonderland as she did up Daphne's buttons.

'Thank you. Oh, look! A spotty dog. The spottiest dog you ever did see. That's from the *Woodentops*, you know.'

'Oh, yes,' agreed Dervla, even though she hadn't a clue what Daphne was talking about.

Kitty was dancing around her heels, smiling at Daphne. 'Here we go looby loo,' said Daphne. 'Here we go looby lay. Can you do my bow for me? It's called a pussy cat bow, you know.'

'Of course.' As she put the finishing touches to Daphne's pussy cat bow, the sound of running footsteps made Dervla look up.

'Daphne! Thank God!' Nemia came careering around the corner like Road Runner, naked but for a bath towel and trainers. She doubled over, clutching her hands to her chest. 'Oh, dear God,' she managed. 'Oh dear God – I thought you might have fallen in the river.'

Looking around, Dervla wondered if this surreal moment would end up on Google Earth, and if so, how could it be explained?

'What happened?' she asked, when Nemia got her breath back.

'I was taking a shower,' Nemia told her, 'and when I got out, I saw that the front door was open.'

'She escaped?' said Dervla, realizing even as she said the words that it was a most politically incorrect observation.

'Yes,' said Nemia, who was probably too distraught to notice that it was equally politically incorrect of her to concur. 'I forgot to deadlock the door. Thank God you found her. Daphne!' she said, turning to her charge. 'You silly billy! What are you doing, sitting under a bush?'

'I went for a walk,' said Daphne. 'And because I was far too hot, I decided to take my vest off. I think that is a perfectly reasonable thing to do, don't you? It's not as if there was anybody around to see me.'

'You're right. It's far too hot to be wearing a vest. I shouldn't have put it on you this morning.' Nemia held out a hand to Daphne, who clutched it like a child holding on to Mummy. 'Come on, darling, let's get you home.'

'Home?'

'Yes. There's egg salad for lunch, and then you can watch David Attenborough or Monty Don before we go off on our jaunt.'

'Not the *Woodentops*? That was a joke, you know.'

'Of course it was. Hup, hup, and away!' Nemia sang as she hoisted Daphne to her feet.

Dervla looked down at the vest she was holding and thought she was going mad.

'I can't tell you how sorry I am,' Nemia said, stooping to brush grass cuttings off Daphne's skirt. 'I hope it's not a firing offence?'

'God, no,' said Dervla. 'It was a mistake anyone could have made.'

Nemia straightened up, and took Daphne's arm. 'Would you like to join us for lunch, Dervla?'

'Do!' said Daphne. 'What are we having?'

'Egg salad,' said Nemia.

'I can't,' said Dervla. 'I – um . . . can't.'

The two women looked at each other. 'I understand,' said Nemia, after a beat. 'Not everybody likes egg salad.'

And Dervla knew that she was being very gently let off the hook.

Turning away, Nemia started steering Daphne back up the driveway. 'Look, Daphne!' she said. 'A pheasant!'

'Where? Where!?'

'You just missed it – it's in the long grass over there. What a splendid day it is! I'm glad we decided on a jaunt to the beach today. It'll be your first time in my new car! You can

111

sit and look at the waves dancing in the sun. And while there are showers forecast, the long-term weather forecast is . . .'

Dervla watched as Nemia and Daphne walked away, hand in hand, their voices receding. Nemia's pace was measured to Daphne's, her attention wholly centred on the old lady, her demeanour that of a guardian angel.

Dervla felt . . . inadequate.

Later, Dervla was sitting behind the counter in Bacchante, wishing that someone would come in. Beyond the window there was a lot of toing and froing: well-heeled tourists were window-shopping, backpackers were consulting their *Rough Guides*, locals were gossiping in shop doorways, a busker was playing a guitar. Ardmore was bigger than Lissamore – a town as opposed to a village. It was a popular tourist venue, and boasted several hotels, one of which – the five-star Demetrius – was situated directly across the road from Bacchante. The Demetrius was where most of the cast and crew of *The O'Hara Affair* were staying, and that was probably what was keeping Bacchante afloat right now: those movie people liked their wine.

There went one of them now: Corban O'Hara, no less. The valet had just pulled up under the porte-cochère in a limited edition BMW, and a porter was hooking a smart leather suiter onto the rear coat hanger. Funny. Dervla thought that Corban always stayed with Fleur when he came west.

Corban paused on the step of the hotel, said something to the porter and handed him a tip. Then he came across the road, and pushed open the door to Bacchante.

'Good afternoon,' he said.

'Good afternoon, sir,' replied Dervla. 'May I help you, or would you just like to browse?'

'I'm quite happy to browse, thank you.'

'You're welcome.'

Corban O'Hara strolled past the display shelves, pausing now and again to examine a label. He was a big man – well, powerfully built rather than big – and he exuded a confidence so rampant you could almost smell it. Dervla could see why Fleur was smitten: Mr O'Hara was a very sexy man. He bypassed the Burgundies, which Dervla thought was odd, given that his wine of choice at lunch last week had been a Meursault, and picked up a bottle of pink *prosecco* with a flamboyant name. It was a most *un*-Corban O'Hara wine, Dervla thought. Not just that, it was a most un-Fleur O'Farrell wine too. A woman as sophisticated as Fleur would never accept pink *prosecco* as a substitute for champagne.

Corban approached the counter and set the bottle down.

'Anything else, sir?' asked Dervla. She wondered if he might recognize her from Chez Jules, but he gave no indication that he did. She looked different, she guessed, with her hair pulled back and no make-up on, and anyway, he'd been too side-tracked by Shane's young fans that day to notice her.

'No, nothing else, thank you,' said Corban O'Hara. His attention was diverted by the display rack of cards by the till. 'Oh – you do cards.'

'Yes. We giftwrap, too, at no extra charge. A lot of people buy wine as presents these days.'

'It's a good idea. Could you giftwrap it for me?'

'Certainly.'

Dervla unfurled a length of wrapping paper, covertly watching Corban as he examined the cards. The one he chose bore the legend 'For the Sweetest Thing!' beneath a bubble-gum pink cupcake.

'That'll be seventeen euros eighty-five, please,' said Dervla, scanning the items.

She watched while he extracted his Vuitton card case. His cufflinks were gold, discreet but heavy. His jacket was Paul Smith, his shoes Italian leather.

'Thank you,' he said, and was gone. Dervla watched him through the window as he slid into the driver's seat of his BMW, and took off.

'Christian?' she said, poking her head around the door that led into the back room, where her husband was busy doing his accounts. 'If you had loads of wealth and a lot of taste and a mistress, what wine would you buy her?'

'What kind of a question's that?' said Christian.

'Just think for a moment. Would you buy her a bottle of pink *prosecco*?'

'Absolutely not.'

'Hmm. What kind of card would you pick for her?'

'Dervla – is this some kind of stupid quiz on Facebook?'

'No. I'm doing a bit of detective work. Would you give her a card with a cupcake on?'

'My putative mistress? No. I'd give her one of those cards with a classy reproduction on.'

'Like the Bonnard nude?'

'Yeah – I guess so.'

'Definitely not a cupcake?'

'No. The cupcake's more Megan than mistress.'

'That's what I thought.'

Christian's phone went, and she left him to it. Looking at the display of cards, she reached for the cupcake one. *More Megan than mistress*. Megan was Christian's eighteen-year-old daughter. Megan would probably love the cupcake card, if it came from a boyfriend. And she'd be delighted with the pink *prosecco*. But Fleur? Fleur most certainly would not.

114

Chapter Eight

'Dervla! Fancy a walk?'

'How funny, Fleur. I was just about to call you and ask that very same question.'

'Serendipity! The beach? Or the bog road?'

'The bog road,' said Dervla. 'Then we can stop off in O'Toole's and have a drink on the way home.'

'I'll see you there in ten.' Putting the phone down, Fleur moved to the door, switched the sign from 'Open' to 'Closed', and turned the key in the lock.

She threw an eye around the interior, checking that none of her precious stock was languishing on the floor. Fleur found the disrespect for garments that some customers displayed quite shocking. She never handled her beloveds with anything other than the utmost reverence. Tweaking here the strap of a charmeuse slip dress, there the zipper on a pencil skirt, Fleur moved through her shop, falling in love with it all over again.

Fleurissima had come into being as the brainchild of Fleur Thérèse Odette O'Farrell and Río Kinsella over two decades ago, shortly after Tom had left Fleur for his Canadian Mountie, and Río had broken her sister Dervla's heart by hooking up with Shane Byrne. They had met at a music festival in Galway, she and Río, and had hit it off at once.

Both women were smart, independent and sassy, and – at the time – both of them dressed boho-style in second-hand threads. It had been fun in those early days, roaming the countryside in Río's battered car, hunting for vintage clothes in house auctions and charity shops. But once Río's baby boy had been weaned and was no longer portable, they had – reluctantly – gone their separate ways. Río was boho still and always would be, but Fleur had cultivated a classier look over the years, as the business took off and she found herself running it solo. Being *Parisienne* helped. Women tended to defer to her on matters of taste, and although half a lifetime spent in Ireland meant that Fleur had lost most of her French accent, she knew how to use it to effect when it suited her.

She had decorated the shop with Río's help, in shades of ivory, cream and eau-de-nil. The interior had been inspired by the fin-de-siècle designs of Charles Rennie Mackintosh: a fusion of Art Nouveau flourish and Japanese simplicity. Carefully placed mirrors lent it the appearance of being larger than it was, and Fleur made sure the L-shaped space was never cluttered. She had designed a boudoir in the foot of the L – where she also displayed and sold Río's paintings – and customers who spent a lot of time and money in the shop were invited to take their ease on a chaise longue with a copy of French *Vogue*, a dish of Fleur's homemade chocolate truffles, and a glass or two of complimentary champagne. It worked every time. Invariably those pampered patrons helped themselves to one last frivolous purchase once the second glass of Laurent-Perrier kicked in. *'What a darling set of lingerie!' 'Such sinfully divine mules!' 'I know I shouldn't, but that little marabou-trimmed cardigan is just irresistible!'* Fleur couldn't help smiling as she enveloped those precious last-minute items in tissue paper and sprinkled them with rose petals. An embossed Fleurissima card was always tucked into the package for good measure. Fleur aimed to please, and she scored mostly bull's-eyes. Patrons came back again and again, and brought new customers with them. To shop *chez* Fleur lent a gal *élan*. Her customers left the shop believing that some of the owner's sophistication had rubbed off on them.

On completion of her inspection of the shop – *Merde!* What philistine had turned that embroidered silk tabard inside-out! – Fleur moved towards the back room to change into her walking gear. But a tap on the window made her turn. A boy in motorcycle leathers was standing beyond the window display. Giving her an appealing smile, he spread his hands.

'We're closed,' Fleur mouthed at him.

The boy spread his hands further, and made his smile even more appealing. It worked. With a shrug and a look of mock-exasperation, Fleur moved back to the door and let him in.

'Thanks a million,' he said. 'I won't take up much of your time. I already know what I want.' He indicated a pair of faceted gemstones in the display case. 'Can you giftwrap them for me?'

'Sure. Present for a girlfriend?'

'No. It's my mum's birthday tomorrow – I nearly forgot about it. I can't tell you how glad I am you let me in.'

'Your mum's a lucky lady. These are tourmaline.'

'She deserves them. It's her fiftieth.'

Fleur unhooked the earrings and reached for a length of tissue paper.

'You're Daisy's aunt, aren't you?' the youth asked, setting his helmet down on the counter.

'Yes.'

'How's she getting on in Africa?'

117

'I haven't heard from her.'

'Neither have I. She's not even updating her Facebook.'

'Her father told me that there's limited access to the internet where she is.'

'Yeah?'

'Yes. I think she has to get herself to a hill station to get online.'

'She probably has better things to do with her time than fool around on Facebook,' said the boy. 'That was a really brave thing she did, giving up her career and all.'

'Yes, it was. I'm very proud of her.'

As she unravelled a length of ribbon, Fleur glanced at the youth's face. He was a cutie, with floppy dark hair and conker-brown eyes. She guessed he was the boy who'd been riding the motorbike that had taken Daisy off on pillion, on the last Saturday morning she'd seen her in Lissamore. He was looking around desultorily at the stock on display: Fleur smiled to herself when she saw him eyeing a lace-trimmed polka-dot bra and panty set.

'Are you here on holiday?' she asked.

'No. I'm working on *The O'Hara Affair*. I'm an assistant director. Well, I'm actually assistant to the assistant.'

'Oh?' Fleur was just about to ask if he knew somebody called Bethany O'Brien, when she realized that if he *did* know her, and word got back to Bethany that Fleur of Fleurissima had been asking about her, well, it would look very odd indeed. So she zipped her lip, and instead she said: 'Do you know my friend Río? She's working as a set-dresser on the film.'

'Río the fox? Sure I know her. She's great gas. Everybody loves Río.'

Fleur filed this tidbit of information away, to tell her friend later. 'Are you paying by cash or credit?' she asked.

118

'Cash.'

'In that case, I'll give you ten euros off.'

'Hey – that's bloody decent of you! Why?'

Fleur shrugged. 'You have a nice smile,' she told him.

He laughed. 'So do you.'

As she handed over the giftwrapped package, there was a moment between them when something unspoken hung in the air, and then the door to the shop opened and Corban walked in.

'Corban!' said Fleur. 'I didn't expect to see you until the weekend.'

'Surprise,' was the laconic response.

Corban stood to one side, and the boy left the shop with a breezy, 'Thanks very much! See you again!' and a cheeky smile at Fleur. Then, producing a bunch of tulips from behind his back, Corban said, 'For you.' He strolled over to her, dropped a kiss on her mouth, and handed her the flowers.

'Thank you!'

'There's more.' He set a carrier bag on the counter.

'You've been shopping in Dunnes?'

'I have.'

'But you never shop in Dunnes!'

'There's a first time for everything.' Corban took a fruit-cake and a packet of Cheerios from the carrier bag, and then he pulled Fleur into him and kissed her properly.

'Tulips in mid-summer?' she said, when he finally released her from his embrace. 'How did you get hold of them?'

'I ordered them specially.'

'Why?'

'They were the only flowers that could adequately express the way I feel.'

'Er . . . you mean, you feel like a tulip?'

'Exactly like a tulip.'

'And the fruitcake?'

'I feel like a fruitcake, too.'

'The Cheerios?'

He grimaced. 'They're to say goodbye. I know we'd planned to spend the weekend in Coolnamara Castle, but something's come up, Fleur, and I have to go to London instead.'

'So you drove all the way from Dublin to bring me tulips and fruitcake and Cheerios? You are a crazy man.'

'Crazy for you. Now shut up shop and come to bed.'

'Oh, Corban – I can't. I've arranged to meet Dervla for a walk.'

He raised an eyebrow. 'You'd rather go for a walk than come to bed with me?'

'No, of course not. But you don't cancel an arrangement with a girlfriend on account of a man. You just don't. It's one of the first rules of friendship.'

'Rules are made to be broken.'

'Not this one. I am sorry.'

Corban shrugged. 'Hey – no worries. I guess I can take care of some business while you're tramping the sand dunes.'

'We're going up the bog road, actually.'

'While you're trotting the bog, then.'

'Let me just turn off the lights and get rid of the cash, and then I'll let you in upstairs.'

Fleur took the cash drawer from the till, and carried it into the back room, where the safe was. She didn't have time to count her takings – she'd be late for Dervla if she did – but she knew they were meagre today. Hallelujah for that last-minute sale!

She wondered what business was taking Corban off to London. It wasn't entirely unexpected that he'd had to cancel their weekend – Corban was always hopping on and off planes and crisscrossing the world at the drop of a hat. But it had been sweet of him to drive down from Dublin to tell her in person. Of course, he probably had movie matters to attend to and was killing two birds with one stone, but still. Time was a precious commodity for Corban, and he never wasted it. Nor did Fleur resent the demands on his time. She'd seen too many relationships capsized by the weight of a needy, clinging woman, and she wasn't about to start dragging Corban under.

How long might he be staying in Lissamore? Just one night? Two? And then Fleur remembered that – yikes – her bedroom was a mess, she hadn't shaved her underarms, and her toenails needed cutting. Maybe she could have a quick shower when she got back from her walk and take care of her beauty treatments then.

Through the door, she could see Corban sauntering past the rail where the lingerie hung, pausing from time to time to check out textures between finger and thumb. She exchanged her work skirt for jeans, her heels for walking boots, switched off the lights, then went back into the shop.

'Men seem to gravitate towards that set, for some reason,' she observed, as she saw Corban unhook the polka-dot number from the rail. 'That boy who was in here before you was eyeing them, too. He's an assistant on the film.'

'An assistant director?'

'Assistant to the assistant. Do you know him?'

'No. Is he first or second unit, lighting or casting?' Corban's studiedly casual demeanour, was, Fleur suspected, a cover-up for the fact that – now he was a big shot in the world of film-making and had learned to speak the lingo – he actually felt like a dog with two tails. Power and all things hierarchical were important to her lover, and it only added to his charisma.

'You mean there's more than one director to be assistant to?' she asked.

'There are several. Just as there are several producers.'

'I don't know whose assistant he is. He didn't say.' Fleur picked up the Dunnes carrier bag and the bunch of tulips. 'Will you put these in water for me? You'll find a vase in the utility room upstairs.'

'Sure,' said Corban, taking the flowers from her. 'What time will you be back?'

'In an hour or so.'

'Perfect. I'll make some phone calls, send some mail, and then I'll be free as a bird.'

He moved across the shop floor to hold the door open for her, and Fleur passed through, loving the feel of his hand on the small of her back. Corban was a quintessential gentleman: standing up when she entered the room; insisting on paying, always; angling the umbrella so that she stayed dry while he took the lion's share of rain . . . For Fleur, nothing was sexier than a man with manners. She locked the shop door behind her, then unlocked the adjacent one to her duplex. 'Do you want to join us for a drink, later?' she asked him. 'Dervla and I thought we might pay a visit to O'Toole's.'

'Yeah, I'd like that. We might eat there, too, afterwards.'

'Cool.' Fleur was glad he'd suggested dinner in O'Toole's. The last thing she felt like doing was rustling up supper. Standing on tiptoe, she kissed him, then backed away down the street. 'A bientôt, darling. It's so nice to see you!'

'Enjoy your walk, Fleur.'

'I will.'

Fleur turned and moved briskly away. She was running late now, and Dervla would be waiting for her. They regularly walked the bog road as an alternative to walking the beach. The beach walk was glorious, especially on a day like today when it had been raining and the air was rich in ozone.

But the bog road was glorious, too, in its own way, meandering as it did between myriad small lakes, and curling around the low-lying hills. At this time of the year the moorlands looked as if they had a rich Turkish carpet strewn across them, the purple of the heather mingling with the pale gold of honeysuckle in the hedgerows, and the tawny brown of peat.

Dervla was sitting on a low dry-stone wall, looking at something through a pair of binoculars.

'Who are you spying on?' Fleur asked as she approached.

'I think it's a merlin.'

'A what?'

'A type of small falcon. It's got the sweetest legs, as if it's wearing little feathered trousers.'

'I wouldn't have taken you for a twitcher, Dervla.'

'I'm hardly a twitcher. But I've taken to checking out bird life since Christian gave me these binoculars for my birthday.' Dervla stood up from the wall, and looped the strap of the binoculars around her neck. 'Come on,' she said. 'Let's walk.'

'How come Kitty isn't with you?' asked Fleur. Christian's Dalmatian was usually a constant companion on their walks.

'I had to leave her at home. I went into Ardmore to man the shop for my main man. If you had an air to that . . .'

'My main man arrived in town earlier!' said Fleur, happily. 'He brought me a really silly gift!'

Dervla raised an eyebrow. 'Pink *prosecco*, by any chance?'

'Pink *prosecco*?' Fleur gave Dervla a curious look. 'No. What made you think Corban would buy me pink *prosecco*?'

'I don't know. Oh, look! Could that be a linnet?' Dervla raised her binoculars and directed them at a thorn bush.

Fleur didn't bother to look. She was preoccupied with the bizarre reference to pink *prosecco*. 'Honestly, *why* would you think Corban brought me pink *prosecco*, Dervla?' she persisted.

'No reason.' Dervla continued to peer through her binoculars. 'I'm probably getting dementia, like my mother-in-law. Maybe it's catching. I found her on the driveway earlier today, trying to take off her vest.'

'Oh, God. How are things with her, generally?'

'I don't see too much of her. Well, I do actually: if I look out of the turret room window, I can see directly into her sitting room. She seems to spend the entire day watching TV.'

'I thought she was half blind?'

'She is, but she loves to listen to David Attenborough programmes. And old musicals.'

'Does she ever get out?'

'Yes. We took her out to lunch not long ago. And we're toying with the idea of having dinner in Coolnamara Castle this weekend.'

'Coolnamara Castle? Corban and I were meant to be spending the weekend there.'

'Meant to be?'

'We had to postpone. Business has claimed him elsewhere. He's flying off to London.'

'Business has claimed Christian, too. It looks as though he's going to have to head off to France for a couple of weeks.'

'Nice break for him.'

'Yes. But not so great for me. The really bad news is that those are the two weeks when Nemia is due to take her holidays.'

'Oo-er. What are you going to do about Mrs Vaughan?'

'We may have to get her into residential care if we can't find a replacement. It's unbelievably expensive, Fleur. I rang a friend in Dublin who had to spend time in a care home when she broke her leg. She says that if she hadn't had private insurance it would have cost her two and a half grand a *week*.'

Fleur shuddered. 'What will become of us, I wonder, when we're old and decrepit?'

'I'd really rather not think about it.'

'At least you have Christian,' observed Fleur.

'And you have Corban.'

'Ah, but Corban has no duty of care to me, since we are not married.'

'Have you ever thought about it?'

'Marrying Corban?'

'Yes.'

'No,' replied Fleur, with a laugh that she contrived to make careless. 'Corban's not the kind of man to marry a second time. He is – how does that phrase go? Once bitten . . . something.'

'Once bitten, twice shy.' There was a pause. 'When will I get to meet him?'

'This evening. He's joining us for a drink in O'Toole's.'

There was another pause, then: 'What exactly does he do, your boyfriend?' asked Dervla. 'I mean, aside from being a hotshot film producer?'

'I've never really asked him. I just know he's loaded enough to sink megabucks into a movie.'

'I'd love to pay a visit to the location. Río tells me that they've reconstructed an entire famine village beyond Ardmore.'

'A visit could be arranged. Maybe we should have a girlie lunch afterwards – you, me and Río. I hear there's a new restaurant just opened in Ardmore.'

'Chez Jules. It's very good. That's where we took Daphne for lunch. Shane was eating there, too, with – with a friend.'

'That must have been Corban!'

'Really?'

'Tall, dark and handsome?'

'Yes.'

'That's my man!' fluted Fleur. 'Isn't he gorgeous?'

'Yes.' Dervla drew her sunglasses from a pocket and slid them on.

'How is Shane? Did you speak to him?'

'I did. He's still in love with Río you know, Fleur.'

'I've suspected that for a long time. Poor Río.'

'I dunno. It must feel pretty damned fine to have a film star mad about you.'

'Not when there's nothing you can do about it. You know as well as I do that Río would never leave Lissamore – especially when there's every chance that her son's on his way back to her.'

'Finn's coming back to Lissamore? How do you know?'

'Oh – I overheard some kid talking about it in the shop.'

Fleur didn't want to tell Dervla that she'd actually read about Finn's homecoming on a Facebook page. She was becoming a tad worried about her Facebook habits: the social networking site was proving more than a little addictive.

Bethany had accepted her as a friend without a quibble, and since then, Fleur had been keeping a regular eye on the girl's profile. She didn't know what it was about Bethany O'Brien that she found so fascinating. She guessed that there was something about her that reminded her of the teenage Fleur: imaginative, vulnerable, romantic – in love with the idea of being in love. And now that Fleur had no Daisy to be a surrogate mother to, she found offering Bethany vicarious advice over the internet enormously satisfying.

The girl was still in town, she knew, working every day on *The O'Hara Affair*. She claimed to find extra work so dull that she'd taken to visiting an online community called

Second Life, and had invited Flirty O'Farrell to meet up with her there. Fleur was tempted, but the first time she'd visited Second Life she'd found it to be full of people whom she perceived to be very young, very bored and rather silly. Bethany had also mentioned that she was living on her own in the family cottage in nearby Díseart, enjoying the freedom it afforded her, and Fleur had IM'd her back immediately, warning her not to broadcast the fact.

It hadn't been on Bethany's profile that Fleur had found out about Finn coming home – it had been on the profile of a girl called Izzy Bolger, his one-time girlfriend, and a Facebook friend of Daisy's. Fleur remembered what a stunning young couple Finn and Izzy had been, and wondered if they were still an item. Izzy's status told her she was in a relationship, but maybe she had moved on from Finn? It felt strange to be able to follow the trail of these young people as they journeyed around the world: Izzy was off to Dubai, next, where her father had won the tender on some new construction project.

'Remember Adair Bolger?' she asked Dervla. 'Río nearly had a thing going with him didn't she?'

'She could have been a contender, all right. But I think she baulked a bit at the idea of becoming her son's girlfriend's father's girlfriend – found the whole thing a bit incestuous. Where is he now, I wonder?'

'He went to Dubai after his business here went bust.'

'And that big house of his never sold,' mused Dervla. 'It was on my books when I was a working girl. I guess it never will sell, now. Finn had some mad dream of converting it into a scuba-diving centre. Thanks be to Christ he didn't. Could you imagine trying to run a destination dive centre in this economic climate?'

'"All's changed, changed utterly,"' said Fleur.

'That's Yeats, isn't it? My dad used to quote from that poem when he was in his cups. And wasn't he right, auld W B? It's incredible to think how this country's changed in the course of a year. Millionaire property dealers forced to go and live in Dubai, house prices plummeting, wine merchants stocking cheap bubbly instead of Cristal . . .'

'But at least we don't live in the city! Look, look around you! It's heaven!'

'It is,' agreed Dervla.

'Give me a go with your binoculars,' said Fleur, reaching for them.

Through the binoculars she saw to the west the navy stripe of the horizon where sea met sky; a shoreline flecked with aquamarine and turquoise; a beach of golden sand fringed with emerald dunes; flanks of hills stippled with blue cloud shadow; a countryside ashimmer with sun and rinsed squeaky clean by rain, and, as her gaze took in the wind-rippled watered silk of the lakes, Fleur decided that if Coolnamara was couture, the only designer responsible for its creation could be Lainey Keogh.

Chapter Nine

Dervla strode along the bog road, wanting to kick herself. *Why* had she mentioned the *prosecco*? Fleur's mention of a silly gift had led her to assume that Corban must have presented her with the pink fizz, but that was quite clearly not the case. So who *was* to be the recipient? A girlfriend? The waitress she'd seen him handing his card to in Chez Jules? Or the girl he'd been ogling through the window of the restaurant?

Oh, stop it – stop it, Dervla! Her imagination was going into overdrive. Maybe the *prosecco* was for his niece, if he had one. Maybe it was a farewell present for a cast or a crew member on the film. Maybe there was an entirely rational explanation for his purchase.

This must be what happened when you were starved for company, living alone in a big empty house. You started making up stories about people you didn't even know. Maybe she should start writing fiction instead of a useless book about how to sell houses nobody wanted to buy. Maybe she should get out more, get herself a proper job. But doing what? Auctioneering? Cue hollow laughter. Working in a shop? Maybe she could ask Fleur if she could help out part time in Fleurissima, or maybe Christian could take her on instead of Lisa? At least if she were working in an environment surrounded by real live human beings she could keep up to spin with what was going on in the world. She hadn't even known that her own nephew was coming back to Lissamore!

Yes. A job would be good: something that would earn her some money, restore a little of her self-esteem, give her a sense of purpose. Hadn't Río used to grab any work that was going, when she'd been a struggling single mother? She'd driven a hackney cab, she'd worked behind the bar in O'Toole's, she'd done odd jobs in people's gardens.

But Dervla had none of those practical skills. She'd lived such a rarefied life in the heady days of Celtic Tiger Ireland that she barely even knew how to wield an iron. And now she was, ironically – ha ha – ironing her husband's shirts for him. She'd thought of offering to pay Nemia to do it, but since she'd given up work, Dervla couldn't afford to splash out the kind of silly money she had once upon a time on ironing services and suchlike. Anyway, she'd have felt too embarrassed to ask Nemia, because in a way, Nemia was family . . .

Nemia! Now there was a job she could do! Nemia earned six hundred and fifty euros a week looking after Daphne. Six hundred and fifty euros was a lot. If she, Dervla, took over Nemia's job while she was off on holiday, she and Christian could save Daphne's estate a fair few bob. Two and a half thousand a week for residential care was ridiculous! And Nemia would need more time off in the future, to visit her family in London. She'd mentioned recently that her own mother was ailing. Maybe, between the two of them, they could work out a roster so that when Nemia took time off, Dervla could take over. It couldn't be that skilled a job, caring for an elderly person. All she would have to do would be cook and clean a little, and set Daphne down in front of the television. Nemia occasionally did the crossword with her, and she'd mentioned something about reading bedtime stories, but that was hardly onerous. If Dervla moved into Daphne's cottage for the two weeks that Nemia was away, she could bring her laptop, get some work done on her book! It was a no-brainer. Well . . . OK, not such a no-brainer. Daphne could be a real pain in the arse sometimes, but that was part of the job description and simply something Dervla would have to learn to put up with.

She and Fleur had been walking in companionable silence for some time, each wrapped in their own thoughts, when Fleur gave a sudden laugh.

'What's so funny?' asked Dervla.

'I was just remembering what some girl said when I was doing my fortune-telling gig. She told me to fuck off, and then clamped a hand over her mouth and apologized profusely.'

'Why did she tell you to fuck off?'

'It's the way kids say "I don't believe you". You know – like the way we used to say "get away!" They say "fuck off" instead – but they don't mean it rudely. She was *so* mortified.'

'I meant to ask you – how did that gig go?'

'Really well, funnily enough.'

'So the Facebook stunt worked?'

'Yes. It's amazing the stuff kids tell each other over the internet. It's like a confessional. Having read some of it, I'd hate to be a mother.'

'You're like a second mother to Daisy.'

'Ah, but Daisy can take good care of herself.'

'Have you ever regretted not having kids, Fleur?'

As soon as the words were out of her mouth, Dervla regretted them. The eyes that Fleur turned on her were tragic.

131

'Oh, Dervla – of course I have. I should have loved to have had a child. I just never found the right man to be the father.'

'It's not too late.'

'Corban would make a fantastic father—'

What? Dervla doubted it, somehow.

'—but a child is a big commitment, and he's a very busy man.' Fleur shook her head. 'I don't even entertain the notion of having a child now. I'd have adored to have had a daughter. A little girl that you could dress in cutesy clothes and read stories to and tuck up in bed and kiss and cuddle and inhale the scent of . . . Oh! Oh, dear. I'd better not go there. What about you, Dervla, now you're settled? Have you thought about children?'

'I've a feeling I might be too old for children, Fleur.'

'Well, I know it's more difficult to conceive at our age, but there's still a possibility, isn't there?'

Dervla shrugged. 'My periods have become a bit erratic. I may be on the cusp of premature menopause.'

'Oh, God. Dread word.'

'They say it can be worse than puberty.'

'Nothing gets easier, does it? Life's a bitch and then you die.'

'Or – as in the case of my mother-in-law, life's a bitch and then you don't even get to die.'

'Dervla! That's a shocking thing to say!'

'Is it? Sorry. It's just that Christian and I have developed a rather black sense of humour around her.'

'Does she have absolutely no quality of life?'

Dervla was about to say 'no', and then she thought about it. What quality of life did Daphne have? She lived in comfort, surrounded by her own beautiful things. She could talk – even though she mostly just talked rubbish. She may not

132

have been able to see much on her flat screen, but she could hear the mellifluous tones of David Attenborough and Monty Don, listen to musical numbers. She had her radio, she had her audio books, she had the soothing gurgle of the fish tank. She had her scent – *Je Reviens* – and the aroma of the excellent food that Nemia prepared for her, plus, of course, the taste. She had the warmth of the sun on her face when she sat on the swing seat on her patio. She had her hair styled for her, and her nails manicured. She had her pashminas and her cashmere throws. She had memories of her lovers – that was evident from the way she'd spoken of Jack, the love of her life who had died in a fire. All in all, Dervla thought, when compared to some people, Daphne had a damned fine life.

'Actually,' she said, 'she's got a lot going for her. I wouldn't mind being taken care of like that, when I reach her age.'

They were nearing the end of their walk now, rounding the bend in the road that led to the outskirts of the village. A rather ugly apartment development had been built here during the boom years. Corban O'Hara had snapped up the penthouse, but as far as Dervla knew, most of the rest remained unsold. It was like a ghost building – even Corban rarely stayed there, preferring to sleep at Fleur's any time he was in town.

Corban O'Hara. Why had Dervla taken so agin the man, when she hadn't even met him properly? How long had he and Fleur been an item now? Six months or so? Dervla had once suggested that he and Fleur join them for dinner in the Old Rectory, but Fleur had told her that when Corban came to Lissamore it was in search of peace and quiet. He spent so much time wheeling and dealing and socializing in Dublin that privacy was a precious commodity for him here. Anyway, the notion of entertaining a millionaire – or was he a billionaire? – in her kitchen did little for Dervla's sense of self-worth. She'd rather wait until her dining room was finished – if they could ever afford to finish it.

Hmm. She wondered now if Mister O'Hara would recognize her as the woman from whom he'd bought the *prosecco* this afternoon, and if so, how it would affect his demeanour? Should she disingenuously ask him if he'd enjoyed it? Let a few worms wriggle out of that can? No, *no*, Dervla! It was none of her affair. It was Fleur's affair. Or maybe even his . . .

Outside O'Toole's, a handful of tourists were perched on windowsills, admiring the view of the harbour. One of them was playing a bodhrán, badly, while another was murdering a tin whistle. All of them were singing 'The Fields of Athenry'. Inside, it was quieter: empty but for a pretty blonde girl reading a book and a mountainy man in a greasy gaberdine, both atop barstools.

'Will you order for me?' Fleur asked Dervla. 'I need to pay a visit to the loo and make myself presentable.'

'Sure,' said Dervla. 'A glass of Guinness?'

'Please.'

Dervla ordered two glasses from the bartender, then sat down on a banquette by the fire. There was always a fire going in O'Toole's, whatever the weather. Because the pub was small and rather dark, it provided a welcoming touch. Someone had left a *Daily Mail* behind. Reaching for it automatically, Dervla steeled herself to read more tales of recessionary doom and gloom.

An article on the ageing population demographic predicted that within a quarter of a century one in four people in Britain would be over the age of sixty-five. One in four! And one in eighty-eight of over sixty-fives was currently suffering from dementia. The caring industry was clearly in for a boom time: more and more people would need to be recruited by agencies as carers. Dervla thought of all those first-time buyers she'd shown around apartments a year or two ago. There'd been lots of girls who'd trained as beauty therapists, employed in luxury spas and five-star hotels all over the Galway and Coolnamara region. In those days, beauty therapy had been big business. She wondered would those hapless girls have to retrain, now that jobs were so scarce; and if they did, would they realize that caring for the elderly was now the new beauty therapy?

'Your Guinness, Dervla,' said the bartender, setting two half-pint glasses in front of her. 'Beautiful evening, isn't it?'

'Yes,' said Dervla, segueing automatically into weather small talk.

'The forecast is for more rain, though.'

'Oh?'

'Spreading from the west.'

'I'll get these!' It was Fleur. She had combed her hair, spritzed herself with scent, and applied a little lip gloss. Her eyes and skin were glowing from the walk: she looked ten years younger than the forty she admitted to. Dervla suspected that since they had first met, shortly after Fleur had divorced her husband, she had shaved five years off her real age. She got away with it, as most French women did. And of course, like most French women, Fleur never got fat.

'Can you bring us some nuts, too, Fergal?' said Fleur, endorsing Dervla's observation about French women. 'I'm ravenous after that walk.'

'Coming up,' said Fergal, moving back to the bar.

'How do you manage to pack away so many calories and stay so slim?' Dervla asked. 'I just have to look at a packet of nuts and I instantly feel about half a kilo heavier.'

Fleur shrugged. 'I guess I inherited it from my mother.

135

She adored her food, but she warned me never to get complacent. That's why I go to exercise classes twice a week. You should come, Dervla. The Irish dancing classes are great fun, and you can vent all your pent-up aggression doing kickboxing.'

'Maybe I should. Maybe I should join Nemia's Tai Chi class, and go along with her on the nights when Christian takes over Daphne-sitting. Although I'm not sure that Tai Chi would burn up a whole load of calories.'

'But I'm sure it's good for the spirit. Didn't you say that Nemia was a kind of saint?'

'You'd need to be to put up with my mother-in-law.'

The door to the pub opened and Corban O'Hara came through. He was more casually dressed than when Dervla had encountered him earlier that day, but the clothes he wore looked expensive. Approaching the bar, he ordered a pint of Guinness, then turned and moved in their direction.

Fleur raised her face for a kiss, and then, as Corban sent a look of polite enquiry in Dervla's direction, she effected introductions.

'Corban,' said Fleur, 'this is Dervla Vaughan.'

'Delighted to meet you at last,' said Corban, smoothly. He scooped up Dervla's hand and brushed the back with his lips, regarding her from under his eyebrows. Had he recognized her? It was impossible to say. 'I've heard so much about you that I feel I know you already,' he added.

'Likewise,' said Dervla, reclaiming her hand with a perfunctory smile.

'You even look the way I'd imagined you.'

Ew! Dervla wasn't sure that she liked the idea of Corban O'Hara 'imagining' her. She picked at a piece of lint on her sleeve.

As Fleur went to extract money from her purse, Corban

put a hand over hers. 'Put that away, darling,' he said, sliding a billfold from his pocket, and handing the barman a fifty. Oh! He was so fucking smooth that Dervla wouldn't have been surprised to hear him say 'Keep the change'.

Turning back to his female companions, he drew out a chair for Fleur before sitting down beside Dervla on the banquette. Dervla got the trace of a light cologne, citrus, with notes of sandalwood. It was a subtle smell. Sexy. A trace of six o'clock shadow stippled his jaw; the hair that curled over his collar had the gloss of a raven's wing. His skin was tanned – a little weathered, even; his teeth white, but not too white. Mr Corban O'Hara's presence was palpable, his charisma undeniable. He looked at Dervla, bestowing upon her the full beam of his attention, and said: 'I understand you're writing a book on the art of selling houses.'

'That's right.'

'What a very clever thing to be doing.'

Dervla raised an eyebrow. 'In the middle of a recession, when nobody's buying? I beg to differ.'

'I beg to differ, too. I think you'll find you have a best-seller on your hands, Dervla.'

'Really? What on earth makes you think that?'

'Well, people aren't selling their homes right now. But they're thinking of little else. How much the value of their property has depreciated, and what they could do to hike the price up by a grand or two – or simply shift the joint so that they can move on. And when the market starts to recover, everyone who is just thinking about selling now will be testing the waters en masse. They're going to want to know the tricks of the trade. And who better to teach them those tricks than a savvy former auctioneer who was in the running for female entrepreneur of the year?'

Dervla gave him a surprised look. 'How did you know that I was up for an award?'

'I read about it in *The Irish Times*.'

The barman arrived with Corban's pint of Guinness. 'Thanks, Fergal,' said Corban. 'Tell me, how are you and Geraldine getting on with the new arrival?'

'Grand, thanks, Corban. He's started to sleep through the night now. And he's the smiliest young fella you ever saw.'

'Have you a photo?'

'I have, of course.'

Fergal slid a hand into his breast pocket, produced a couple of colour photographs, and handed them to Corban. Dervla was struck dumb with horror. She hadn't even known that Fergal and Geraldine had had a new baby! How could she have missed out on that nugget of news?

'He's a grand head of hair,' observed Corban, holding the photos at arm's length so that Fleur and Dervla could have a look, too. 'Takes after his daddy.'

'Ah, but lucky for him, he's his mammy's nose.'

'Look at the feet on him!' Corban said, laughing, as he scrutinized the second picture. 'He'll be playing for Connaught as soon as he can walk!'

'Pah! You men!' said Fleur. 'Even looking at a picture of a baby, all you can think of is football!'

'Here, Fergal,' said Corban, taking another fifty from his billfold, 'take that to wet the babby's head.'

Fergal accepted the banknote, and slid it into a pocket. 'That's very good of you, Corban,' he said. 'You're a dacent skin.'

'Here's to you. And to little Manus.' Corban raised his pint, and Dervla realized that not only had he known the fact that Fergal had had a baby, but he even knew the infant's name! Oh, God – how inadequate she was! Had spending her days solitaire in the Old Rectory made her undergo a personality change, rendered her socially inept? She raised her glass, and echoed, 'To Manus!' and then she started rummaging in her pocket for her purse so that she, too, could contribute towards the wetting of the baby's head.

Fergal departed with a thank you, a smile and seventy euros, and Dervla cursed herself for not having had the nous to ask after his family earlier, rather than exchange banalities on the bloody weather.

Corban leaned a little closer to Fleur. 'Fleur O'Farrell,' he said, 'are you wearing a new scent?'

'You noticed, *Monsieur*!'

'Of course I noticed.'

'You approve?'

'Mmm. I approve. It suits you. Feminine . . . and – mmm – not quite so innocent as it smells at first. Tell me what it is, and I'll bring you some back on my next business trip.'

'It's *Narcisse Blanc*. You'll have to write it down. It's not the kind of name a man would remember.'

'I'll remember it.'

Corban then turned his attention back to Dervla. 'May I ask who's publishing you?'

Dervla told him.

He considered, then nodded. 'They're great. They're small, but they're keen, and once they get behind an author, they do their best to push. Have you an agent?'

'No,' said Dervla. 'Is that a problem?'

'Not with a first book. But you might want to think about acquiring one before you sign your next deal.'

'My next deal!' scoffed Dervla.

'Why shouldn't you get another deal?'

'Because I don't have anything else to write about.'

'I can think of a title straight away.'

'Yeah?'

'Yeah. How about: *Women Entrepreneurs – Kicking Ass and Getting Results*.'

'Nice aphorism.' Dervla gave him a challenging look. 'But is it true?'

'It doesn't have to be true,' Corban told her, 'as long as it sells.'

'Aren't you being a little cynical?'

'Hello? This, coming from a former estate agent?'

Dervla laughed, despite herself.

'Cynicism's all right,' he told her. 'It's a carapace that allows us to function.'

'A survival mechanism?'

'Exactly. If we didn't allow ourselves to be cynical from time to time, we'd be stumbling around with no protective membrane. It's the same with humour. If we didn't distil a grain of humour from the dark side of life, we'd be banjaxed.'

Dervla thought about the myriad times she and Río had used gallows humour as a way of coping with their father's alcoholism, and the politically incorrect jokes that she and Christian shared about 'the elderly', and knew that Corban was right.

'It's true, of course,' sighed Fleur. 'How could we have laughed at George Bush otherwise?'

'Or our current Taoiseach?' Corban took a swig of his pint, then set it down. 'How was your walk?'

'Excellent,' Fleur told him. 'Dervla saw a – what kind of a bird was it, Dervla?'

'A merlin.'

'Wow,' said Corban. 'They're scarce enough. Male or female?'

'Male.'

140

'They're such elegant-looking birds, aren't they? Apart from—'

'Their silly little legs, like feathered trousers!' exclaimed Fleur. 'That's just what Dervla said about them, earlier.'

'That's it, exactly!' Corban said with a laugh. 'What's that breed of chicken that has feathery legs, too? Some kind of bantam.'

'Silkies?' said Dervla.

'That's it. Hey – cue for a joke. A chicken and an egg are lying in bed together. The chicken is smoking a cigarette, and the egg is looking cross. "Well," says the egg, "I guess that answers *that* question."'

Dervla spluttered on her Guinness.

'I don't get it,' said Fleur, looking perplexed.

'Which came first?' prompted Dervla.

Fleur shrugged. 'I still don't get it.'

'Never mind, my little French poodle.' Corban put an arm around her shoulder and pulled her close. 'It's probably something to do with the fact that English is not your first tongue.'

'I must run that joke by my sister Río,' said Dervla. 'She collects them.'

'Río? Why is that name familiar?' asked Corban.

'She's working on *The O'Hara Affair*,' Fleur told him. 'She's the set-dresser. By the way, can Dervla and I visit the set some day?'

'Sure. Just let me know in advance and I'll tell one of the ADs to expect you. You could come this weekend, if you like.'

'But you won't be there!'

'Where will I be?'

'In London, of course, you noodle.'

Corban struck his forehead with the heel of his hand.

'See? Your memory *is* rubbish,' Fleur remonstrated. 'What's the name of the perfume you're supposed to be bringing back for me?'

'That's easy. *Narcisse Blanc.*'

'Go to the top of the class!'

Dervla suddenly felt superfluous. She drained her glass and rose to her feet. 'I'd better make tracks,' she said. 'I'll have to get dinner on the table.'

'Why don't you and Christian join us here?' said Corban. 'We're eating upstairs in the restaurant this evening.'

Dervla shook her head. 'We can't. I promised I'd cook for my mother-in-law.'

Corban looked grave. 'She has Alzheimer's, hasn't she?' Clearly registering her surprise that he was so clued-up, he added: 'Fleur told me. I am sorry – for you and your husband as well as your mother-in-law. Living with Alzheimer's is tough. I have a cousin who cares for her father twenty-four/seven.'

'It's actually dementia that Daphne has.'

He sucked in his breath. 'Ow. That's worse.'

'It is?'

'Yes. Alzheimer's is fatal, in the end. With dementia, a person can go on for years.'

Was this indeed the case? Dervla decided she'd better do a little online research.

'But isn't that a good thing?' said Fleur.

Corban gave her a questioning look. 'What do you think? Scientists have calculated that, in theory, modern man could be capable of living to a hundred and twenty.'

Fleur shuddered. 'Oh. I guess that *isn't* a good thing.'

'I wouldn't want to live that long,' said Corban, 'which is why I carry a living will.'

'You do?' said Fleur. 'I didn't know that.'

Corban reached for his billfold again. He took a folded sheet of paper from it, and handed it to Fleur.

"'If',' she read out loud, "'I suffer an incurable, irreversible illness, disease, or condition and my attending physician determines that my condition is terminal, I direct that life-sustaining measures that would serve only to prolong my dying be withheld or discontinued.'" She gave him an admiring look. 'Wow. Well done, you, Corban O'Hara.'

Dervla found herself sitting down again. 'How do you make one of those?' she asked.

'It's easy,' Corban told her. 'You'll find hundreds of sample living wills on the internet.'

'Now, that is something I would be interested in doing.'

'My own mother was a card-carrying member of Exit.'

'Exit?'

'The Voluntary Euthanasia Society. She contracted terminal cancer, and self-delivered.'

'You mean . . . she committed suicide?' asked Dervla, hesitantly.

'Yes. She did it very beautifully. Filled her house with flowers, enjoyed a glass of Bordeaux, put some Mozart on the CD player. Then took the pills. She wrote us – my brother and me – a beautiful letter, to say goodbye.'

'Oh, Corban,' said Dervla. 'I am sorry.'

He smiled at her. 'I wouldn't have wanted it any other way. She would have hated to have died in hospital, all tubed up. She was a free spirit.'

'What age was she, when she died?'

'Sixty-two.'

'That's heartbreaking.'

He shrugged. 'It's the way of the world,' he said. 'Or it should be.'

Dervla found herself wanting to reach for his hand.

Corban's cosmopolitan exterior and facile charm clearly concealed a soft centre. She decided that she liked this man after all. She was about to ask him how his cousin coped with her senile parent, when her phone alerted her to a text message. She accessed it to find the following: **Dropping into care home to check it out for mum. Home around 8. Will you record the match?**

She smiled. Fleur had been so right earlier, when she'd said that all men thought about was football. She started to text back.

'Well,' said Fleur with a sigh. 'That was a jolly conversation.'

Corban laughed. 'I'll tell you another joke then, shall I? To cheer you up.'

'Yes. Do!'

'How many Germans does it take to change a light bulb?'

'How many?'

'One,' said Corban.

There was a pause, and then suddenly all three of them were rocking with laughter. And in fact, Dervla noticed, as she looked up from her phone – it wasn't just the three of them who had found the joke funny. Over by the bar, the girl who had been sitting reading had raised her eyes from her book and was looking obliquely at Corban with a coquettishly raised eyebrow.

Later, Dervla was stocking up on basics in the village shop when she realized she'd left her binoculars behind in O'Toole's. Back she went to reclaim them, exchanging pleasantries with the village folk as she strolled down the street. How funny it was, she thought, that in the Sugar Stack – the exclusive apartment block in Galway in which she had lived during her estate agent days – she had known nobody. Here in Lissamore she knew almost everyone. It was a good feeling.

As she drew level with the pub window, she saw that her binoculars were no longer on the table. Fleur had mentioned that she'd need to go home to change before dinner: presumably she had taken them with her. The joint was empty now apart from the blonde girl and Corban, who was leaning against the bar. The pair were deep in conversation, and the girl was smiling: Corban was clearly working that facile charm again. His back was turned to her, and even though the door to the pub was open, something about his demeanour made Dervla stop in her tracks. Their voices came to her faintly: they were discoursing in German.

As Dervla observed them, she could see that their body language was as fluent as the German they were speaking: she recognized those little telltale signs that indicated mutual attraction; the touching of hair, the looping of a thumb in a belt, the fiddling with an earring . . .

Turning away, she walked back down the main street of the village. There was no sign of Fleur on her deck: she must be getting ready to join Corban in the restaurant. As Dervla zapped the locks on her car, she wondered what Corban and the blonde girl had been talking about. She suspected, somehow, that it was not a conversation they might have had had Fleur been present. How she wished she spoke German.

Dervla was feeling knackered. She'd come home to find that Kitty had been sick on the kitchen floor. There were emails backed up – most of them spam that she had to filter through to find the genuine articles. She'd made a pasta sauce from scratch because there wasn't any in the freezer and she'd promised Christian something scrummy for supper (to cheer him up after she'd forgotten to record the match); and then she'd had to do all the dishes by hand because the brand new dishwasher was on the blink.

They were standing together at the kitchen sink, she in her Marigolds, Christian with a drying-up cloth in his hand. Dervla emptied the washing-up bowl with an emphatic 'Thank fuck that day's over!' and lunged for a bottle of wine. Daphne had joined them for dinner this evening, and when Daphne came to dinner, they didn't have wine because Nemia had told her that alcohol made her tetchy. Tetchi*er*, you mean, Dervla had wanted to say, but she'd kept her lip zipped.

'Don't bother drying the rest, darling,' Dervla told Christian. 'Just leave them, and I'll put them away in the morning.' She took a couple of glasses from the cupboard, and set them on the table. 'You open it, will you? I love the way you do it, like a proper sommelier.'

Sitting down at the table, she watched as Christian expertly stripped the foil from the neck of the bottle, inserted the corkscrew and pulled. Dervla thought the sloshing of the liquid into the long-stemmed glasses was the most welcome sound she'd ever heard.

'Cheers,' they said simultaneously, chinking crystal and smiling at each other.

'Tell me the story of your day,' said Dervla. She loved to be able to say this. In all her years as a singleton, there'd been nobody to swap stories with, nobody to give out yards to about what a shite day it had been or how badly people had behaved, or – conversely – nobody to celebrate with on those days when life had been joyous and profitable and people had made her laugh. Now, for Dervla, this was the most important time of the daily routine, when she and her husband could finally kick off their shoes and sit down and talk.

'You tell me your day, first,' said Christian.

Dervla gave him a wry look. 'Well, you already know about my eventful morning.'

'Mum's bid for freedom?'

'Uh-huh. The next thing you know she'll start digging secret tunnels like Tim Robbins in *The Shawshank Redemption*.'

'Or take off on a motorbike like Steve McQueen in *The Great Escape*.'

'Escape,' mused Dervla. 'It's such a wonderful word, isn't it? The very thought of it lifts your spirits. I heard a good joke today, incidentally.'

Christian and Dervla had taken to searching for jokes on the internet as – how had she described it earlier to Corban O'Hara? – as a kind of survival mechanism. Most of them were rather un-PC.

'Shoot,' said Christian, and Dervla launched into the story of the chicken and the egg, rather well, she thought. Dervla had never been very good at telling jokes, and she was pleased when Christian gave a gratifying laugh.

'Who told you that?'

'Corban O'Hara.'

'Corban O'Hara? Fleur's bloke?'

'Yes. We met him for a drink in O'Toole's after our walk.'

'I thought you didn't like him?'

'Correction. I mistrusted him. Erroneously, as it turns out. He's actually really sound. Although he is a little over-partial to flirting with young wans. I spotted him chatting up a German backpacker.'

Christian shrugged. 'You can't deny a man his midlife crisis. I love a good opportunity to flirt. It's when people stop flirting back that it's time to get worried.'

'I suppose you're right. Gather ye rosebuds, and all that.'

'If he enjoys a good joke maybe we could entertain him in our kitchen after all,' suggested Christian.

'Maybe we should. It would be nice to have company.'

'It would make a change from having my mother to dinner.'

They shared another smile, and then Dervla said: 'Your turn.'

Christian heaved a sigh. 'OK,' he said. 'Here goes. The wine-tasting *tour de France* can't be cancelled, Dervla. There are too many people already booked, and if we pull out at this stage we'll create an awful lot of ill will, and an awful lot of problems.'

Dervla reached for his hand across the table. 'I'm glad, for your sake,' she said. 'It means the business can't go under just yet.'

'There's more.'

'Yes?'

'I did as you suggested,' Christian told her, 'and book-marked a couple of old people's homes to investigate on the way back this evening.'

'And?'

'And . . .' he broke off. 'Look, Dervla, just let me tell you about them before you come to any conclusions.'

'Fair enough. Go on.'

'I did some trawling on the internet, this afternoon, like you did. I found out that the two homes I visited would be cheaper options than getting the professionals in.'

'That's what I thought.'

'But – oh, Dervla, all I can say is that if your mother were still alive, you wouldn't ever, ever want her to end up in a place like the two I saw today. You'd sooner she died than be – be incarcerated in one of those homes from hell.'

'They're that bad?'

'What can I tell you? They smell of cabbage and wee and chemical air freshener. The inmates – I mean, the *residents*

148

– all sit around the four walls of one room, strapped into their chairs, and there's a television high up on the wall, blaring *Sky News* – all war and earthquakes and bickering politicians. And in the other place I visited, it was *Deal or No Deal*, and nobody was watching it.'

'Oh, God.'

'I had a look at the bedrooms, too.'

'What were they like?'

Christian shrugged. 'There were a few singles, but they're all occupied, and there's a waiting list. The only option for Mum would be to share, and can you imagine how hard that would be for her?'

And for the other inmate, Dervla thought, but did not say.

'Most of the rooms are poky and dark,' continued Christian, 'with no space for visitors, so you'd have to go to the day room any time you called in. They're awful places, Dervla. Just awful. I'm sorry. I know it's expensive, but there's no way around it. We'll just have to get the health care pros in.'

Dervla laced her fingers through his, and took a deep breath. 'It's OK, darling. You don't have to worry about this any more. I've been doing some thinking, and I may have come up with a solution.'

'Oh?'

'I'll do it.'

'You'll do what?'

'I'll take over Daphne's care while Nemia's away.'

The expression on Christian's face said it all. He was swamped with relief, and Dervla felt a fresh, fierce, pull of love for him.

'Dear Jesus, Dervla – would you? That would be the solution to everything! Oh, God – this is like a gift from heaven!'

He raised her hand and pressed his lips to the palm. 'But tell me,' he said, when he released her hand. 'You've really and truly thought this through?'

'Yes. It makes perfect sense. I'll move into Nemia's room and live with Daphne in the cottage for the two weeks you're away. If I need anything, sure I'm right next door to my own home. And once Daphne's settled for the day, I can work on my book.'

'Have you run this by Nemia yet?' asked Christian.

'No. But I suspect she'll be thrilled. It means that if she needs to take a break in future, I can step in and hold the fort.'

'You'll have to be paid for your trouble, from my mother's funds.'

'I agree. That's only fair – and we could certainly do with the money. Hell, darling – maybe we should even encourage Nemia to take more time off!'

Dervla kept her tone light, watching Christian with an encouraging smile as he refilled her glass, but in the cavity of her chest, her heart was pounding with anxiety. What if something went wrong? What if Daphne fell and broke a bone? What if her false teeth went missing and she couldn't eat? What if Daphne missed Nemia and Christian so much she pined away? What if she died in her sleep, and Dervla went into her bedroom in the morning to try and wake a corpse? What if . . . what if . . .

Dervla *was* doing the right thing, wasn't she? Yes, she was! Could she stick fourteen days with Daphne? Come on, Dervla. Fourteen days was just two weeks. She could do it, she *would* do it, for Christian.

Chapter Ten

Bethany was flying high, high over Shakespeare Island, searching for signs of life below. There were none. She was bang on time for Hero. They'd been meeting up, same time, same place, for over a week now. They'd checked out all kinds of landmarks on Second Life: they'd visited a rainforest and a book shop and a music store and a Hollywood backlot and a tropical island, where they'd even been able to explore underwater, and where they'd seen a whale and been threatened by a shark! They'd spent hours chatting and laughing together, and making private observations about all the strange-looking, taciturn (a word she'd learned from Hero) loners who tended to hang out in the overly populated locations, looking lost.

Hero was exactly the kind of guy that Bethany would love to meet in real life. He was a maverick, a free spirit who wouldn't think twice about breaking a few rules. He enjoyed the same music as she did, read the same books, loved the same films. He'd told her about the theatre he'd seen in Dublin recently: a fantastic production of Chekhov's *Three Sisters*, a lousy adaptation of *Lady Chatterley's Lover*. He was intelligent, he had a GSOH. The only problem was that he was an avatar, not a living, breathing boy.

She was excited about seeing him again. Last night Hero

had teleported her to a club called Sweethearts, where they'd danced together. They hadn't talked, just danced. And Bethany had loved it. It sounded mad, but it had been romantic – something had definitely been shimmering in the air between them. And then Hero had told her that he had to take a phone call in real life, and had left her forlornly sitting alone, refusing dance invitations from other single-tons. The last thing he'd said to her was **Same time, same place tomorrow?** And she'd replied – very uncoolly, she realized in retrospect: **Yes! Can't wait!**

And now she *was* waiting, because a glance at the bottom right-hand corner of her screen told her that Hero was late. Dropping down next to the great door of the high-raftered library, she passed through. The fire in the hearth was the only animated thing there.

Pah. She'd have a better view from upstairs, on the mezzanine. As she negotiated the stairs, she thought how weird it was that somebody had gone to all the trouble to create this entire virtual village of Tudor buildings, and furnish them – and even light fires in them! – and nobody ever seemed to come to visit. She took a seat, then decided to amuse herself by activating some expressions. She yawned. She laughed. She cried. She shrugged. She waved to nobody. She beckoned to nobody. She blew a kiss – to nobody. She fidgeted.

In real life, Bethany was feeling fidgety, too. Hero was usually early for her. So far in their encounters she had not once had to hang around waiting for him. She felt horribly lonely, sitting there on the divan in the Elizabethan library. Or was she sitting on her bed in her cottage in Díseart, Lissamore? Was she Bethany or Poppet? Was she a real girl or a virtual being? Flesh and blood or ether? She would have laughed if she hadn't been feeling so unsettled.

But hang on – what had Hero said to her last night? *Same time, same place tomorrow* . . . Maybe he had meant that club, Sweethearts – not Shakespeare Island! Maybe he was there now, waiting for her . . .

Oh! She was an idiot! With clumsy fingers, Bethany clicked on 'Landmarks', scrolling down until she found Sweethearts. Another click or two, and she was teleporting to the dance club. The rushing sound in her earphones as she was transported through time and space made her feel heady – and a little sick. What if Hero wasn't there? What if something awful had happened to him in real life?

The club was more crowded than it had been last night when Hero had held her in his arms and swooped with her across the dance floor. There were women in beautiful ball gowns preening themselves, and men in tuxedos checking them out. Couples were smooching, gazing into each other's eyes, moving in time to the cool jazzy music that played non-stop in Sweethearts.

Poppet set off on her quest to find her date. There were lots of other heroes in here tonight. There was Theseus, Rambo, Byron and Shrek. But of the real hero – *her* hero, she could see no sign. As she manoeuvred her way around the club, several male avatars hit on her, but she ignored them. Bethany felt her heart rate quicken. Her progress was being impeded by a couple locked in an embrace, and she found herself careering into them. **'Sorry'**, she managed, before moving on: left, right, forward, back. Oh, this was hopeless, hopeless! He wasn't here. Should she teleport back to Shakespeare Island? Or should she sit down at a table by the dance floor and wait a little longer? But then, if Hero *was* on Shakespeare Island, he might give up and go away . . .

Take it easy, a Beyoncé lookalike told her, as Bethany's avatar collided into her.

Sorry, said Poppet again. And then she realized that the Beyoncé lookalike, whose name was Candy, had been in here yesterday. **Can you help me?** she asked. **I was in here last night with a guy called Hero. Have you seen him?**

Yeah. He was here earlier, looking lost.

How long ago?

Ten minutes or so. You want to be careful. A lot of gals were hitting on him.

Oh! Oh, God. She had to get out of here, get back to Shakespeare Island.

Thanks, Candy. Excuse me.

As she brushed her touchpad, Bethany realized that her palms were sweaty. Shakespeare Island, Shakespeare Island, quick, quick, quick. That swooshing noise in her cans told her she was on her way.

As usual, the place was deserted: a town peopled by ghosts, echoing with the sound of virtual applause and the dialogue of non-existent actors.

On the divan in the library, Poppet sat down, looking bereft. And on her bed in the cottage in Díseart, near Lissamore on the west coast of Ireland, Bethany began to cry.

Fleur put the cork back in the bottle, and rinsed the wineglasses. She was tired, now. Walking the three miles of the bog road always took more out of her than she expected, and while dinner in O'Toole's had been a treat – she'd made sure that they ordered lobster, to keep Seamus Moynihan happy – she and Corban had been joined by an accountant friend of his, which meant that the entire evening had been hijacked by talk of profit margins and tax breaks and investments. It had cost Fleur an effort to keep an interested expression pinned to her face.

She yawned, and turned towards the spiral staircase that would take her to the bedroom. From the en suite bathroom, she could hear Corban singing the toreadors' chorus from Carmen. He was singing lustily, clearly still full of energy, and Fleur's heart sank a little. It sank further when she saw the outfit he had laid out on the bed for her to wear. Red satin garter belt. Peephole bra. Those panties she hated. He clearly expected her to be a whore tonight. Maybe she could plead tiredness? But they had so few nights together – it was unfair to ask him to abstain just because she wasn't in the mood. Besides, it had been established from day one that when it came to sex Corban called the shots, and Fleur sensed that their relationship was still too – what was that word again? – too *nascent* to challenge the status quo.

She peeled off her fine cashmere sweater, unzipped her pencil skirt, and stepped out of her heels. Then she strapped herself into the bra and garter belt, pulled on the panties, and went to her lingerie drawer to find a pair of black stockings. As she slid the sheer nylons up her legs and hooked them onto the belt, she gazed yearningly at her collection of La Perla and Chantelle brassieres, and her neat piles of French lace and Swiss cotton panties. Why did men find red such a turn-on? She'd lost count of the number of men who'd come into her shop, handed over a perfectly beautiful balconette bra in pale blue or pink, and said: 'Do you have this in red, please?' She was just stepping into a pair of even more vertiginous heels, when Corban's voice made her turn.

'Feeling a little slutty, are we?'

He was lounging against the doorjamb, watching her lazily. She knew that look. It was her cue to bite down on her lip and lower her eyes. And as she did so, she felt herself assume a character, a character who bore no resemblance to the real-life Fleur. And as the character took possession of her, her apathy lifted as she felt the first stirrings of sexual arousal.

'Because no one but a whore wears stuff like that,' resumed Corban. 'You should be ashamed of yourself. You *are* ashamed of yourself, aren't you, Fleur?'

She glanced up at him from under her eyelashes and nodded.

'Something tells me you need to be taught a lesson, madam. It's not a nice thing to do, to parade around the streets looking like butter wouldn't melt in your mouth, wearing stuff like that under your chic little sweaters and skirts. What would people think, if they knew? They'd think that you needed to be taught a lesson, and they'd be right, Fleur, wouldn't they?'

'Yes,' she managed. Her body had begun to betray her already. She could feel her nipples harden, and she saw Corban's eyes go to them, where they jutted from the embroidered eyelets in the crimson satin.

'Slutty little bitch.' He reached between the folds of his heavy towelling robe and began to stroke himself. Fleur felt her breath coming faster, and her head drooped a little. 'Stand up straight when I'm talking to you.' She raised her chin and set back her shoulders. His eyes were still on her nipples. 'Get your lipstick.' She moved to her dressing table and took YSL's *Rouge Pur* from a drawer. 'Paint them,' Corban commanded, and she raised a hand and circled her nipples in red. His lip curled in contempt. 'What would your customers say if they could see you now?' he said. 'The fragrant Fleur O'Farrell playing with her own tits, gagging for it. You *are* gagging for it, aren't you, Fleur?'

'Yes.'

156

'Yes, what?'

'Yes, sir.'

'And you'd like me to give it to you, wouldn't you?'

'Yes, sir.' There was an ominous silence. Corban narrowed his eyes at her. 'Yes . . . please, sir,' she amended.

'That's better,' said Corban, with a humourless smile. Under the robe, he was still working on his erection.

'So, my little French whore, how are you going to go about getting what you want?'

Fleur got to her knees. 'I'm begging you, sir,' she whispered.

'Speak up, you pathetic bitch. I can't hear you.'

'I'm begging you.'

'Begging me to . . .?'

'To fuck me. Sir.'

'Hmm. Corban gave an ostentatious yawn. 'To tell you the truth, sweetie, I'm not sure I could be bothered.'

Oh, God. She'd have to earn it. She crawled across the carpet, parted the folds of his robe, and took him in her mouth. 'Good girl,' he said, laying his hands on the back of her head and exerting a little pressure. Fleur was gratified to hear the moan of pleasure that was her reward for being compliant. And she knew she was good at this: Corban had once told her jokingly that she had missed a vocation as a fellatrix. After several minutes, when he was very, very stiff, he withdrew. 'Get to your feet,' he commanded. 'At once.'

She obeyed, rising clumsily from the carpet.

'Turn around.'

Again, she did as he ordered.

'Bend over, Fleur.' And this time his voice was velvet smooth, indulgent as a paterfamilias and gentle as a caress. 'I think you're going to like what I've got for you, darling. I think you're going to like it very much.'

She did like it. And as she felt him thrust into her, she heard him say the words she longed to hear. 'Oh, God – you're beautiful, Fleur. You're so, so beautiful.'

'Am I?' she asked.

'Oh, yes. You're – oh, God!'

'Say it. Say it again.' This time there was nothing obsequious in her tone; this time *she* was in command.

'You're beautiful. You're beautiful, Fleur. You're so, so beautiful . . .'

The next morning when she awoke in Corban's arms, he raised himself on one elbow, kissed the tip of her nose and smiled down at her. 'You stay there, *mon petit chou*,' he said. 'I'm bringing you breakfast on a tray. *Café au lait* and croissants?'

'Mmm. Yes, please. Sir.' They shared a smile.

And as he made his way down the spiral staircase, Fleur hugged herself, then stretched from her pretty painted fingertips all the way down to her tippy tippy toes. This must be how Scarlett felt, she decided, the day after being ravished by Rhett, smug in the knowledge that she had her man where she wanted him. Corban might perceive himself to be a master of the universe, but savvy Fleur O'Farrell knew that it took two to tango.

It was the second night in a row Bethany had spent on Second Life, waiting for Hero to show. She'd revisited all their old haunts, but there was no sign of him. Now she was sitting on the mezzanine in the library again, all alone. She knew that she should shut down her computer and do something else – take a bath, take some exercise, read a book – but she felt a compulsion to remain online, hunting for Hero.

Her mother had phoned today, to make sure all was well in Bethany's world, and Bethany had told her that yes, everything was fine – she was eating properly and enjoying her work and keeping the place tidy. But in fact, that had been a big, fat lie. She didn't bother preparing food for herself other than cereal, the only good thing about work was the fact that she was fed for free, and the cottage was looking sadly neglected. She hardly even bothered with Facebook any more. Bethany was spending all her spare time roaming a brave new virtual world.

But what was the point of exploring a virtual word if she had no fellow adventurer to explore it with? Tara had found herself a real live boyfriend, Hero had gone AWOL, and Bethany was lonelier than ever.

Diddle-ip! The convo button on her toolbar lit up. Flirty. Who was Flirty? Oh yes – the girl who'd asked to be her friend a couple of weeks ago. They'd chatted a little on IM since then – she seemed nice. Bethany remembered that she'd used a funky font.

She clicked, and read: Hi! I see you haven't updated your Facebook status for a coupla days. How are things?

How were things? Things were . . .

Bloody awful, typed Bethany.

Oh no! What's up?

Before she could even register what she was doing, Bethany had typed: **I'm in love.**

What? Who are you in love with?

Oh, it's too stupid.

Tell me.

I can't. I feel like such a loser.

Maybe I can help.

How?

I'm a good listener. But don't just take my word for it. Check out Daisy de Saint-Euverte's

159

profile and you'll see that she describes me – Flirty O'Farrell – as her favourite agony aunt in the world. But if you don't want to talk to me, there are lots of places on the internet where you can look for advice.

I'd rather talk to a real person like you.

That generally makes more sense. So. Tell me about it.

OK. Have you been on Second Life yet?

Once only. But I could give it another go.

OK. The problem is that I met a guy on there. He's really cute.

But he's only an avatar, Bethany!

I know. That's what makes this so stupid. But he's just – I don't know how to explain it.

Perfect?

Yes!

What makes him perfect?

He's just everything I want and everything I've ever imagined. He loves all the same things I do and wants to do all the things I want to do. He's a dreamer and an adventurer and he's really intelligent and he makes me laugh.

Hmm. He sounds pretty perfect, all right. Have you been spending a lot of time on SL?

Well I can't during the day cos I have work. But in the evening I do.

How long?

An hour maybe.

That was a lie. Bethany actually spent much longer on Second Life. In a way, it gave her the same kind of comfort that she'd garnered from all those hours spent alone in her

160

bedroom as a child, acting out fantasy scenarios. But she didn't want Flirty to think she was a *complete* loser.

Maybe not even that, she added, for good measure.

And how did you meet this guy – what's his name?

Hero.

Cool! What's your avatar's name?

Poppet.

Where did you meet this Hero?

In an empty theatre.

Was that not a little scary?

No. He looked kinda lost. I showed him around.

And you've met up with him since?

Yeah. Loads of times. He teleported me to a club the other night. It was cool. There were loads of couples dancing.

Like – cheek to cheek?

Yeah.

And did you dance?

Yeah.

How did it feel?

Kinda warm and fuzzy.

Weird?

No. Not really. It felt right. And then I was meant to meet him again there last night and I blew it because I was late and he'd gone. And then I tried looking for him again tonight and I couldn't find him anywhere.

What does Hero do in real life, Bethany?

He has something to do with casting.

Like in theatre casting?

Yeah.

In LA?

No. In Dublin.

Dublin, Ireland?

Yeah.

There was a hiatus in the convo. Bethany filled it by bringing up Second Life, where her avatar, Poppet, was still sitting on the divan in the library, waiting for Hero to show up. She scrolled down the actions menu, wondering whether to make Poppet stand up or fall down and cry, and then she froze. There was someone downstairs. Bethany felt a rush of apprehension mixed with adrenaline. She moved to the balustrade and peered over.

Hello, said Hero. **Did you miss me?**

Bethany didn't waste words. She sped down the library stairs – stumbling, banging off walls – and into his virtual arms.

Chapter Eleven

Dublin, Ireland?

Yeah.

Fleur sucked in her breath and reached for the wine bottle. Uh-oh. What had she stumbled across? She quickly reread the final few exchanges in the convo, then typed:

Bethany, you haven't let him know where you are, have you?

There was no response.

Because she had had nothing better to do this evening now that Corban had called off their Coolnamara Castle weekend, Fleur had decided to see who was available to chat on IM. She was glad she had – she was concerned about Bethany. Poor little lamb, wasting her time consorting with strangers on Second Life – strangers who, for all she knew, could turn out to be unscrupulous manipulators.

Bethany – are you there?

Nothing. But Bethany was still online. Maybe she was chatting to somebody else? Maybe she'd gone back to Second Life? Maybe she'd finally touched base with Hero?

Hero! Fleur had lied when she'd told Bethany it was a cool moniker. It was a very clever moniker – what girl didn't want a hero in their life? – but anyone could be a hero on

163

Second Life. Anyone at all. Hell – even *she* could be a hero on Second Life.

Hmm. Maybe she should check out the online community. But before she went to the Google tool bar, she typed in one last question:

Bethany – promise you'll keep in touch? I am concerned for you.

Fleur had decided to do some detective work. Her Second Life account was all set up, and she was just waiting on confirmation via email that she was good to go. She poured herself a glass of wine, wound a pashmina around her shoulders, and stepped through the French windows onto the deck. It was dusk now, and the village was quiet. The only sound was that of the water lapping against the keels of the boats and the occasional lonely call of a curlew. A heron was standing in the inky water by the slipway, perfectly motionless, waiting for some hapless fish to pass by.

Fleur reached for Dervla's bird-watching binoculars. She'd left them behind in the pub the other day, and Fleur had realized that actually, binoculars were quite a handy item to have around. Apart from making the view more immediate, it channelled her inner nosy neighbour. She'd had fun spying on the residents of the holiday houses around the marina and making up stories about them. Was that the wife, daughter, or mistress of the man whose Merc was parked outside his picture window? Did the honeymoon couple realize that she could see straight into their bedroom? Were those rather mannish elderly ladies sisters, or lesbians, or just very good friends? You could write a soap opera about what went on in the holiday houses around Lissamore.

And as for the locals: Fleur didn't much care to think

about what 'Peeping' Tom Hunter got up to on the shiny MacBook Air he'd recently treated himself to.

Fleur trained the binoculars on the heron and watched as, with a lightning-bolt dart of its head, the bird plunged its beak into the shallows, gulped down its dinner, and took off with a melancholy squawk in search of new hunting grounds.

As she followed its flight, the boat that belonged to Corban came into view. Corban wasn't a serious sailor: the *Lolita* was a small pleasure craft, which he used for trips to neighbouring islands. The last time she'd boarded it Fleur had packed a picnic, and they'd spent an afternoon sunbathing and skinny-dipping, feeling as if they were the only two people in the world. Now that she knew just how powerful a pair of bird-watching binoculars could be, she might think twice about skinny-dipping.

She took a sip of her wine, then leaned her elbows on the table and scanned the horizon. There was Sean the Post coming out of O'Toole's, there was Mrs Murphy closing her curtains, there was Río, watering the miniature garden of Eden she'd created on her balcony, there was . . . someone on Corban's deck! Someone – a girl? – with long blonde hair . . . Was there? Fleur adjusted the focus so that she could zoom in closer, but instead of zooming in, the image became blurred. She twisted the dial in the opposite direction, but by the time she'd refocused, the deck that ran the length of Corban's penthouse was deserted. Had she imagined it? She wasn't used to viewing things through binoculars: maybe it had been a trick of the fading light. Still, she'd hate to think that someone had broken in to his apartment. Should she call the guards? No – they had enough on their hands without someone dragging them all the way from Ardmore to investigate a crime that might be wholly imaginary. But maybe it mightn't be a bad idea to phone Corban.

She reached for her phone and pressed speed-dial. It rang and rang, and just as she thought her call would be diverted to voice mail, he picked up.

'Hello, darling,' he said.

'Corban – I think there might be someone in your apartment.'

There was a pause, then Corban said: 'What makes you think that?'

Fleur didn't want to say that she'd been checking the joint out through a pair of binoculars – that would make her sound like some spooky stalker type – so instead she said: 'I was strolling down towards Río's and happened to look up. I could have sworn I saw someone on your deck.'

'Darling, have you been drinking?'

'Well yes, I have had a couple of glasses of wine. But not enough to give me hallucinations. I was wondering whether I should call the guards.'

There was another pause. 'OK,' Corban said finally. 'I'll come clean with you. One of the ADs knew I had a place in the village. He's conducting an illicit affair with one of the extras – a girl from Lissamore. He knew he couldn't entertain her in his hotel room because you can't keep something like that secret on location, so I gave him a key to my apartment.'

Fleur's perplexed expression broadened into a smile. 'Oh – aren't you sweet! What a generous thing to do, *chéri*. But why is the affair illicit? Is he married?'

'No. She is.'

'Oh!' Fleur's nosy neighbour antennae stiffened. 'Who is she?'

'Darling – if I told you that, I would have to kill you.'

'Spoilsport! Go on, Corban, tell me! I promise I won't breathe a word.'

'Fleur – do you consider me to be a man of integrity?'

166

'Of course I do.'

'Well, I am not going to compromise that integrity by revealing the identity of someone who swore me to secrecy.'

'Oh.'

Fleur felt a little small, suddenly. She knew perfectly well that if Corban furnished her with the identity of the mystery girl she'd spotted on his deck she couldn't have resisted the temptation to share the knowledge with Dervla and Río. But she couldn't prevent herself from speculating. Who in the village did she know with long blonde hair? How many extras had long blonde hair? How many married extras had – oh, stop it, stop it, Fleur! She was behaving like a busybody.

'All right,' she conceded. 'I'm ashamed of myself for being a nosy parker. You can give me a rap over the knuckles next time you see me.'

'I'd rather give you something much more vigorous than that. By the way, darling – do let me know if you see any lights on in the apartment, will you? I did ask them to be discreet and not turn on any lights that can be seen from the street.'

'Why so?'

'I didn't want anyone calling in and expecting to find me there.'

'Good point.'

'Oh – there's another thing you could do for me. Could you let – what's the name of your cleaning lady?'

'Audrey.'

'Could you let Audrey have your set of keys so that she can do a clean-up job on the place some day next week?'

'Can't they clean up after themselves?'

'Think about it. How would you like to have a romantic weekend and then spend the next day doing laundry and cleaning the bath and scrubbing floors?'

'You *are* a thoughtful man, Corban O'Hara. How was your trip, incidentally?'

'Uneventful.'

'It's a shame Río isn't still driving a hackney. She'd have been great entertainment on the run into Galway. Who drove you?'

'Somebody local. I didn't catch his name.'

'Where are you staying?'

'In one of the Grange hotels. I've a great view over the City.'

'Have you raided the mini bar yet?'

'Yep. And I'm on my way to chill in the steam room – if that isn't too much of an oxymoron.'

'Oxymoron?'

'Contradiction in terms, my little French maid. Be off with you now. If I don't get to the spa before nine o'clock they won't let me in.'

'All right, my darling. Enjoy your steam.'

'Enjoy your wine. Are you sitting on the deck?'

'Yep.'

'I can just picture you. How's the weather?'

'Fine. It's a beautiful, balmy evening.'

'Lucky girl. It's raining here. Bye, darling.'

'Bye, lover.'

Fleur hung up, then speed-dialled Río's number.

'Hello, Mrs Monty Don!' she said.

'Mrs Monty Don?'

'I saw you on your balcony earlier, tending your garden.'

'Why didn't you come up and say hello? I haven't seen you in ages.'

'I didn't see you from the street – I was on my deck.'

'God bless your eyesight.'

'It was much improved by a pair of binoculars. I've been spying on people.'

168

'Spying on people? Oh, hello, Fleur! Are you turning into the village curtain twitcher? Next thing you know you'll have a telescope installed on your deck.'

'The binoculars aren't mine,' confessed Fleur. 'I borrowed them from Dervla, when we were out walking the other day. I'll have to return them to her, otherwise you're right – I could turn into the village curtain twitcher. Binoculars are addictive.'

With her right hand, Fleur reached for the binoculars, and started to pan over the hump of an island that lay to the west. It was rimmed with red-gold light, from where the sun had set behind it.

'How is Dervla?' asked Río. 'I haven't seen her in ages, either.'

'She seems all right. I think she's a little worried about business in Bacchante.'

'I'm not surprised. Have you taken a hit in Fleurissima?'

'But of course.'

'I thank God every day for this film,' said Río. 'If I was still driving a hackney, I'd be in deep shit. I ran into my ex-boss the other day, and he says fares are down by twenty per cent.'

'You'll be glad to know that Corban will have boosted business for him. He took a hackney all the way to the airport today.'

'I thought the pair of you were having a romantic tryst in Coolnamara Castle?'

Fleur shrugged. 'He had to go to London on business.'

'Not again!'

'That's what happens when you're involved with Mr Big. You don't get to see as much of him as you'd like. Haven't you met him yet?'

'No. But someone pointed him out to me on set last week. He's some dude, Fleur.'

'I know,' said Fleur, smugly, as she scanned the purple mountains to the east. Venus, the evening star, was just climbing into the sky above them. 'Oh, by the way, Río, did you know that one of the ADs on your film is having an affair with one of the extras?'

'What's so unusual about that?' said Río. 'Loads of people have affairs on a movie set. There's even an acronym for it. DCOL. Doesn't Count On Location. Shane told me.'

'How is Shane?'

'Charming, nimble-witted and generous of spirit, according to one of his fan sites.'

Fleur remembered what Dervla had said to her on their walk. *He's still in love with Río* . . . She wondered if Río knew that the father of her son was still crazy about her after all these years.

'I think it's great that the pair of you get on so well,' she hazarded.

'Well, it would be nightmarish for Finn if we didn't. He's coming back to Lissamore soon, you know.'

'Does that mean he and Izzy have split up?'

'I think they're on a break. In a way I'm glad. She may have been an excellent business studies student, but that idea of turning her daddy's mansion into a scuba-diving outfit would have been bonkers in the CEC.'

'CEC?'

'Current economic climate.'

Fleur allowed her binoculars to abseil down the mountainside. They landed on a woody area near the lake at Coolnamara Castle. 'What about your plans for building on your land by Coral Mansion?'

Coral Mansion was the name Río had come up with for the ostentatious house that had belonged to Adair Bolger, Izzy's father.

'Can't afford to. But it's still a nice feeling to be a landowner. Once this film's over, I'm going to set up a stall selling organic produce.'

'Apples from your orchard?'

'And honey. I've started keeping bees. And I'm going to plant a load of vegetables. I'll be just like W B Yeats on his lake isle. My daddy used to recite "The Lake Isle of Innisfree" when he'd a few jars on him. "Nine bean rows will I have there, a hive for the honey bee." And very likely the only house I'll ever afford to build there will be one just like his – "of clay and wattles made". I wonder would you need to get planning permission for a cabin made from clay and wattles?'

'Probably. I've had planning permission for my extension turned down.'

'Oh – poor Fleur. Will you appeal?'

'I can't be bothered, to tell you the truth. The way things are going, this country will soon be as wound up in red tape as France.' Fleur set the binoculars down and sloshed more wine into her glass. She made a 'yikes' face when she saw how much the level in the bottle had gone down. 'So – tell me, who do you think is having the affair? Apparently the woman involved is married, and from the village.'

'How do you know all this, Fleur?'

'Corban told me.'

'I wouldn't have taken Corban for a gossip.'

'He's not. He's actually helping them out by lending them his apartment to conduct their liaison in.'

'Wow. That's big of him.'

'I told you – he *is* my Mr Big.'

'I'm dying to meet him. Maybe I should introduce myself next time he's on set.'

'Do that. Dervla met him for the first time the other day.

171

I think she was impressed – and you know what an astute judge of character she is.'

'I wonder where that came from. She can hardly have inherited it from our parents.'

Fleur laughed. 'I bet *she'd* be able to work out who's having this dangerous liaison.'

'How? By skulking around the set spying on the extras' body language? What has you so intrigued, Fleur?'

'That's what living in a village does to you. I guess I'm just a small-town gossip at heart.'

'Concealed by an *über* elegant exterior, like one of the Wisteria Lane gals.'

'The Wisteria Lane gals would never be caught dead in wellies.'

'Ah – but they don't live in the wild west of Ireland.'

From the kitchen table beyond the sliding doors, Fleur heard the 'ping!' of an incoming email. 'Ooh – some email's just arrived that I've been expecting. I'd better go check it out.'

'It's probably from Neighbourhood Watch, thanking you for your contribution to security in Lissamore. By the way, if you see a man in a black polo neck climbing over my balcony, please don't phone the guards. I'm expecting the Milk Tray man this evening.'

'Lucky you! Enjoy!'

Fleur put the phone down and went back into the kitchen. When she clicked on her in-box, this is what she found:

Welcome to Second Life, Flirty LittleBoots! Please keep this email in case you need to retrieve your account name later. CLICK HERE TO ACTIVATE YOUR ACCOUNT

She clicked, and there was her avatar, suddenly, a blue-haired little Gamer girl with a funky helmet and combats and hardcore boots, standing in Arrivals, looking for some action. The first thing she had to do, obviously, was ask for help, and the Helper of the Week who approached her was only too happy to oblige. Within the space of an hour, Flirty LittleBoots had been equipped with an inventory of sparkly stilettos, leatherwear, hairstyles and accessories. She'd learned how to teleport, how to gesture, how to have private conversations with other avatars, and how to fly.

By the end of the evening, Fleur was ready to try something else new. She poured herself another glass of Dutch courage, and sent Flirty LittleBoots off on an adventure. She was keen to find out for herself just how far you could push the parameters in the curiously seductive virtual world that was Second Life.

Chapter Twelve

It was another beautiful day in Lissamore. If Dervla could have been arsed to get into the car, she would have driven to the nearest signpost and added a capital B to the place name.

She had been woken in the most delightful way of all, with her husband's hard-on nudging her hip. She'd put Mozart on the CD player after he'd gone off to work, and blasted it through the house as she'd had her shower. She'd juiced carrots and ginger and apples and pineapple, and then she'd ruined the beneficial effects to her health by having a mega hit of caffeine and a bowl of Honey Nut Loops (Christian adored them), while sitting on the front doorstep, admiring her view. From Finnegan's farm a mile away she could hear the crowing of a cockerel, bees were buzzing loudly in the lavender, and a mile high above her, a skylark was singing its heart out.

But bliss could not be prolonged. There was much to be done. Dervla washed up her breakfast things, then crossed the courtyard to Daphne's house and rang the doorbell. Nemia came to the door, wiping her hands on a cloth.

'Oh – it's you!' she said. 'Come in, come in – it's not often we have visitors. Will you have tea or coffee?'

'Tea would be lovely, thanks.'

Dervla followed Nemia into the kitchen. It was pristinely clean and tidy. A stock pot was simmering on the hob, and Ryan Tubridy was on the radio, talking to someone about the ageing demographic. Nemia reached to switch it off.

'Oh – don't let me interrupt your radio,' said Dervla.

'No worries. I'll get it later, on a podcast. It's interesting stuff. Sit down, sit down.'

Dervla took a seat at the kitchen table, while Nemia set about making tea. A half-filled in Sudoku puzzle lay beside a vegetarian cookbook. From the sitting room floated the gently authoritative tones of David Attenborough. 'How's Daphne?' she asked.

'She's in good form today.'

Nemia's voice was lovely, Dervla thought – lilting and slightly accented. She had a fantastic smile, too. It seemed a shame that she was stuck here in a cottage in the middle of the countryside when she should be out being sociable – even finding herself a man, maybe. She was a good-looking girl.

'Are you looking forward to your holiday, Nemia?'

'Yeah, yeah,' said Nemia. 'I am so glad that the weather forecast is for lots of rain here! I would hate to go to Malta and know that back in Ireland it is sunny still.' She reached for the teapot. 'How have you got on with finding a replacement for me?'

Dervla took a deep breath. 'I'm going to do it,' she said.

'You!' Setting down the teapot, Nemia clapped her hands. 'What a fantastic idea! Why didn't we think of it before?'

'It does seem like the obvious solution.'

'But of course it is! Will you move Daphne in with you?'

'No. We don't have a spare bed yet, and she'd find the stairs hard to manage. I'll move in to your room here – that is, if you don't mind?'

176

'Of course not. What about Christian?'

'He'll be away for that fortnight.'

'So you will be here on your own with Daphne?'

'Yes.'

Nemia looked doubtful. 'Are you sure that you will be able to handle it?'

'What do you mean?'

'It can get pretty lonely.'

'Oh.' Dervla felt guilty, suddenly. She really ought to have made more of an effort to befriend Nemia. 'How do you manage?'

Nemia shrugged. 'I keep myself busy. I have my Tai Chi, and I spend a lot of time in the evening online. I have many friends to Skype.'

'Friends in Mauritius?'

'Friends from all over. I have Facebook. I have Twitter.'

Dervla thought about who she might talk to while Christian was away. Río, obviously, and Fleur. But aside from that, there was virtually nobody. In her estate agent days she had had numerous contact details in her organizer, but they were all business contacts. Dervla had been too busy making money to make friends.

'I intend to keep myself busy, too,' she said, with a bravado she did not feel. 'I'll be working on my book.'

'That's a good idea. Hey – this could really work out, couldn't it? Maybe, if I needed more time off, we could take turns? Share the caring?'

'That's exactly what I had in mind.'

'Fine, fine! It is better for Daphne, also, you know, that she is looked after by somebody she knows and likes.'

'Daphne likes me?'

'Sure. She says you have a lovely speaking voice and excellent manners. The way people talk to her is important. Once,

177

in London, I organized a girl to replace me for a week. She was from Texas, and Daphne just hated her. She could not bear to listen to her, and even refused to eat for her.'

'Refused to eat?'

'Yes. You know, like a spoilt child. She can be very childish sometimes. You will find that sometimes you will just have to put your foot down. And of course, bribery helps.'

'How?'

'Well, for instance, if she refuses to go to bed, I tell her that she will not get a story until she is there. Sometimes she wants to stay up until midnight, and that is too late for me. I like to make time to record *Eastenders* and watch it on my own because she cannot bear it. She hates the way they talk, and just sits and shouts at the television.'

A timer buzzed, and Nemia reached for it and turned it off. 'My stock is ready,' she said, taking the pot off the hob. 'I'm making tomato soup. It's Daphne's favourite.'

Dervla felt inadequate. She'd have to make sure the freezer was stocked with ready meals before Nemia headed off on holiday. She'd taught herself to cook since marrying Christian, but her repertoire was limited to one-pot meals and pasta sauces.

'It smells delicious.'

'My grandmother's recipe. I miss her cooking. She made the best *gateaux piments* I ever tasted.'

'*Gateaux piments*?'

'Chilli cakes. A Mauritian speciality.'

'What made your family leave Mauritius?' Dervla asked. 'I holidayed there once, and thought it was heaven on earth.'

Nemia shrugged. 'Economic necessity.'

'I need help here. *I need help*!'

It was Daphne's voice, coming from the sitting room.

'Oopsie. *Coming*!' Nemia swung out through the kitchen door.

'What's the problem, Daphne?' Dervla heard her say.

'*I can't hear it*! I can't hear the television. There's something wrong with it.'

'OK. No worries.' The decibel level of the television rose a notch. 'That better?'

'Yes. Thank you.'

'Oh – you've finished all your apple juice, Daphne. Do you need to spend a penny?'

'Do I? Yes, maybe I do.'

'Let me help you.'

'Oh! Your hands are like stones.'

The voices receded as they trundled along the corridor, and Dervla turned her attention to the cork board on the wall. There was a list of memos and contact numbers, postcards, a flier for fitness classes at the Lissamore community hall. Maybe Dervla should start attending, as Fleur had suggested? She could choose from Tai Chi, Kick-boxing, Irish Dancing, Strength Training, Aerobics and Yoga. But Dervla practised yoga every morning before her run. Maybe she should start up some classes herself, on the property market. But would there be any takers for night classes on home improvement with a view to selling? She suspected that nobody in their right mind who lived in Lissamore would ever dream of moving elsewhere. Since she had moved into the Old Rectory – even though the place was unfurnished – she felt as if she had come home at last.

Beside the flier was pinned a brochure featuring aids for the elderly. It included such devices as safety frames, 'donut' ring cushions, alerting devices, long-reach toenail cutters, lotion applicators and Bottom Buddies. Bottom Buddies? Oh, OK. Let's not go there, thought Dervla, pinning the brochure back onto the cork board as Nemia came back into the kitchen.

She was wearing a broad smile. 'Well! Daphne actually remembered to say thank you! She forgets, sometimes, to mind her manners.'

'I've noticed.'

'The worst thing is when she whistles for you, like a dog.'

'No! She doesn't, does she?'

'Sure. But you can't let it upset you. I just say, "Look, Daphne – I am not a dog, OK?"'

Dervla had to admire the girl's laid-back attitude. Her sanguinity verged on the saintlike. She watched as Nemia strained her vegetable stock through a colander, then added a little ground pepper. Stock from scratch! The only 'home-made-style' soup that Dervla had ever prepared had been the kind you got in the fresh soup section of the chiller cabinet in Tesco.

'So, how does your routine go?' she asked.

'Let's see. In the morning, I bring her breakfast in bed. Crunchy Nut Cornflakes, with a little banana chopped up, or strawberries. Tea and toast, buttered already and with marmalade. That gives me time to do my Tai Chi, and have a shower. Then I get her up and wash her—'

'You wash her?'

'Of course. But sometimes she tells me no wash, and I leave her alone because I do not want an argument. Arguments are a waste of energy. It's OK to leave her for one day with no wash, but no more, because then she will start to smell.' She tasted her stock, and made an appreciative face. 'Mmm. It's good.'

'Oh, God. How do you manage it?'

'Manage what?'

'The washing.'

180

'I put her standing by the basin in the bathroom because that way she has something to hold on to. I do her face with a flannel, and use a sponge for under her arms and between her legs. Front bottom first, then back. And sometimes I give her a toothbrush and ask her to do her teeth. She hates to clean her teeth, so any time I see her dentures lying around, I grab them and give them a scrub.'

Dervla sucked in her breath. 'What about dressing her?' she asked.

'There's no need to bother fussing around with buttons and zips – except if she is going out. She finds dressing too exhausting.' The strained vegetables went into the compost bucket, the colander into the dishwasher. Nemia helped herself to a Sabatier from the block, and started chopping onions. 'Most days I just put on a clean nightdress, and a gilet or a long cardigan. She prefers the cardigan to a dressing gown. She says it is more elegant.'

Dervla remembered the nappies she'd seen on the day Daphne had arrived, and gave an internal shudder. 'Has she had any – um – accidents recently?'

'No. She is good. But sometimes early in the morning she gets out of bed and does poo poo before I am awake, and I cannot wipe her.'

'You *wipe* her?'

'Sometimes. She cannot do it herself, see? I use baby wipes, and there are disposable gloves on the shelf above the loo.'

Dervla just stopped herself from saying *Gross!* 'How often do you change her bed linen?' she asked instead.

'If things go good, once a week. But you check every day to see if they need changing. I have a complete fresh set ready to go in a plastic bag in the airing cupboard, in case of accidents. And there are pants with pads in the top drawer of her chest of drawers, in case of emergency. In case a urinary tract infection kicks in.'

'Does she wear them at night?'

Nemia laughed – a warm gurgle of a laugh. 'I have tried, but she just yells and throws them at me. She's not used to wearing panties in bed.'

'She *throws* them at you?'

'Sure, sure. She has a temper! Sometimes she uses bad language. She say things like "Fuck off you fucking bitch – who do you think you are, ordering me about?" But I just say: "Don't talk to me like that, Daphne. I'm just trying to take care of you. Don't you know how lucky you are to have a family who care so much about you that they make sure you are comfortable in your own home with someone to wash you and cook for you?"' Another laugh. 'And then she says, "I'm perfectly capable of looking after myself, thank you. And I'll have you know I'm an excellent cook."' Nemia mimicked Daphne very well, but in an affectionate way.

'So . . . she's abusive?'

'Sure. Sometimes she can be violent. If she does not get her own way, she pulls my hair, and pinches me. She grabs my arm if I'm on the phone, in how do you say? – a Chinese burn, yes? – and takes the phone from me. She gets jealous, you see, that I am talking to someone else and not giving all my attention to her. She throws water at me when I try and get her in the bath—'

'How often do you bathe her?'

'Once a week, on the electric chair.'

'The electric chair?' There was a joke to be found here somewhere, but Dervla didn't bother to go looking for it.

'You know – the chair in her bath that raises her and lowers her electronically. I call it her throne.'

Dervla pictured a naked Daphne sitting on her bath chair

– a parody of Aphrodite rising from the waves – and felt a surge of something between laughter and revulsion. Nemia seemed utterly impervious to the fact that this was – from Dervla's point of view – the job description from hell. But it was too late now to back out. She'd promised Christian she'd do this thing, and she would damned well do it to the best of her ability. Besides, they had no choice.

'You look nervous, Dervla,' remarked Nemia. 'There's no need to be nervous. You'll do fine. You can handle her, no problem.'

Dervla managed a nod. 'Where did you train, Nemia?'

'Train?'

'To be a carer?'

'I have no training. Just experience. I helped my mother care for my grandmother in Mauritius, before we moved to London. I joined an agency there, but then decided to go freelance. The agency was taking too much money. I worked for an old man who used to expose himself to me—'

'No, Nemia! Are you serious?'

'Oh, yes. You learn to live with it. You know? The behaviour of demented people ceases to be shocking after a while. They can't help it. But sometimes I think that the Japanese had the right idea. They used to take their old people to the mountains in winter, and leave them to die there, from exposure. They were talking about it on the radio earlier, on the Ryan Tubridy show.'

Oh! Dervla found this shocking, coming from the mouth of a woman whom she'd just compared to a saint.

'But isn't that a form of euthanasia?'

'I guess so.' The smell of cooking onions intensified. 'But it was an established tradition in Japan – and in many other countries, before political correctness became commonplace. Old people didn't want to be a burden to their young any

183

more than the young wanted to see the elders they loved and respected become ruins of themselves. It makes sense to me. I'd hate to see my mother infirm and incontinent, and she would hate it even more. She's always been a strong, independent woman.'

Dervla remembered the story Corban had told in the pub the other day, about his mother filling her house with flowers and knocking back a glass of Bordeaux along with the pills that would kill her. Not a bad way to go, all things considered. She'd seen a fly-on-the-wall documentary recently about state health care and the elderly. It had shocked her to the core – but after what Christian had told her about the homes he'd visited, private health care didn't seem to be very much better. Nemia had been right when she'd said earlier that Daphne was lucky to have a family who looked after her.

'Go on,' she said, 'telling me about your routine.'

'Well, after she is washed and dressed, I bring her out to the patio if it is fine, where she can sit on her swing seat and listen to the radio, or into the sitting room, where she can have the television. Any time you find a programme about gardening, record it. She adores gardening programmes. She says she always wanted to be a gardener, not a stupid model.'

'She did?' Dervla was reminded of Fleur's niece Daisy, who had chucked in modelling and gone off to work on the land in Africa.

'Yes. But her husband didn't approve. She talks to him sometimes, you know.'

'Sorry? Who does she talk to?'

'Her dead . . . husband.'

The slight pause made Dervla wonder if Nemia knew about Daphne's true love who had died so tragically.

'Oh, Christ. Isn't that really spooky?'

'It's like everything. You get used to it.' Multi-tasker Nemia stirred the onions in the pan with one hand, poured boiling water into the teapot with the other. 'Around half-past one, I serve lunch. And then I am free again until four o'clock, when she has tea and a biscuit. I usually try and have dinner on the table at seven.'

'It all sounds pretty regimented.'

'It's better that way. Establish a routine and stick to it. It will make life easier for both of you.'

'Do you enjoy your work, Nemia?'

Nemia looked thoughtful. 'Do I enjoy my work? I think I am lucky to have a job that is so well paid. In Mauritius, they might think I am a millionairess! And I am lucky too that I get on well with Daphne. To be honest with you, I am a man's woman, and Daphne likes me for that. I get the feeling that she doesn't much care for women, you know? Does that make sense?'

'I'm not sure.'

'Daphne was a very beautiful woman once. A sexy lady. She preferred always the company of men to that of women. I can understand that. I adore men.'

'That must make it difficult for you, living in the back of beyond.'

'Ah – but I will make up for it on holiday!' Nemia's phone went, and she checked out the display. 'Excuse me, Dervla. I need to take this – it's the travel agent.'

'No worries. I'll go and talk to Daphne.'

Dervla got up and went into the sitting room. Daphne was wearing a fleecy gilet over her nightgown, and a pair of velvet slippers. There was a Beanie Baby polar bear on her lap. She turned stony eyes upon Dervla as she came through the door.

'Hello, Daphne,' said Dervla.

'Who is it?'

'It's Dervla, your daughter-in-law.'

'Are you my daughter?'

'No. I'm your daughter-in-*law*. What's David Attenborough talking about today?'

'Yes. It's very interesting. But I've had enough of him now.'

'OK. I'll turn him off. Shall we do the crossword?'

'Yes. I'd like that.'

Dervla reached for the crossword book on the coffee table and a Biro, then sat down in the armchair across from Daphne. Clearing her throat she said – very loud and clear – 'One across. "Old-fashioned rural roof covering." Six letters.'

Daphne thought for a minute, then: 'Thatch,' she said.

'Yes. It must be thatch.' Dervla moved on to two down. '"Suspend canine with shamefaced look."'

'Suspend what?'

'"Suspend *canine* with shamefaced look."'

'With what look?'

'Shamefaced. Seven letters. The first letter's H.'

'What does that mean?'

Dervla wrote HANGDOG along two down. 'I don't know,' she said. 'It's a tough one, isn't it? Let's go on to the next one.'

She ran her Biro along the clues, trying to find an easier one, then skipped to thirteen across. '"Old Nick. Satan."'

'Old who?'

'"Old Nick", or "Satan". Five letters.'

Daphne thought again.

'It might start with a D,' prompted Dervla.

'Devil!' pronounced Daphne triumphantly.

Dervla wrote DEVIL, then moved on to another clue. '"Sign of the fishes. Six letters."'

'What do they *mean* by "sign of the fishes"?'

'I think it might be a Zodiac sign, Daphne.'

'Oh. I had a car once called a Zodiac,' said Daphne, proudly.

'What a lovely name for a car. "Lie back and relax",' continued Dervla.

'What? I'm perfectly relaxed, thank you very much.'

'No – it's a crossword clue. "Lie back and relax." Seven letters.' Dervla wrote RECLINE, and waited.

'I don't know what that is. Go on to the next one.'

'"Sound of a horse." Five letters.'

'Gallops.'

'Yes. It must be gallops,' said Dervla, writing NEIGH along twenty across. '"A wheeled vehicle." Three letters.'

'Pram.'

'Pram. Hmm. That's a good guess, but it's one letter too many. How about this? "A child's dog." Six letters.'

'Bow-wow,' came the immediate response. 'I think I'll buy a dog. I used to have a dog. It was a Lakeland terrier. They're known as toy dogs, you know.'

'How now, Daphne!' Nemia said brightly as she came into the room. 'Doing the crossword, are we?'

'Yes. Who is it?'

'It's Nemia, Daphne.'

'Oh, Nemia! I love Nemia.' Daphne's stony eyes softened. 'Did I tell you about my giraffes?'

'Giraffes?' Nemia and Dervla exchanged glances.

'I looked out of the window the other day, and there were two giraffes in the garden. The people in the house down the road own them, you know, and they came to visit me.'

'Oh, Daphne!' Nemia reached for the remote, and aimed it at the television. 'It's time for *Murder She Wrote*. You mustn't miss it. Would you like some tea?'

'Yes.'

'OK. I'll bring you a cup.'

Nemia left the room, and Dervla followed her back into the kitchen.

'What did she mean by giraffes? Has she been hallucinating, do you think?'

'No. I think she must mean the peacocks. There are white peacocks living in the garden of the house down the road, and they fly onto the patio sometimes. I got quite a fright when I first saw them. They have a really spooky call. Haven't you seen them?'

'No. They haven't been around to our side of the house. How weird that she would get giraffes mixed up with peacocks.'

Nemia poured tea into two mugs, and reached for a cup and saucer. 'She likes her tea in this porcelain cup,' she told Dervla. 'And she prefers Hermesetas to sugar.'

Dervla watched Nemia stir Daphne's tea with a silver spoon.

'She's a very lucky lady,' she said, 'to have someone like you looking after her.'

'Yes,' said Nemia, as she headed for the kitchen door. 'She's a very lucky lady indeed.'

Chapter Thirteen

The Second Life adventure that Fleur had planned for Flirty LittleBoots hadn't happened. She'd fallen into the virtual sea around Welcome Island and hadn't been able to get out, so in the end she'd logged off and called it a day. But this evening –her second on Second Life – things were looking up. She'd worked out how to emerge from the sea and had been flying around, searching randomly for a likely location, before finding herself outside a lap-dancing club. Walking through the door, Flirty took a look around. Inside, all was shiny chrome and glass, but the place was empty. There were, however, two people above on the mezzanine level. She could read their conversation as it appeared on her screen, but she could not see them.

I'm not sure I can do this, someone called Ariella was saying.

Come on, baby, her partner replied. **It's cool. I'll help you**.

I don't think I want to, Dave.

Is it your first time?

Yes.

It's easy, Dave reassured Ariella. **The camera is at the very top of your screen. Just activate—**

I can't. I'm sorry.

And suddenly Ariella was gone.

Aha! thought Fleur. It looks as though I may have a candidate in Dave. If he's been sweet-talking his ladyfriend, he may be in the mood for some action.

Making her way over to the staircase that accessed the mezzanine, Flirty sashayed up the steps. At the top stood a hunk of beefcake, wearing tight jeans and a tighter T-shirt that displayed musculature and tattoos to effect.

Hello, Dave, said Flirty.

Hi.

Not a great buzz in here tonight.

Well ma'am, that might be because it's only 7 p.m. in Austin, Texas, and most folk are eating.

Texas! That's where you're from?

Yep.

Fleur settled back and flexed her fingers.

Do you own this place? she asked.

No. I'm the manager.

Hmm. Fleur decided that the manager of a virtual nightclub that featured pole dancers would know his stuff. Casting aside any reservations as to whether or not she was doing the right thing, she opted for the upfront approach.

Do you mind if I ask you some questions, Dave?

Shoot, came the laconic response.

In Second Life, avatars can touch, kiss, make out, yes?

Sure, Dave told her.

Can you help me?

You want to make out?

Yes. I'm a journalist, and I'm doing a little research.

LOL. I'd be glad to help.

Thank you, said Flirty. **That's very kind of you.**

My pleasure, ma'am.

Um. So how do we get started?

It's easy. See those two coloured balls to your right?

Flirty turned. To her right was a dodgy-looking contraption resembling a dentist's chair, but with stirrups and restraints. She hoped that this would not come into play in her little experiment. Next to the chair were suspended two spheres, one of which bore the legend 'Missionary M', the other 'Missionary F'. Missionary, she was sure she could manage.

I see them.

They're pose balls. Touch the one marked Missionary F.

Fleur clicked and touched. Nothing happened. She turned back to Dave and shrugged.

LOL. Try again, he said.

She repeated the action. This time, something definitely did happen. Flirty suddenly appeared to have tumbled backwards onto the floor. Dave, from her POV, was standing above her.

Oh! she exclaimed. **That worked. Um. Now what?**

Hang on. Another kind of tumbling moment occurred. **There. How's that?** Dave asked.

You're on top of me?

Yes. What can you see?

Um. I can see your arm . . . Or is that mine?

LOL. Try moving your mouse.

It doesn't seem to be working. Everything's blurry . . . although it looks like you're moving to and fro. Are you *sans culottes*?

Culottes?

Pants.

LOL. No. I still have them on.

Pah! said Flirty. **This is useless.**

You must be in mouse-look mode. Go to esc.
Esc?
The key at the left-hand top of your computer.
That doesn't seem to be working either.
Hmm. Let's see if there's anything I can do at my end, while I pump away. Where are you from, Flirty?
Ireland.
And you're a writer?
Journalist.
Cool. What's the research for?
A magazine feature on Second Life. *Merde!* This feels ridiculous. To judge by the image on her screen, Flirty was still lying in 'Missionary F' with Dave working away in 'Missionary M' on top of her. What do you do? she asked, conversationally, keen that no embarrassing silences should descend upon her time in the sun with Dave. It reminded Fleur of the last time she'd been spread-eagled in her gynae-cologist's chair, talking about the weather and Barack Obama.

I'm with Brinks Mat, Dave told her.
So you have a secure job. Ha ha.
Yeah. I'm very lucky. Times are hard everywhere these days.

Another conversational gambit was clearly called for. Do you come here often? Flirty asked.
I have to put in a few hours a week cos I'm manager here.
Do you enjoy SL?
Passes the time, Flirty. Hmm. Not sure I can do anything about this.

But if I can't move my cursor, does that mean that my avatar is going to end up here humping for all eternity? Fleur twiddled her mouse. Hey – I've got a great view of the ceiling now.

LOL. Try pressing esc again. Keep your finger down hard on it this time.

OK.

She aimed a forefinger at the key marked Esc, and pressed long and hard.

Suddenly she was on her feet again. She and Dave were erect at last, standing proudly face to face, no longer stuck in supine 'Missionary F' and 'Missionary M' on the shiny floor of the mezzanine.

Yay – it worked! typed Fleur, before clicking on 'Laugh'. Then she clicked again and again.

Phew! Dave followed suit, and suddenly there they were laughing like virtual drains in a virtual nightclub in a virtual world, and in real life, Fleur was laughing too.

When they'd finished laughing, Fleur resumed her businesslike demeanour.

Well, that was very useful, Dave, she said. **Thank you for your time.**

You're welcome, ma'am. Glad to have been of service. I hope you got the info you needed?

Enough to know that I never want to do something as deadly dull as *that* again, Fleur wanted to say – but didn't. She was clued-in enough about heterosexual men to know that any disparagement cast upon their masculinity – even their virtual masculinity – was a kick to the *cojones*, and Dave had done her a real favour. She did, however, draw the line at telling him the earth had moved for her.

I got the info, she told him. **Thanks. You're a gent.**

My pleasure, ma'am.

All of a sudden Dave's avatar went skittering like a gibbon to the other side of the mezzanine. Flirty turned to see a girl climbing the stairs. It was Ariella. She was Barbie, resplendent in hot pink hotpants, belly top, body-piercing and glittering heels, and she had a determined look about her.

Hello, Dave, she said, marching towards him.

Hi, Ariella. If it were possible for an avatar to look sheepish, Dave was that avatar.

Ariella turned and glared at Flirty.

Hi, Ariella, Flirty said.

Ariella responded by putting her hands on her hips.

Oops, thought Fleur, hoping that she hadn't been responsible for the end of a beautiful virtual romance. She'd leave them to it.

Looks like I may be *de trop* here, she said. ***Au revoir*, Dave. Thanks again for your help.**

Good luck with your article.

And as Fleur moved her cursor to cut the connection, in her headphones she heard burly Dave chuckle.

So, she thought, leaning back in her chair, it really was possible to have sex in Second Life. Clicking on her Google toolbar, she typed in 'Sex in Second Life'. There were 25,300,000 results. Doh – hello, Fleur? Why didn't you do that earlier instead of going to the trouble of having virtual sex with Dave?

But at least Dave had made her laugh. There wasn't anything very funny about the some of the sites she clicked on now. Second Life was awash with sex, from regular liaisons to orgies, from lovemaking in the clouds to bestiality. Fleur had simply been tiptoeing on top of the iceberg.

She went to Bethany's Facebook page. There was a picture there, of her avatar. Poppet looked a little like the real-life Bethany – shy-eyed, ingenuous, unsophisticated, and very beautiful. She wondered if Poppet were active now, in Second Life. It could be easy to find out. Bethany had told her that she and Hero met up at the Globe Theatre. Fleur searched, clicked, and teleported.

She was there – sitting on a cushion facing the stage! And so was he. He turned to her as she landed and rezzed in ungainly fashion, and then said **Hello, Flirty. Welcome.**

Thank you, said Flirty.

Poppet said nothing. She was clearly miffed that someone had come barging in on her tryst. And, actually, she was right to be miffed, because that's exactly what Fleur had done. *Merde!* She was behaving like a nosy neighbour in Second Life, as well as in real life. Who did she think she was, busybodying around like this? Was she going through some midlife crisis, obsessed as she seemed to be with Bethany and her virtual amour? Was she missing Daisy so badly that she needed a surrogate? Really, what Bethany got up to was none of her affair. If the girl did have virtual sex with this Hero, what business was it of Fleur's? It wasn't as if Bethany was going to contract an STD or lose her real-life virginity or get pregnant. She should leave them to it.

Why don't you join us? asked Hero. **We were talking about films. Poppet's an actress in Real Life.**

I'm only an extra, protested Poppet.

Oh? What are you working on? Flirty asked.

A film called *The O'Hara Affair*. It's being shot in Coolnamara on the west coast of Ireland.

Silly girl, thought Fleur. That's a bit location specific.

What's it about? said Flirty, feeling a tad duplicitous. She knew damned well what the film was about, because she'd read the script.

It's about Scarlett O'Hara's Irish family.

Come and sit down, invited Hero.

Fleur could hardly say, **No**, and leave. She'd learned enough about Second Life to know that good manners here were as important as they were in real life. She pressed the key to activate her avatar, and moved over to where Poppet and

Hero were sitting, feeling self-conscious. For some reason the leather skirt in her inventory of outfits had attached itself to her, and she didn't know how to take it off. The combination of leather skirt over combat trousers and hardcore boots was bizarre, to say the least. No one would ever dream that in real life, Flirty LittleBoots was the owner of an exclusive boutique.

That's an interesting combo you're wearing – LOL, remarked Hero.

LOL, echoed Poppet.

I know, said Flirty. **I don't know how to get rid of it.**

Sorry for laughing, said Poppet, **but it really does mark you out as a newbie. You should teleport to a store and find some free stuff**.

I already have free stuff in my inventory. Sparkly shoes and leather gear.

Dodgy, said Hero.

There's a great store called aDiva Couture, Poppet told her. **It does beautiful designer gowns. I can't afford them – that's why I'm in a generic girl-next-door outfit.**

I think you look adorable just as you are, Hero told her, and Poppet gave him a coy look.

What brings you here, to the Globe, Flirty? Hero asked.

I'm passionate about theatre, lied Flirty.

Not many people come here, when there isn't a show on, said Poppet.

They do shows?

Yes. I could have auditioned for a part in *Twelfth Night* last week.

Maybe you should try out, Flirty, suggested Hero.

I'm not an actress.

I have a friend called Flirty in Real Life, said Poppet.

Yikes! **You do?**

Well, on Facebook.

Oh, God. Fleur was out of her depth here. There were too many strands to this virtual imbroglio, too much potential for things to spiral out of control.

Where are you from in RL? asked Hero.

Sydney, Australia.

What time is it there?

Fleur hadn't a clue. **Dunno,** she typed.

All you need to do is check on your screen, he pointed out.

Yikes, again. What time *was* it in Sydney, Australia? Were they twelve hours behind, or twelve hours ahead? There was nothing else for it. Fleur clicked on Teleport.

Well, she'd made a right mess of that! She'd blown her cover spectacularly. If she were to be even remotely plausible on Second Life, she'd have to be a little savvier. Maybe she should get rid of her generic clothing, for a start. She'd pay a visit to aDiva Couture, and have a look around.

aDiva Couture was a vast parquet-floored showroom displaying representations of elegant models posing in evening wear. Fleur was spoilt for choice. She could dress as a slave girl in a harem, or as a disco diva, or as a forties femme fatale. She could be pretty in pink or slinky in a LBD. In the end, she chose a gown modelled by a Victoria Beckham lookalike that cost her six hundred Linden dollars, cheap at the real-life price of around three US dollars. It was not unlike the one worn by Scarlett O'Hara in *Gone with the Wind*, the one she wore when Rhett carried her upstairs to bed and ravished her.

Fleur felt more comfortable in her virtual skin, now that she was dressed in something stylish. Maybe she should

197

register under a new name, too, and modify her appearance – get rid of the blue hair. Flirty LittleBoots had made such an ass of herself that she could do with a complete makeover. She could call herself Scarlett Something-or-other, adopt a more sophisticated persona.

She went shopping in a virtual plaza. In Platinum World, she helped herself to a golden glow and Rita Hayworth hair. In Flirts' Nails (*Sassy, Sexy and Sensual*) she got herself a manicure. In French Elegance she bought a pair of Louboutin lookalikes and some glittering emerald jewellery. Leaning back, she scrutinized herself. She looked sensational; she was good to go. Glad to have re-established her sartorial nous, Fleur logged off as Flirty LittleBoots and reinvented herself as ScarlettO'Hara Sahara. If Bethany were in danger of being seduced by some manipulative predator, her virtual agony aunt would be there in Second Life to help her.

Chapter Fourteen

Corban was back from London. He had a present for Fleur, he told her on the phone from Dublin, but he wouldn't be able to see her next weekend. He'd try to fly down for the weekend after next.

'But your car's here!' she protested. 'How are you going to manage without it?'

'I have a runabout Lexus convertible in town.'

Doh. Of course he had. 'Maybe I should get the train up there?' she suggested.

'I'm going to be too busy, sweetheart.'

Fleur made a moue. Two weekends in a row! The movie would be wrapping next month, too, which meant that Corban would have fewer reasons to come to Lissamore. But she wasn't about to start putting pressure on him.

'Remember I was hoping to have a guided tour around the movie set before it wraps,' she said.

'I'll get one of the ADs on your case.'

'And it's all right for Dervla to come too?'

'Sure. So, what have you been up to while I've been away, sweetheart?'

Fleur wasn't sure she wanted to tell him. She'd read an article about how some people considered Second Life to be a Land of Losers, while others thought it had the potential to change the world. And then she recalled Corban's penchant for role-playing. He might find the idea of Second Life quite a turn-on. It would mean that – once they worked out how to do it – they'd be able to have virtual sex any time he was away globetrotting. Better than phone sex.

'I've become a member of Second Life,' she told him.

'Shit. Hang on a sec, Fleur. My BlackBerry needs me. I'll call you back.'

'OK.'

While she waited for Corban to call back, Fleur reached for her binoculars – or rather, Dervla's binoculars. There was little Bethany, walking along the street in a cotton frock, looking absurdly like her SL avatar. She was lost in thought, dreaming perhaps of her virtual companion. What weird parallel worlds they inhabited! If Fleur had managed to activate more than one avatar, how many other people might have done the same? She guessed there could be places on Second Life crowded with avatars, all of whom were aspects of just one individual. You could be a queen in your own court, a sultan in your own harem, the ringmaster of your own circus.

The phone rang.

'Sorry about that,' said Corban. 'What were we talking about?'

'I was telling you about Second Life.'

'What's that?'

Fleur explained.

'So it's kind of virtual role-play?'

'Yes. You can even make out on there, Monsieur O'Hara.'

'I trust you've refrained, Madame O'Farrell?'

'Of course I have,' she lied, remembering her clumsy rumpy-pumpy with Dave in the lap-dancing club.

'Good. I don't want to be upstaged by a virtual – what did you call them again?'

'Avatars.'

'What have you called yourself?'

Fleur was just about to say Scarlett O'Hara, when she felt a rush of mortification. If she told Corban that she was using his surname on Second Life, might he interpret it as some kind of coded invitation to become man and wife in Real Life? She decided to call herself by her old name instead.

'My virtual name,' she said, 'is Flirty LittleBoots.'

There was silence on the other end of the line.

'Corban? Are you still there?'

'Yes.'

'What's wrong?'

'Don't you think that Flirty LittleBoots is a rather provocative handle, Fleur? You could attract a lot of unwanted interest.'

'Oh, Corban – don't worry! Half the avatars on Second Life are called things way more provocative than that. And you should see what some of them go around dolled up in.'

'Hmm. Maybe I *should* take a look. How complicated is it to register?'

'It's surprisingly simple.'

'And would I be able to locate this Flirty LittleBoots and befriend her?'

'I guess so. I'm just a newbie still – I'm not quite sure how things work.'

'So what kind of a get-up does Flirty LittleBoots wear? A French maid's outfit?' There was a smile in his voice. 'You know I've always wanted to see you in one of those.'

'I could get one. They've all kinds of outfits for sale. Unfortunately, right now Flirty's made a big sartorial gaffe. She's somewhere out there in the ether sporting a leather skirt over combat trousers.'

Corban laughed. 'Most un-you.'

She wondered whether she should tell him that she'd met Bethany in a virtual world, and then decided against it. There was only so much explaining a gal could do, and since Corban could hardly handle his own Facebook, he certainly wouldn't be able to get his head around SL. Picking up the binoculars again she watched Bethany come out of Ryan's corner shop with an ice cream.

'I've become such a nosy neighbour since I acquired Dervla's binoculars,' she said.

'You have binoculars?'

'Yes. Well they're Dervla's. I'll get them back to her next time we meet up.'

'When you go on your visit to the set.'

'Yes.'

'In that case, I'll organize that excursion asap.'

'There's no hurry, lover. I rather enjoy spying on people.'

'Who are you looking at now?'

'That little Bethany. The one you found work for on the film.'

'Oh? What's she doing?'

'She's sitting on the sea wall, licking an ice cream and swinging her legs. I wish she'd find herself a boyfriend.'

'What makes you think she wants a boyfriend?'

'She told me that time when I dressed up as Madame Tiresia for the fortune-telling gig. I'm so glad you were able to get her that job, Corban. She's a very lonely girl. She's living all on her own in that holiday cottage down in Díseart.'

'How do you know?'

How did she know? She was hardly going to confess to Corban that she'd been having IM conversations with a new Facebook friend who was young enough to be her daughter.

'Río told me,' she said.

Another lie! She'd been telling Corban rather a lot of lies recently. She'd better cut herself some slack, or the mendacious web she'd woven could become too intricate to maintain.

No more lies, Fleur, she told herself sternly. And no more spying on the village, either.

She was just about to set the binoculars down on the table when Bethany turned and looked directly at her. *Merde!* Fleur dropped the binocs as if they were hot stones. How uncool to be caught out spying! In the past, women had been put in ducking stools for being nosy parkers and village gossips. She'd better watch her step, or people might start crossing the road when they saw her coming.

'Río, the set-dresser? Another friend of yours I've yet to meet.'

'She's coming for dinner this evening, with Shane.'

'Shane Byrne?'

'Yes. They used to be an item, way back. They have a grown-up son together.'

'Oh, yes. I remember he mentioned a son, that time we had lunch together. He's a scuba-diving instructor, yeah?'

'Yeah. And now I think of it, perfect boyfriend material for little Bethany.'

'Don't you think you should leave this Bethany to her own devices, Fleur? You've already done her a big favour by getting her a job.'

'But she and Finn would be perfect together . . .'

'You've forgotten something, I think.'

'Oh?'

'That little matter of location, location, location. Bethany lives in Dublin.'

'*Merde!* You're right, of course.' Something struck Fleur as being a bit odd, here. 'How did you know?'

'That Bethany lives in Dublin? I saw the form she filled in for the casting director. She gave both her addresses, and you've just mentioned that the house in Díseart was a holiday home.'

'What sort of info do extras have to fill in on those forms?'

'Contact details, appearance, availability. That kind of

thing. They always lie about their riding ability, apparently – to go by the claims on the forms, all extras are excellent horsemen and women.'

'I remember in the old days, Shane used to lie about that, too.'

'Well, he can certainly ride now. He's a natural in the saddle.'

Over on the sea wall, Bethany had swivelled around, and was talking to someone. It was Río.

'There's Río now.' Fleur glanced at her watch. 'Heavens – is that the time? I'd better set the table.'

'What are you cooking?'

'Bouillabaisse, from my own fish stock.'

'I'm jealous.'

'I'll do one for you when you're next down. Weekend after next, yes?'

'Hopefully. Unless something crops up in the meantime.'

'*Au revoir*, then, *chéri*.'

'*Au revoir*, Fleur.'

Fleur put the phone down and went into the kitchen. It would be like old times, having Fleur and Shane to dinner. Except in those old times they hadn't eaten off Bridgewater plates or drunk from John Rocha crystal. In the days when Fleur and Río and Shane had lived in a squat in Galway city they'd often been too poor to afford to buy food. How things had changed! Now Shane was a Hollywood hotshot, Río a woman of some substance, and Fleur a fully-fledged fashionista.

She was uncorking wine when the door bell rang. 'Come up, darling Río,' she said into the entry phone, pressing the button that would release the lock.

'How did you know it was me?' said Río, as she came up the stairs. 'I could have been an axe-murderer. Shane always pretends to be a murderer when he calls.'

'I saw you on the street just now, talking to that little Bethany girl.'

'Oh, yeah? She's a sweetie-pie. She's an extra on the movie.'

'I know. I got her the gig.'

'How?'

As Fleur led Río into the kitchen, she told her about the ruse she'd devised to secure a job for Bethany.

'What a kind thing to do,' remarked Río.

'I like to spread a little happiness. And I warmed to her. She's an unusual kid.'

Río sniffed the air. 'Hey! Fantastic smell.'

'It's bouillabaisse.'

'It'll be nice to get some real food for a change.'

'Aren't the caterers any good?'

Río shrugged. 'To call them nondescript would be paying them a compliment.'

'Go on out to the deck,' Fleur said, 'and I'll bring you a glass of wine.'

The Burgundy in the fridge had been a present from Christian, to say thank you for help in choosing lingerie for Dervla. He certainly knew his wine. She'd have to invite him to dinner next time Corban was in town: being a wine buff himself, they'd have a lot in common. And then she remembered Dervla's bizarre remark about pink *prosecco*. What on earth had made Dervla think that Corban would ever present her with a bottle of pink *prosecco*?!

She poured two glasses and took them out onto the deck, where Río was sitting with her bare feet up on the railing, looking like a 1940s land girl in dungarees, with a scarf tied around her head.

'*Santé*!' said Fleur, handing her a glass.

'*Sláinte*!'

'Here's to the safe return of Finn. When's he due?'

'Tomorrow. I don't imagine he'll stay long, though. His wanderlust's bound to get the better of him. He's really just checking in to say hello to his ma and pa because it's not often he gets to see me and Shane in the same place.'

'How do you feel about him and Izzy taking a break?'

Río shrugged. 'Izzy never really warmed to me for some reason. I think she saw me as a rival for her daddy's affections. She's a real daddy's girl – she's gone off to work for him in Dubai.'

'Have you heard from Adair?'

'We stay in touch via Facebook. He's doing all right out there.'

'Any regrets about not going out to join him?'

Río gave Fleur an incredulous look. 'Hel*lo*, Fleur? Can you *picture* me in Dubai? My heart belongs here in Lissamore. I'll never leave. I want to be buried in my orchard. That's where Finn was conceived, you know.'

'I can't say I've ever been that into alfresco sex.'

'I'd be into any kind of sex, these days,' said Río ruefully. 'Lucky you, to have a lover.'

'Whom I rarely get to see. That's the one disadvantage of going out with a Mr Big – everybody wants a piece of him. We're going to be visiting the location some time this week, by the way. Me and your sister.'

'What for?'

'Curiosity. I've never been on a movie set before.'

'If you're lucky you'll get a chance to laugh at Shane's acting.'

Fleur gave her a reproving look. 'You give him such a hard time, Río.'

'I'm allowed. He fathered my child and then fucked off to LA.'

'He did ask you to go with him.'

'Sure Fleur, *acushla*, I'd be as out of my depth in LA as I would in Dubai.'

'There he is now.'

'Who?'

'Shane. Coming out of O'Toole's.'

As Río swung her feet off the railing and stood up to get a better look, Fleur clocked her expression. Uh-oh, she thought. Río Kinsella was still plainly smitten with Shane Byrne, even after all these years. She remembered how the pair had larked together, back in the Galway squat days, when Río had been pregnant with Finn and before Shane had 'fucked off' to LA, how the sound of laughter from their bedroom would echo around the cavernous old building they shared with artists and musicians and actors and film makers. They'd all been so carefree then.

The phone rang.

'Hello?' said Fleur, picking up.

'Hello,' came the response. 'Am I speaking to Fleur O'Farrell?'

'You are.'

'Hi, Fleur. My name's Jake Malone. I'm an AD on *The O'Hara Affair*, and I was asked to phone and arrange a time that would suit you to visit the set.'

'Oh! That was quick. Thank you, but I'll need to check with my friend, to see when she's available.'

'No problem. Save my number to your phone and call me when you've decided.'

'Will do. Sorry – did you say your name was Jack or Jake?'

'Jake. We've met, actually. I bought a pair of earrings in your shop the other day.'

'Oh, yes. I remember you. I hope your mother liked them.' Fleur recalled the youth's wicked eyes, the way his hair flopped over his forehead, the interested look he'd given her. She wondered if he was the AD Corban had told her about – the one who was having the affair with a married woman from the village. 'Will you be available, Jake, to show us around?' she asked.

'I'll make it my business to be available, ma'am.'

'Thank you. I'll look forward to it.'

'My pleasure.'

Fleur set the phone down with a minxy smile. What an accomplished flirt the boy was, and how good it felt to flirt back! She'd have to check out his profile on Daisy's Facebook.

Her doorbell rang again. 'Are you the murderer?' Fleur said into the entry phone.

'Yes,' came the reply.

'Come on up.'

Fleur opened the door to her duplex, and watched Shane lope up the stairs. He was, if anything, better looking than when she'd first met him, twenty odd years ago – more rugged, a little rougher around the edges, but fit, still.

'Come on in, Monsieur Byrne.'

'Thanks, darlin'.' Shane stooped to kiss her on the cheek, before handing her a bottle in a brown paper bag. 'I hope I'm not late. I stopped off to get wine in O'Toole's and my arm was twisted into staying for a pint.'

'Let me pour you a glass. Río's out on the deck.'

'I saw her from the road. She looked like the figurehead on the prow of a ship.'

'I'm not sure she'd thank you for the comparison. Figureheads tend to have *embonpoint*.'

'What's that?'

'*Embonpoint* means . . . um . . .' – Fleur described an hourglass shape in the air with her hands – 'curvy.'

'And that's a *bad* thing? I can't agree with you on that one.'

Fleur watched as Shane joined his ex-ladylove, his smile reflected in Rio's face.

How sad, she thought, that fate had kept them apart. She wondered if there was any way she could encourage a reunion, manipulate it somehow that they might see sense and become an item once again.

No, no, Fleur. Stop it at once! Stop all this nosy-parkering in other people's business. It was absolutely none of her affair.

She poured Shane's wine and took it out to him. Río had produced a copy of the *National Enquirer* from her basket, and was leafing through it.

'What are you doing with that rag, Río?'

'I had to buy it when I saw the headline. Look.' She held up the tabloid, and three words leaped up at Fleur. SHANE BURNS OUT she read.

'Yikes,' said Fleur. 'What's that all about?'

'I'm having a nervous breakdown,' said Shane equably, 'according to the *Enquirer*. Apparently I'm so distraught at working on the same set as my erstwhile lover and mother of my child – flame-haired Irish colleen, Río Kinsella – that I've been locking myself in my trailer for hours on end, knocking back whiskey and gulping down painkillers.'

'Is it true?' asked Fleur.

'I was given a present of a bottle of vintage Reserve by Jameson – which I haven't opened yet. And someone must have seen me going into the pharmacy in Ardmore for a pack of paracetamol.'

'Listen to this,' said Río, scanning the article. '"The flame-haired temptress refused to comment." Hello? Nobody even *asked* me to comment. "But the *Enquirer* can reveal in a bombshell world exclusive that according to an insider Ms Kinsella spends a lot of time in Shane's trailer begging him not to open another bottle of his favourite Special Reserve

Jameson whiskey, which costs a staggering $239.00 a bottle. Shane and Río's relationship goes back many years – they first met when Shane was a struggling young actor in Galway. Río immediately fell pregnant with their love child, but Shane left mother and baby Finn behind in Ireland to pursue a career in Tinseltown. He first came to prominence as Seth Fletcher in the mega successful TV series, *Faraway*, and since then has gone from strength to strength as an actor. He has won an IFTA (the Irish equivalent of a BAFTA) and owns homes in LA and the south of France. The whiskey-voiced star is also rumoured to be interested in buying a property in his native Emerald Isle in order to be close to his estranged family . . ." *What*?' Río looked up from the *Enquirer*. 'Is that true, Shane?'

'Yeah. I miss you guys.'

'Oh.' Río looked a little nonplussed. 'Well, Adair Bolger's house is still up for grabs. Apparently he's reduced the asking price by half. If you bought it, we'd be neighbours.'

'What do you mean?' asked Shane.

'I own the adjoining orchard, remember?'

'Hmm. I have to say it would give me no little satisfaction to buy out Baldy Bolger. I haven't forgiven him for trying to annexe you, Río.'

'I can't be annexed,' retorted Río, 'because I don't belong to anyone. And don't you forget it, buster.' Río returned her attention to the *Enquirer*. 'And Adair isn't bald.'

'Yes, he is,' said Shane. 'Turn to page five for the "full and exclusive story" and you'll see a picture of him.'

'*What*?' said Río again, tearing the paper in her haste to turn the pages. 'Oh, my God! Where did they get this?' She scanned the column inches rapidly, then dropped the paper onto the tabletop and regarded it incredulously. 'What on earth makes them think that anybody *cares*?'

'Show me.' Fleur reached for the paper. 'Tousle-haired Río has been linked to millionaire property developer, Adair Bolger,' she read, 'and in a bizarre twist, the love child of Shane and Río – Finn Byrne, who is now all grown up and works as a professional scuba-diver (see left) – has been linked to Bolger's daughter, Irish beauty Isabella Bolger, who is currently working for her father in glitzy Dubai.' The photograph on the left showed Finn and Isabella larking on a beach, and had clearly been lifted from a Facebook page. The picture of Adair was bog standard picture library. Sweet Jesus, thought Fleur, was there no privacy left in the world? 'According to a close Byrne pal,' the article continued, 'the pair never stopped loving each other. But Shane's drink problem has triggered an avalanche of concern, and until he kicks the habit, the former love of his life will not consider a reunion.'

Fleur couldn't help it. She burst out laughing. 'Who are the "insiders" and the "close pals"? Where do they source all this info?'

'Beats me,' said Shane. 'Maybe I should start doing something to justify all the fuss.' He reached for his wineglass, and held it aloft in a mock toast. 'Look, Google Earth!' he pronounced in stentorian tones. 'Here I am, whiskey-voiced Shane Byrne, knocking back booze and triggering an avalanche of concern. I am clearly a roaring drunk, and neither can I stay away from the love of my life, flame-haired temptress Río Kinsella.' He slung an arm around Río, who had started laughing too.

'Quick, Fleur!' she said. 'Take a picture so we can sell it to the *Enquirer*.'

But a flash from the street told Fleur that a tourist had got there first. It was official. There was no privacy left in the world.

The next day Fleur set off for the recycling centre. As she was enjoying chucking her wine bottles into the bins (she loved the sound of breaking glass), she was joined by her cleaning lady, Audrey. Fleur sometimes felt guilty about having a cleaning lady, but she had inherited her mother's antipathy for housework. She didn't mind doing the ironing because she found it soothing, but dusting and Hoovering and polishing bored her senseless. The other plus about having Audrey in from time to time was that she was an inveterate gossip, and gossip in a village as small as Lissamore was a valuable commodity.

'Hi, Audrey. Beautiful day, isn't it?' said Fleur, as she lobbed a bottle into the 'green glass' bin. They'd got through rather a lot of wine last night, and it had been good to hear the sound of their laughter competing with the jangling of halyards against masts in the marina. 'Did you get the keys I left for you in Ryan's?'

'I did, thanks, Fleur. In fact, I'm just after cleaning up Mr O'Hara's place. Here – I'll give you the keys back.' She rummaged in her bag and produced an envelope.

Fleur was tempted to ask in what state Mr O'Hara's place had been left, but then realized that it might look as if she was snooping for info on Corban. Audrey wasn't to know that the penthouse was being used for illicit trysts – at least, she *hoped* Audrey didn't know.

'Had you a party yourself?' Audrey's gimlet eyes were clearly calculating the number of bottles Fleur was slinging into the maw of the bin.

'Yes. I had some friends around last night.' Fleur moved on to the 'drink cans only' bin.

'It's good to know that there's still fun to be had,' said Audrey, shaking her head lugubriously. 'I'd love it if I could afford to drink stuff like this.'

Fleur turned to see Audrey examining the label of an empty wine bottle. It read *Riondo Pink Prosecco Raboso*.

'Ooh. Who's been drinking pink fizz?' asked Fleur.

'Whoever's been staying in Mr O'Hara's penthouse,' said Audrey.

Fleur found herself smiling. If the culprit was Jake Malone, she hoped he'd had a lot of fun.

After the bottle bank, Fleur dropped by Ryan's corner shop to pick up French *Vogue*, which was on perpetual order specially for her.

'*Bonjour*, Fleur,' said Peggy Ryan. '*Comment ça va, aujour-d'hui?*' Because Peggy was doing a Linguaphone course, she loved to practise on Fleur. It was another great way of finding out the village gossip, Fleur had discovered, because the locals seldom understood what they were saying. She segued into her native tongue, glad to be able to converse *en Français*. The only time she spoke French these days was on the phone to her brother and – on occasion – to Daisy.

'*Bonjour*, Peggy,' she said. 'What's new?'

'Well,' said Peggy, in her Irish-accented French, 'the latest from the film set is that Noreen Conroy found a bag of what she thinks is cocaine when she was cleaning that Nasty Harris's trailer.'

'That doesn't surprise me,' said Fleur. 'It might explain those mood swings she's prone to. Río says she's a nightmare to work with. If she's not careful she's going to end up as box-office poison.'

'Noreen says so too. Apparently she insists that her sheets have a thread count of at least 250, and the door handles are to be disinfected every half-hour. And did you know that poor Pat "Hackney" Carmody was instructed to polish the upholstery in the car every time he chauffeurs her? He's got so pissed off now that he just sprays the inside of the car with leather polish so it smells like he's done it. And her latest food fad is for fresh lobster.'

'I'm glad, for Seamus's sake. Yikes – there she is now! Doesn't Des look stupid in those shades?'

Big Des O'Shaughnessy – who worked occasionally as a bouncer in a nightclub in Galway – had been hired as Anastasia Harris's bodyguard. It was yet another of the riders her contract had insisted on, but Corban had drawn the line at flying in her personal goon from LA. Since Big Des had got the gig, he had taken to wearing baseball caps and wrap-around shades and T-shirts with slogans like 'Live Fast, Fight Hard', 'Harder than Hardware' and 'Kicking Ass for Cash' emblazoned upon them. Fleur wished he'd wear one with 'I'm with this Idiot' on it, and an arrow pointing to Nasty Harris, but she didn't think that even big Des would be that thick.

As Nasty passed the shop, she pointed at something in the window and gave a disparaging little laugh. The object of her derision, Fleur saw, was the photograph on the front of the *Coolnamara Gazette* of the current Rose of Lissamore, who was wearing a dress that she had designed herself. 'How parochial!' trilled Nasty.

Fleur bridled. She'd show Nasty Harris just how 'parochial' people in Lissamore were.

'*Au revoir*, Peggy,' she said, moving towards the door.

'*Au revoir*, Fleur! *Bonne journée!*'

Fleur was glad to see the expression on Nasty's face change, as she got a load of the *Vogue* under Fleur's arm. 'Oh!' she exclaimed. 'They stock *Vogue* in that quaint little store?'

'But of course,' said Fleur, with a sweet smile and in her classiest Parisienne accent. 'French *Vogue*. But I'm afraid I got the last copy.'

And Fleur strode down the street, very glad that today she'd been channelling Coco Chanel in No 19, matelot stripes, loose trousers and a little straw cloche.

Chapter Fifteen

Dervla found visiting the famine village that had been built specially for *The O'Hara Affair* quite harrowing. The famine was a period of Irish history that had fascinated her when she'd studied it at school, and to see it now represented in the burned-out cottages and the wretched hovels that comprised the fictional village sent shivers along her spine. She remembered an account she'd read of starving children looking like decrepit ancients with wrinkled faces and bent bodies and dead eyes, and she wondered how these well-fed-looking extras could convey the real horror that had been inflicted on Ireland by the famine, which had killed a million people and sent another million – including Scarlett O'Hara's father – overseas.

It was unsettling, somehow, to witness these people knocking back their skinny lattes and cans of Diet Coke while kitted out in rags and smeared with cosmetic filth. It was even odder to see starving peasants idling over Amazon Kindles and electronic notebooks and talking on their mobile phones. But then Dervla had been feeling odd and unsettled for days. The red star in her diary marking the date when Christian would fly to France and Nemia to Malta was encroaching ever nearer, and every day when she consulted her calendar, Dervla felt her stomach lurch.

She'd done a lot of thinking about her future. She'd finish the damned book asap: she'd have to, otherwise she'd be in breach of contract. But Dervla had realized that the life of a writer didn't suit her. It was too sedentary, too insular and too lonely. She missed the buzz of buying and selling, missed the competitive element of the auctioneering game, the cut and thrust. She was restless: once the book was done and dusted, she would need to embark upon a new project.

She'd thought about getting an art gallery going in Ardmore, but two had recently gone out of business. She'd thought about maybe acquiring the plot of land next to Río's and setting up an organic vegetable suppliers with her sister. But Río was still vacillating about the future of her small-holding. If Finn came home still full of plans for starting his scuba-diving outfit with Izzy, it wouldn't surprise Dervla if Río surrendered the two acres to him. Well then, maybe Dervla should go into business with Finn? Scuba-diving holidays abroad might be less popular nowadays, but staycations were proving more and more attractive alternatives. Or maybe she could set up a travel business aimed at ex-pats hoping to trace their Irish roots? Maybe she could do tours of Irish movie sets, like this one? But then, maybe *The O'Hara Affair* would bomb and there would be no demand for visits to the repro famine village.

Maybe, maybe. There were so many maybes. But surely there was a project out there that was right for her? She hadn't forgotten Corban's suggested book title: *Women Entrepreneurs: Kicking Ass and Getting Results*. As soon as her stint as Daphne's carer was up and her book was finished, she'd start kicking ass again. She'd earned her place on that short list for female entrepreneur of the year, and she damned well wouldn't relinquish it.

Corban wasn't available today to show them around the

set: Fleur had told her he'd been detained by business in Dublin. Instead a very good-looking assistant director called Jake took them on a grand tour of the location. He showed them the Big House, which was supposed to belong to the evil landlord played by Shane. It was a genuine castle, built by a wealthy industrialist in the nineteenth century, and Dervla longed to explore. It was the kind of joint that – if she'd had it on her books in the glory days of the Celtic Tiger – she would have adored to show off, with the proviso that only rock stars need apply. As she walked through the main entrance hall, she began to compose the sales blurb, a habit she hadn't been able to kick. *A grand oak staircase, six feet wide with oak-panelled dado, massive newel posts and ornamental balustrade, lit by beautiful tracery windows with rich stained-glass panels in sixteen divisions, with above a handsomely decorated ceiling with corbels, moulded panels, centrepieces, bosses and openwork cornice of artistic design . . .*

Beneath the openwork cornices of artistic design, oblivious to the beauty of the stained-glass window and impervious to the crew members going about their business around him, Shane Byrne was sitting in a canvas chair studying his script.

'I'd introduce you,' said Jake, 'only I don't want to interrupt while he's working.'

'It's OK,' said Fleur airily. 'We've known Shane for years. I even shared a squat with him once.'

'You did? I can't imagine a classy dame like you living in a squat.'

'Oh, I was a wild young bohemian in my time,' said Fleur, with a baroque gesture and an entrancing smile. 'Still am, at heart.'

'It's just as well Corban isn't here,' Dervla told Fleur later, when they were ensconced in the canteen bus, having coffee. It was crammed with extras on their tea break.

'You've spent the entire afternoon flirting with that boy Jake.'

'I can't help but flirt with preposterously good-looking men,' said Fleur. 'It's wired into my DNA. Don't you remember that before Corban I'd never dated anyone who was older than me?' She looked admiringly through the bus window at Jake, who was now sitting on a dry-stone wall, gazing intently at the screen of his BlackBerry. 'It's true, you know, what they say about young men in bed. They can keep it up for hours.'

'Yeah?'

'Oh, yes.' Fleur made a moue. 'But sometimes that can get a little boring. I find that sex with Corban is more . . . imaginative.'

Dervla didn't ask. She never talked about sex with anyone other than Christian, and simply couldn't understand why those *Sex and the City* gals were so vociferous on the subject. She picked up her phone to check the time. 'Río's late,' she remarked. Río had arranged to meet them for coffee on the bus.

'I'm not surprised,' said Fleur. 'She looked run off her feet.'

Dervla had watched her sister earlier as she'd gone about her set-dressing duties, assessing objects with that critical eye that Dervla remembered so well. In the days when Río had worked for her as a home-stager, she had been a perfectionist: today she'd prowled the set dismissing here a clock as being of the wrong period, or there a bowl of fruit for being out of season, and at one point telling off an extra who was sporting lip gloss. Most of the extras lolling around on the bus were now wearing hoodies over their rags, but there was one girl sitting at the back dressed in a ladies' maid get-up, complete with lacy cap and apron. She was, incongruously, working away on a laptop.

'Have you read the script of this film?' Dervla asked Fleur, who was rummaging in her bag for something.

'Yes.'

'What did you think?'

'I enjoyed the scenes set in the great houses,' said Fleur, opening a little compact and inspecting her face. 'And the character that Shane is playing is a real out-and-out villain. And the double bluff played on him by the O'Hara family is brilliant. But I'm not sure about the famine scenes. I prefer my movies to be escapist. There's a lot of dead and dying and weeping and wailing in this film.'

'The Irish famine wasn't pretty.'

'No famine is.' Fleur produced a lipstick, and retouched her mouth. 'They say that we French hit upon frogs' legs and *escargots* as a source of nutrition during times of war and famine when there was nothing else to eat.'

Dervla looked down at the controlled mayhem below, at the sparks unrolling spools of electric cable, and the lighting men angling klieg lights, and the make-up girls powdering faces, and thought how odd it was that a multi-million-dollar movie was providing jobs for people whose ancestors may have starved to death in Coolnamara.

Oh! Why was she allowing such morbid thoughts into her head? She had to snap out of this, have some fun, do some positive thinking. Shane had invited them to join him in his trailer for a drink once work was done for the day: that would be something to look forward to. She'd change the subject.

'It's weird to see someone in period costume working on a laptop, isn't it?' she observed, nodding at the black-clad ladies' maid.

Fleur followed the direction of Dervla's gaze. 'Oh! It's Bethany,' she said.

219

'You know her?'

'I told her fortune when I was Madame Tiresia.'

'I wonder has it come true yet,' joked Dervla.

'You'd be surprised. Some aspects of it very well may have.'

'No shit! How do you know?'

Fleur tapped her nose. 'Intuition,' she said.

In Second Life, Poppet and Hero were building their very own cottage. Hero had paid for it in Linden dollars: Bethany hadn't a clue how much it might have cost him in real money, and was too embarrassed to ask. They'd furnished it with a pleasing rustic simplicity: a grandfather clock that ticked and told SL time, a table with a gingham tablecloth, two reed-bottomed chairs. There was a fire burning brightly in the grate, a kettle steaming on the hob, and a jug of marguerites on the windowsill. Upstairs wasn't finished yet, but Bethany pictured a bed with crisp linen sheets and plump pillows and a patchwork coverlet. She hummed as she swept the floor with an old-fashioned besom. She was pleased with the way she looked today, like an olde-worlde serving wench, with a puff-sleeved blouse, full ankle-length skirt, and bare feet. She'd given herself the kind of boobs she'd have loved in real life (nothing too ostentatious – more Cheryl Cole than Jordan), and she'd grown her hair down to her waist.

The grandfather clock struck the hour. Hero would be here any minute. How lucky she was to have met him! Tara seldom bothered with Second Life any more since she'd got herself a boyfriend, and now that the evenings were drawing in, Bethany might have found living in Díseart more than a little lonely.

Drumming her fingers on the tabletop, she looked around her at real life. Below her, a chauffeur was holding the door of a Merc open for Elena Sweetman, one of the older stars of the film. The actress emerged from the back seat wearing wraparound shades and jeans, yawning, her hair dishevelled. Soon, Bethany knew, she would be transformed by hair, make-up and wardrobe into a flawlessly coiffed and gowned nineteenth-century beauty. The animal wrangler was leading a horse across the car park – the one that Shane Byrne had been riding around on all last week. One of the ADs – the hot one – was sitting on a dry-stone wall, working away on his BlackBerry. She watched him push a wing of dark hair back from his face, and then he looked up, and their eyes met. He gave her a smile that could, she supposed, be described as 'winning'. Bethany blushed, bit her lip, and smiled back at him before returning her attention to her screen.

In Second Life, Hero had arrived.

From her vantage point on the top of the bus, Fleur watched Bethany go through her paces. She'd observed her half an hour earlier, when she'd been tip-tapping away on her laptop. Had she been floating around Shakespeare Island? Fleur wondered. Had she hooked up with Hero? Had she been laughing, crying, blowing kisses, dancing?

Where might Bethany's Hero be in real life? Dublin was his home town, he'd told her, but he could be anyone, anywhere. He could be burly Dave, with whom Fleur had had that clumsy cyber sex. He could be 'Peeping' Tom Hunter, who spent every evening hunched over the screen of his MacBook Air. He could be that charming AD, Jake, who'd been messing about on his BlackBerry earlier. He could be a rock star, a politician, an astrophysicist. He could be the Queen of England for all anyone could ever know.

Now, watching Bethany in her role as lady's maid, she wished she'd remembered to bring Dervla's binoculars –

spying wasn't nearly as much fun when you couldn't get close-ups.

Bethany's brief was to emerge from the front door of the big house, walk to where a groom was holding the leading rein of a horse, and 'chat animatedly'. A party was being thrown by the evil landlord, and all over the driveway, starving peasants were raking gravel and weeding flowerbeds. Bethany looked good in her lady's maid outfit. Her hair was tucked up under her lacy white cap, displaying to advantage her delicate bone structure. The 'animated chat' may have consisted of nothing more than the usual 'rhubarb rhubarb rhubarb', but when Bethany was animated, it made her pretty face even prettier. Fleur could see that she was attracting a deal of attention – especially from the male members of the crew. Whether she was aware of it or not, Bethany was blossoming, and Fleur felt privileged – and not a little proud – to witness her protegée's transformation from gawky girl to beauty.

She herself remembered the pain of the transition period. While Bethany had been called 'pleb' and 'loser', Fleur had been called '*bon à rien*' and '*crétine*'. She had been slow to develop physically, she had been mildly dyslexic and – like Bethany – she had been no good at games. She might not have got through this difficult time if it had not been for her mother, who every day would leave a message for her under a fridge magnet. These took the form of quotes from famous women, such as this from Colette: 'Be happy. It's one way of being wise.' From Brigitte Bardot: 'Every age can be enchanting, provided you live within it.' And, from Coco Chanel: 'The most courageous act is still to think for yourself.' Fleur had started to do the same for Bethany – although technology meant that she could dispense with the fridge magnets. Every day – under the guise of Flirty O'Farrell – she sent the girl affirmations on Facebook. From Jeanne Moreau: 'People's opinions don't interfere with me.' From Claudette Colbert: 'It matters more what's in a woman's face than what's on it.' And from Françoise Sagan: 'One can never speak enough of the virtues, the dangers, the power of shared laughter.' It might be as facile as dressing up as a fortune-teller and offering specious advice, but as the Tesco ad famously declared – 'every little helps'. And Bethany really did seem to be emerging from her cocoon.

Again and again she was required to walk down the front steps and approach the extra playing the groom, and again and again she hit her mark, no problem. On the penultimate take, the horse – who was clearly bored at being kept standing – helped himself to Bethany's mob cap and her hair came tumbling riotously over her shoulders. But instead of looking mortified and blushing, as Fleur knew the girl would once have done, Bethany laughed, and grabbed the cap back. It was a lovely, spontaneous moment, and Fleur hoped that the editor would have the nous to keep it in.

It looked as if Bethany was embracing her inner butterfly.

Later, a knackered Río fell into Shane's trailer where Dervla and Fleur were sitting on a leather-upholstered banquette, quaffing champagne.

'You jammy bastards,' said Río. 'Swigging back champagne while I was setting a dinner table for twenty poncy actors with Sèvres porcelain and an artillery of cutlery.'

'So we'll be getting a real meal tomorrow?' said Shane, rubbing his hands like Jamie Oliver. 'Yes! What's on the menu?'

'Four and twenty blackbirds baked in a pie.'

Shane gave her a 'grow up' look. 'Seriously, Río. What are we getting to eat?'

'I am serious,' she said. 'Live songbirds in a pie was a famous olde-worlde recipe for special occasions. I hope those birds crap all over you, Shane Byrne. You deserve it, for skiving off like this.'

'I'm not skiving off!' protested Shane. 'I had a really tough day today.'

'You call snogging Elena Sweetman tough?'

'Somebody's got to do it.'

'Children, children – stop bickering,' said Fleur. 'Pour Río a glass, Shane.'

Shane sloshed fizz into a glass, and handed it to Río, who accepted it ungraciously.

'Hey, sis,' she said, turning to Dervla. 'I haven't seen you in a while. How are things?'

Dervla sucked in a stoical breath. 'Things are great,' she said. 'I have a new job.'

'A new job? Doing what?'

'I'm going to take over caring for my mother-in-law.'

Río's jaw dropped. 'Permanently?'

'No, no. Just while Nemia's away on holiday. It's actually going to work out really well. I plan to move in there with my laptop, and finish my book. It'll be like killing two birds with one stone.'

'I'd better remember to fill my pockets with stones tomorrow,' said Shane, glumly. 'I'll need at least a dozen, if I'm going to kill off two blackbirds per shot.'

'Sounds like a really good idea, Dervla,' said Río, ignoring Shane. 'What made you decide to do it?'

'We can't find anyone else. And the money's good.'

'How much?'

'Six hundred and fifty a week.'

'Sheesh,' said Río. 'I'd be up for that if I weren't working on this caper. What does it involve?'

224

'A little cooking, a little cleaning, a little ironing.' Dervla didn't mention the washing, or the scrubbing of the dentures.

'Nice work if you can get it.'

'I think I'd rather be paid to snog Elena Sweetman,' said Shane.

'How much do you get for that?' Río gave him a curious look.

'An obscene amount of money.'

Dervla wondered what, exactly, constituted an obscene amount of money. In her estate agent days, she had earned what might have been considered an obscene sum. But she bet it was nothing near what Shane earned. Looking around at the state of the art trailer, she calculated how much it must be costing the film people to accommodate their stars in this kind of luxury. She'd explored it earlier, while Shane made a phone call. There was a pull-out TV housed in an opaque glass and pear-wood cabinet; there was a bar, a kitchen, a bedroom and a bathroom. Integrated halogen lighting illuminated the joint, and it was carpeted from head to toe in pure new wool. Shane's home from home was, Dervla thought ironically, probably better furnished than the Old Rectory. Maybe she and Christian should sell up, buy a state-of-the-art camper van and go travel the world? But there was, of course, the small matter of his mother. Daphne could hardly come careering around the world with them.

Christian had spent the previous evening devising a list for Dervla, of phone numbers and email addresses to contact in case of emergency while he was away, plus Daphne's bank and Bupa details. He'd printed it out for her, and titled the document 'Mum Matters'. Dervla wasn't sure whether the emphasis should be on the first word or the second. 'Mum Matters' sounded like the kind of miniature book you'd stick in a Christmas stocking, full of sentimental aphorisms about motherhood.

Nemia had promised to do something similar: she was going to compile a list of activities for Dervla to engage Daphne in if she happened to get bored with David Attenborough and Monty Don. Going through old photograph albums worked a dream, Nemia told her, because even though Daphne couldn't decipher details, once the places and people in the photographs were described to her, they restored long-dormant memories.

Long-dormant memories . . . Maybe, Dervla thought, she might access some of the memories that pertained to Daphne's string of lovers? Would it be un-kosher if she took out the letters too, that she had found hidden away on the bookshelves? She might find out a little more about what had motivated her mother-in-law to do the things she'd done.

'More champagne, Dervla?'

'Oh! Yes, please. But just a tad.'

Dervla smiled at Shane as he refilled her glass. There was still a little make-up – kohl possibly – smudged around his eyelashes, and she could understand how women worldwide fell for his easy charm. 'Stop there!' she said. 'I'd love more, but I'm driving.'

Maybe this evening she should open one of the bottles of fizz that Christian's partner had given them as a wedding present. To celebrate . . . what? To celebrate the fact that she was married to a lovely, lovely, *lovely* man, and how lucky was that? She remembered the cherry stone game she used to play with Río when they were children. *Tinker, tailor, soldier, sailor* – well, Christian was none of those. *Rich man, poor man, beggar man, thief* . . . Neither was he beggar man nor thief. He *had* been a rich man when they first met – Dervla remembered him buying the ring, booking the honeymoon and approving the architect's plans that had been drawn up for the restoration of the Old Rectory. But he was now – thanks to the recession – a comparatively poor man.

Not as poor as some baby-boomers, though – those forty- and fifty-somethings who had sold off parents' houses to pay for their care, and who were now scraping the bottom of the barrel to maintain it. She'd heard a man on the radio recently talking about how he had been forced to take his mother out of the home in which she had been living for a decade, and have her admitted to hospital via A&E, because he could no longer afford private care. Nobody was inheriting anything any more, and Dervla just hoped that whatever Daphne had got from the sale of her house in London would last her until the end. They'd have to be careful.

But in a way, she decided, as she watched Shane fetch another bottle of champagne from the fridge, the *nouveau pauvre* status conferred upon her and Christian had made them richer. Two years ago, Dervla had spent money in a spurious attempt to address what was missing in her life. She had helped herself to the wardrobe, the gadgets, the fuck-off penthouse. Now she had acquired more valuable things. A lazy-eyed smile to greet her upon waking. Text messages that read: **I am horny just thinking about u sexy wifelet xxx** or **I cannot WAIT to get home.** Little gifts secreted in unexpected places: a cartoon clipped from *The Guardian* slipped between the pages of her library book; more favourite tunes downloaded to her iPod; rose petals from the garden sprinkled on the surface of a bath run for her when she was bone tired. Immeasurable riches.

Dervla looked at her sister, she looked at her friend. Both Río and Fleur had been unlucky in love. Río had had two great loves in her life and lost them both, while Fleur had

had a team of toyboys, and was now involved with a man who was rarely there for her.

Yes, Dervla told herself as she reached for her glass, of the three women sitting here in this miniature mobile palace, she was by far the richest.

'What are we celebrating?' asked Christian, on hearing the popping of a cork from the utility room.

'Everything and nothing,' said Dervla. She dropped the champagne cork into the bin, half-filled two glasses, and moved through to the kitchen. Christian was sitting at the table, the itinerary of his forthcoming French tour in front of him and Kitty at his feet. Dervla set the bottle and the glasses on the table, and came clean with him. 'To be honest, I just feel like getting a little drunk,' she said. 'And you certainly look as if you could do with a hit of alcohol.'

'I do?'

'Yes. You have a furrow on your brow.' Dervla ran a finger over her husband's forehead, tracing the line that ran from temple to temple. It had not been there a year ago.

'Move over, Kitty,' said Christian, levering the dog's head off his lap, and pulling Dervla down. 'There's a new girl in town.'

She drew him against her, loving the feel of his face against her breasts, the way his hands automatically moved over her hips to cup her ass.

'What's worrying you, love?' she asked.

'Everything and nothing.'

'I know exactly how you feel. It's weird, isn't it? As if there's something hovering in the atmosphere. A kind of universal malaise.'

'I've stopped listening to the radio in the car. I can't bear to hear the news.'

'I've started playing classical music very loud. It drowns out the clamour in my head.'

They looked at each other and laughed.

'We're talking like people in a radio play!' said Christian.

'It's fun! Let us continue to bemoan our lot.'

'Vent our anguish.'

'Shake our fists at the heavens.' Dervla dropped a kiss on his forehead. 'Have you ever noticed the way we talk when Daphne's here?'

'Well, we talk louder, that's for sure.'

'It's not just that. The dialogue's all stilted. It's like – "Are you enjoying your supper, Christian?" "Yes, Dervla. It is delicious. Did you happen to hear the weather forecast earlier?" "Yes, I did. It looks like rain tomorrow." "Oh, dear. I shall have to have the old wellies handy, so." "Ha ha ha."'

Christian slumped. 'Oh, God. I'm sorry, Dervla.'

'Sorry? What for?'

'My mother.'

'Tush, tush, my love. What do you do? It's the way of the world.' Dervla reached for the champagne bottle, and topped up the flutes.

'D'you know, sometimes I envy her,' said Christian.

Dervla looked at him askance. 'Why on earth would you envy Daphne?'

'Because she has no worries. She just expects to be fed and clothed and watered and kept warm. Like a baby. Except babies aren't imperious.'

Imperious was putting it mildly, Dervla thought, handing Christian his glass.

'Well, here's to no worries,' she said. 'There will come a time, mark my words, when the gods will smile upon us and things will be more propitious.'

'Propitious. That's a good word. May we never forget that the cornucopia of plenty is half full, not half empty.'

'Amen,' said Dervla, adding 'Oh!' and jumping up. 'Talking of cornucopias, I nearly forgot. We have salted almonds. Fleur gave me a bag of them as a thank-you present for doing the driving today. She does the best salted almonds in the world.'

Swinging into the utility room, Dervla emptied the ziplock bag of almonds into a bowl, noticing as she did that she'd left the door of the freezer open. Shit! More wasted energy! Their electricity bill had arrived today, and she hadn't dared to open it.

Back in the kitchen, Christian was leafing through *Essential Interiors* magazine, looking morose.

'I'm sorry,' he said again.

'What are you sorry for now?'

He indicated the glossy magazine. 'For not having the money to furnish your dream house.'

'Oh, love! I don't need any stupid dream house. Haven't I a dream husband, and isn't that enough to make any woman happy?'

'You really are so sweet. Let me kiss your pretty nose.'

But before Christian could kiss Dervla's pretty nose, a knock came at the kitchen window. It was Nemia.

'Hi,' she said, putting her head around the door. 'Sorry to interrupt, but I need your help, Christian.'

'What's up?'

'Daphne is trying to phone her mother. She's getting anxious because she can't get through to somebody she calls the operator.'

'Unsurprisingly enough,' said Christian, getting resignedly to his feet, 'since the operator has been redundant for about twenty years. I'll come and try and explain things to her.'

230

He turned to Dervla, and added, 'In the words of Lawrence Oates, "I am just going outside, and may be some time."'

As Christian followed Nemia through the door, Dervla heard the carer say, 'What might she have meant by "the operator"? Who *is* the operator?'

Who is the operator? The question had a metaphysical ring to it. How weird it must be, to live in Daphne's world, a world that was probably populated by such antique trades-persons as cobblers and smiths and milliners and milkmen. And estate agents.

Swigging back champagne, Dervla reached for *Essential Interiors*.

The house featured on the page that Christian had been perusing was a beauty – a nineteenth-century Gothic Revival mansion, all bay windows and floor-to-ceiling library shelves and grassy parklands and Carrara fireplaces. There was, of course, an Aga in the kitchen, which was charmingly cluttered with copper pots and pans and mismatched china. Bedrooms were furnished with four-posters dripping with tassels and tiebacks and swagged with faded brocade; bathrooms featured throne-like loos and scroll-topped, claw-footed baths; there were designated rooms for boots and coats, a schoolroom and a night nursery, and Farrow & Ball was splashed everywhere.

A house like this had been, once, the vision at the fore-front of Dervla's mind's eye. This is how she had pictured the Old Rectory in her childhood dreams. She had popu-lated it with a rosy-cheeked housekeeper and a gnarled gardener, a husband, a dog, and children. She had the husband, now; she had the dog. But there was no rosy-cheeked housekeeper and no gardener, and instead of the children, she had another dependent.

Christian had compared Daphne to a baby, earlier. But

231

babies were bundles of joy. They epitomized hope, growth, a future where anything was possible. Aside from that, you could pinch babies' chubby bits, stroke their peach-like skin; you could squeeze them and kiss them and rock them and rough-house them and inhale their glorious babyness. You could teach them and learn from them and laugh with them and applaud their hand–eye coordination. Babies were a brave new world.

Draining her glass, Dervla decided that Daphne wasn't like a baby at all. She was more like an incubus, sucking energy from others to maintain her own wellbeing. The analogy was so appalling that she found herself clamping her hands over her mouth. Then she lunged for the bottle, and poured.

Thank God the alcohol helped.

232

Chapter Sixteen

Fleur waited for ScarlettO'Hara Sahara to rezz on the screen of her Apple Mac in all her red velvet glory; but for some reason, Flirty LittleBoots materialized instead. She must have entered the wrong password. Flirty was still wearing the leather skirt over her combats, her helmet hadn't rezzed, and neither had the blue hair. Flirty looked worse than ever: maybe Fleur should change the avatar's name to Baldy LittleBoots instead.

She was about to consult the file in which she stored her passwords so that she could breathe life into ScarlettO'Hara Sahara, when lo! suddenly a request for Flirty LittleBoots's friendship popped up. It was from Bethany's virtual boyfriend, Hero. Hmm. Maybe it wouldn't be a bad idea to get to know this Hero better, find out how kosher he was, work out whether he was truly worthy of Bethany O'Brien. Fleur accepted his invitation, then set about trying again to divest Flirty of her leather skirt. It worked! Now all she needed was to reinstate her helmet and her hair.

Her Instant Messenger sprang suddenly into life.

Hero says: Hi, Flirty, she read.

Oh! He was online.

Hi, she said back.

Wanna come and see the place I made?

Um. Did she want to see it? What kind of place is it?

233

she asked, cautiously. She didn't want to end up in another lap-dancing club.

It's real cosy. I have a kitty cat.

His invitation to teleport popped up on her screen. Fleur hesitated, then typed in **On my way,** and clicked 'Accept'.

She found herself in the kind of cottage Walt Disney might have dreamed up. There was a fire burning in the hearth, and a kettle steaming on the hob. A vase of marguerites sat on the windowsill, the cat was snoozing in a basket, and a framed picture of Bethany's avatar had been hung over the mantelpiece. Hero was standing at the foot of the stairs, watching her.

Nice place you've got here, she said.

TY.

Flirty moved to the window. Virtual waves licked at golden sand, and she could hear the call of a curlew. **You've a great view of the sea.**

It's my little Irish cabin.

You're Irish?

Begorrah, and I am. You?

French.

Ooh la la! Bienvenue, Madame!

Merci, Monsieur.

There was a hiatus, then: **You managed to get rid of the leather skirt, LOL**, he said.

Yes. Finally.

But I'm not sure that the bald look is right for a sophisticated French lady. Maybe you should go shopping for some new hair and help yourself to a French maid's outfit while you're at it. LOL.

Hmm. Fleur hoped that the tone of the convo wasn't going to become prurient. She'd raise the bar a little.

A French maid's outfit is a little too Feydeau farce, don't you think?

Hello! An educated French lady! Maybe we could discuss Proust next.

Or Yeats.

Or Voltaire.

Or Synge.

Or Pauline Réage. Hero took a step towards her. **Would you like me to show you around my humble abode?** he asked.

Yes, please.

He turned back towards the stairs, and Flirty followed.

Mind your head, he said, as she banged her head on the ceiling. **Pity you forgot your helmet LOL.**

Upstairs was a little bedroom, with a dormer window and a sloping ceiling. The bed boasted piles of snowy pillows and a patchwork quilt. A candlestick stood on a rustic bedside table, there was a rag rug on the floor, and a white nightgown hung from a peg on the back of the door. Hero moved to the bed and sat down. Flirty elected to keep her distance, and sat instead on a reed-bottomed chair just inside the door.

What are you in RL, Flirty? Hero asked.

You mean, what do I do?

Yes.

I own a boutique.

Cool! Where?

Paris, she lied. And then she remembered that the last time they'd met she had told him she was in Sydney, Australia. She thought fast, then typed: **I've just come back from a buying trip in Sydney.**

Paris! Lucky you, to live in the city of lovers! What kind of clothes do you stock?

Designer gear.

Lingerie? French knickers? Pretty little brassieres?

No, she lied again. **Are you trying to be provocative?**

235

Provocative? *Moi*?

Let's keep it clean, my friend. I saw the picture of your girlfriend downstairs, and I wouldn't like to think I'm muscling in on her territory. What are you in RL, Hero?

Hmm. What would you like me to be?

How about a matador?

Fleur watched as Hero rezzed into a matador, complete with cape and tight bolero jacket.

Wow! she said. **I'm impressed.**

Anything else?

Show me a fire fighter.

This time he morphed into a Village People-style fireman, booted and helmeted.

Very good! How about a handsome prince? she asked.

Like in the fairy tales?

Yes.

Your wish is my command, Madame LittleBoots.

Again he obliged. His prince sported an ermine-trimmed cloak, a gold medallion on a chain, and a glittering crown. He also sported an enormous erection. It poked angrily out of his breeches, swollen and red.

Come and join me on the bed, *chérie*, he said. **I've got something for you that I think you might enjoy. I bet you're wet just looking at it. suck me off suck me off suck me off i'm gonna make you gag oh god i'm so horny for you i'm gonna cum all over the screen—**

Fleur lunged for her touchpad and teleported the hell out of there.

Oh. Oh, God. She leaned back in her chair and realized she was hyperventilating. What a sleazeball! What a scumbag! What had made him think she'd be up for virtual sex? The fact that she'd told him she was French? She'd heard warning

236

bells go off when he'd mentioned Pauline Réage, author of erotica, but when he'd moved on to brassieres and French knickers she'd made it perfectly plain that she wanted to keep things clean. Oh! Had he been masturbating from the moment he'd invited her into his cutesy cottage? Did he invite Bethany there? Was the white nightgown on the back of the bedroom door intended for her? The thought of some pervy middle-aged guy getting his rocks off while Bethany danced around his cottage like Snow White made her feel sick. Oh, God. Maybe things had gone further between the virtual couple since she'd last spoken to Bethany, maybe Hero was grooming the girl? Maybe he'd been encouraging her to dress up as a French maid or something even tackier – pornographic permutations on Second Life were infinite; Fleur had seen stuff for sale that had made her blench . . . No. She shook the thought from her head: she couldn't countenance the idea.

Going to 'Search', she typed in 'Poppet'. But Poppet wasn't online. *Merde* – even if she had been, what would Flirty tell her? That the Hero of her imagination was in fact a jerk-off drooling in front of his computer screen? Bethany was too blindly in virtual love – she'd never believe it.

Merde. Suddenly Fleur felt grubby. She went upstairs to run herself a bath.

Five minutes later, she was lying in L'Occitane-scented water, glass of wine to hand, book on the lectern of the bath tidy. She was still feeling a bit shaky after her brief encounter, but there was no one she could talk to about it. She hadn't told Dervla about Second Life because she'd heard Dervla refer to it one day as 'Sadville', and Río was a Luddite who wouldn't have a clue. How about Corban! She'd filled him in on her Second Life persona – maybe he could calm her down. She was just about to reach for the phone when it rang. Corban's name was on the display.

'Lover!' she said. 'I was just thinking about you.'

'Serendipity,' he said. 'I was just thinking about you.'

'Nice thoughts?'

'*Very* nice thoughts. What are you up to?'

'I'm in the bath.'

'Hmm. And what exactly are you up to in the bath?'

'I'm having a glass of wine and reading a book.'

'Is it a sexy book?'

'I guess bits of it are sexy.'

'Read me some of it.'

'A sexy bit?'

'Yes.'

'Very well,' said Fleur, flicking through the pages, 'how about this? "Leisurely I changed into fifties-style garter and bra, in stiff pink satin. Bra made breasts high and jutty – when leaned forward could see nipples. Garter went from waist to top of legs, giving extreme hourglass curve. Rosy glow from fabric made thighs look creamy and smooth and I sat on brocade chair, liking rough feel of fabric against naked bottom. Slowly rolled silk stockings up legs and attached them to rubber suspenders on garter . . ."'

'Oh, Fleur . . .' Corban's voice in her ear sounded thick. 'Don't stop.'

Later, when she had topped up the bath with more hot water, feeling smug that when it came to phone sex, she indubitably cracked the whip, Corban said: 'You know, if your business ever fell through, you could make a living doing that. There's nothing quite like having a bedtime story read in a sweet French accent.'

'What is it about all things French that men find such a turn-on? French kissing, French letters, French knickers? I had some sicko come on to me in Second Life this evening, and the minute I mentioned I was French he assumed I was sexually available.'

'Really? What did he say?'

'Oh – just horrible stuff. I think he must have been jerking off during our entire conversation.'

'That'll teach you to go to Loserville.'

'Ha, Dervla calls it Sadville.'

There was a pause. 'Is Dervla on Second Life, too?'

'Not as far as I know. She's going to have enough to cope with in real life soon. She's taking over as her mother-in-law's carer.'

'Tell her to take care of herself, while she's at it. There's little to be gained in caring for an elderly relative when you're exhausted and rundown. There was a first-person account in the *Guardian* yesterday. I'll keep it for her.'

'That's sweet of you, but she'll be grand. She says she'll get lots of work done on her book.'

'Another multi-tasking woman! How I admire the fairer sex.'

'By the way, thanks for organizing the *O'Hara Affair* tour for us. Dervla was really impressed. There's clearly a lot of money being sunk into it.'

'Let's hope I make it back.'

'Of course you'll make it back. You promised me a night at the Oscars, remember?'

'Dream on, babe. The wrap party might be the height of our celebrations.'

'Do I get an invite?'

'You're on the list already.'

Fleur stretched out a foot and studied her toenails, which needed repolishing. Not only that, but her feet could do with a good slathering with moisturiser. All that time spent in the bath had made them look leprous.

'I'd better go, *chéri*,' she said. 'I'm starting to look like a prune. I'll see you this weekend, yes?'

'Looking forward to it. Do you think you might get hold of some of that lingerie you described earlier?'

'I'll see what I can do, *Monsieur. Au revoir*!'

Setting her phone down on the edge of the bath, Fleur reached for a towel. As she dried herself, she inspected her body in the cheval glass. She wasn't in bad shape for a forty-four-year-old, thanks to all the walking she did, and to her two weekly exercise classes in the community hall. But could she still carry off sexy lingerie at her age? It wasn't just the bath water that had had a crinkling effect. Her skin was starting to look a little thin. She remembered a joke that Río had told her about reaching a stage in life when you bend down to pull up your socks before remembering you aren't wearing any. It had made her laugh at the time, but now, looking at her reflection, she didn't find it quite so funny. No wonder people had virtual sex in a parallel universe, where all the participants were young and nubile, with no saggy bits in sight.

As she slid into her robe, she thought of the perv who'd invited her into his Second Life home. There'd been something really sinister about the fact that the cottage had a kind of picture-book prettiness about it, while harbouring a – a *pauvre con*. Who was he? There was no way of finding out, and no way of warning Bethany to be careful. Was she there in the cottage with him now? Fleur remembered the virtual portrait over the virtual fireplace, and shuddered. One thing was certain, there could be no more logging on to Second Life as Flirty LittleBoots. Next time she went there, she'd have to make sure her alias was ScarlettO'Hara Sahara. *Merde!* Maybe she should back off altogether. Dervla was right, Second Life was Sadville, and she, Fleur, actually had a life. Or did she? When she thought about it, real life hadn't been much fun lately. No wonder Second Life was so huge. She imagined that all over the world, *femmes d'un certain age* like her were making more virtual friends than real ones.

Her phone went again. She didn't recognize the number in the display. Who was JM?

'Hello?' she said, cautiously.

'Is that Fleur O'Farrell?' It was a man's voice.

'Yes. Who is this?'

'It's Jake Malone.'

'Oh, Jake! Hello. Thanks for the tour today. It was kind of you to spare the time.'

'It was my pleasure.' There was a pause, then: 'Fleur, I hope you don't think I'm being cheeky,' he said, 'but I'm just being straight with you. I'd really like to see you again.'

'Oh!'

'You can tell me to bog off, no problem. I promise you I won't be offended.'

'Oh, I wouldn't tell you to bog off! I'm actually very flattered. But – um – to be perfectly honest, don't you think you're a little young for me, Jake?'

'I don't see how that's a problem. We could just meet for a drink. Or a walk. I don't want to put any pressure on you.'

Just a drink . . . The thought was very appealing. But word would be around the village like wildfire that Fleur O'Farrell had bagged herself another toyboy. And of course there was Corban . . .

But Corban was on the other side of the country, and it wasn't as if she was in purdah. And she was feeling a little lonely and this boy had made her laugh and he had flirted with her, and Fleur had always adored flirting. The moniker that Daisy had dreamed up for her aunt had been bestowed upon her for a good reason. Still . . .

'I need some time to think about this, Jake,' she said.

241

'I'm sorry. I guess I ambushed you.'

'I'll call you back in a day or two.'

'Cool. I look forward to it.'

Fleur put the phone down and regarded her reflection again. What was she doing, even considering meeting up with this boy? She'd looked at herself unsparingly just minutes ago, and hadn't much liked what she'd seen. She was ageing, she was feeling insecure about her naked body . . .

Fleur's eyes widened suddenly, and she bit down on her lip. *Quelle folie!* There could be no question of sex! That would have to be understood from the start. But to have a new friend to have a laugh with would be fun, uplifting. Fleur had always surrounded herself with young people: she adored their vibrancy and optimism – they made her feel young again herself – and since Daisy had gone off to Africa, she hadn't had a decent fix of teen spirit. Not that Jake was in his teens – she'd put him at around twenty-three, twenty-four. Come to think of it – that wasn't too horrendous an age gap. Look at Demi Moore and Ashton Kutcher . . .

Oh, stop, Fleur, stop, Fleur, stop, stop, stop!

She needed some advice on this. Picking up the phone, she speed-dialled Río. But Río didn't pick up. She went to speed-dial Dervla, but then remembered that Dervla had enough on her plate without Fleur phoning to engage her in girl talk. Christian was leaving for France in the morning.

She was tempted to simply phone Jake back straight away and say, 'Yes – I'd love to meet up!' – but she'd had a couple of glasses of wine and she knew about the dangers of drunk dialling. Also, she didn't want to look like a cast member of *Desperate Housewives*.

Fleur turned her phone off, cleaned her teeth, and went to bed.

Chapter Seventeen

Dervla zipped up her laptop case and hefted it on to her shoulder. She threw an eye around her study to make sure she hadn't forgotten anything, then went down to her bedroom and slung some essentials into a weekend bag. The bathroom still smelled of Christian's aftershave, a pillow on the bed in which they'd made love last night still bore the imprint of his head. She had said goodbye to her husband earlier that day, and clung to him, feeling a little weepy.

'Are you having second thoughts?' he'd asked, and Dervla had shaken her head vigorously.

'No, no,' she assured him. 'We're doing the right thing. It's only two weeks.'

But when he'd got into the car and driven off down the driveway she'd allowed the tears to fall.

It's only two weeks . . . Repeating the words to herself like a mantra, Dervla went downstairs. Oh! There on the kitchen table was a small giftwrapped package. Christian must have left it for her there after lunch – she hadn't noticed it until now. She set down her case, reached for the package and untied the ribbon. Inside was a photograph, enclosed in a mother-of-pearl frame. The photograph showed herself and Christian sitting hand-in-hand on the sea wall in Lissamore. In the foreground Kitty smiled to camera, in the background, sun gilded the peaks of the Coolnamara mountains and bounced off wavelets in the harbour. It was a picture of pure happiness.

Dervla tucked the photograph carefully away in the pocket of her case before leaving her house through the back door. She locked it behind her, and called for Kitty. Then she crossed the courtyard to Daphne's house, where Nemia's bags were waiting on the front step, and rang the bell.

'Welcome, welcome!' sang Nemia, throwing open the door and leading the way into the house. She was looking radiant, dressed in holiday hues of yellow and blue. 'Hello, Kitty!' She stooped to pat the dog, then said, 'Let me show you the ropes, Dervla. I've made up a bed for you in there –' she indicated her bedroom door '– and cleared some wardrobe space. There's cannelloni in the oven for dinner and the freezer's well stocked. Don't worry if you have to run into town for basics – as long as you've made sure she's been to the loo, she'll sit in front of David Attenborough for hours. I often spend an hour doing Tai Chi after I've given her breakfast, and leave her listening to the radio or one of her audio books in bed. It's important you keep fit and make some time for yourself.'

'Yes. I read something about that in the paper recently.'

Nemia swung into the kitchen/breakfast room, where the table was set for dinner. 'There's prawn cocktail for starters, and I've given Daphne her gin and tonic—'

Dervla was aghast. 'I thought she wasn't allowed alcohol.'

'No, no! I play a trick, see? I bring her a glass of tonic with ice and lemon, and just rub the rim of the glass with a little gin. So she thinks she's having her pre-dinner drink, the way she always did in the past. And at dinner, if I'm having red wine I give her a glass of blackberry cordial, and if I'm having white wine, I give her a glass of apple juice. The same colour, see? That way she feels included.'

'Clever,' said Dervla.

'You have to be a little cunning, sometimes. See – on the fridge, there is my routine. It's important to stick to a routine, because otherwise she gets unsettled.'

Dervla slid the A-4 sheet out from under the fridge magnet and scanned it. 'Thanks,' she said. 'This will be useful to know. Bedtime's ten o'clock? Yikes! That late?'

Nemia shrugged. 'Sometimes I try and get her to go a little earlier, but it's difficult to persuade her that it's time to go to bed when it's still sunny outside. And if she does go to bed early, it means that she sometimes wanders at night.'

Dervla looked at Nemia apprehensively. 'You mean she wanders around the house?'

'Yes. She's looking for reassurance, see? She needs to know that there is someone here with her and she is not all on her own. That's why it is important to make sure that all the outside doors are securely locked, and the sliding doors in her bedroom, too. Come with me, and I'll show you how to lock them.'

Nemia left the breakfast room, and passed by the sitting room, where Dervla caught a glimpse through the door of Daphne in her armchair, gazing stonily at the telly. Attracted by the howling of wolves on David Attenborough, Kitty veered into the room, whereupon Dervla heard Daphne exclaim: 'A spotty dog! Where did you come from?'

In Daphne's bedroom, Nemia picked a little silver dish up from the dressing table.

'This is where the key to the windows belongs.'

The windows were wall-to-ceiling sliding glass doors. Dervla wished they were open now: the room was stuffy, and there was an old-lady smell of urine mixed with talcum powder. She took a look around, to familiarize herself with the room: she hadn't been in here since she and Christian had moved Daphne's possessions into it, all those weeks ago.

Things had changed. There was a railing on one side of

the bed, to prevent Daphne from falling out, and the head-board now boasted a white vinyl backrest. Dervla was rather touched to see that the counterpane was strewn with Beanie Babies, some of them well worn from all the attention they'd received. A table stood next to the bed, upon which a glasses case and a magnifier lay next to a large-print book.

'Does she still read?' Dervla asked.

'Not at all. But she likes to pretend she can.' Nemia opened the wardrobe door. 'If you decide to take her out for a jaunt, she prefers to wear the silk blouse with the pussy-cat bow, and the herringbone trousers. They're easy to get her into because they have an elasticated waist.'

Dervla looked into the wardrobe. Lined along the base was a row of shoes, all of which wore a patina of dust.

'Bathroom next!' breezed Nemia.

Opening the door of the bathroom cabinet, Nemia gave Dervla a guided tour. The shelves were stacked with jars and bottles and tubes: some of them with instructions written on them: 'To rub onto back, legs, feet, etc'. Dervla tried to repress a shudder.

'This is important,' said Nemia, holding up a blister pack of pills. 'Daphne must take one of these before bed each evening.'

'What is it?' asked Dervla.

'It's her ARICEPT. If she doesn't take it, her dementia symptoms will become worse.' Nemia set the blister pack down beside a box of disposable latex gloves.

'Anything else I need to know?' asked Dervla.

'You know about the spare bed linen?' Nemia opened the door of the airing cupboard. 'It's there, in that bag, ready to go if there's an emergency.'

Dervla nodded, then blanched as she caught sight of a pack of disposable adult nappies. 'Oh, God,' she said. 'I hope to high heaven I'm not going to need those.'

'There's no need to be nervous, Dervla,' said Nemia. 'You'll do fine. When I told Daphne today that Dervla's coming to stay, she said, "Oh, good! Dervla is such a well-mannered person". You can handle her, no problem. Now,' Nemia's tone changed, became brisker, 'I'd better go. There's no way I'm gonna miss that flight.'

Nemia shimmied down the corridor, with Dervla floundering in her wake, feeling as if she'd been set adrift.

'Front door keys,' said Nemia, indicating a bunch of keys on the telephone table. They were attached to a plastic tag that bore the legend: *A woman has the age she deserves –* Coco Chanel.

'Let me help you with your luggage,' said Dervla, stooping to pick up a Gladstone bag. 'Wow! This is heavy.'

'Books and shoes,' said Nemia, zapping the locks on her car, and pulling open the boot. 'Shoes for dancing every night of the week, and books to catch up with all the reading I never seem to have time for.'

What? Dervla'd thought that Nemia should have had all the time in the world for reading; which meant that she, Dervla, should have had all the time in the world for writing. Her heart sinking a little, she dropped the bag into the boot, then gave Nemia a kiss on the cheek. 'Enjoy your holiday!' she said, as she watched her slide into the driver's seat.

'I will!' returned Nemia. 'Any problems, just give me a call.' And then she gunned the engine and was off down the drive. Dervla heard the receding strains of Madonna's 'Holiday' as the car rounded the bend and disappeared from sight.

'Well, Kitty,' she said to the dog who had joined her on the step. 'It's just you and me and Daphne now. Let's go check out what scintillating stuff is on the telly this evening.'

In the sitting room, David Attenborough was coming to an end.

'Hello, Daphne,' said Dervla.

'Who is it?'

'It's Dervla, Daphne. I'm here to take care of you while Nemia's away.'

'What nonsense. I don't need taking care of. I'm perfectly capable of taking care of myself.'

Dervla helped herself to the television guide, and sat down.

'What did you say?' asked Daphne.

'Nothing. I'm just looking to see if there's anything on television. 'Hmm,' Dervla murmured into Kitty's ear, as she scratched the dog's head. 'How about *Badly Dubbed Porn*? Or *Sexy Cam*? *Pimp My Ride*? Or *Dirty Sanchez*?'

'What are you muttering about?' demanded Daphne.

'I'm looking at the television page. There's a programme on the National Geographic Channel about elephants. D'you fancy watching it?'

'Would that be interesting?'

'It might be.'

'All right, then.'

David Attenborough's theme tune faded away.

'I'll just go and check how long dinner's going to take,' said Dervla, aiming the remote at the telly and leaving the room. In the kitchen, the timer on the oven told her that the cannelloni would be ready at twenty past seven. She poured herself a generous shot of gin, added some tonic, and went back into the sitting room.

Shit! She'd got the wrong channel. MTV was blinging on the screen, and some muthafucka was rapping about slapping his bitches and hos, while a gang of nubile girls in thongs and minuscule bikini tops gyrated around him.

Daphne's stony eyes were fixed on the television. She frowned, then leaned forward. 'What's going on there?' she said. 'I can't see. What are they *saying*?'

Dervla lunged for the channel changer.

'Oh, it's just a pop video, Daphne,' she said brightly.

'Keep it on. I like pop music. 'Congratulations and celebrations'. That's Cliff Richard, you know.'

'Yes.' Dervla zapped the telly, and a close-up of an elephant's face came on.

'I love Cliff Richard.'

'Yes.'

'Who's that?'

'It's an elephant.'

'What's it doing?'

'We'll soon find out.'

The camera pulled back to show them that it was mating with another elephant.

'Is it having sex?'

'Looks like it.'

'It's very overrated, you know. Sex.'

'Mmm.'

A man walked onto the screen. 'G'day,' he said jovially, and Dervla's heart sank. He was Australian, and his accent was impenetrable – at least, to Daphne's ears it would be. 'The elephants behind me have just finished rutting. This means that – if the rut has been successful we can expect to see—'

'What's he saying? I can't understand a word. Turn it up.' Dervla obliged, but it was a pointless exercise, because, '*What's he saying?*' shouted Daphne.

'He has an Australian accent, Daphne,' explained Dervla.

'I don't have a clue what he's saying. Turn him off.'

'OK.' Dervla's jaw was clenched as she tossed the channel changer onto a pouffe. Taking a swig of gin, she reached randomly for some reading material – a small volume of famous quotes, called *In Praise of Grandmothers*. It had, presumably, been given to Daphne by Megan, Christian's daughter from his first marriage. The first aphorism Dervla lit on was this, from Virginia Woolf: 'I don't believe in ageing,' Dervla read. 'I believe in forever altering one's aspect to the sun.' Well, that was rich, coming from a depressive who famously took her own life before she hit sixty.

'Isn't there anything on the TV?' said Daphne plaintively.

'Well, I suppose we could watch some news before dinner.' Dervla reached resignedly for the remote again.

A celebrity with enhanced tennis ball breasts was posing on a red carpet.

'What is she *wearing*?' said Daphne.

Dervla hadn't the energy to talk her way out of this one. She decided to distract Daphne by drawing her attention to a finch that had chosen that moment to alight on the windowsill.

'Oh, look, Daphne! What kind of a finch is that?' she said brightly.

Daphne swivelled her head and peered at the window. 'What colour is it?'

'It has a reddish face and a blue head.'

'Then it's a chaffinch. I must put some nuts out for it. Finches love nuts. I had an art teacher called Miss Finch. Oh – off he goes. Bob bob bob. What are they doing on the television?'

'They're posing.'

'You call *that* posing? I used to be a model, you know.'

'Excuse me, for a minute, Daphne. I just want to check on something in the kitchen.'

Dervla got abruptly to her feet, picked up her glass and left the room. In the kitchen, she took another swig of gin, then covered her eyes with her hand. She could feel a headache coming on.

Later that evening, after Dervla had put Daphne to bed, she took the phone out into the courtyard to call Christian.

'How are things?' he asked.

'Oh. Things are fab. Daphne and I had a sparkling conversation over dinner about the weather. Noel Coward might have envied us our repartee.'

'Is she in bed now?'

'Yes.'

'Good girl. How did you manage that?'

'I told her I'd read her a story.' Dervla started to pace. 'And she demanded that a story be read to her there in the sitting room, and I said no – I'd feel ridiculous reading a bedtime story to someone who wasn't in bed, and I said that if she didn't want a story I'd make myself useful by getting the dishes out of the way. So I went off and banged about in the kitchen for a while, and next thing I hear her stomping down the corridor into her bedroom. So I go down, and say – all enthusiastic: "Oh, Daphne! You've decided it's bedtime after all! That's great. I'll be able to read you a story, now." And then I gave her her ARICEPT and read her the story—'

'What did you read her?'

'That Roald Dahl one about the woman who murders her husband with the frozen leg of lamb.'

'Nice one!' Christian laughed over the phone.

'I realized too late that it wasn't the best choice. I think it left her feeling a little . . . nonplussed.'

'Is she settled now?'

'I hope so. I rubbed some of that lavender balm on her temples and told her it would help her sleep. And then I kissed her on her forehead and said, "Night night, sleep tight".'

'Sweet of you.'

'Oh – I nearly forgot,' said Dervla, with a little laugh. 'After I'd tucked her in and put the balm on her temples and kissed her forehead, she said, "But you said you'd read me a story!"'

'No shit!'

'No word of a lie.'

'She'd forgotten already?'

''Fraid so, darling.'

'How completely, utterly bloody this disease is.' She heard him sigh down the line. 'You're doing great, Dervla. You're a star. You carry on like this, and you'll get through. As Nemia says, the important thing is to establish some kind of a routine. And whatever you do, don't let her get to you.'

'That's the thing I'm scared most of happening. That she'll say something awful, and I'll let it get under my skin, and then we'll have a row. Nemia says that rowing is a complete waste of energy.'

'She's right. You've just got to keep strong and not let her get to you. And what did we decide was the best way of doing that?'

'By being perfectly pleasant at all times. So far, I've been a positive amusement palace of pleasantness. A veritable stately pleasure dome.'

'So don't let her undermine your foundations. What's the weather like there?'

'It's nice. The forecast is good. I'll be able to go for a run in the morning.' Dervla paused in her pacing to take a sip of her drink.

'Are those ice cubes I hear?'

'Yes. I'm having a G&T. A large one.'

'You've earned it. You'll sleep well tonight.'

'Damned right.'

There was a pause, then: 'I'd better go, love,' Christian said. 'I've some oenophiles to take care of.'

'OK.'

'But wait. I've got a good one for you before you go.'

'Bring it on.' Dervla took another sip of gin.

'An old man hobbles up to an ice-cream van and orders a cornet. "Crushed nuts, granddad?" asks the ice-cream man. "No," replies the old man. "Rheumatism."'

Dervla laughed. 'Goodnight, darling. Thanks for that. I love you.'

'I love you too. Goodnight, Dervla.'

There was a click and the line went dead, just as a white peacock rounded the corner of the house.

'Look, Kitty!' exclaimed Dervla. 'A white peacock! Are they supposed to be lucky, or unlucky?'

But Kitty wasn't listening. She was off after the peacock, ears stiff with excitement.

Dervla went back into the house. 'Here we go looby-loo,' she said.

The next morning, Dervla slid out of bed nursing a mild hangover. It had been stupid of her to drink gin last night. She wasn't used to it.

In the bathroom, it was clear that the loo had been used. Good. That meant that Daphne had done her morning poo. Dervla flushed away the evidence, then padded into the kitchen, and set about making her mother-in-law's breakfast as per Nemia's instructions.

Grapefruit juice. Tea with milk and one Hermeseta. Toast with butter and marmalade. Chopped strawberries with Crunchy Nut Cornflakes. Except there weren't many cornflakes left in the packet. Dervla poured in what remained and set off with her tray.

'Good morning, Daphne!' she said, breezing into Daphne's bedroom, and setting the tray down on the breakfast table, sliding the L-shaped legs under the bed. Then she moved to the window and pulled back the curtains. 'It's a beautiful day! The weather forecast was right, for a change!'

'Who's that?'

'It's Dervla, Daphne. I'm staying here while Nemia is away. She's gone to Malta on holiday.'

'Oh, yes.'

'Shall I hoosh you up?'

'I can hoosh myself up.' Daphne made an ineffectual hooshing movement, and Dervla took advantage of this to slide another pillow behind her back. Daphne reached for her teeth, slid them in, then picked up her spoon and started to eat the cornflakes. Her expression changed from one of resigned routine to one of thunderous outrage. 'They taste of dust!' she fumed. '*Dust!*'

Dervla almost expected her to add: 'Dust – I tell you! Dust!', and felt a giggle rise. But instead of giggling, she found herself ducking as a spoon came hurtling across the room. Picking it up, she flinched, half-expecting Daphne to hurl the bowl after the spoon, but Daphne sank back against her pillows, and murmured '*Dust!*' again.

'Oh, dear,' said Dervla, determined not to be riled. 'I'd better fetch you a fresh bowl, then, hadn't I?' She picked up the bowl and left the room, then marched across the yard to her own kitchen to fetch Christian's Honey Nut Loops, congratulating herself for behaving with such – what would Fleur call it? Sang froid – that was it, the literal translation of which was 'cold blood'. Dervla decided she would need intravenous antifreeze if she was going to get through the next two weeks.

'Well, Kitty,' she said as she returned to Daphne's cottage. 'Let's hope the Honey Nut Loops do the trick.'

She chopped up more strawberries, added milk and cream to the bowl, and went back down the corridor to the bedroom. In the doorway, she paused.

Daphne was lying back against the pillows, looking as if

254

she was wearing a death mask. 'Dust,' she said again. Oh, God! She was still harping on about the Crunchy Nut Cornflakes. But in fact, she wasn't, because: 'This room is dusty,' she added.

Actually, the room was spic and span. Nemia had obviously done a big cleaning job before she'd absconded.

'And it's very messy,' continued Daphne. 'Why are your clothes strewn all over the place?'

What? For a moment Dervla wondered if Daphne was talking to her, but she'd given no indication that she'd seen her. And there were no clothes strewn over the bedroom floor. What was she talking about?

'Well, Maurice?' said Daphne, in a peremptory voice. 'Do you expect me to pick up after you? I must say that I have no intention of doing so. I did not marry you to be your servant, and if you think I did, then you have another think coming. I *beg* your pardon? Then we are clearly going to have a row. My mother told me that I must never tidy up anyone's mess other than my own. You make your bed, you must lie in it. I am going to pick up the phone to Mother right now and tell her to come over here. I might even get into the car and drive myself to her house. Yes. That is exactly what I am going to do. I am going to drive to Mother's. And when I come back, I want every trace of your clothing hung back in the wardrobe. Is that loud and clear?'

Dervla looked at Daphne with an expression that was half-apprehensive, half-fascinated. She took a step into the room, and Daphne said: 'Who is it?'

'It's Dervla, Daphne, with a fresh bowl of cereal for you.' Dervla set the bowl on the breakfast table, then left the room without a backward glance and went back into the kitchen.

'She was talking to Maurice. Oh, God help me. She was talking to her dead husband. Oh, God. How spooky is that?

Oh, oh, oh – where's the phone where's the phone where's the phone?'

It was on its recharger, on the window ledge. But there was something else there, too. A spider. The biggest, blackest spider Dervla had ever seen.

'Oh, crap, oh, crap. Oh – oh, how do I get rid of it?' she said in a panicky voice.

Dervla never killed spiders. She didn't even find them scary, although if they were really big she'd ask Christian to get rid of them for her. But this arachnid was like a CGI spider from a horror film, and Dervla found herself hyperventilating as she rummaged in the cupboard beneath the sink. She emerged with a can of fly spray.

'Oh God oh God oh God.'

Wresting off the cap, Dervla stretched out an arm, aimed the can at the spider, depressed the nozzle – and suddenly the creature was covered in toxic white foam. It went into a spasm, sprang to the far end of the ledge, shuddered once or twice . . . and then it went still.

Dervla set down the fly spray, then leaned up against the central island. She allowed herself time to calm down, then reached again for the phone.

No! It lived! The bugger made a kind of bouncy movement, and Dervla shrieked and lunged for the fly spray with her free hand, spraying the insect as if it were on fire and she was trying to put it out. The spider went apeshit – like an ink doodle in motion – and then it fell off the window ledge into the recycling bin.

'Oh God oh God oh God.'

Dervla's thumbs twinkled over the keypad as she sped along the hall, heading for the front door. Christian picked up on the third ring. By now she was out in the courtyard, starting to pace.

'Hi. It's Dervla calling from the house of horrors,' she said, trying to catch her breath.

'Oh, God. What's happened?'

'The Crunchy Nut Cornflakes tasted of dust. She tried to brain me with a spoon. She's giving out yards to your dead father for not hanging his clothes back in the wardrobe, she's threatening to drive to her mother's house, and I've just had a close encounter with an arachnid that even her beloved David Attenborough would find repellent.'

'Oh, darling. I'm sorry.'

'I know you are.'

'How are things in the – er – hygiene department?'

'What do you mean?'

'Has she been to the loo?'

'Definitely,' she said with assurance.

'OK.' Christian gave a sigh. He always sighed when he was thinking hard. 'Here's what I suggest. I suggest you leave her alone for an hour. You need some time to yourself. Plug yourself into your iPod and get out your yoga mat.'

'Oh ho!' said Dervla. 'Are you mad? There's no way I'm plugging myself into my iPod while I'm living in this house.'

'But you love your iPod.'

'I know. But I'll need to keep my wits about me in case your mother sneaks up and starts firing missiles at me. Come to think of it, I'd better hide the fly spray in case it gives her ideas.'

'OK. Go for a run.'

A run! A run was exactly what she needed. 'Good idea. I'll go right this minute. Talk to you later, love.'

Dervla went back into the house and cleared away the remains of Daphne's breakfast. She dumped the dishes in the dishwasher, put an audio book on Daphne's CD player, then changed into her running gear. Before she left the house, she put her head around Daphne's door and said: 'I'm off for a quick run, Daphne. I'll be back in half an hour.'

'You may do as you please.'

Dervla swung through the door of the cottage and locked it behind her. Then she called for the dog, who was lying on the doorstep of the Old Rectory, clearly waiting to be let back into her own house. Dervla knew how the poor thing felt.

'Come, Kitty! Come on, girl!'

Together they raced down the driveway, then diverged onto a path that would take them down to the river. Dervla was glad she hadn't bothered with her iPod: it was much more satisfying to hear the rush of the river, the thud of her feet on the hard-packed earth, the ebullient birdsong above. She wondered what it might be like to have your movement restricted, as Daphne's was, what it must be like not to be able to dress yourself or wash yourself, or wipe your own bum. Not to be able to dance or do yoga or vault a gate – as she herself had just done. Not to be free to go wherever on God's earth you wanted to go, not to be able to make love, not to be able to exult in the sheer pleasure of feeling your own body move at full tilt, not to be able to count your blessings.

Dervla ran and ran and ran, as if her life depended on it.

Chapter Eighteen

Poppet and Hero were sitting together on their divan in the library, talking about poetry.

Have you ever read any of Rochester's poems? Hero asked her.

No. Who's he?

I'm surprised you haven't heard of him. Your real-life hero Johnny Depp played him in the film, *The Libertine*.

What's it about?

It's about this bloke the Earl of Rochester, who meets an aspiring actress at the theatre, and sets out to make her a big star.

How romantic!

You should get it out on DVD. Are you still stuck in Lissamore?

Yes.

I don't think the local store would stock it. It's more arthouse stuff.

Poppet stood up and performed a twirl. **Will we visit our cottage tonight?**

I'm not going to be able to stay online much longer. I have a play to go to.

Are you helping your casting friend again?

Yes.

What are you going to see?

A Rough Magic production of *Mother Courage*.

Lucky you. I'd love to be able to go to the theatre.

Actually, she wouldn't much fancy *Mother Courage*. Bethany didn't enjoy political theatre. She preferred the romantic comedies of Oscar Wilde and Noel Coward, or the heady drama of Shakespeare. She performed a series of twirls along the balcony, hoping that by reminding him how well she danced, Hero might realize that he hadn't taken her to Sweethearts since that first time.

When she stopped, she turned to see that Hero wasn't looking at Poppet. He had been joined by a very glamorous avatar, at whom he was blowing a kiss. The avatar was dressed in a full-length red gown with a train and fluted sleeves, and she had green eyes, thick dark hair and magnolia-white skin. Her name was ScarlettO'Hara Sahara, and Bethany disliked her at once. What kind of a stupid name was that for an avatar, and how dare she come and interrupt her tryst with Hero?

'**Good evening, madam, and welcome**,' said Hero, and Bethany suddenly felt incandescent with rage. How dare he blow this ScarlettO'Hara Sahara a kiss when he thought she wasn't looking? How dare he welcome her to 'their' library? She'd teach him. Poppet turned her back on the pair of smirking idiots in a huff, and teleported.

The minute she'd done it, she regretted it. What had she done, leaving her Hero alone with a Vivien Leigh lookalike? Scarlett O'Hara was famous for her craftiness and her flirting skills. What if the green-eyed temptress tried to seduce him? But Poppet couldn't go back now – she'd look like an eejit. Stupid, stupid, *stupid* Bethany!

She got up and went to the window. It was a beautiful

night. The moon was peeking out from behind a mantilla of cloud, like a lovely lady giving a come-hither look, and the sea was gleaming like polished pewter. She was admiring her reflection in the surface, the lovely lady, waiting for the cloud to clear so that she could admire her cloak of stars. The words of a Yeats poem she'd loved at school came back to her:

> Had I the heavens' embroidered cloths,
> Enwrought with golden and silver light,
> The blue and the dim and the dark cloths
> Of night and light and the half-light,
> I would spread the cloths under your feet:
> But I, being poor, have only my dreams;
> I have spread my dreams under your feet,
> Tread softly because you tread on my dreams.

Oh, why had she teleported in a huff? She could have told Hero about the poem. Stupid Bethany. You're back to being bored now, and it's all your own fault.

She left the window, and went back to her computer, to try to find something to amuse herself with. Going to the Eircom home page, she clicked disconsolately on random news items. There was nothing of any interest. If she'd been at home in Dublin she could be curled up on the sofa with her mother watching reruns of *Friends*, but there was no television here in the cottage in Lissamore, and anyway, watching *Friends* on your own was no fun. YouTube beckoned. You could waste hours on YouTube.

What had she used to do, before her parents had allowed her unsupervised access to the internet? She'd played games on her Xbox, but she'd grown out of that now. She'd devoured books as a child – it had been her way of escaping from real life – but she hardly read at all now. She was, she realized, as dependent on Second Life as a means of escape as she had once been on books.

Oh, God. Was she turning into a loser? Would she end up like one of those big fat people who sit around in front of screens and stuff their faces with junk food all day? She couldn't be a loser. She was a well brought-up, well educated girl. She talked about poetry and plays on the internet, not loser crap!

But without Second Life she was feeling a little lost. Maybe she could do some research, find out stuff about the Earl of Rochester to impress Hero with next time they met up. She went to her Google toolbar and typed in 'Earl of Rochester'.

He was, she learned, a famously debauched member of the court of Charles the Second. He had seduced the actress Elizabeth Barry when she was just seventeen. He had written obscene verse, had had a string of lovers both male and female, and he had died of syphilis. His poem – 'A Ramble in St James's Park' – was the most disgusting thing Bethany had ever read. Oh. He wasn't romantic at all. Why had Hero brought him up?

She felt dirty, having read the poem. She'd expected 'A Ramble in St James's Park' to be something lovely and buoyant and pastoral, not the corrupt musings of a sex-addicted sicko, which was clearly what this Rochester had been.

Bethany went into the bathroom and ran herself a bath. Her phone rang, just as she was stepping into it. She checked out the screen, hoping it might be her mother, but a private number was displayed. Bethany never picked up private numbers. She set the phone down on the bath rack, and slid under the water.

As a little girl she'd pretended to be the Little Mermaid any time she took a bath. The film had been her all-time favourite: she adored Ariel, and to her mind the handsome prince was the handsomest of all the Disney heroes. But when she got around to reading the Hans Christian Andersen original, she was shocked to find that it did not have a happy ending. In the Hans Christian Andersen version, the little mermaid sacrifices herself so that the prince may live happily ever after with his human bride. Bethany wished afterwards that she hadn't read the original fairy tale. She wanted to believe in happy endings. Still did – even now. But Bethany knew that growing up meant putting childish things behind her. Her Facebook friend, Flirty, had sent her a new message recently. Something from Simone de Beauvoir . . . *One is not born a woman. One becomes one.*

Bethany guessed that – like Wendy in *Peter Pan*, she had to come to terms with the fact that becoming a woman meant she couldn't fly any more. Or maybe, she wondered, as she reached for the soap, she should try flying in a different direction?

Her mother's dog-eared copy of Erica Jong's *Fear of Flying* was in the bookcase downstairs. Maybe she'd try that as her bedtime reading tonight.

Dervla took a deep breath, and opened the door of Daphne's bedroom. This morning she would endeavour to get her mother-in-law washed. Yesterday, after the spoon incident, she had decided that she'd skip the bathroom bit, but Nemia had told her that Daphne couldn't go more than forty-eight hours without a wash, and Dervla knew she couldn't postpone the ablutions any longer.

'Who's that?' asked Daphne, turning to the door.

'It's Dervla, Daphne. I'm staying here while Nemia is away. She's gone to Malta on holiday.'

'Oh, yes.'

'I thought you might like to have a wash before lunch.'

'What? What do you mean?'

'Well, I've run some water into the basin, and put on the heat in the bathroom, so it's nice and warm for you in there. And after we've had a wash, you might like to go into the sitting room. There's a present waiting for you in there.'

'Who's it from?'

'It's from me.'

'Oh! How kind! Who did you say you are again?'

'I'm Dervla, Daphne.'

'Dervla? *Dervla?* Did you marry someone I know?'

'Yes, Daphne. I married Christian.'

'You married Christian? My son, Christian?'

'Yes.'

'You don't mean to tell me that you two are married?'

'We are.'

'Why did nobody ever tell me? That's great news! I'm so happy to hear that! Well, welcome to our family, Dervla!'

'Thank you. Would you like me to help you out of bed, Daphne?'

'Why do I have to get out of bed?'

'We're going to have a wash, before lunch.' Dervla moved to the chest of drawers and took out a nightdress. 'And I'm going to look out a fresh nightdress for you. Let's see – this one's pretty. You're wearing a white one, so let's ring the changes and wear blue today.'

Dervla tried very hard to sound bright and upbeat, but she was dreading what was coming next.

'What's that you've got wrapped around your head?'

'It's a scarf, Daphne.'

'Aha! Fancy yourself, do you?'

'No. It's to keep my hair back from my face. Now!' said Dervla, pulling back the duvet cover. 'If you take hold of my hands, I'll help you up.'

Daphne reached out and grasped Dervla's outstretched hands. 'Oh! Your hands are like stones!' she cried.

'No worries. It's lovely and warm in the bathroom.'

Daphne was on her feet, teetering a little. 'Which way do I go now?' she asked.

'Through this door, to the right. Follow me.'

Dervla had turned on the electric heater that hung high up on the wall and it was warm in the bathroom. She stood by the basin, testing the temperature of the water. 'Hmm. Yes. I think that's about perfect.'

'What do you want me to do now?' asked Daphne.

'If you stand here, and hold on to the basin, I'll give your face a wash.'

'There are bubbles in there. I don't like soap.'

'It's not soap,' improvised Dervla. 'It's an emollient.'

'A what?'

'A kind of moisturiser.'

Dervla dipped a flannel into the water, wrung it out, then proceeded to wipe Daphne's face. Daphne had her eyes squeezed shut, and her expression was that of someone doing penance. 'There's a thing,' she said, 'on my face.' Raising a bony hand, she pointed at a small growth sprouting from the corner of her jaw.

'Yes, I know. Don't worry about that. Nemia has made an appointment for you with the doctor. She's going to take you to see him once she gets back from Malta.'

'And there's another one, here.' Daphne pointed at a similar growth on her forehead. She must have been worrying at it: it had formed a scab.

'The doctor will have a look at that too,' Dervla told her. 'You must try not to fiddle with it, Daphne.'

'I don't *like* it!'

'No. Of course you don't. But the doctor will take care of

it.' Dervla dipped the flannel in the water, squeezed it, then assayed another gentle swipe at Daphne's face.

'That's enough!' said Daphne.

'Fair enough. I'll get a towel.'

Dervla reached for a bath towel, and handed it to Daphne. 'It's heavy!'

'All right. I'll dry your face for you.' She did so, then draped the towel over a rail. 'Now.' She steeled herself. 'Arms up, and I'll help you off with your nightgown.'

For an awful moment, Dervla thought Daphne was going to refuse to cooperate. But then she raised her arms, and Dervla drew the gown over her head.

Dervla had never seen an old person naked before.

Daphne's skin was as thin and transparent as clingfilm, apart from the skin on her bum, which was leathery, and a mottled purplish colour. Daphne's tummy was like a deflated balloon, her breasts sagged like empty silk purses, and the folds of her sex drooped like some exotic dying flower.

'Raise your arm for me, Daphne, will you please?' Dervla took a sponge, and wiped first under Daphne's left arm, then the right. She wiped the folds under the left breast, then the right. Then she got to her knees. 'Can you part your legs for me?' she asked.

'It's a long time since anyone's asked me to do that!' quipped Daphne, and Dervla managed a laugh.

She did as Nemia had told her to: first front bottom, then back. 'Hmm,' she said, trying not to gag and hastily dropping the sponge back into the basin. 'I think we're going to need baby wipes for this job.'

'Baby wipes! I'm not a baby!'

'I know that, Daphne. But we have to look after your hygiene.'

'Oh – you're such a fusspot! Little Miss Finickity Boots!'

'Bear with me.' Dervla reached for the baby wipes on the shelf, and peeled away three. 'You're very good, Daphne. Very patient. I know it can't be easy.'

She performed the task in silence, and when she had finished, Daphne slumped and said, 'Can I sit down now?'

'Yes. Let me just put a towel on there for you, to make it more comfortable.'

Dervla laid a towel across the seat of a Perspex chair, and Daphne sat down with an 'Oof!' She really did look exhausted. She'd been standing for maybe all of four minutes.

'Now. How about a little talcum powder, to help dry under your arms?' Dervla reached for a tub of baby powder, and sprinkled some onto her palms. Daphne obediently raised her arms, and allowed Dervla to anoint her with the talc before drooping again. 'And now let's get you into a clean nightgown. Here we go.'

Dervla managed to get the collar of the blue gown over Daphne's head, but the armholes were problematic. Sliding her hand inside a cuff, she invited Daphne to take hold of it. That way she could draw first one arm through the sleeve, then the other.

Oh, yay, Dervla! You've done it! she congratulated herself. You're nearly there!

She knelt again, and guided Daphne's feet into a pair of slippers. Daphne's feet were like misshapen claws, the bones jutting out so far they looked as if they might break through the skin. There was a massive bunion on the right foot.

'My foot hurts,' said Daphne.

'I'll mention that to Nemia. She can ask the doctor to have a look at it when she takes you to see him.'

'And I have an itch.'

'Yes. I noticed that you've been scratching yourself.'

There had been red score marks on Daphne's back.

Dervla supposed the skin was so thin that even scratching damaged it now. 'Now,' she said, all businesslike. 'Shall I do your hair for you, or can you do it yourself?'

'I'll do it myself.'

'OK.'

Dervla handed Daphne a wide-toothed comb, and she raked it through her hair. She was a little thin on top, and there were flaky patches on the bald bit. When she'd finished, she handed the comb back to Dervla, who immediately rinsed it under the tap.

'What do you want me to do now?' asked Daphne.

'Here's some moisturiser for your face,' Dervla told her, unscrewing the top of a tub of Nivea. She scooped out a dollop, and transferred it to Daphne's fingers.

'What do you want me to do with it?'

'Rub it onto your face. You can sit there and do your moisturiser while I tidy up. And then we'll go through to the sitting room and I'll give you your present.'

'A present? Who's it from?'

'It's from me.'

'Oh! How kind!' Daphne proceeded to rub her face with the white cream, pausing to inspect the growth on her jaw with her forefinger. 'I don't like this thing on my face!'

'Try not to fiddle with it, Daphne. The doctor will have a look at it when Nemia takes you to see him.'

Dervla moved to the basin, and pulled the plug. The sponge went into the pedal bin, the flannel was rinsed in hot water and folded, and then Dervla washed her hands again and again. She could be Lady Macbeth in the sleep-walking scene, she washed them so thoroughly.

After drying her hands, Dervla picked Daphne's discarded nightie up from the floor. What she found on Daphne's nightie did not make her a happy bunny. She dropped the garment into a plastic bucket, and reached for the long ribbed cardigan that Nemia told her Daphne liked to wear in preference to a dressing gown.

'Now, Daphne!' she said, automatically adopting the bright tone of the professional carer. 'Let's go through into the sitting room, shall we? And then I'll organize lunch for us.'

'Where do you want me to go?' asked Daphne.

'The sitting room.'

'You mumble, you know. It's difficult to hear.'

'Sorry.' Dervla helped Daphne to her feet. 'Let's get this on, first,' she said, angling the cardigan so that Daphne could negotiate the sleeves. 'It's nice and warm in here, but it might be a little chillier in the sitting room. I'll give the heating a boost. The weather's taken a turn for the worse.' She moved to the bathroom door and held it open.

'Where are we going?'

'The sitting room.'

'Which way is it?'

'It's this way. Follow me.'

Dervla started to walk slowly down the corridor and Daphne trailed after her, moving like one of the cast members of *Night of the Living Dead*. When she reached the right turn in the corridor, she halted abruptly.

'Where have the stairs gone?' she asked.

'There are no stairs in this house, Daphne.'

'Oh, yes. I forgot. There were stairs in my old house, weren't there?'

'I think so.'

'I forget these things, you see.'

'It's perfectly natural to forget things at your age.'

Daphne sniffed the air. 'What's that smell? Is something burning?'

'No. It's our lunch. We're having macaroni cheese.'

269

'Oh, good. I love macaroni cheese.'

Dervla flicked the booster switch on the wall to re-activate the heating, and then opened the sitting-room door for Daphne. Now Daphne seemed to have a better idea of where she was going, for she headed towards her chair like a heat-seeking missile. Well, not *exactly* like a heat-seeking missile – more like Wall-E over rough terrain.

'It's chilly in here,' said Daphne.

'I'll put the fire on, until the central heating's warmed up, shall I?' Dervla stooped, and flicked a switch on the gas fire. Then she reached for a blue cardboard box that was sitting on the table beside Daphne's chair. 'Here is your present, Daphne,' she said.

'Oh! Thank you. What is it?'

'It's a bottle of your favourite scent. *Je Reviens.*'

'Oh! How kind.'

'Shall I put some on you?'

'Yes, please. That'd be lovely.'

Dervla opened the box that contained the perfume, unscrewed the little blue bottle and dabbed first Daphne's left wrist, then her right, with *Je Reviens.* 'Did you know that this is the perfume traditionally given by departing soldiers to their sweethearts? Hence the title.'

'What's it called?'

'*Je Reviens.*'

'Oh, yes. "I'll be back."'

Dervla didn't articulate the thought that came into her head, the one that related to Arnold Schwarzenegger as The Terminator. Instead she said 'Mmm!' and put the bottle back in its box. 'How heavenly! We'll have this as a treat every day after your wash, shall we?'

'That'd be lovely! But it's wasted on an old bag like me.'

'You're not an old bag, Daphne. You're my *belle-mère.*

That's French for "mother-in-law", you know. It translates as "beautiful mother".'

She really was labouring at keeping Daphne sweet.

'Now. I'll put your CD player on, so that you can listen to one of your stories before lunch.'

'What are we having?'

'Macaroni cheese. It'll be ready in ten minutes or so.' Dervla inserted a CD into the player, and after a moment or two of white noise, a voice boomed into the room. '*She's got to be killed!*'

'Is that loud enough for you?'

'No it's not. Turn it up a bit.'

Dervla adjusted the volume to an even higher decibel level, and then she said – raising her voice so that she could be heard above the actors bellowing their way through Agatha Christie's *An Appointment with Death* – 'I'll just finish tidying up, and then I'll bring lunch in.'

She left the room, and went to gather up Daphne's discarded night clothes, her demeanour faltering a little. *Stay strong, stay strong, stay strong,* she told herself. She fetched the bucket from the bathroom, then went to check on the bed sheets. The bottom sheet would have to be changed. She pulled the duvet off the bed, then bundled up the sheet. Then she went into the utility room, and reached for the stain removal spray on top of the washing machine.

From the sitting room came the sound of a whistle. Daphne was calling her.

Later that afternoon, Dervla opened up her laptop and went to *How to Sell Your House – What Every First-Timer Needs to Know.* CHAPTER FOURTEEN, she typed. And then she sat and stared at the blank screen for forty minutes, waiting for something to happen while the David Attenborough theme music on the DVD menu mode went round and round on a loop in the sitting room. She'd have to change the DVD – she never wanted to hear that theme tune again in her life.

Getting to her feet, she stretched and yawned. She'd have to think about what they would have for supper soon. Lunch had been a pallid affair. Literally. Macaroni cheese had not been a good idea because the food was the same colour as the plate and Dervla had had to keep spearing bits of macaroni for Daphne. And every time she did so, Daphne would ask what was on the fork. Dervla must have said the words 'macaroni cheese' twenty times.

She closed over the lid of her laptop, and moved down the corridor. Daphne was staring – not at the screen of the television – but at the fish tank, seemingly lost in thought. What might she be thinking, wondered Dervla. Were past memories crowding her brain? Ghosts of lovers, friends and family? And if so, were they pleasant memories or unsettling ones? Nemia had said that going through old photo albums was always a good way of keeping Daphne entertained: she'd left a pile of them on the book shelf nearest the door. Dervla reached for the topmost one.

'Daphne?'

The old lady emerged from her reverie, and adopted an imperious expression.

'Yes. That's me. What do you want?'

'I thought you might like to look at some old photographs.'

'Yes.' She waved a dismissive hand at the television screen. 'Turn it off.'

Dervla zapped the DVD player, then drew a chair alongside Daphne's and set the album on her mother-in-law's lap, open at the first page.

'Look!' she said. 'It's a picture of you! Isn't it extraordinary! What a beauty!'

The photograph was a studio-type portrait, taken when Daphne could have been not much more than sixteen or seventeen. Her unlined face was a perfect heart shape, her mouth curved in a demure Cupid's bow. Her eyes were luminous below sleekly groomed brows, the glossy mass of her hair was held back with a simple ribbon. Her bone structure was exquisite: the nose aquiline, the cheekbones high, the jaw as defined as that of a Modigliani drawing. This face bore no resemblance to the parchment-covered skull that Dervla saw lolling on the pillow every time she entered Daphne's bedroom.

'Yes,' conceded Daphne graciously. 'I was extraordinarily beautiful.'

'Let's look at some more.'

Dervla turned the page to reveal picture after picture of Daphne. Daphne in a feathered cartwheel hat; Daphne modelling Dior's New Look; Daphne looking haughty in a pleated satin evening dress.

She reached for another album. This contained mostly snapshots. They showed Daphne playing tennis; Daphne larking on a beach in a swimsuit; Daphne hiking with a rucksack on her back; Daphne with a party of girlfriends – linking arms and smiling to camera. As Dervla turned page after page she saw more images of a vibrant young woman, the picture of *joie de vivre*.

A third album was devoted to married life. Daphne on her wedding day, decked out in white mousseline; Daphne on a cruise ship, dining at the captain's table, surrounded by much older people; Daphne kneeling before an exquisite doll's house with a little girl; Daphne holding a baby. Christian?

Daphne confirmed it. 'My son, Christian,' she said, gazing at the last page. 'I wish . . .'

'What do you wish, Daphne?'

'I wish I had been a better mother to my children. I didn't want to marry, you see. I didn't want to marry my husband.'

'His name was Maurice, wasn't it?' prompted Dervla.

'Yes. His name *was* Maurice. My parents wanted me to marry him. And in those days you did what your parents thought best. I wanted to marry . . .'

'Who?'

'I forget.'

'But were you happy with Maurice?'

'Happy? No. I was never happy with him. Maurice was old, you know. He was the same age as my father. And I was quite young when I married him – just twenty. I was a virgin, of course.'

'That must have been difficult for you.'

'Yes. I didn't know anything. My mother had told me nothing. All she told me was that I had to do exactly what my husband wanted, no matter how odd it seemed. And it *was* odd. *Very* odd.'

Dervla watched as Daphne turned over a page of the album. There was a photograph of her standing on a terrace, her arm linked with that of a barrel-chested man with a ruddy face and a comb-over, dressed for golf in checked plus fours and a pullover that strained against his paunch.

Dervla felt a sudden surge of pity for the young girl who'd been married off against her wishes, the girl who had missed out on her twenty-something years when she should have been testing her wings, flirting and partying and falling in and out of love every six months or so. This girl who had instead ended up in a marital bed offering her virginity to a man who looked – and possibly behaved – like a bull.

No wonder she had had affairs later on in her marriage. No wonder she had become bitter and twisted. No wonder she had sent the evidence of her intimacy with her husband – her two children – off to boarding school at the earliest opportunity. But, Dervla calculated – Josephine and Christian had been born very late into the marriage. Christian had been just twelve when his father had died. Did that mean that Maurice had not been their real father, that someone else had sired the Vaughan children? Or did it mean that Daphne had mellowed, and that there had been some *rapprochement* between the ill-matched pair? It might be easy to find out. It might simply be a question of leafing through the diaries that Daphne had concealed in the volumes of Dickens . . .

Daphne had turned another page. The photograph on this one showed her with a lean, blond Adonis. He had an arm around her shoulders and was looking into the camera with an amused expression; she was gazing up at him with adoration writ clear on her face. Was this the man she had wanted to marry, the dancer who had died in a fire? Was this her first love? What had happened to him? Had she written about him in her diaries?

'Did you used to keep diaries, Daphne?' asked Dervla.

'Diaries? Yes, yes – I did. But I destroyed them. They were dreadful diaries, really. I was an unhappy creature when I wrote them.'

'Why did you write them?'

'It eases unhappiness, to put things into words. But nobody else should ever be privy to those words. Diaries are not written to be read. That is why I destroyed them.'

'Are you sure you destroyed them?'

'Oh – I hope I did!' Daphne looked anxious now. 'I certainly hid them away somewhere no one could find them.

Dear me – how dreadful that would be, if they ever saw the light of day. I should die of shame.'

'Don't worry, Daphne,' Dervla reassured her. 'If they still existed, Nemia would have found them when she was moving all your stuff from London.'

'Stuff? What is *stuff*?'

'I mean, your things.'

'I think you mean my personal *effects*, don't you?'

'Whatever,' said Dervla, sotto voce.

'Speak up!' commanded Daphne. 'You're a dreadful mumbler, you know.'

Oh, sweet Jesus! *Plus ça change* . . . thought Dervla.

Her eyes went to the bookcase where the complete works of Dickens were aligned neatly on their shelf. She'd take their contents up to her office in the Old Rectory later when Daphne was sleeping, and put them through the shredder. Allowing her mother-in-law to die of shame simply wasn't an option. The diaries had been a record of her life, they had been for her eyes only, and Dervla had no right to pry.

A movement beyond the window caught Daphne's attention. 'When the red, red robin . . .' she sang.

Once, to have added the line about 'bob bob bobbin' along' would have made Dervla feel foolish. This time, she joined in con brio. Christian would have been proud of her.

Chapter Nineteen

In the library on Shakespeare Island, ScarlettO'Hara Sahara was behaving very cautiously. She hadn't spent long talking with Hero last night because he was going to the theatre, he'd told her. It had disturbed her that he and Bethany were still consorting in Second Life, but she was glad to see that they were consorting openly, rather than in that Disney-esque cottage. Bethany had clearly been nonplussed to have Scarlett O'Hara muscle in on her man – Fleur assumed that that was why she'd teleported away last night – but Fleur was determined to protect her. If this man was as toxic as she suspected, she didn't want any of that toxicity rubbing off on a girl who could so easily be frightened, living as she was on her own in that cottage down in Díseart.

This evening Hero was nothing other than gentlemanly. She half-expected him at any moment to come out with some obscenity or display his priapic prowess as he had done when he'd lured Flirty LittleBoots to his cottage, but so far he'd been perfectly mannerly. Maybe it was because Shakespeare Island was a public place, whereas his cottage was private. She knew that people could be expelled from Second Life for abusive or obscene conduct in public places, so it was likely that Hero was on his best behaviour, in case she reported him.

This public Hero was charming, educated, and interested in the things she was interested in: walking, art, music, travel, theatre. He had a GSOH, he loved dogs, he ticked all the boxes. This Hero was very, very clever, and Fleur was determined to let slip no personal details.

Where do you live? he asked her.

Not Sydney, not Paris. Definitely not Lissamore. **Elysium,** she said.

LOL. Nice. What made you choose Scarlett O'Hara?

I'm a big fan of Vivien Leigh.

Me too. Those forties film stars were the most glamorous of all.

I couldn't decide between Vivien, Rita Hayworth or Veronica Lake.

Sad women, all three of them.

He knew his film stars! Forties film stars were Fleur's passion – she could be a *Mastermind* contender on the subject.

Veronica Lake was the saddest case of all, he told her. **She was so broke in the end that she couldn't even cover the cost of her own funeral**.

He really *did* know his film stars! Fleur was impressed, despite herself. She was just about to volunteer some interesting facts of her own about Veronica Lake, when her phone rang. It was Dervla.

'Hey, Dervla,' said Fleur. 'What's up?'

'I just wanted a chat. I'm feeling a bit lonely.'

'Oh – of course! Christian's gone, hasn't he?' Fleur cradled the phone between her jaw and her collarbone, and typed, **Gotta go. RL phone call.**

Adieu, Ms O'Hara, came the response.

'Yes,' said Dervla morosely. 'Christian's gone, and Nemia too, and now I'm all on my own with Daphne.'

Closing over her laptop, Fleur topped up her wineglass. 'You've moved in with her?'

'Yes.'

'How are you getting on?'

'It's tougher than I thought.'

Dervla's voice sounded slightly slurred. Fleur remembered how Río had used to do a lot of drunk dialling when Finn first departed on his travels and she was suffering from Empty Nest syndrome. She hoped the same thing wasn't happening to Dervla. She was glad she'd picked up, glad she was here for her friend when she needed her.

'What age is Daphne now?' she asked, conversationally.

'Eighty-five, and suckin' diesel, as they say. I hope I never get to be that old.'

'Well, "Old age ain't no place for sissies." Bette Davis said that – and she was younger than Daphne when she died. Still, I guess Bette had a better innings than poor Veronica Lake.'

'Veronica Lake? Who she?'

'Oh, don't get me started on forties film stars, Dervla! I'd rather we talked about you.'

'No – go on please. I mean it. It's good to listen to some-body sane for a change. Daphne was reciting nursery rhymes earlier.'

'Well, Veronica Lake was known as the Peekaboo Girl on account of her hairstyle. She was only fifty when she died, destitute.'

'What killed her?' asked Dervla.

'She was a chronic alcoholic. A lot of those forties film stars drank heavily, or were mentally unstable. Frances Farmer's addiction got her locked away in a mental institu-tion, even though she was one of the most intelligent actresses in Hollywood. Tallulah Bankhead died yelling for codeine

279

and bourbon. Vivien Leigh suffered from bipolar disorder, which wasn't helped by her drinking. She died – alone on the floor of her bedroom – at the ripe old age of fifty-four.'

'Vivien Leigh? She was Scarlett O'Hara, wasn't she?'

'Yeah. She was quite exquisitely beautiful, but strangely unsexy. The sexiest of them all had to be Rita Hayworth. She was the ultimate temptress – the Angelina Jolie of her day.'

'How did she die?'

'Alzheimer's and alcohol – at sixty-eight. Most of those stars had dismal private lives, you know.'

'Mine's pretty dismal right now. I've started hitting the bottle, too.'

'Oh, do be careful, Dervla! You ought to be taking care of yourself, as well as Daphne.'

'Don't worry, Fleur. I'll be all right if I keep off the gin—'

'Gin! You never drink gin, Dervla!'

'I know, I know. I'll stick to wine from now on. But that hit of alcohol at the end of the day is such a sweet feeling, I tell you.'

'I feel guilty. I should have been in touch with you before now. Maybe I should call in some evening?'

'No. I'm brain dead by the evening. But you know what would be great, Fleur? If you could come and take me and Daphne out for a drive, or something. I really feel like getting out of here, but there's no way I could manage to get Daphne in and out of the car on my own.'

'Of course I'll come. When would suit? Name your day, and I'll ask Angie to take over in the shop.'

'God – you're so kind!'

'I'm your friend, Dervla.'

'Oh – I'm excited already about being sprung! I feel kind of entombed here.'

'Then you must get some fresh air. We'll go for a walk.'

'Oh. You're forgetting something. Daphne can't walk.'

'She can't walk at all?'

'Well, she can kind of stumble between rooms, but that's the extent of it.'

'No worries. I'll organize a wheelchair. We'll go somewhere glorious, like Arnoldscourt. We can have lunch, and then wheel Daphne around the gardens.'

'I'd love that!'

'I'll book a table for . . . let's see. Sorry – tomorrow's not good. I have a delivery. How about the day after?'

'Can't wait. You're a pal, Fleur.'

'Yes, I am, and don't you forget it. Phone me any time you need me, day or night.'

'I will. Thank you.'

'And stay off the gin.'

'Yes, Fleur,' said Dervla, sounding meek.

'Goodnight, Dervla.'

''Night, Fleur.'

Fleur put down the phone, and took a thoughtful sip of wine. What was the word Dervla had used to describe how she felt? Entombed. Oh! What must it be like to be entombed with a demented eighty-five-year-old? She could understand why Dervla had taken to the gin.

Old age ain't no place for sissies . . . Bette Davis had been one of the lucky ones, Fleur supposed. She thought of all those tragic stars, burned out and abandoned as soon as their looks began to fade. Suicide blonde Carole Landis made her final exit aged twenty-nine. Lupe Velez's Seconal overdose led to her vomiting into her toilet bowl and drowning. Mae Murray ended up sleeping on park benches; June Duprez kept herself alive by eating dog biscuits, and Louise Brooks found work as a salesgirl in Saks Fifth Avenue before turning to prostitution. Beautiful women, all: all victims of ageism. Was it, Fleur wondered, better to get out while the going was good, or to grow old disgracefully? Hadn't Sophia Loren appeared in the Pirelli calendar recently, aged seventy-two? And what about Madonna, several years older than Fleur? Or Tina Turner, who had been strutting her stuff for fifty years? Whatever fate had in store for her, Fleur decided, she ought to live each day as though it were her last. She lunged for the phone and punched in Jake's number.

'Hello, Fleur,' he said, a smile in his voice.

'Hello, Jake. About that drink?'

'Are you free right now?'

Fleur looked down at her chipped toenail polish.

'No. Tomorrow?'

'I've a night shoot tomorrow. Day after?'

'Sorry. That doesn't suit.' Corban was due to visit her this weekend. 'How about this day next week?'

'Cool. In O'Toole's?'

Fleur didn't want to go for a drink in O'Toole's. It was too public.

'I don't think I'd be comfortable with that. Why don't you come to me?'

'I'd like that. What'll I bring to drink? Pink fizz?'

Fleur smiled. How very young he was! 'Pink fizz sounds perfect,' she said.

Dervla woke with a start. What had woken her? She sat up in bed, and listened hard. *Stump, stump, stump*. Uh-oh. Daphne was on walkabout.

Her heartbeat accelerated. How strange, she thought, for a grown person to be afraid of a little old lady. But Dervla knew she had reason to be afraid. She'd noticed, when she washed Daphne, that her charge sometimes looked so testy that Dervla was fearful she might aim a right hook at her. Her mother-in-law was surprisingly strong – Dervla could tell by the way she gripped her hands when she was helping her to get up from a chair. And Dervla hadn't forgotten what Nemia had said to her about Daphne lashing out at her, and pinching her, and giving her Chinese burns in her efforts to wrest the phone from her. She had reason to be on her guard.

Daphne was still stumping, outside in the corridor. The footsteps stopped outside Dervla's door, and she dropped back against her pillows, feigning sleep. She heard the handle turn, and through her half-closed eyes, saw Daphne's face peer around the door like a gargoyle. Dervla lay quite still, certain that Daphne could hear the beating of her heart. Then the old lady shut the door and continued her pacing. What was she doing? Checking to see that she was not alone – that was what Nemia had told her. Who did she expect to find in the rooms she peered into? Her parents? Her husband? Her long-dead lovers? The children she felt she'd let down?

Dervla knew that she wouldn't be able to go back to sleep until the stumping stopped, and Daphne had finished checking on her loved ones. But the stumping didn't stop. Finally, Dervla sat up again and switched on the bedside lamp. She listened hard, trying to pinpoint exactly where in the house Daphne might be. But all had fallen silent.

She slid out of bed, got into her kimono, and went to the door. Outside, an amber lozenge on the floor of the corridor told her that the light was on in the bathroom and she saw through the open door that Daphne's bed was empty. She wasn't in the bathroom, but her nightdress was. It was on the floor, and when Dervla went to pick it up, she realized that it was saturated with wee. She dropped it into the laundry bucket as if it was on fire. Then she steeled herself to go back along the corridor. The light was on in the kitchen, but

283

Daphne wasn't in there. The sitting room was in darkness. Dervla flicked the light switch. Daphne wasn't in her usual armchair, but she was in the one behind the door. Dervla didn't see her until she turned to leave the room, and she jumped out of her skin, with a shriek.

'Oh! Daphne! You gave me such a fright! What are you doing there?'

'I think I have every right to be here, don't I?' said Daphne. She was wearing her slippers and her long ribbed cardigan, and that was all. Her cardigan was pulled tightly around her. 'I need someone to light my fire,' she added. 'I'm freezing cold.'

Dervla shook her head as if to clear her mind of the surreal situation she'd found herself in, then leaned down and switched on the gas fire. It *was* cold in the sitting room. Then she straightened up and looked down at Daphne. Daphne was biting a fingernail.

'Did you have an accident, Daphne?' asked Dervla.

'What do you *mean* by "an accident"?'

'Did you not manage to make it to the loo in time?'

'I don't know what you're talking about.'

'OK. I'd better check this out.'

Before Dervla left the room, she took a backward glance at Daphne. She was sitting very erect, like the Queen at a gala performance, and her eyes were staring into the middle distance. She was still chewing on her fingernail.

In the bedroom, she whipped the duvet off Daphne's bed. It was drenched. Wee had soaked through the sheet and the so-called 'protective' underblanket to the mattress. It had even got onto the carpet. For Dervla, it was a fight or flight moment. She took a deep breath and opted for the former, swinging into action.

She took the soiled bed linen into the utility room along

with the dripping nightdress, loaded the washing machine, and activated it. Then she unlocked the sliding doors in Daphne's bedroom and hoisted the mattress off the bed and out into the patio, where she dumped it against the wall. A pillow was dumped as well.

She diverted into the kitchen and – wearing rubber gloves – came back with a bottle of Dettol and a roll of kitchen towel, a scrubbing brush and a bin bag. After cleaning the carpet, she dumped the cleaning equipment in the bin bag, then moved on to her own room, and started pulling the bedclothes off her bed. When it was stripped, she lugged the mattress down the hall, and heaved it onto the base of Daphne's bed. She stood there for a moment or two, looking at the unprotected mattress. Then she went into her own bedroom, emerging with her yoga mat. This she unrolled and laid upon Daphne's mattress, before setting to and making up the bed with fresh linen.

Finally it was done. Hospital corners and all. Into the bathroom, next, to run a bath. Then back to the sitting room.

Daphne was still sitting up dead straight in the armchair, gnawing at the skin on her index finger. Dervla could tell that she sensed she'd done something wrong, and that she didn't want to be reminded of it.

Dervla looked at her and said: 'Daphne. We're going to have to get you into a bath.'

'What? Don't be so stupid! It's the middle of the night.'

'I know it's the middle of the night, but you've got to have a bath.'

Daphne turned her Medusa gaze on Dervla and said: 'I will *not* have a bath.'

'You don't have any choice, Daphne.'

'I do have a choice. I shall do as I please, and I will not get into a bath at this hour of the night.'

'You will not do as you please. I am trying to help you, and I am simply telling you what has to be done. Once you've had a bath you can get back into bed.'

'I want to go back to bed.'

'I know you do. But you can't go back to bed without having a bath first.'

'Oh, don't be such a ridiculous little fusspot.'

'I am not being a fusspot, Daphne. I am telling you that you have to have a bath for reasons of hygiene.'

'What do you mean? Are you saying that I smell?'

'Yes, you do, Daphne. You wet your bed.'

Daphne went very still.

'You wet the bed, Daphne, and I have put clean sheets on it. Now I need to get you into a bath and into a fresh nightgown. Once you've done that, you can go back to bed and rest.'

Dervla could see Daphne thinking, hard. Then: 'I'll do whatever you say,' she said.

'That's good. We're doing the right thing, now.' Dervla held out her hands, and Daphne got to her feet with an effort. In the bathroom, Dervla helped Daphne off with her cardigan and slippers, then guided her towards her electric bathing chair.

'Now. Sit on there, and I'll lower you in.'

Dervla pressed the button on the control, and down Daphne went, into the foamy water.

'I don't like bubbles,' she said. 'I don't like soap.'

'It's not soap,' said Dervla tiredly. 'It's an emollient.'

'What's an emollient?'

'A kind of moisturiser.'

'Oh.'

Dervla then started to sponge Daphne all over, finally saying: 'OK. We're all done.'

Beyond the window a pallid dawn was starting to make its presence felt: the dawn chorus would start soon.

Dervla wrapped a bath sheet around Daphne, and started to pat her dry. Despite the heat from the electric bar on the wall, the old lady was shivering.

'We're nearly there now, love.' Dervla took a nightdress and dropped it over Daphne's head. Then she negotiated the sleeves. 'Take my hand and follow through,' she said. 'Good. And now the other one. Good. Good girl. Now. You're all set for bed.'

'What do you want me to do now?' asked Daphne.

'You can go back to bed, now.'

'Which way do I go?'

'Out through here, and to your left.'

Daphne shuffled into her bedroom and gave her usual 'Oof!' as she sat down on the bed. She looked nearly as exhausted as Dervla felt.

Dervla lifted Daphne's legs, slid them under the duvet. Then she moved to the door and switched off the light. 'Goodnight, Daphne.'

'Goodnight, Dervla,' said Daphne. 'Thank you.'

Thank you! She'd said thank you. Dervla knew it had cost her to say it. For Daphne to express any form of gratitude after going through something that must have been profoundly humiliating for her indicated that she sensed a kindness had been done. Maybe, maybe, they could pull through this together.

Dervla went back into Nemia's room, improvised a bed from cushions and pillows, and lay down. But she could not sleep.

At around six o'clock, there was movement from Daphne's bedroom. Dervla sat up at once, listening. Then she reached again for her kimono and slipped into it, knotting the sash as she made her way along the corridor.

Daphne was sitting on the edge of the bed, chewing on one of her fingernails.

'Do you need to spend a penny, Daphne?' asked Dervla.

'No. I don't believe I do.'

'Are you sure? I'll help you into the bathroom, if you like.'

'Why should I want to go to the bathroom?'

'To spend a penny.'

'Oh, no. I don't need to spend a penny, thank you very much. I've already spent one.'

Dervla's eyes travelled downward. There was a puddle on the floor.

Chapter Twenty

Fleur usually adored delivery day. She revelled in pulling frock after frock out of boxes, taking a sensual pleasure in the look, the feel, the smell of the garments. The slipperiness of silk, the crispness of organdie, the svelte, pelt-like nap of velour, even the darling little buttons, all combined to make Fleur long to fling the frocks onto the floor and roll wantonly around on them. She had, of course, far too much respect for them to do that; besides, anyone passing the window would surmise that the eccentric Frenchwoman who dressed in forties film star threads had lost the plot completely.

But today Fleur's nerves were a little jangled. Her assistant had phoned in sick, and without Angie to help her unpack, Fleur was working overtime. She'd put up a sign on the door that read 'Closed 'til Midday', but she'd clearly forgotten to lock the door, because the bell tinkled as someone came through.

Looking up, Fleur saw Elena Sweetman standing on the threshold. She was just about to tell her that she wasn't open yet, when something made her stop. Miss Sweetman had to be channelling Jayne Mansfield in *Panic Button*. She was sporting a black beret and slim black trousers, into which was tucked a white French-cuffed shirt. Pearls dangled from her earlobes, and the sexy, summery scent she was wearing was, unmistakably, Balmain's *Vent Vert*.

'Oh!' said the film star, clocking Fleur sitting on the floor in a sea of satin and taffeta. 'I'm sorry. I can see you're busy. I'll come back later.' Her attention was arrested by a charmeuse sheath that Fleur was unfurling from its cocoon of tissue paper. 'Or maybe . . . I could help you?'

'Help me?'

'Yes. I worked in a boutique once, way back when I lived in Little Rock, Arkansas.'

'Like Lorelei in *Gentlemen Prefer Blondes*?'

Elena's eyes widened in delight. 'That's right! I even lived on the wrong side of the tracks. But then, waddayaknow –' Elena's velvety voice went up a register, became a breathless little purr '– I suddenly found myself being wined and dined and ermined.'

Fleur smiled at this meeting of minds. She moved to the DVD player, pressed 'Play', and the sugary voice of Marilyn Monroe came floating through the speakers, crooning 'A Little Girl from Little Rock'.

'Come on in,' she told Elena. 'I'd be glad of your help, if you're absolutely sure you don't mind?'

'I'm sure.' Elena stepped across the threshold and Fleur locked the door behind her. 'I'd actually love to help. It means I'll get a sneak preview of your stock.'

Fleur smiled. 'And the best pickings. Coffee?'

'I'd love a cup. Shall I get started?'

'Sure. There's a box of hangers by the counter.' Fleur moved into the back room to put on the kettle. As she fetched from the cupboard a tin of Illy and a box of homemade madeleines (baked to her mother's recipe), she heard Elena's voice drift through from the shop.

'I love the way you have proper padded hangers,' she was saying. 'Everything about this shop reeks class.'

'Thank you!'

'It's kinda surprising to find a shop like this in a sleepy joint like Lissamore.'

'I make hay while the sun shines. And I hibernate in the winter.'

'What an enviable way to live. Ooh – look ! This is just like the dress Gina Lollobrigida wore on the motor scooter in *Come September*.'

Fleur went back into the shop to see Elena holding up a burned orange cotton dress. 'Isn't it pretty?' she said. 'I would have earmarked that for myself, once upon a time.'

Elena gave Fleur a look of assessment. 'Why not bag it?' she said. 'It's very you.'

'I know. I'd love it. But I'm having to be more cautious with my cash these days. Although, I can't say I'm sorry to see the decline of the economic boom,' she added conversationally. 'I saw a side to human nature that I didn't much care for then.'

'Red in tooth and claw about sums it up.'

As Elena hung the dress on a rail and drew another from its tissue paper nest, Fleur began to attach discreet price tags to tiny gold safety pins. 'How's the movie going?' she asked.

'*Comme ci, comme ça*,' said Elena. 'It's like everything. We have our good days and our bad days.' She shot Fleur an oblique look. 'You have a thing going with Corban O'Hara, don't you?'

'Yes,' said Fleur, surprised. 'How did you know that?'

'Shane told me. He's very fond of you, you know.'

Fleur smiled. 'Shane and I go back forever.'

'You were part of an arty clique, weren't you? You and Río?'

'Yes. You know about Río, too?'

'Well, everybody knows about Río since that *Enquirer* piece spilled the beans.'

Fleur laughed. 'The *Enquirer* is hardly a reliable source of information.'

'For sure. But that rumour has been dogging Shane since his *Faraway* days.'

'Has it done his career any harm, do you think?'

'On the contrary. I think it's been responsible for sparking a lot of interest in him. Every wannabe in LA is determined to be the one who'll finally snatch him from the arms of his long-lost colleen.'

'Are you serious?'

'Yes. It's a perpetual source of speculation for the press. Every time he goes out in public with a hottie on his arm, Perez Hilton's on his case.'

'Poor Shane.'

'We're all stuck between the same rock and hard place in LA. We're damned if they pap us, damned if they don't.' Elena cooed as she held up a periwinkle cashmere sweater. 'Funnily enough, if Shane did end up with his childhood sweetheart, I think his stock would plummet. The tabloids and the paparazzi don't like happy endings. They're like a pack of jackals bringing down a gazelle: the more it bleeds, the more blood they crave.'

'Does all the fuss bother Shane?' asked Fleur.

Elena shrugged. 'I don't think he cares much either way. I've known Shane since we worked on *Faraway* – he's one of the most laid-back individuals in la-la land. And one of the most respected.'

'I'm glad for him. He didn't have it easy in the early days. I guess none of us did.'

'I certainly didn't, coming from the wrong side of the tracks. I'm the first film star to crawl out from under Little Rock since Julie Adams.'

'Of *Creature from the Black Lagoon* fame?'

'Yep.' Elena swooped on a fitted, knee-length dress with a scoop neck and a fishtail, and held it up against her. 'This I gotta have!' she said. 'This is just perfect for my birthday party.'

'When is it?'

'Day after tomorrow. Wanna come?'

'Thank you. I'd love to, but I can't.' Corban was due. Fleur suddenly found herself wondering why he hadn't been invited to Elena's party, but resisted the unmannerly impulse to ask. 'Why don't you go try it on, and I'll bring the coffee out?'

Back in the kitchen, Fleur bit into a madeleine, then spooned coffee into the cafetière, all the time thinking about Shane and how he had spent his life yearning for Río the way Rhett yearned for Scarlett in *Gone With the Wind*. Stupid Scarlett hadn't seen sense until it was too late, and she hoped that a similar fate wasn't in store for Río. Elena Sweetman had spoken of Shane with real warmth, and she fancied that the actress might look very tasty in that scoop-necked dress. She was right. When she went back into the shop with the tray of coffee things, Elena was assessing her reflection in the cheval glass.

'Wow,' said Fleur. 'You look just like Jayne Mansfield in the baby shower scene in—'

Elena finished the sentence for her. '*Promises! Promises!*' she said.

Fleur laughed. Had she found a soul sister in Elena Sweetman? What a shame she couldn't go to the party on Friday. Maybe she should suggest it to Corban, and they could turn up together? But then what would she do if Corban knew nothing about the event, and was miffed that he hadn't been invited? It was better to say nothing. Besides, she hadn't seen him for a while: it would be nice to have him all to herself.

293

Fleur set the tray down and reached for a straw coolie hat that had arrived in the morning's consignment. Setting it on her head at a tilt, she turned to Elena and said: 'Guess who? Clue: *Macao*.'

Elena didn't miss a beat. 'Jane Russell,' she said, with a smile.

Having said goodbye to her NBF, who had left with her party dress sprinkled with rose petals and enfolded in a glossy Fleurissima carrier, Fleur chucked the cardboard boxes into the recycling cupboard and turned the sign on the door to OPEN. Within moments, the jangle of the little bell made her look up from the jumpsuit she was teaming with a silver belt.

'Hello, beautiful,' said Shane Byrne.

'Shane! How are you?' Fleur stood up and presented her cheek for a kiss.

'I'm good, thanks.' He gave the smile of a proud pater-familias. 'My boy is back from his travels.'

'So you're a happy family again?'

'We're so fucking happy we could be a family in an adver-tisement for washing powder. What's that?' he added, nodding at the jumpsuit.

'It's a jumpsuit.'

'Why's it called a jumpsuit?'

'Skydivers wore them, originally.'

'I can't see anyone jumping out of a plane in a flimsy yoke like that. They'd be in their nod by the time they hit the ground.'

Fleur put the jumpsuit on a hanger, and moved to the costume rail. 'What brings you into my emporium, Shane?'

'I want to buy a present for my leading lady. It's her birthday.'

'So I heard. What age is Ms Sweetman?'

'She's not saying, but my guess is she's a deal older than she looks. Random fact: did you know that Americans spend more each year on cosmetic surgery than they do on education?'

'Have you had anything done yourself?' she asked.

Shane looked aghast. 'Fleur! Get real! Don't you know that I have a pathological fear of needles?'

'But there must be serious pressure on you in your industry to look youthful.'

'Of course there is. I swear by haemorrhoid cream for my eyebags.'

Fleur laughed. 'Aren't you embarrassed to be seen buying it?'

'Nothing much embarrasses me, Fleur. I'm an actor. I played a horse's arse once. What keeps you so youthful, beautiful?'

'Good red wine, lots of butter and cheese and the occasional glass of champagne. You know we French women don't get fat.'

'You're a gal after my own heart.'

The phone went. 'Fleurissima: good morning!' said Fleur into the mouthpiece.

On the other end of the phone was a journalist from the local newspaper, wanting to pick Fleur's brains about the current trend for jumpsuits. 'They're incredibly versatile,' said Fleur, segueing into fashionspeak. 'They're perfect for daywear, but can be glammed up for evening with heels and accessories. Stella McCartney does a fabulous one in silk, but it's expensive—'

'How much?' asked the journo.

'Over two thousand euros.'

Shane's eyes widened and his jaw dropped in disbelief,

then, as Fleur blurbed on about jumpsuits, he reached for one of the glossy magazines on the counter.

'What the fuck is going on in the world?' he said, when she'd finished her phone call. 'Take a look at this. One thousand two hundred and sixty euros for a pair of shoes! And see this ridiculous pair of hooves? They don't even have the nerve to give the price. It just says, "Price on request". I thought there was supposed to be a squeeze on.'

'People have to be allowed to dream, Shane.'

Shane shook his head. 'One thousand two hundred and sixty euros could feed a third-world village for a year. It's obscene.'

Fleur didn't like to think about it. The rag trade *was* obscene, but the pleasure she got from examining the detail on a couture gown – while morally reprehensible – was indescribably intense.

'What had you in mind for your leading lady's birthday present?' she asked.

'I dunno. Ooh. These are nice.' Shane was fingering the polka-dotted silk knickers.

'You can't buy underwear for somebody unless you're having an affair with them,' Fleur told him, with authority.

Shane raised an eyebrow. 'Who's to say I'm not having an affair with her?'

'What! Shane Byrne! *Are* you having an affair with Elena Sweetman?'

'Sadly, no.' He gave her a careful look. 'How's your affair faring?'

'With Corban?'

'Hello? Who else?'

Fleur flushed, suddenly. For some reason, she had thought that Shane might have been referring to Jake Malone, with whom, of course, she had no intention of having an affair.

'Fine. I don't see as much of him as I'd like.'

'He's pretty obsessed with his pet project. He's one of the most hands-on executive producers I've met.'

'He is?'

'Yeah. Most of them just hand over the money and let the creatives get on with it. I suspect he's going to want to direct something himself once this is in the can.'

'What makes you think that?' Fleur asked.

'Well, he's kind of a control freak, ain't he? No disrespect.'

Fleur was a little taken aback. *Was* Corban a control freak? He enjoyed the power he wielded, that was for sure, but any Mr Big worth the name played power games.

'"Control freak" is a little harsh, don't you think?' she said.

'Sorry. I guess I don't like taking direction from anyone but the main man.'

'The main man being?'

'The director, of course.'

'You mean Corban tries to direct you?'

'Not just me. He tries it on with Elena, too. We tend to ignore him.'

Oh! Fleur found this information not a little embarrassing. Was Corban unpopular? Maybe she should ask Río what she thought – after all, she was on location every day.

'How about jewellery?' she said, changing the subject. 'Take a look at these earrings – aren't they gorgeous? Or this dinky charm bracelet. Or how about this perfume atomiser? Isn't it sweet? And you can never go wrong with a scarf. Just look at this beauty!' Fleur unfurled a length of shimmering silk chiffon.

Shane was looking at her with amusement. 'You're such a girl, Fleur, aren't you?'

'Unapologetically so.'

'Which option would you go for?'

297

'The earrings.'

'Aren't they a bit *über* dangly?'

'Earrings can never be too dangly or too glittery,' Fleur assured him. 'They draw light to the face and add radiance.'

'I'll take your word for it.' Shane took his card out of his wallet and handed it over.

'You'll be wrapped on the film, soon, won't you?' she asked.

'Yep.'

'Are you heading back to LA?'

'No. I'm thinking of hanging on here for a while longer. I might have a look at some property.'

'It's the right time to buy.'

'Sure is. I'll pick Dervla's brains.'

'If she has any left. She's half demented, you know, looking after her demented mother-in-law.'

'No shit. I thought she paid someone to do that?'

'The carer's gone on holiday. And Christian's gone off to France.'

'Oh, yeah. I'd forgotten. Dervla shouldn't really be taking on that kind of responsibility.'

Fleur nodded. 'That's what I think. But she really has no other option.'

'Why not put the mother-in-law in a care home?'

'Christian won't hear of it. You should pay Dervla a visit, Shane. She'd be delighted to see you.'

'I'll try and find time. You know my mother suffered from dementia?'

'Río mentioned it, yes.'

'Caring's a highly specialized job. I forked out a small fortune to have Ma cared for, and I felt lucky to be able to afford it.'

Fleur sucked in her breath. 'I know it's an awful thing to say, Shane, but sometimes I feel lucky that my parents died when they did, before something like that could happen to them.'

'It's not an awful thing to say. I hope I have the nerve to take things into my own hands when the time comes.'

'Oh!' Fleur shuddered. 'Let's not think about it! Let's think about something lovely instead.'

'Like chiffon scarves. And dangly earrings.'

'And pink poodles. And champagne.'

'Pink champagne?'

Fleur shook her head. 'Not my style. I'm a Laurent-Perrier girl, myself.'

'Nasty Harris is big into pink *prosecco*. The fridge in her trailer is crammed with the stuff.'

Riondo Pink Prosecco Raboso. The label on the bottle that Audrey had chucked into the recycling bin a couple of weeks ago flashed across Fleur's mind's eye. Audrey had said she'd found it in Corban's apartment. Could it be that Anastasia Harris was the woman having the affair with the assistant director? But no. Corban had told Fleur that the woman in question was a local. And then she thought back to what Jake Malone had said to her on the phone last night. *What'll I bring to drink? Pink fizz?* Was Jake the male half of the couple whose affair Corban was facilitating?

'You're looking very thoughtful,' Shane observed.

'Sorry.' Fleur snapped out of gumshoe mode and resumed giftwrapping Elena Sweetman's birthday present. 'I was just wondering about something that Río told me about. I think she called it "Doesn't Count On Location".'

'DCOL, yeah.'

'Affairs are commonplace among movie people, then?'

Shane shrugged. 'Always have been, Fleur. It's a cliché as old as the casting couch.'

'The casting couch? Is that still going on?'

'Yep.'

'Sheesh. I remember the story about Marilyn Monroe. When she signed her first major contract she said, "Well, that's the last cock I'll ever suck".'

'Unfortunately, some poor girls are still doing a lot of cock sucking.'

'*Plus ça change, plus c'est la même chose,*' she said.

'You wha'?'

'It's a French proverb. It means, the more things change, the more they stay the same.'

'Oo-er. That's a bit profound for me. I'm only a dumb actor.'

'Not so dumb, Shane.'

Fleur completed the transaction, then handed over Shane's credit card and the pretty package. She'd taken extra care with the giftwrap, seeing as how the earrings were for a bona fide movie star. Maybe she'd see them on the red carpet some day!

'Thanks, babe,' said Shane. 'And thanks also for the advice.'

'Advice? What advice?'

'About wearing glittery earrings to add radiance to the face,' said Shane, flouncing towards the door. 'Maybe I should try diamanté instead of haemorrhoid cream.'

'You'd look good in earrings, Shane. *Salut*. Enjoy Ms Sweetman's birthday party.'

The bell tinkled as Shane left the shop, then tinkled again a minute later as Río entered it.

'What was Shane doing in here?' she demanded.

'He was buying a birthday present for his co-star.'

'The enigmatic Elena?'

'The very one.'

Río's lip curled. 'Huh. What did he buy her?'

'A pair of earrings.'

300

'Expensive?'

'No,' lied Fleur.

'Hey! You've new gear,' remarked Río, pouncing upon the rails. 'Maybe I should get myself something nice to wear for the wrap party.'

'How about this?' Fleur swung a poppy print tea dress off a hook.

'Ooh! It's sweet,' said Río, holding it up against herself and checking out her reflection in the mirror. 'But is it too young for me?'

'Río, dear one – you are the epitome of the Bob Dylan song.'

'Which one?'

'"Forever young",' said Fleur.

Río laughed. 'Sure, aren't we all going to be that, soon? I had a spam email today telling me I could live a healthy and productive life until I'm a hundred and twenty. Yikes – just think! That would mean that my son would be over a hundred. Could you imagine a hundred-year-old Finn?'

'How is he?'

Río looked thoughtful. 'How is he?' she echoed. 'D'you know, Fleur, I'm not too sure how he is. I think the split with Izzy hurt more than he's letting on.'

'How did it happen?'

'She wanted to go to Dubai, and he didn't.'

'A bit like you and Adair?'

'I guess.'

'What's he going to do now?'

'His father's got him work on the film, as a stunt double.'

'Wow! Is he standing in for Shane?'

'No. He's standing in for the actress who's playing the lady dowager.'

'Are you serious?'

'Yes, I am. She can't ride. So all that donkey-riding and messing about with Coolnamara ponies when he was a kid is going to stand Finn in good stead.'

'Is he going to have to dress up in women's clothes?'

'Yes.'

Fleur laughed. 'I love it! A beautiful piece of beefcake like my godson all dolled up in bombazine. How does he feel about it?'

'No worries. You know Finn. He takes after his father. He's laid-back about most things.'

Río hung the poppy print dress back on its hook, and helped herself to a swirl of turquoise cashmere. 'Ooh,' she said, 'I *love* this cape.'

'Río – may I ask you something?' said Fleur.

'Fire away.'

'Have you had any dealings with Corban on location?'

'No. I'm just the humble set-dresser. Why do you ask?'

'It's just that Shane said something earlier, about Corban muscling in on the director's territory.'

'I guess he's allowed. He is the money man. If it weren't for him there'd be no film and we'd all be out of a job.' Río swung the cape over her shoulders. 'Imagine having that kind of power. Where did he get all his money from?'

'I've never really asked.'

'Maybe he's in the Mafia,' joked Río. 'Wow! Look at this! Can I try it on?' She unhooked a rainbow-hued ruffled silk dress from the rail.

'Sure,' said Fleur abstractedly, and Río disappeared behind the curtain of the changing cubicle.

Maybe he's in the Mafia . . . For all Fleur knew, maybe he was. She realized that, actually, during the six months she'd been dating Corban, she'd learned very little about him. She'd never been to his house in Dublin, which was in an upmarket area of D4. He never talked about his ex-wife, or the girl called Rachel, for whom he had mistaken her on the night of the Tudor-themed ball. He never even talked about his responsibilities as CEO of a group dealing in something called decentralised review aggregation. Fleur didn't even know what decentralized review aggregation meant, and felt far too embarrassed to ask. Corban's private life was exactly what it said on the tin: private. And something told Fleur that that was exactly the way he wanted to keep it.

As she moved towards the counter where her laptop stood, something on the floor caught her eye. It was Shane's credit card. She stooped to pick it up, and as she did so, the bell on the door tinkled again and the owner of the card came through.

'I forgot—'

'Your credit card,' said Fleur, handing it to him with a smile.

But Shane wasn't looking at her. His gaze was fixed upon the vision that was Río emerging from the changing cubicle.

She looked a little nonplussed when she saw Shane. 'What are you doing here?' she asked. 'Back to buy your film star girlfriend more presents?'

'She's not my girlfriend,' he replied. 'And God, you look lovely in that.'

'I do?' Río pinkened. 'Do you think I should buy it? I thought it might be good for the wrap party.'

'I'll buy it for you,' he said.

'You will not, Shane Byrne. I'll buy my own clothes, thanks very much. What do you think, Fleur?'

'I think you should allow Shane to buy it.'

'No. I didn't mean that. I meant, what do you think of the dress? Is it a bit too ruffly?'

'I love ruffly stuff,' said Shane.

'No. Shane's right. It's a perfect party frock.'

'OK. I'll take it, so.' And Río swished back in behind the curtain.

'Here,' said Shane in an undertone, handing Fleur his credit card. 'Take it, quick.'

Fleur gave him a warning look. 'She won't be pleased, you know.'

'Maybe not. But if I do this, she can hardly refuse to dance with me at the wrap party.'

Oh, God, thought Fleur, as she swiped Shane's card. The *National Enquirer* was right. Shane was still smitten.

Chapter Twenty-One

Dervla was on the phone to the doctor's surgery.

'Can you bring your mother-in-law in here?' said the receptionist, after Dervla had filled her in.

'No, I can't,' said Dervla, feeling her cheeks flush with anger. 'I can't get her into a car without help. I need a house call.'

'All right.' The receptionist sounded pissed-off. 'Can you hold, please?'

'Yes.' She would hold for as long as it took.

'Greensleeves' seemed to go on for ever. Dervla felt her anger mounting like a geyser.

Then the receptionist was back on the line. 'We can send a doctor out,' she said, 'but she can't be with you until after surgery hours.'

The geyser subsided. After surgery hours was better than having to shoehorn Daphne into the car.

'Thank you,' said Dervla. 'I appreciate it.'

'And please have a urine sample ready.'

'A urine sample?'

'Yes. Dr Doorley will need to test your mother-in-law's urine. She may have an infection of the urinary tract.'

'Oh, God. OK. I'll see what I can do. Thanks again.'

Dervla put the phone down, resisting the temptation to

pick it up again and call either Fleur or Río. They were busy gals with their own agendas, and Dervla should be handling this herself. She had taken this responsibility on her own shoulders, was being well renumerated for it, and she'd damned well see it through. Swinging into the kitchen, she searched for something with a lid that could serve as a container for Daphne's wee. The only thing she could find was a tin that had once contained handmade chocolates.

She steeled herself, then went into the sitting room, where Daphne was gazing at swans on David Attenborough while simultaneously listening to *Appointment with Death*. 'Make that appointment sooner rather than later,' were the shameful words that went through Dervla's head. Oh, God, God – what was happening to her? She was turning into Ms Bitter and Twisted of Coolnamara. She'd have to start chanting positive mantras when she practised her yoga – except, of course, her yoga mat was now serving as Daphne's mattress protector.

'Daphne?'

'Who is it?'

'It's Dervla, Daphne.'

'Oh, yes. What do you want?'

'I've been speaking to the doctor on the phone.'

'The doctor? What about?'

'About the fact that you might have a urinary tract infection.'

'A what?'

'You might have a problem with your urinary tract, Daphne. That's probably the reason you had that accident last night.'

'What accident?'

'You wet the bed.'

Daphne looked away. Her finger went to her mouth. It

was clear that she had no recollection of the events of the early hours of this morning.

'Not being able to control your bladder is symptomatic of a urinary tract infection, Daphne, and the doctor has asked me to get a sample. She's going to call later today, and she will need to do a test.'

'What sort of a test?'

'She's going to need a urine sample.'

'And are we going to give her one?'

'Yes. You're going to have to pee into this, Daphne.'

'What is it?'

'It's a tin. It used to have chocolates in it.'

'That's ridiculous!'

'Yes.' Dervla managed a smile. 'It is ridiculous. But I couldn't find anything else. How do you feel about spending a penny?'

'Now?'

'Yes.'

'I don't know.'

'If you think you could manage it, Daphne, I will help you.'

'How can you help me spend a penny?'

'I can catch your wee in this tin so that the doctor has a sample to test when she comes later today.'

'Then I'd better do as you say, hadn't I?'

'Yes. Let's give it a go.'

'We'll give it a go!' said Daphne, gamely.

Dervla set down the chocolate tin, and held out her hands.

'Oh! Your hands are like stones!'

'Yes. I have poor circulation.'

Dervla and Daphne left the study and trudged along the well-worn carpeted path to the bathroom. Once there, Dervla helped Daphne onto the loo before donning a plastic glove. *Please, God – give me an out-of-body experience*, she thought.

'Now,' she said. 'This is going to be awkward, but we can do it, Daphne!'

'Yes! We're a team, aren't we, Dervla, you and I?'

'We're a team.'

Dervla hunkered down. 'If you can just raise yourself a little on this side, Daphne, I'll try and angle the – um – receptacle under you like . . . so. Yes. This could work.'

'Do you want me to spend my penny now?'

'Yes. Go for it.'

For a couple of antsy seconds Dervla heard the sound of Daphne's wee hitting the ceramic side of the loo, and then there was the sudden tinny ring of liquid on metal.

'Yes, Daphne! We've done it!'

'Yippee!'

Dervla extricated the chocolate tin from beneath Daphne's bum, checked that there was sufficient urine for a sample, then snapped the lid back on and set it on the edge of the hand basin.

'Well done!' she said, helping Daphne off the loo.

Daphne teetered a little, then grabbed the basin for support. 'Hello! What's this?' she said, her hand hovering over the chocolate tin, making as though to pick it up and open it.

'No, no! Don't touch!' cried Dervla in alarm. 'We don't want to spill all that precious wee!'

'Oh, no!' said Daphne. 'That would be dreadful, wouldn't it? After going to all that trouble! To think that there were chocolates in there once. Nobody would want to eat a chocolate out of that box now, would they?'

'That's for sure!' Dervla was laughing with pure relief.

'Where will I go now?' asked Daphne.

'I think you should go back into the sitting room, don't you? And you can watch David Attenborough until the doctor arrives. But why not take a little rest –' Dervla pointed to the Perspex chair '– while I finish clearing up.'

'Why is the doctor coming? Oof!'

'Because we think that you may have a urinary tract infection, Daphne.'

'Oh, yes. But we were clever, weren't we?'

'Yes. We were very clever to get a sample. The doctor will be very pleased with us.'

'We're a team.'

'We certainly are.'

Dervla stripped off the glove, dumped it in the pedal bin, then washed her hands over and over, Lady Macbeth style. And then she led Daphne back into the sitting room, and turned up the volume on David Attenborough, who was saying: 'For many of the birds, this will be their first journey across the Himalayas, but for some, it will be their last.'

'Enjoy, Daphne,' said Dervla. She reached for a cashmere throw and draped it over her mother-in-law's knees before leaving the room and listing into her bedroom. Then she got onto her makey-up bed of cushions and pillows, and pulled the duvet over her head. Within minutes she was fast asleep.

Ding dong! The doctor was here.

Dervla stumbled to the front door, pulling on a sociable expression.

Oh! she thought, thank God. She could tell immediately that this doctor was lovely. She was younger than Dervla, and she had a crinkly smile and glasses that were not trendy.

'I'm Dr Doorley,' she said.

'Come in, please!' said Dervla. 'Oh, God – I'm so glad to see you!'

'No worries,' said Dr Doorley. 'I'm here to help.'

Dervla led the doctor into the kitchen, and because the woman had such a kind face and seemed so concerned, Dervla started to cry. She told Dr Doorley everything. She told her about Christian and Nemia going away, and about Daphne wetting the bed, and how wrong she had been to think that she might be able to care for her mother-in-law on her own.

And Dr Doorley listened and said, 'You shouldn't be doing this, Dervla.'

Dervla blew her nose and said, 'I know. What do you think the problem is? Will she have to be hospitalized?'

'No. It's almost certainly a urinary tract infection,' said Dr Doorley, 'and antibiotics will clear it up. Will I be able to get a sample, do you think?'

'I've already got one for you. It's in the bathroom.'

Dr Doorley looked impressed. 'Brave of you!' she said. 'That can't have been easy.'

'No,' said Dervla with a mirthless smile. 'I won't go into details.'

'Where's the patient?'

'I'll take you to her now.'

Dervla led the way to the sitting room, tapped on the door, and opened it. 'Daphne!' she said. 'The doctor's here to see you.'

'Who?'

'The doctor. She's here because we think you may have a urinary tract infection.'

'Oh. Yes.'

Dervla stood aside to allow Dr Doorley into the room.

'Hello, Mrs. Vaughan. I'm Dr Doorley,' she said, hunkering down beside Daphne's armchair.

'Oh, hello,' said Daphne, proffering a regal hand. 'How do you do? It's a pleasure to meet you.'

'Thank you,' said Dr Doorley. 'How are you feeling, Mrs Vaughan?'

'I'm feeling perfectly fine, thank you. It's very kind of you to enquire after my health.'

'No pain anywhere? No discomfort?'

'None at all.' Daphne smiled benignly. It was a beautiful performance, thought Dervla. She was the picture of the gracious dowager.

'May we have a little chat?' asked Dr Doorley, taking a pen and a notepad from her bag. 'I'd like to ask you some questions. I have a form here that I'm going to fill in – a kind of questionnaire.'

'Certainly. I love doing questionnaires.'

'Now. First question. Your name is?'

'Daphne Beaufoy,' said Daphne, giving her maiden name without hesitation.

'Mmm-hmm. And your address?'

The address in Coolnamara that Daphne gave was completely unfamiliar to Dervla. It must have been her childhood home.

'And can you tell me, Daphne – I may call you Daphne, may I?'

Daphne considered, then nodded her head once, as if bestowing a favour.

'What season of the year is it?'

'It . . . it's winter.' Daphne knew immediately that she'd made a mistake. Her eyes went to the window. 'But to judge by the weather,' she amended gamely, 'you'd almost think it was summer!'

Wow. Dervla was impressed. Daphne was like a swan paddling like hell beneath the surface to maintain that illusion of serenity, so afraid of being perceived to be non *compos mentis* that she was working her ass off to appear clued-in.

311

'And can you tell me who our current Taoiseach is, Daphne?' asked Dr Doorley.

'Cosgrave!' she announced triumphantly, citing the name of a man who had been Taoiseach decades ago, and who was now dead. 'I'm very interested in politics, you know.'

'And who is this person?' Dr Doorley indicated Dervla, who was still standing by the door.

'That person,' said Daphne, 'is . . . not as stupid as she looks.'

Dervla felt like applauding her mother-in-law. What an inspired answer!

'Very good!' said Dr Doorley, putting away her pen and notepad. 'Now. Dervla here tells me that you had a little accident.'

'An accident?'

'Last night, Daphne.' Dervla was careful not to say 'Remember?' If she did, that would imply that Daphne had forgotten the 'accident', and if Daphne was confronted with proof of her completely non-existent memory it would upset her. 'Actually, it was very early this morning,' Dervla continued. 'When you didn't make it to the loo in time.'

'Oh, yes.' It was impossible to tell from Daphne's expression whether or not she really remembered, or if she was bluffing. 'That was dreadful, wasn't it?'

'Yes, it was. And we don't want it to happen again. So Dr Doorley's going to do some tests.'

'What are you going to do to me?'

'I won't need to do anything to you,' said Dr Doorley, 'because Dervla tells me that you've been very forward-thinking and have a urine sample all ready for me.'

'Oh, yes!' Daphne beamed. 'We thought that would be a good idea, didn't we? Dervla and I are a great team.'

'Yes,' said Dervla. 'So Dr Doorley and I are going to go to the bathroom now.'

'Why do you need to go to the bathroom?'

'Because that's where the urine sample is.'

'Oh, yes.'

'But I'll bring you a Cornetto first, Daphne, because I stupidly forgot to bring you your tea and little pancake this afternoon.'

'I'd love something to eat. I'm very hungry, you know.'

Dervla zapped the TV on. '*Inspector Wexford*! Yay!' she enthused, before ducking into the kitchen for a Cornetto. She peeled the wrapper halfway down for Daphne and then she and Dr Doorley departed on their assignation to the bathroom.

'It's in here,' said Dervla, holding up the chocolate tin.

Dr Doorley smiled. 'Interesting choice of receptacle,' she remarked.

'I searched the place high and low for a jam jar with a lid before I came across this.'

Dr Doorley poured a small amount of the sample into a phial, and then did deft things with a little stick. 'Yep. Urinary tract infection,' she pronounced finally, squinting at the stick.

Dervla looked stricken. 'But I try to be so careful with her personal hygiene!'

'Don't blame yourself. It happens a lot at this age. The skin is so thin.'

'She – um. Most mornings there's a little excrement on her nightdress. I suppose it migrates south.'

'That'd do it every time.' The doctor tucked the phial with Daphne's urine sample into a plastic bag. 'I'll send this off for tests, and write a prescription for antibiotics when I get the results next week. In the meantime I have some broad-spectrum antibiotics that I can let you have. These should help.' She rooted in her bag, and produced a blister pack. 'Twice a day, after meals.'

313

'How long before they start to kick in?'

'Two, maybe three days.'

'Oh, God. So there could be more accidents in store?'

'It's a possibility. Have you nappies, or padded pants?'

Dervla slumped. 'Yeah. But the usual carer says she kicks up a stink if she's made to wear them. Oops. Sorry. The pun was unintentional.'

Dr Doorley laughed. 'Try telling her that the doctor insists that she wear them until the infection clears up. Those two words – *The Doctor* – have a lot of authority.' She snapped her bag shut, and left the room. Dervla followed her along the corridor, not wanting her to leave.

'Will you have something before you go?' she said. 'A cup of tea or coffee?'

'No, thanks,' said Dr Doorley. 'I've a baby to get home to.'

'Oh! Lucky you!' What would Dervla have given to have a baby's nappies to change, rather than the nappies of an eighty-five-year-old!

'Any problems, give us a call,' said Dr Doorley, when they reached the front door. 'And remember to look after *yourself*, too.'

'Thank you. I will,' said Dervla, gratefully. 'You're very good.'

She let the doctor out, then went back into the sitting room.

'Did you enjoy *Inspector Wexford*, Daphne?' she asked.

'Yes. Who was that you were talking to?'

'The doctor who was here to check out your urine sample.'

'Oh, yes.'

'You have a urinary tract infection, Daphne. That's why you had the accident last night.'

'Oh.' There was a flicker that told Dervla she remembered something. 'Oh, yes. That was dreadful, wasn't it?'

'Yes, it was. Truly dreadful. And we don't want it to happen again. So *The Doctor* has suggested that you wear pants with pads in them, until the infection clears up. I think it's a good idea, and I think you should get into them now.'

There was a silence, and then Daphne said: 'All right. Whatever you say.'

'We'll go to the bedroom, and put them on there.'

In the bedroom Dervla took a pair of padded pants from a drawer, knelt at Daphne's feet, and took off her slippers. 'Here we go,' she said, manoeuvring Daphne's feet into the elasticated pants, then drawing the garment up as far as her knees. 'Now – if you stand up, I'll lift your nightdress, and you can pull them up yourself.' Daphne did so. 'By the way, *The Doctor* says it's a good idea to keep them on at night, until the urinary infection clears up.'

'All right. I'll get into bed now, shall I?'

'No, no. It's not bedtime yet. I'll go into the sitting room and put a new David Attenborough DVD on for you. I'll call you when it's ready to go.'

And off Dervla went, feeling like a zombie in *Groundhog Day*.

Once Daphne was settled in front of David Attenborough, Dervla shambled back into the bedroom to air it a little. She was distracted by her own haggard reflection in the mirror on Daphne's dressing table, surprised to see that she had definitely lost weight. Maybe she should open a weight-loss clinic here, she thought: "Spend time looking after Mrs Daphne Vaughan and we guarantee the weight will drop off as if by magic." Ha ha. Gillian McKeith eat your heart out.

Her gaze dropped to the objects littering the surface of the dressing table. Christian had told her that it was important for Daphne to have familiar objects around her as reassurance – her handbag, her glasses, old house keys,

315

her wallet, with a little cash in it. Here on the dressing table was a dusty address book, full – Dervla conjectured – of the addresses and phone numbers of dead people. There was a silver-backed hand mirror that she didn't suppose Daphne looked into any more, along with a powder compact, and a lipstick. Christian had told her Daphne had once been such an expert at putting on lipstick that she could do it without the aid of a mirror. There was a photo in a worn velvet frame. Behind the flyblown glass two young people regarded the camera solemnly. The man was wearing a top hat, the woman a wedding veil. Daphne's parents on their wedding day, Dervla surmised. Their daughter hadn't been born when this photo was taken. She wondered if Daphne's parents had ever dreamed they would have a baby who would be back wearing nappies at the age of eighty-five. She wondered how Daphne's mother had ended up. Daphne thought her mother was still alive, of course. While watching the news the other night, a feature about bereavement support had come on, and Daphne had said: 'I don't know how I'd cope with the death of my parents. They're all I've got, you know.'

It had made Dervla feel oddly glad to know that her own parents were really and truly dead, and would never be inveigled into the twilight zone that Daphne inhabited. She picked up the phone to her rock, Christian, and told him all about her day.

'You star! How did you manage to get hold of a sample?'

'I don't know. Whatever fighting spirit got me through last night, when she wet the bed. Maybe it's my beloved mama, watching over me still.'

'I don't know what to say to you. I'm speechless with admiration. You know what you have, girl?'

'What do I have?'

'You have pluck.'

Tears sprang to Dervla's eyes. 'No, I don't, Christian,' she told him. 'It's all bravado. I'm on the ropes now, completely wrung out. I'm sorry – so, so sorry, I know I sound like a wimp but you're going to have to organize a home for her – it's time the health-care professionals were called in. It's not fair on Daphne and it's not fair on me. All the money in the world isn't worth what this job is doing to me. And it won't be fair on Nemia either, once Daphne's fully incontinent. And you know that that day can't be too far away.'

There was a pause, then: 'OK. I'll make some phone calls when I get back,' said Christian.

The awful resignation in his voice made Dervla start crying in earnest. 'I'm sorry, love. I really am. I thought I could make this work, but it's no good. I'd rather get a job stacking shelves somewhere.'

'There there,' said Christian, and he kept saying it over and over until her sobs had dwindled into snuffles. Then he adopted a more matter-of-fact tone. 'Are you looking after yourself?' he demanded. 'Are you eating properly?'

'No,' she said. 'I've lost my appetite. I had to resort to your mother's emergency Complan today. Actually, it wasn't bad. If I mixed a little gin in it, it might taste even better.'

Christian laughed. 'I'm glad to see your sense of humour's still intact.'

'It's keeping me sane. Bring on those black jokes.'

'I have one. Here goes: Three old men are talking about their aches, pains and bodily functions. One seventy-year-old man says, "I have this problem. I wake up every morning at seven and it takes me twenty minutes to pee." An eighty-year-old man says, "My case is worse. I get up at eight and I sit there and grunt and groan for half an hour before I finally have a bowel movement." The ninety-year-old man says, "At seven I pee like a horse, at eight I crap like a cow."

"So what's your problem?" ask the others. "I don't wake up until nine," he replies.'

Dervla made an effort to laugh, even though she hadn't really been listening. After she put the phone down on her husband, she headed to the kitchen and mixed four heaped dessert spoons of Complan into a glass of milk. Studying the info on the side of the pack, she wondered how much of the stuff she'd get through before matters were resolved. And then she thought some more about Christian's joke, and started to smile. Forget about the gin, forget about the Complan. Black humour and a man with a generous spirit were what were going to get her through this season in hell.

Chapter Twenty-Two

That evening, Fleur phoned Dervla to arrange a time for their jaunt to Arnoldscourt the next day. Dervla's voice sounded strained, but she didn't appear to have been drinking, and she assured Fleur that all was well.

'Have you managed to get much work done on your book?' Fleur asked.

'Are you joking? Looking after Daphne is a full-time job. Oops. Gotta go. She's calling for help. I'm always terrified that I'll go into the room and find she's fallen.'

'OK. Off you go, beauty.'

As Fleur put the phone down, she spied Dervla's binoculars hanging from the back of one of her patio chairs. She'd have to remember to return them tomorrow – she'd forgotten last time they'd met up. *Merde!* She'd miss her newfound hobby of spying on the village.

Raising the binoculars to eye level, she scanned the main street. Hmm. It looked as if shenanigans were going on again in Corban's apartment. Those curtains had definitely not been closed earlier today. Amused, she dialled his number.

'Well, hello, *Monsieur*. Your pals are up to more hanky-panky in your penthouse.'

'How do you know?'

'The curtains are closed.'

319

'Oh? Do me a favour, Fleur, and ask your cleaning lady to pay another call tomorrow, will you?'

'Will do.' Fleur took up a pen and wrote 'Phone Audrey' on a Post-It. 'I'm taking the day off tomorrow, and going to lunch in Arnoldscourt.'

'They're shooting some of the film there. I have to confess I've never visited the place.'

'Oh – it's beautiful. I must take you there someday, Corban. It's a big Palladian mansion with the loveliest gardens, open to the public. They do a very good lunch.'

'Good for you. You deserve to treat yourself.'

'I'm not sure how much of a treat it's likely to be. I'm actually taking Dervla's *belle-mère* along.'

'*Belle-mère*? Beautiful mother?'

'In French, it translates as mother-in-law.'

'How lovely. Talk French to me, Fleur. *Qu'est ce que tu portes, ce soir?*'

So Fleur spent the best part of twenty minutes sweet-talking her sweetheart, and when she put the phone down, her attention was drawn to the reminder on her Post-It pad to phone Audrey on behalf of the amorous duo in Corban's penthouse.

'Hello,' she said into the phone. 'Is Audrey there?'

'No. she's not, Fleur,' came a man's voice – Audrey's husband. 'She's gone up to Dublin to visit her mother in hospital.'

'Oh, I'm sorry to hear that. When will she be back?'

'There's no way of telling. Her ma's real sick.'

'Please send my sympathy.'

'Will do.'

Fleur put the phone down. Should she call Corban and tell him that there was no cleaner available? No. She couldn't be bothering Mr Big with mundane domestic matters. She'd overcome her aversion for housework, don her Marigolds and do the job herself.

The next day dawned bright and beautiful. Well, Fleur – being a night bird – didn't actually see the dawn, but by half-past nine when she took her coffee onto her deck, the sun was climbing steadily towards the zenith. She'd have to lash on SPF 50: the heat would be at its most intense when she picked up Dervla and Daphne at midday.

Before she'd gone to bed last night, she'd had a quick canter around Second Life but there'd been no sign of Bethany, and no sign of Hero. On Facebook, Fleur was glad to see that Bethany had garnered more friends. Maybe, if the girl befriended more people she'd lose interest in her virtual life, and pay more attention to her real one. But were those Facebook people real friends? Or just self-publicists? The same faces seemed to come up again and again, and some of the banalities were – well, truly banal. Did Bethany really need to know that someone called Trixie had visited Boots and knocked down a display of toothbrushes? Was she supposed to be tickled pink by the fact that somebody's baby's first word was 'poo'? Or concerned that the house of a girl called Janet had become infested with ants? Did she really want to look at five hundred and fifty-seven photographs of an up-and-coming DJ and his girlfriend?

Merde! Fleur was too old for Facebook. She was too old for Second Life. She was too old for toyboys. Maybe she should stop trying to embrace her inner child, and embrace herself, warts and all. Well – she'd draw the line at warts.

Draining her coffee cup, she went upstairs to shower.

Dervla had served Daphne breakfast in bed. She'd washed and dressed her, and done her hair, and now Dervla was sitting out by the water feature in the courtyard, waiting for Fleur to arrive, Kitty by her side. Thank God she had Kitty to talk to!

'D'you know something, Kitty?' she said. 'I always thought I was a good person. I mean, I know I don't go to church, but I've never hurt anyone intentionally, and I've never stolen anything, and I've never broken a law apart from trespassing sometimes in my estate agent days. So why am I thinking such bad thoughts? I know I said to Fleur last night that I'm scared I'll go into a room and find that Daphne's fallen over, but actually, sometimes I wish she would fall over. Because when old people fall over, they break something, and then very often they get pneumonia, and then they die. And do you know, Kitty, what pneumonia used to be called? It used to be called "the old man's friend", because at last the old person was being put out of his or her misery. But now nobody gets pneumonia any more, because of the flu jabs they give out every autumn. And Daphne won't ever die of an infection because she'll be prescribed antibiotics that didn't exist once upon a time.'

Kitty cocked her head sagely.

'I wonder how many women of my age are doing exactly what I'm doing, Kitty, without even getting paid for it?' continued Dervla. 'I wonder how many forty- and fifty- and sixty- and even seventy-year-old women are caring for their parents? Maybe loads of these women have just finished rearing a family, and have been looking forward to their so-called "Golden Years", and getting to enjoy their grandchildren. Maybe loads of them had babies late in life now that IVF is so commonplace, and are still rearing infant children? And maybe in the not-too-distant future, fifty-something-year-old women will be breastfeeding their babies and spoon-feeding their mammies at the same time.

Do you know, Kitty, I read just recently that a sixty-six-year-old has given birth thanks to IVF.'

She glanced down to see that Kitty was looking aghast.

Dervla laughed, and rubbed her velvet ears. 'I'm sorry, doggy. That was some polemic. I'm prone to them. If Christian were here, he'd tell me I should go into politics. Cheer up, now, and I'll give you your grub. Oh! Here's Fleur.'

As Fleur's sexy little Karmann Ghia rounded the corner of the driveway, Dervla led Kitty back to the Old Rectory. The dog hadn't adapted well to living in Daphne's cottage, sleeping fitfully and growling at imaginary burglars, so Dervla had decided to allow her to sleep in the kitchen of the big house. She was glad of her company during the day, though, because Kitty was such an excellent listener. And, of course, the phone calls with Christian helped, and Río had checked in on her every other evening on her way home from location, and Shane had phoned last night and promised to visit, and now Fleur was ferrying her off to lunch and – all things considered – Dervla was getting there. She had just one more week to go, and then Nemia would be back.

She refilled Kitty's bowl, checked to see if there were any messages on the landline, then joined Fleur in the stable yard. Fleur was looking fabulous as usual, in a flounced black-and-white polka-dot dress, and when Dervla told her so Fleur said, 'Well, thank you! Today I am channelling Rita Hayworth in *Lady from Shanghai*. Here are your binoculars.'

'Thanks. Today I am channelling Dobby the House Elf,' replied Dervla, taking the binoculars, 'and Daphne's channelling the Wicked Witch of the West. She's in a vile mood. Come and meet her.'

Dervla led the way into the house and through to the sitting room, where Daphne was sitting with her teeth beside her on the occasional table.

Quickly, Dervla grabbed a tissue, seized the teeth and – with a brusque 'Excuse me!' to a surprised Fleur – carried them off to the bathroom like a hard won trophy. This was only the third opportunity she'd had to clean Daphne's dentures and she set about the chore vigorously, donning a disposable glove and scrubbing with a toothbrush, keeping her eyes averted all the while. The teeth could not be considered an object delightful to behold by anyone – with the possible exception of Damien Hirst or Tracey Emin. Come to think of it, Tracey Emin would *love* Daphne's bed, thought Dervla. Maybe she should take a photograph of it and send it to Charles Saatchi? Daphne's unmade bed could fetch a fortune at an art auction.

Job done, Dervla returned with the teeth to the sitting room, where Daphne and Fleur were conversing in French.

'*Elle a la figure d'une bonne congédiée,*' Daphne was saying, '*et un regard très, très mauvais.*' Well, hell. Dervla didn't have much French, but it would appear that Daphne's mastery of *la langue française* was more adroit than her English.

'*Mais, non, Madame,*' answered Fleur. '*Elle est tout simplement fatiguée.*'

Daphne gave her an autocratic look. '*Savez-vous où habitent mes parents?*'

Fleur and Dervla exchanged glances. Daphne was asking Fleur if she knew where her parents lived.

'*Je regrette que non, Madame,*' said Fleur.

'Are we ready for our jaunt, Daphne?' Dervla interjected, with exaggerated cheeriness.

'Jaunt?'

'Yes. We're going to Arnoldscourt for lunch. Do you need to spend a penny before we go?'

'No, I do not need to spend a penny.'

Dervla felt insouciant: it didn't matter either way. Dr

Doorley's psychological trick had worked a treat: any time Dervla came out with those three magic words '*The Doctor says*', Daphne had become uncharacteristically acquiescent. Last night she had kept her incontinence pants on, and this morning after Dervla had washed her she'd allowed herself to be manoeuvred into a fresh pair. And there was a spare in Dervla's tote bag, 'just' – as Nemia had once so memorably said – 'in case'.

Dervla discreetly handed Daphne her teeth, and between them, she and Fleur got the old lady out of her chair, through the front door, and into Fleur's car. Dervla was glad to be allowed to sit in the back, even though the back seat of the Karmann Ghia was as narrow as a shelf. As they bowled down the drive, she let her head fall back against the leather upholstery, listening to Fleur and Daphne sing '*Sur le Pont d'Avignon*' and '*La Vie en Rose*', and soon she was fast asleep.

She was woken by Fleur gently shaking her. 'We're here,' she said. 'Daphne's complaining that she's hungry.'

'Oh. Right.' Dervla rubbed her eyes. What was wrong with her? She *never* fell asleep during the day. She knew now that when in the past she'd complained of being exhausted after a hard day's work, she simply hadn't known the true meaning of the word. She slid her legs out of the car, feeling as if they were made of lead, and helped Fleur lever Daphne out of the front.

'What's the story with the wheelchair?' she asked Fleur.

'I reserved one when I booked the table. We can take her around the gardens after lunch.'

Lunch was excellent. Dervla had a plate of tapas and Daphne had lasagne, and Fleur had herb-crusted cod, which she pronounced delicious but wasn't able to finish because Daphne sneezed on it. And a baby burst into tears when Daphne smiled at it. And Fleur and Dervla got a fit of the giggles when Daphne peered at the waiter and said, 'How do you . . . Long John Silver?' But aside from that, lunch was uneventful. After cappucinos (Daphne sipped hers from a teaspoon), they went out into the garden where a wheelchair was waiting for them.

The gardens were ablaze with scarlet flame creeper, magenta salvia, and free-flowering rambling rose. Dervla hadn't had much interest in things floriferous until she'd moved into the Old Rectory, and had looked to Río for her help, because Río knew more about gardens than anyone else in Lissamore. She remembered how she had pictured life in the Old Rectory once, how she'd imagined herself dressed in white linen, drifting around a garden with a basket on her arm, plucking flowers – old-fashioned ones like lupins and dog roses – that she would arrange later in the kitchen with the help of her rosy-cheeked house-keeper. What a joke!

Dervla and Fleur wheeled Daphne between geometrically laid-out flowerbeds and lawns that sloped down a steep incline to a central walk. There were lots of other old people being pushed about in chairs, and Daphne was clearly deter-mined to distance herself from these ambient geriatric types, because she insisted on talking to Fleur very loudly in French. '*Qui sont ces vieux gens?*' '*Pourquoi suis-je dans cette chaise roulante?*' '*Regardez cette vieille! Elle a un visage à faire peur!*' And then she would laugh very loudly, and turn her face up to Fleur and smile. She was clearly entranced by Fleur's Frenchness, and Dervla felt a rush of gratitude to her friend for taking over all the small talk and letting her off the hook for the afternoon. It felt good to stroll in the sun.

Rounding a corner, they were confronted suddenly with a bizarre spectacle. A courtyard had been cordoned off, where cameras and lights and sound equipment were being set up.

People in sunglasses were contriving to look cool and business-like at the same time, and a posse of horses was surmounted by ladies in riding habits and men in red coats.

'What's going on?' said Dervla.

'It's *The O'Hara Affair*,' said Fleur. 'And look – there's Finn!'

'Finn?'

'Yes. See? He's the one on the big black horse.'

Dervla followed the direction in which Fleur was pointing. Her nephew Finn was sitting side-saddle on a stallion. He was wearing a billowy black skirt, a riding coat and a topper with a veil.

'What's he doing in women's clothes?' Dervla asked.

'He's a stunt double,' Fleur told her. 'Shane got him the job.'

Dervla laughed. 'But he looks ridiculous! Finn! Finn!'

Finn turned, and, spotting them, vaulted off the horse's back, handed the reins to the wrangler, and strode towards them, his veil streaming out behind him.

Dervla ran to him. 'Hey, honey! I didn't know you were into cross-dressing!'

Finn wrapped his arms around her and gave her a big bear hug. 'Hey, auntie,' he said, looking down at her with his best smile. 'How's it going? Good to see you.'

'Come and say hello to Fleur,' said Dervla, 'and allow me to introduce you to my august mother-in-law.'

'Hi, Fleur,' said Finn, drawing abreast with Fleur and the wheelchair that contained Daphne. But the minute Daphne caught sight of a man in a black top hat and veil and what looked like an undertaker's outfit, she shrieked, 'Death!', propelled herself backward, and took off down the hill.

Because the slope was terraced, it was like watching something being replayed over and over in slow motion. Daphne

327

slalomed down one terrace, then skidded to a virtual halt before toppling over the next one.

'Daphne!' screamed Dervla, sprinting in hot pursuit. But Finn got there first. Daphne had parted company with the wheelchair halfway down the last embankment and was lying on the grass gazing serenely up at the sky. She didn't appear to be fazed at all.

'How did I get here?' she asked.

Finn hunkered down beside her. 'My name is Finn. I'm an Emergency First Responder. Can I help you?' he said.

Daphne looked at Finn and smiled. 'Yes, you may. I'm pleased to meet you.'

'What's your name?' he asked.

'My name is Earl.'

Finn looked at Dervla. 'She's confused. She may be concussed.'

'Not necessarily,' Dervla told him, fishing wildly in her bag for her phone. 'She often comes out with things like that.' Dervla dialled, shouted, 'Ambulance!' into the mouthpiece, then gave details to the service provider. 'Please be quick!' she begged. 'She's a very frail old lady.'

By now, Daphne's tumble had attracted quite a crowd. People were milling around, proffering advice.

'Put her in the recovery position!'

'Don't move her!'

'Loosen her clothing!'

'Is her airway blocked? She may need mouth-to-mouth resuscitation.'

'Are all these people here for me?' said Daphne. 'Help me up, young man, so that I may address them.'

'I don't think you should move, Daphne,' said Dervla.

'I'm perfectly fine. I just took a tumble. That's perfectly normal at my age. I'm eighty, you know.'

'Please don't move, madam,' said Finn. 'Not until the ambulance gets here.'

'An ambulance is coming? For me?'

'Yes.'

'What fun. I've never been in an ambulance before. Nenagh, Nenagh.'

Daphne continued to gaze up at Finn, who was removing his riding coat. Underneath, he was buff in a black T-shirt. He rolled the coat into a compact bundle, and handed it to Dervla. 'Put that under her head,' he said, as he gently took Daphne's face between his hands. Dervla did as she was instructed, and watched as Finn carefully laid the old lady's head upon the makeshift pillow.

'Why are you wearing a skirt?' Daphne asked him. 'Are you homosexual?'

'No.'

'I think you call homosexuals "gay" now, don't you? I think it's rotten – *rotten* – that the word "gay" has been taken over, and made to mean something that it's not. I like to say that I'm in a "gay" mood or such and such, or that I'm singing a "gay" song, but nowadays I suppose people would laugh at me if I said such a thing. I'm eighty, you know.'

'She's actually older than that,' Dervla told Finn in an undertone.

'I took a tumble, didn't I? It's just as well I'm not an egg.'

An egg? thought Dervla. 'Where did that come from?

'Humpty Dumpty sat on a wall,' said Finn, and Daphne joined in with enthusiasm.

She continued to converse blithely with Finn for the next twenty minutes, as if it were quite normal to be lying on her back on a green baize lawn, all the time gazing up at him as if she were worshipping at the shrine of Adonis.

Once the ambulance men arrived she transferred her

adoration to them, and once she was ensconced on a trolley in A&E, she transferred it to the doctor. She positively blossomed under the attention that was being lavished upon her – all the nurses wanted to have a look at the plucky old dear who had survived a tumble down a forty per cent gradient without a hair on her head being disturbed. Nothing was broken, there wasn't a mark on her (although there was a ladder in her pop sock), and she had – pronounced the beaming doctor – the haemoglobin of a twenty-one-year-old. After a few hours observation, Daphne was given a clean bill of health and the all-clear to go home.

Daphne, Dervla decided as she escorted her *belle-mère* into the cottage with the aid of a taxi driver, was clearly cut from the same indestructible cloth as Keith Richards.

Chapter Twenty-Three

Later that evening, Finn called in to see Fleur.

'I hope I'm not disturbing you, godmother.'

'How many times have I told you not to call me "godmother". It makes me sound like a superannuated old bat. Come in and have a drink. Beer?'

'Please.'

'Help yourself from the fridge and join me on the deck.'

Fleur wandered onto the deck, reached for the wine bottle in the cooler and poured herself a glass of Chablis. On the main street, a tour bus operator was herding the last of his passengers on board. They were looking a little morose, clearly reluctant to leave this picture-postcard-perfect village on such a glorious evening.

How lucky she was to live here! How many blessings could she count right now? She had a beautiful duplex, a fabulous shop, wonderful friends, an enviable lifestyle, and a handsome Mr Big for a partner – whose apartment, she remembered, rather ruefully, required some housework. Still! She had the evening sun on her face, a glorious view to gaze upon, a glass of wine, a bowl of Picholine olives, and the prospect of excellent company. She had money worries, yes – but didn't everyone?

Far out to sea, a scintillating disturbance in the water

spoke of dolphin activity. Another blessing! But why on this evening of all evenings, when she had no binoculars to hand?

'Finn – quick!' she called. 'Come and look! There's a pod of dolphins out there, just beyond Inishclare. Doesn't that mean good luck or fine weather or something?'

'No,' said Finn, snapping the tab on his Budweiser. 'It just means that the herrings are in. Why have you Bud in your fridge, by the way? I've never seen you drink beer in your life.'

'My boyfriend's partial to a can from time to time.'

Finn shaded his eyes with his hand and squinted at the horizon. 'I dived with dolphins once, in Killary harbour.'

'You privileged person!'

'Yep. It was seriously special.'

'Sit down. Have olives.'

'Thanks.' Finn took a seat, stretched out his long legs. 'Any word on Mrs Vaughan?'

'Yes. I spoke to Dervla earlier. She hasn't a mark on her, apparently.'

'Wow! How did she manage that?'

'They reckoned her padded gilet helped.' Fleur did not share with Finn the fact that the padded pants had probably helped, too.

'She's some tough old bird. Maybe I should ask Dad to see if he can get her a job as a stunt double.'

Fleur laughed, and helped herself to an olive. 'You're doubling for some actress playing um – a dowager, isn't that what Río said?'

'Yeah. She's a great big horsy woman who's meant to lead the local hunt. She said on her CV that she could ride, but she's actually scared shitless of horses.'

'Nice opportunity for you.'

'It'll see me through until I head off on my travels again.'

'*Sans* Izzy?'

'What's "*sans*" mean?'

'Without.'

'Yeah.' Finn's indifferent shrug looked a little too studied. 'We're on a break.'

'What does that *mean*, exactly? I've never really understood that phrase.'

'It means that we've decided to spend some time apart.'

'Oh, Finn – I am sorry. You made such a beautiful couple. And I liked Izzy. She was a minx.'

Finn smiled. 'That would be Izzy, all right. She's in Dubai now, you know, working for her dad. She asked me to come with her, but I really didn't want to end up in the world capital of bling.'

'Not your style, I wouldn't have thought. You're clearly more Bud than Bolly.'

Finn looked thoughtful. 'So was Izzy in a funny kind of way. She was real down-to-earth for a D4 princess. But it always made me feel weird, knowing that she could just snap her fingers if we were in trouble, and have her dad send money by Western Union. And if we had gone into business together and set up that dive school in Adair's place, I think I'd always have felt like the hired help. It meant that I sometimes acted a little weird around her, and she couldn't understand it. And when she told me her dad could find me work on a construction site in Dubai, I kinda flipped. Not because I felt it was beneath me or anything – it just made me feel like I was some kinda charity case. So we decided to go our separate ways for a while.'

'Was she upset?'

'We both were. It was just awful at the airport, heading for different gates. But hey – Izzy's a beautiful girl with prospects, and she can't waste time hanging around with a no-hoper like me. Mum was right – I should have studied marine biology instead of becoming a diving instructor.'

'You are emphatically not a no-hoper, Finn Byrne,' Fleur told him sternly. 'You are one of the kindest, funniest, most free-spirited, beautiful young men I have ever had the pleasure to meet, and I am proud to be your godmother. Of course you're feeling dispirited now, but I guarantee you that you will bounce back. It's in your genes, after all. Look at Río and Shane – they've always landed on their feet.'

'I guess Ma and Pa are resilient, all right.' Finn reached for an olive, then pushed the bowl back across the table to Fleur and gave her a curious look. 'What has me blabbing my mouth off to you? I haven't even confided all this stuff in Ma.'

'That's because you don't want her to worry about you. That's why she made me your godmother, because she knew that at times like this you'd need someone you could take your troubles to.' She popped an olive into her mouth. 'Is Izzy seeing anyone else, Finn?'

'I don't think so.'

'Are you?'

'No.'

'But since you've inherited your father's good looks as well as his temperament, I imagine there's no shortage of takers.'

Finn shrugged. 'That Anastasia Harris is kind of flirty around me. She insisted on coming for a drink with me and Dad the other night, and I got a vibe. But Dad warned me not to go there.'

'Because she's married?'

'Well, not just that. Look, this is classified information, Fleur. She's involved with one of the producers.'

'Which one?' Fleur popped another olive into her mouth.

'Corban O'Hara.'

Suddenly Fleur was standing up from the table and clutching her throat, and Finn had leaped to his feet and wrapped his arms around her from behind, thrusting his fist into her solar plexus. At the third thrust the olive came shooting out of Fleur's mouth and landed like a bullet on the deck. Finn ran into the kitchen, and emerged with a glass of water.

'Drink this,' he commanded. 'Sit down. Try and breathe easy.'

Fleur did as he instructed, pulling in long, shuddering breaths, and steadying herself by placing her palms flat upon the tabletop.

'Well, hell,' said Finn. 'Am I glad I was here. Are you OK, Fleur?'

She nodded, and Finn handed her a paper napkin so that she could wipe her streaming eyes. She took a swig of water, and followed it with a swig of wine.

'Shit,' she said. 'That was scary.'

'Two separate emergency first responses in one day is a little more than I bargained for when I took my training. I've never done the Heimlich manoeuvre in a real-life situation.'

'First time lucky. Thank you, Finn. You saved my life.'

'Wow. That's a first, too. Nobody's ever said that to me before.' He took hold of Fleur's shoulders and looked penetratingly at her. 'Are you sure you're OK?'

'Sure. I'm just a little shaken-up.'

From the kitchen came the sound of her ring tone. She didn't feel like talking to anyone right now. The only person she felt like talking to was—

'Oh, look. There's Dad,' said Shane.

'Where?'

335

'On the street, by the tour bus. He's signing autographs.'

'I want a word with him. You stay here, Finn, and finish your beer. I won't be long.'

Fleur grabbed her keys and left the flat without stopping to put on her shoes. She joined the queue waiting for Shane's autograph, and when her turn came, she laid a hand on his arm and annexed him by forcing him into the doorway of her shop. Her fierce expression told him resistance was futile.

'Sorry, folks,' he said, looking back apologetically at the fans who'd missed out. 'Another time.' He looked down at Fleur. 'What's going on?' he asked.

'Why didn't you tell me that Corban's been having an affair with Nasty Harris, Shane?'

Shane adopted a guarded expression. 'Um. Who told you that?'

'Finn.'

'Aw, *shit*! That's highly classified information.'

'So it's true?'

'Yes,' said Shane, sheepishly.

'How long's it been going on?'

'Pretty well from the start of filming.'

'Oh!' Tears sprang to Fleur's eyes, but this time they were tears of rage. '*Quel con!* Oh – Shane, why didn't you *tell* me?'

'I didn't want to see you get hurt, Fleur.'

'But I'm your *friend*! You don't allow your friends to make fools of themselves! And you let me carry on seeing – seeing *ce con horrible* when all along you knew he was betraying me? Oh! Don't you realize, don't you realize . . . *comme je me sens stupide*?'

'I'm sorry, Fleur. But if word got out, Nasty's marriage would be over, and I've heard rumours about Jay David. His last wife kept walking into doors – d'you know what I mean? Nasty's a silly, spoilt little girl, but it was seriously stupid of her to think that she could handle the DCOL thing, and I wouldn't want to see her get hurt. And, anyway, I kinda thought the thing you had going with Corban wouldn't last – you're far too good for him, sweetheart, you know that. I just assumed that he was one of your – um – *plaisirs d'amour*, is that what you call them?'

Fleur dashed away a tear with such force she hurt her cheek.

'I'm sorry,' Shane said again. 'Please don't cry. I felt awful about it, but I just couldn't get involved.'

'Does Río know?'

'No.'

'So the only people on the planet who know about this are you and Finn?'

'Yes. Well, Elena guessed, but she'd never breathe a word. She's discretion personified.'

'You're quite sure?'

'Yeah.'

'So where have they been conducting *cette affaire torride* – this – this steamy liaison?'

Shane looked uneasier than ever. 'In his apartment.'

Fleur's hands flew to her mouth.

'Oh, Jesus, Fleur, don't look at me like that. You look like you want to kill me.'

'It's not you I want to kill, Shane. It's Corban fucking O'Hara. *Je veux le tuer avec mes mains à moi* – I want to cut his fucking dick off.'

Shane flinched. 'Couldn't you just cut up his suits?'

'*Mais bien sûr!* I'll do that too. I'll cut up his suits and cover his car with paint and sew prawns into his fucking curtains.'

The thought of Corban's curtains filled her with renewed rage. She remembered how she'd phoned him to tell him that his 'friends' were using his apartment again, when all the time Corban had been behind those closed curtains, fucking Nasty Harris. Did he laugh when he thought of Fleur, on the other side of the village, phoning to advise him that he might need the services of her cleaning lady again? A shriek of fury escaped her, and the last tourist to board the coach turned around in alarm.

Shane laid a hand on her forearm. 'Calm down, Fleur. Calm down and let me buy you a drink.'

She shook her head violently. 'No. I need to do something.'

'Oh, God. What are you going to do? Nothing illegal, Fleur, promise me. Please don't get yourself into trouble over this.'

She shook her head again. 'Don't worry, Shane. I just need to think about this. *Viens avec moi.*'

Opening the door to her duplex, she marched up the stairs, Shane following with a 'What have I got myself into' expression on his face.

On the deck, Finn was looking blissed out, leaning back in his chair, feet up on the rails, nursing his beer.

'Hey, Da,' he said. 'Are you joining us for a beer?'

'Um. Am I?' said Shane.

'Yes,' said Fleur, with authority. 'I'll get you one.'

She swirled into the kitchen and took a beer from the fridge. From the deck she could hear urgent muttering, and the occasional expletive. Shane must be giving out to Finn about spilling the beans. Her phone was on the kitchen table. Picking it up, she saw that the missed call had been from Corban. Fuck him, *fuck* him! She took a deep breath, and tried to think. From the marina beyond came the low buzz of an outboard motor and the slop, slap wet silk sound of its wash against hulls.

'Finn?' she said, going back out with Shane's beer.

'Yeah?'

'Are you going to be doing much diving while you're here?'

'I promised to get Da up to advanced standard.'

'So you have all your scuba kit with you?'

'Yeah.'

Fleur looked thoughtful as she handed Shane his beer. She reached for the wine bottle and poured herself a large glass; she helped herself to an olive – then changed her mind when she caught Finn's apprehensive look. She strode to the rail and glared down at the sea, and then her phone rang again. It was Dervla.

'Fleur – I'm so sorry to have to ask for your help again.'

'What's wrong?'

'It's Daphne. She's started talking funny.'

'What do you mean?'

'She sounds like she's speaking ancient Egyptian.' Dervla sounded as if she was about to cry. 'I can't do this any more, Fleur. I'm going to have to get her into a home.'

Setting aside her own concerns, Fleur morphed instantly into the relationships equivalent of an Emergency First Responder. 'How can I help? Shall I come over?'

'No. She's kind of back to normal, and I've put her in front of Monty Don, but she gave us both a bad fright.'

'Have you called the doctor?'

'No. I can't be dragging the doctor out again.'

'Could you take her to A&E?'

'I've had too much to drink, Fleur. Even if I could get her into the car, I wouldn't be fit to drive.'

'An ambulance?'

'I don't think she's a candidate for an ambulance. I think she might find it distressing this time, rather than a jaunt, and A&E at this hour of the night could be a bit harrowing. She's awfully tired.'

'So what can I do to help, beloved?'

'What I need is some time off tomorrow, to check out residential homes. She's going to need professional care. Do you know anyone who could look after her for a few hours? Your cleaning lady, maybe? I'll pay her the going rate.'

'She's in Dublin right now. And I'm so sorry, Dervla, but I just can't take two days off in a row.' Finn had wandered into Fleur's field of vision. 'Hang on. Finn is here. He might be able to help.' Fleur covered the mouthpiece with a hand. 'Are you working tomorrow, Finn?' she asked.

'No.'

'Would you be able to mind Mrs Vaughan while Dervla checks out some nursing homes for her? She likes you, and there'll be a few bob in it for you.'

'Sure.'

'Finn will do it,' Fleur told Dervla.

'Oh – thank God! Tell him thank you from me. I'll phone him in the morning after I've set up the interviews.'

'I'm sorry I can't be of more help, Dervla.'

'No worries. You've done enough. Oh – I'd better get back to her. She's whistling for me.'

'Sounds like she's back on form, then.'

Dervla gave a tired laugh. ''Night, Fleur.'

'Good night, Dervla. I'll talk to you tomorrow.' Fleur set her phone down, and looked at her godson. 'You, Finn Byrne,' she said, 'are a living saint.'

'I am?' said Finn.

'Yes. That's the third life you've saved today. Go register for canonization now.'

'Um. OK. But here, Fleur – there's something I find a bit puzzling. Why did you want to know if I had my scuba gear?'

'Just how difficult is it,' said Fleur, regarding the *Lolita* bouncing jauntily on her mooring, 'to scupper a boat?'

340

Chapter Twenty-Four

After phoning Fleur, Dervla went back into the sitting room. Daphne fixed helpless eyes upon her, and launched once again into ancient Egyptian.

'Roug ge ug oh her wrds,' she was saying. 'Cuming cuming al rong out. Wat rite say. I no dont—'

'Daphne, Daphne – take it easy!' said Dervla, hunkering down and taking Daphne's hand.

Daphne looked not so much unnerved as befuddled. 'Wrds al rite no rong. Al cum wardback. U no . . .'

'I know, I know. I'm listening. I'm trying to make sense of what you're saying.'

Daphne was talking complete gobbledegook. But after Dervla had listened for a few minutes, she kind of got the gist of what she was saying. It translated as:

'Happen me not right.'

'No. You're not right,' said Dervla, trying to sound matter-of-fact. She'd got quite good at that matter-of-fact tone over the course of the past week. 'But don't worry, Daphne. I'm here to help.'

'I'm not right, you see. I need to do the right thing. I'm stuck on the wrong side. I'm not *right*, you see.'

'I will help you find the right thing. I can try.'

'Will you tell me what to do?'

'I can't *tell* you what to do, but I can suggest the right things you are looking for. Would that do? Maybe it's time to go to bed? It is after your bedtime, you know.'

'I am not right. I am telling you I am trying I am trying to be right and I'm not. I'm not making sense. I'm on the wrong side now and wroug ge uz oher wrds . . . Oh!'

Daphne had reverted to indecipherable ancient Egyptian. She clamped her hands over her mouth and gave a shaky laugh as she registered the absurdity of what was pouring out of her mouth.

'Well, if you're on the wrong side, we'll have to try getting you back on the right side, won't we?' Dervla was trying hard to be upbeat, but she was feeling very scared. Was the fall earlier that day to blame? Had they missed something in A&E? Should she make arrangements for Daphne to have a CAT Scan? But she'd heard that there were mile-long waiting lists for CAT Scans. Fuck the HSE! In the meantime, she'd just have to cope as best she could. 'Come on, Daphne. I think you may need to lie down.'

Dervla stood up and reached out her hands, and when Daphne took them, Dervla realized that things must be really bad because for once she didn't tell Dervla that her hands were like stones. Daphne was really unsteady on her feet as she moved out into the hall, so Dervla led the way down the corridor with her arms out behind her and Daphne clutching onto her going 'qua qua qua'. When she got into the bedroom, she sat down heavily on the bed with her usual 'Oof!' and carried on about being on the wrong side and not being right, and then finished up with 'I. Am. Dead.' And she really did look dead – white and exhausted and her eyes stonier and more unseeing than ever.

'Let's get you into your nightdress, Daphne. You'll feel better once we've got you into bed.'

Very gently, Dervla eased Daphne's arms out of her gilet. Then she removed the fawn cashmere jumper, and slowly managed to pull off Daphne's herringbone trousers. Vest and bra and incontinence pants came next, and then Daphne was shrouded in her nightdress, and Dervla was helping her into fresh incontinence pads because *The Doctor says*.

'I'm not terribly comfortable, you know,' said Daphne, as Dervla manoeuvred her legs around, trying to straighten them. 'It's always difficult to make yourself comfortable in an unfamiliar bed.'

'This *is* your bed, Daphne,' said Dervla.

'You mean this is the bed I slept in last night?'

'Yes. You're in your own bed, in your own bedroom, in your own house.'

'Is this my house?'

'Yes. Now. Here's your pill.'

'Why do I have to take a pill?'

'Because if you don't, you'll get cranky.'

'And I'm cranky enough, says you.'

'Ha ha. There you go. And here's a little water to wash it down.' Dervla held the glass of water to Daphne's lips, then set it down on the table. 'I don't think we'll bother with a story tonight, will we?' she said, leaning down to give Daphne a kiss on the forehead. 'You must be tired after talking all that fascinating gobbledegook!'

And Daphne managed a little laugh, and said: 'Good night, love. Thank you.'

'Goodnight, Daphne. Sleep tight,' said Dervla.

After Fleur had said good night to Shane and Finn, she sat glowering at the darkening view, thinking thoughts equally dark. She finished the Chablis and opened another bottle. She wished she'd kept hold of Dervla's binoculars, so that she could train her sights on the penthouse at the other end of the village – check out whether the curtains were open or closed, whether there might be a maverick figure on the deck, a giveaway glint of light from a window. And then she thought – *hello Mesdames et Messieurs*. I can go down there. I told Corban I'd arrange for his cleaning to be taken care of. And since Audrey is unavailable, I'm doing him a big favour by donning the Marigolds myself. What matter that it's nearly midnight? You're not going to be there, Mister O'Hara, are you? And if you are, then I simply take some pictures of you and *la belle* Anastasia and threaten you with the tabloids.

After a bottle and a half of Chablis, all this made perfect sense to Fleur. She drained her glass, located the envelope containing the spare keys to Corban's penthouse, and left her darling duplex, kissing the front door on the way out.

She was still barefoot, she realized abstractedly, as she stepped on to the street, bottle of Chablis clutched in her hand. *Je m'en fou!* Do I give a shit? No, I don't! There was nobody on the street. The lights were off everywhere in the village, apart from in the O'Reilly household, where she knew a new baby had recently arrived. Fleur rather loved walking drunk and barefoot at midnight through Lissamore. Who would believe, if they happened to look out of their window, that the chic French owner of the village's only boutique was swaggering along towards her lover's apartment with steel in her heart and revenge on her mind?

She got there at last, sat on the steps and drooped a little. Then she took a swig from the wine bottle, pulled herself up by the handrail, and leaned hard on the doorbell to Corban's apartment. Nothing happened. She did it again. Still nothing. She inserted the key in the lock. The lobby smelled new, still, of hard wood and putty and paint. The lift had not yet been installed – and anyway, Fleur decided, she hated the idea of a lift that would take her just five storeys to the top of the building. Couldn't Corban and his paramour just fucking *walk*? She climbed the stairs to the penthouse, thrust in the keycard, and entered the password that was scribbled on the envelope. theoharaaffair. Ha ha ha.

There was no one there. She sensed as soon as she passed through the front door into the lobby that the penthouse was empty. Recklessly, she pressed the keys on the panel that would turn on lights all over. The kitchen was her first port of call. There were the half-cleared remains of a fingerfood feast – asparagus, clab claws, shucked oysters. Aphrodisiacs all. Half-a-dozen bottles were lined up on the counter: *Riondo Pink Prosecco Raboso* was the label that leaped up at Fleur. The label that had been on the bottle that Audrey had re-cycled. *Prosecco* was Nasty Harris's tipple of choice: Shane had told her that the fridge in her trailer was crammed with the stuff.

The bedroom next. Fleur leaned against the doorjamb, curled her lip, and looked dispassionately upon the king-size bed with the crumpled sheets and discarded negligée. There was a tripod at the foot of the bed. There was an ashtray on the bedside table. She smoked! Ew! Had Corban given a thought to how poor, elderly Audrey might feel at being expected to clear up after his so-called 'friend's' sex-fest? Evidently not. Corban quite clearly did not give a fuck about anyone other than himself.

In the sitting room there was evidence that they'd been watching a DVD. Fleur aimed the remote at the screen. It was, as she had expected, a pornographic home movie, starring the 'child' star of *The O'Hara Affair* and its executive producer, Mr Corban O'Hara himself. She slid the DVD out of the player. It might come in handy sometime.

His study, next. A snooper's paradise, *on y va!* Fleur turned on the desktop, and typed in theoharaaffair. The word 'Welcome' shimmered onto the screen. What an idiot! What a plonker! How careless of Mr Hotshot O'Hara to use the same password twice!

While she waited for the computer to purr into life, Fleur picked up a folder marked CASTING that was lying beside the keyboard, and rifled through the contents. There was page upon page of printouts of casting forms, attached to colour headshots. All the headshots were of beautiful young women, and all of them were gazing at the viewer with yearning in their eyes. Fleur recognized many of them as local girls, some of whom she'd seen in costume the day she and Dervla had visited the movie set.

She scanned the details on the casting forms: wannabes not only were expected to include such personal information as hair colour, birth date, body shape and measurements (including bust and cup size), there was also a wealth of contact details: day phone, evening phone, mobile, terrestrial address, email, URL to personal website. Corban had at his fingers an assortment of girls who would come running at the click of a mouse and the touch of a key: he was like a gourmand with his hand hovering over a box of delicious sweetmeats, wondering which one to pick next.

He'd got the icing on the cake with Anastasia Harris: how many more of these little cupcakes had he drooled over? Fleur felt bile rise in her throat. Dropping the folder, she reeled into the bathroom and threw up. His aftershave was on the shelf above the basin. She never wanted to smell Giorgio Armani again. Holding the bottle at arm's length, she unstoppered it, poured the contents down the loo, and flushed. Then she wove her way back to the study.

The printouts and photographs lay scattered on the floor:

all those images of exquisite young girls, blossoms all of them, waiting to be plucked. In the nineteen forties, Fleur knew, Hollywood executives had organized beauty pageants all over America and the UK, offering as prizes six-month contracts and a chance to become a movie star. The winners were flown to LA and kept for the delectation of the money men, in an arena known as the Talent Department. Nothing much would appear to have changed.

As she stooped to pick up the photographs, one face leaped up at her. It was Bethany O'Brien. Bethany was smiling a little shyly to camera, hair looped behind one elfin ear, chin on her hand. She had scrupulously filled in all her contact details, including her Dublin address and her address in Coolnamara. Curlew Cottage, Díseart. All her telephone numbers were there, all her measurements had been filled in to the exact centimetre. She'd described her body shape as 'slender', her personal look as 'a young Winona Ryder'. At the very top of the form, in Corban's handwriting, was the single word 'Poppet'.

Fleur rose shakily to her feet. The screen of Corban's desktop was all aglimmer with icons. Organizer. Google Earth. Media Player. The O'Hara Affair. Second Life. She reached for the mouse, and clicked. 'Welcome Hero Evanier' she read. In the password bar, Fleur typed theoharaaffair with numb fingers. Outside the Globe Theatre, like Frankenstein's monster, Hero came to life.

Oh, God. Oh, God. Scared that she might be sick again, Fleur clamped her hands over her mouth. Hero Evanier, Bethany's virtual boyfriend, was Fleur's lover. No, no! He was her ex-, ex-, her *ex*-lover. Corban O'Hara would never set foot inside her home again. Sitting down at his desk, she stared at his avatar, then depressed a key and sent him walk-about. There was nobody on Shakespeare Island for him to prey upon. She went to 'Locations' and scrolled down. There were listed all the places Bethany had told her about during one of their MSN conversations. The Hollywood backlot, the book shop, the pool hall, the Blarney Stone pub, Sweethearts dance club. There was Bethany and Hero's cottage.

Taking a deep breath, Fleur teleported. The cottage was empty. Unsurprising. It was one-thirty in the morning: Bethany was probably tucked up in bed in her real-life cottage down by the sea in Díseart.

It would appear that some housework had been done: it was unlikely that Hero had been responsible. There was a broom by the door, and new curtains at the window – curtains printed with little pink hearts. The flowers had been changed, the marguerites replaced by yellow tulips. And there was something else new. A bookcase. Fleur checked out the titles on the spines. Yeats, Keats, Christina Rossetti. Romantic poets all. Bethany had hoped to invite romance into her life, and instead she had opened her door to a monster.

Fleur thought back to the last time she'd been in this virtual cottage, when Hero had taken her upstairs and barraged her with obscenities. He'd known who she was. She'd told him that her avatar's name was Flirty LittleBoots. Why had he invited her to the cottage? What had been in it for him? Had he got off on the fact that he could verbally assault her? What was his *thing*?

Fleur knew now that she'd been having an affair with a complete stranger. Nothing about Corban O'Hara added up; nothing was as it seemed. He was all façade: as fake as the famine village that had been built with his money. It felt horrible; it felt sordid. She remembered how he'd first approached her, mistaking her for someone called Rachel. Had Rachel even existed? Had he made her up, used a fictitious persona as a device to seduce a gullible woman in fancy dress, just as he had used a fictitious persona – an avatar called Hero Evanier – to seduce . . . *to seduce Bethany O'Brien*? Fleur felt a nauseating flash of fear. Bethany was safe enough right now, but for how long?

Touching the keypad, she pressed X, and sent Bethany and Hero's cottage spiralling into the ether. Then she tidied the casting folder, extracted Bethany's photograph and its attached details, turned off the lights, and left Corban's lair.

On the street, it had started to rain. Fleur welcomed the sweet coolness of the water as she walked barefoot through puddles. She would take a shower when she got home: wash away some of the filth she felt had accumulated on and around her since she'd entered theoharaaffair into Corban's security system.

By the pier, she stopped to look down at the sea. Its pewter surface was dimpled and pockmarked with raindrops. On its mooring, the *Lolita* slumbered, rocked to sleep by waves. *Lolita*. She should have known. Young girls were Corban's thing. That's why he'd abused her in his virtual cottage – because he wouldn't get away with it in real life, without blowing his cover. Fleur was his 'beard' – that term they used in Hollywood to describe the woman who was reeled in to marry the gay film star, because otherwise his career would be toast. That, Fleur realized now, was why sex with Corban had always had to have something a little kinky about it, some element of make-believe. All that role-playing had been necessary to stimulate his appetite. Corban wasn't interested in forty-something flesh. He wouldn't ever have bothered with Fleur if he hadn't needed a mistress nearer his own age and conveniently resident in Lissamore as a decoy to distract attention from the real objects of his lust: girls who were only just legal. All those teenage hopefuls who had filled in their casting forms so diligently, not knowing that they would be perused by a salivating predator.

Lolita. The name of Nabokov's nymphet. Fleur would never be seduced onto that boat again – and she'd make sure that Bethany O'Brien would never be seduced onto it either. Fleur O'Farrell was armed and dangerous now, and she had two lethal weapons. She had her ex-lover's pornographic home video. And she had Hero Evanier's password.

Chapter Twenty-Five

Dervla had approached her mother-in-law with extreme apprehension when she'd brought her breakfast that morning, fearful that Daphne might start to talk in tongues again. But Daphne was more than usually chipper, and had even said a gracious 'Thank you', before tucking into her Crunchy Nut Cornflakes.

Now she had been washed and anointed with *Je Reviens*, and was ensconced in the sitting room, listening to *Appointment with Death* again.

Dervla was due to leave soon for her recce of care homes. She made tea for Daphne and coffee for herself and for Finn, who was sitting by the edge of the pond in the courtyard throwing a ball for Kitty. Kitty was in seventh heaven: nobody had played with her for days. As Dervla left the kitchen, she gave a little shriek. On the hall carpet was a beetle the like of which she had never seen before. It was big, with horny things growing out of it and a pattern like leopards' spots.

Dervla put down the mugs she was carrying, fetched a glass from the kitchen, and trapped the insect underneath. Then she ran to the open front door. 'Finn!' she called. 'Can you help?'

He got to his feet. 'What's up?'

'There's a thing – a kind of beetle – on the floor. Could you do something about it for me, please?'

'Sure.' Finn joined her in the hall. 'Wow,' he said, hunkering down and examining the creature through the glass. 'The last time I saw something like that was in Thailand.'

'How could it have got here?'

Finn shrugged. 'It probably came into the country in a container of bananas or something.'

'That must be how that spider got in too,' said Dervla. 'I had to kill a spider the size of your hand the other day.'

'Go get me a postcard or something, Dervla, so I can slide it under the glass and get rid of this yoke in the garden,' said Finn.

Dervla went into the kitchen and came back with a coaster. She watched as Finn slid it under the glass and flinched when the beetle scuttled to the wall of its prison.

'Who is it?' Daphne was standing in the doorway of the sitting room looking suspicious. 'Is it a man?'

'Yes,' said Dervla. 'Finn is here to look after you because I have to go out.'

'Are you having an affair?'

'What?' Dervla looked startled, and Finn laughed. 'No! Finn is my nephew.'

'A likely story! Get out of here, young man. And you too, madam. Who do you think you are, consorting with paramours under my very roof? Go on – be off with you!'

'But Finn is here to look after you—'

'I don't need looking after. Fuck off the pair of you.' And Daphne stumped back into the sitting room.

Dervla gave Finn a look of entreaty. 'What'll we do?' she whispered.

'Let's take our coffee outside. By the time we've finished, she'll probably have forgotten all about us.'

'Good idea.' Dervla fetched the mugs, then joined Finn,

where he was back sitting by the side of the pond. 'What did you do with the beetle?' she asked.

'I dumped it in the compostor. It'll love it in there.'

'As long as it doesn't start breeding.' Dervla sat down beside her nephew, and handed him his coffee, then: 'Holy *shit*!' she screamed, and clutched his arm. A fat frog had landed right next to her foot.

'Another of your mother-in-law's familiars,' observed Finn.

Dervla started to laugh. She laughed and laughed until the tears came. 'Oh, Finn,' she said finally, after the frog had leaped back into the pond, 'what am I going to do?'

'Don't worry, auntie dear. I'm here to help. And if I can't help, Ma will. And if Ma can't, Fleur will, and if Fleur can't, Da will. We're family. We won't let you down.'

Dervla linked his arm and hugged it to her. 'You have a very wise head on such young shoulders, d'you know that?'

'I'm a scuba diver,' said Finn. 'Scuba divers are pretty zen about most things. My next challenge is to get Da down to a hundred and thirty feet.'

'Correction. Your next challenge is to win over my mother-in-law.'

He smiled at her. Finn's smile was like his father's – crinkly-eyed and warm. 'I'll do it. No worries, Dervla. You finish your coffee and get on with your mission. Kitty and I will hold the fort.'

Dervla took a swig of coffee. 'How are you getting on with the film?' she asked.

'Looking forward to the wrap party, if truth be told. But not half as much as Da. He hates this fucking film.'

'Oh? Why?'

'Corban O'Hara's started behaving like a megalomaniac. He's even making changes to the script. That is so not kosher.

It's like all the power his money has bought him has gone to his head.'

Shit. Maybe they wouldn't be inviting Corban to dinner in the Old Rectory after all. Dervla wondered if Fleur knew about this. 'Well, you know what they say, Finn. Power corrupts, but absolute power corrupts absolutely.' Dervla drained her mug, and got to her feet. 'I'd better take you in to Daphne and reintroduce you.'

'OK.' Finn got to his feet. 'Stay, Kitten,' he said authoritatively, and Kitty gave him a reproachful look.

In the sitting room, Daphne was looking as enraptured as if it were the first time she'd ever heard *Appointment with Death*.

'Daphne,' said Dervla brightly. 'You have a visitor!'

'Who is it?' she snapped, annoyed at being interrupted.

'It's my nephew, Finn.'

Daphne looked up, and her stony expression softened when she beheld the vision that was Finn. 'Good evening, young man,' she said. 'Would you care to join me for a gin and tonic?'

'It's a little early for a gin and tonic, Mrs Vaughan,' said Finn, diplomatically. It was actually just midday. 'But I would love to join you for a cup of tea.'

'Yes. Maybe that would be better,' said Daphne, adding, 'fetch this young man a cup of tea!' to no one in particular.

Dervla slid out of the room. She slipped into her shoes and located her bag, and then she tiptoed out of the house. On her way past the sitting-room door, she heard Finn say: 'So this photograph is of you! Well. You were a good-looking woman, Mrs Vaughan, that's for sure. Still are!' Dervla smiled. Like father, like son . . .

'I've never been too coy to accept a compliment,' replied Daphne graciously. 'Thank you, young man. What did you say your name was, again?'

*　*　*

354

The first care home Dervla visited – La Paloma – looked promising. It was only twenty minutes' drive from the Old Rectory, the gardens were beautifully maintained, and the reception area was bright and modern and airy, with a high ceiling and big Velux windows. In a glass porch to the right of the front door, a coffee table surrounded by easy chairs had a magazine rack attached to it, in which were copies of today's *Irish Times*. An elderly man looked up from the paper he was reading with the help of a magnifying glass and smiled at her as she made her way across the foyer to the reception desk.

'I'm here to see the matron,' Dervla told the security guard behind the desk.

'Dervla Vaughan?' he asked, consulting a desk diary.

'Yes.'

'Through there, first on the left.' The security guard picked up the phone and said, 'Ms Vaughan is here to see you, Pauline.'

Dervla crossed the foyer to a pair of double doors, which opened automatically as she approached. Beyond the double doors was a second set of automatic doors, and beyond them stretched a long corridor that led down to what Dervla took to be a nurses' station. The colour scheme was soft apricot and dove grey.

So far, so good, she thought, breathing in a sigh of relief. Oh. So far, so good – apart from the smell. The smell was: top note, antiseptic; middle note, 'Neutradol'; base note, nappies. Dervla knew the base note was nappies because it was a smell she had become increasingly familiar with over the past week.

She knocked on the door marked 'Matron'.

'Come in,' a voice called, and Dervla entered to find a pretty woman in her thirties sitting behind a desk. She rose as Dervla came through, and extended a hand.

'Nice to meet you, Matron,' said Dervla.

'Please call me Pauline,' said the woman with a warm smile. 'And take a seat. Now. What can I do for you?'

It all came flooding out, as it had that time with Dr Doorley, and as Dervla spoke, Pauline nodded reassuringly.

'Well,' she said, when Dervla had finished her tale of woe, 'we shall have to pay a home visit to make an assessment, of course.'

Oh, God. Maybe Dervla shouldn't have been so honest. Maybe she should have played down her mother-in-law's dementia; maybe this place didn't accept cases as advanced as Daphne's.

'Does your mother-in-law wander?' asked Pauline.

'No,' lied Dervla.

'In that case, she could probably be accommodated in the ground-floor wing. Upstairs is the secure ward, for the more at-risk dementia and Alzheimer's patients.' Pauline got to her feet. 'Let me show you the accommodation.'

She went out into the corridor, and Dervla followed her along the spotless dove-grey linoleum. Here and there, doors were open, and Dervla couldn't stop herself from looking. Televisions were on in most of the rooms, and in many of them the occupants were lying on their beds, eyes closed, mouths open, oblivious to the sound coming from their plasma screens.

Pauline stopped in front of a door, and peered through a glass panel. 'This one's empty,' she said. 'Mrs Ellis must be in the day room. Come in and have a look around.'

Holding the door open, she allowed Dervla to precede her. The room was scrupulously clean. There was a high bed backed up against one wall; floor-to-ceiling windows occupied another. A maple-veneered unit housed wardrobe, dressing table and bookshelves, upon which a variety of ornaments, books, DVDs, postcards and framed photographs was displayed. One of the postcards bore the legend: 'God couldn't be everywhere, so He made grandmas.' A plant protruded from a decorative pot, a Lalique vase was host to a bouquet of artificial flowers.

But on closer inspection, the room was not as pristine as Dervla had first thought. The silk flowers were dusty, the plant was parched for want of watering, and the upholstery on an old-fashioned fireside chair was stained with mysterious fluids. The lotions and potions on the bathroom shelves were not high-end: no anti-ageing or expensive night creams necessary. At least Mrs Ellis had been liberated from the diktats of the beauty industry.

'Mrs Ellis will be celebrating her hundred and first birthday soon!' announced Pauline.

'Hundred and first?' echoed Dervla. 'Goodness! What's the average age of the inmates here?'

'We don't like to call them inmates,' said Pauline. 'It sounds a little institutional. We prefer to call them residents. Most of them are in their eighties and nineties. Would you like to see the day room?'

'Yes, please.'

Along the corridor again they went, past the nurses' station, where two pretty Filipino girls were poring over a chart, and into a room where sun streamed in through the windows, and ambient music poured out through wall-mounted speakers. All four sides of the room were lined with mobile armchairs, in which sat old ladies. Except, Dervla thought, they didn't sit. They lolled, heads on their chests like drooping flowers. Some of them looked awkward, twisted, their elbows bent at odd angles. Each of them was strapped into their chair, and in front of each of them was a wheely table upon which small stuffed toys were ranged alongside feeding cups of orange squash.

'We're just about to serve lunch,' said Pauline. 'That's why we're wearing bibs. Good day, Mrs Lennon! How are we today?' Mrs Lennon looked blankly at Pauline and muttered something.

On the other side of the room, another lady was becoming agitated. She was gazing around with big bewildered eyes as words cascaded out of her mouth, and it seemed to Dervla that she was talking a strange language. But no – here and there came a phrase that was distinctly English. She was talking gibberish – not unlike that uttered by Daphne the previous night. None of the other residents took any notice: they were all sunk inside themselves, unseeing, existing isolated from the real world.

'Excuse me,' said Pauline, as her phone sounded. 'I would have turned this off, but it's a call I've been waiting for.' She moved back out into the corridor to take her call, and left Dervla standing in the middle of the day room surrounded by the moribund. She remained frozen to the spot, keeping her eyes fixed unseeingly on the wall-mounted clock that ticked away the livelong seconds that these poor creatures had yet to endure. How many minutes, hours, days, months were left to them? How many birthdays had they yet to 'celebrate'? How many New Years to ring in? The hands of the clock met with a judder at twelve midday.

And then a beautiful young black man came into the room, pushing a trolley piled with dishes. He was joined by the Filipino girls, who began to distribute lunch, setting plates before each of the inmates – no! the *residents* – then hunkering down beside this individual or that, persuading them to eat, holding forkfuls of food to their mouths, and gently inserting a tidbit or wiping a chin, all the while crooning and smiling encouragement.

Dervla couldn't bear it: she felt as if she'd stumbled upon some arcane ritual – one that she should not be privy to.

She backed out of the day room and fled down the corridor and through a side door into the garden, blinded with tears and gasping for air.

That's where Pauline found her.

'Are you all right?' she asked.

'Yes. I – it's just that I've never seen so many old people together. I never thought that old age could be so incapacitating.'

What was it Fleur had said recently? *Old age ain't no place for sissies* . . . Except now the word 'old' had become as politically incorrect as the word 'fat'. You couldn't say things any more like, 'pity that fat old loony'. You'd have to say 'show consideration for that obese, elderly, mentally challenged person' instead. Oh! What was the world coming to? Why were these people who had once run and danced and sung and argued and wept and felt the wind in their hair and the rain on their faces – why were they cocooned in chairs, strapped in and bibbed like babies, spoon-fed and nappy-clad? Where was their dignity? Was life so sanctified that it had become a grotesque parody of itself? Dervla realized that she was shaking.

'I can understand you're upset,' said Pauline, laying a hand on her arm. 'It can be disturbing to see the inside of a care home for the first time.'

'They were all – they were all *women*,' said Dervla.

'That's only to be expected. Women have a longer life expectancy than men. We do have a few men – there's Mr Slater, for example. He's still going strong at ninety-two.'

Dervla looked over at one of the paths that crisscrossed the garden geometrically. A man was moving slowly between the flowerbeds, assisted by a zimmer frame. He was accompanied by a uniformed nurse; yet another Filipino.

'Your staff seems to be mostly foreign,' remarked Dervla.

Pauline smiled. 'That's because they still have reverence for the elderly in their cultures,' she said. 'They consider grey hair to be a crown of glory – a sign of wisdom. Young people in this country are reluctant to train as geriatric carers because it's perceived as being unglamorous – which, of course, it is.'

Dervla looked at Mr Slater hunched over his zimmer frame, and thought, He's one of the lucky ones.

'How mobile is your mother-in-law?' Pauline asked.

'Well, she doesn't need a zimmer frame. Yet.'

'So she's lively enough. She'll benefit from our animators.'

'Animators?'

'We get entertainers in from time to time – musicians, magicians, that kind of thing. There's a wonderful young man with a guitar who plays folk songs.'

Dervla had a sudden mental image of Daphne being serenaded by an earnest young folk singer, and telling him to fuck off and stop his bloody racket.

'We play games like bowls,' continued Pauline. 'And we have singsongs and art classes.'

'Oh – Daphne might like art classes. She's a very cultured person.' Dervla felt awfully confused, suddenly. She couldn't picture Daphne playing bowls or singing along with a room full of strangers. 'Look, Pauline, I'll have to speak with my husband about this. We may not need to avail ourselves of residential care right now—'

'Oh – I'm afraid there'd be no question of that. We have a two-year waiting list.'

'Two *years*?'

'Yes. A place might become available sooner, but there's no guarantee. It depends on how many of our residents pass away, and the mortality rate is low, thank God. As I'm sure you know, we're all living longer.' Mr Slater was inching his way along the path towards them. 'Hello, Mr Slater!' shouted Pauline. 'Isn't it a beautiful day?'

There was no response from Mr Slater, but the Filipino youth accompanying him beamed at Pauline and Dervla and said, 'It surely is a beautiful day to be alive.'

Dervla resisted the impulse to add, 'For some of us.' She was feeling more and more desperate to get out of there. She looked at her watch and said: 'Oh, I'd better go. I have an appointment.'

'Are you looking at another care home?'

'Yes. Green Meadows. Do you know it?

Pauline looked inscrutable. 'I do. I think you'll find it's not as high spec as this facility. It's . . . a little on the old-fashioned side. Come past my office on the way out, and I'll give you a brochure.'

The brochure was glossily presented in hues of apricot and dove grey, to reflect the La Paloma decor. It featured photographs of white-haired people looking up at the sky laughing, or smiling into the eyes of a Filipino carer, or sitting at an easel with a paintbrush. In the section on rates, Dervla read that 'fees reflect the cost of providing suitable accommodation and care for residents'.

'How much, approximately, are the fees likely to be?' she asked Pauline.

'Well, we can't give you an accurate quote until we've assessed Mrs Vaughan, but they usually even out at just over five thousand a month.'

Dervla tried not to suck in her breath. Five thousand a month! Five thousand a *month*! She felt sweat break out under her arms.

'Thank you so much for your help, Pauline,' she said. 'I'll have a chat with my husband and I'll get back in touch. Goodbye.'

'Goodbye, Dervla. A pleasure to meet you.'

'Likewise.'

Dervla passed through the two sets of automatic doors and back across the foyer, where the man who had been reading the paper was now fast asleep in his chair. Outside, she felt the warmth of the sun on her face, felt a breeze snatch her hair. Above her a seagull wheeled through a bright blue sky; on the topmost branch of a mimosa tree, a robin was singing. There was a scent of wild garlic in the air. What privileges had she taken for granted! Privileges that were denied now, to the 'privileged' five thousand euro per month incumbents of La Paloma.

In the privacy of her car, Dervla laid her forehead against the steering wheel. Of course it would cost in the region of five grand a month for that level of care. There were so many factors to be taken into consideration: nursing, insurance, utilities, nutrition, medication, laundry, housekeeping, entertainment . . . What had Pauline called the entertainers? Animators. It was unlikely that Jim Carrey himself could breathe life into the old people she'd seen in that day room earlier. Dervla couldn't begin to imagine what things might be like in the dementia ward on the first floor – what Pauline had called the 'secure' ward. But what still appalled her most was the fact that the vast majority of the residents were women.

She couldn't – she just couldn't subject Daphne to that kind of care. Her mother-in-law might be a belligerent old bat, but at least she had life in her still. Maybe Green Meadows would be more suitable. It might not – as Pauline had told her – be quite so high spec as La Paloma, but maybe there would be something more homely about it.

It was homely all right, in that it had once been the home of a wealthy Victorian engineer, but as soon as Dervla stepped across the threshold, she knew that she could not commit Daphne to this place. In the foyer, an old lady was sitting very erect upon a moulded plastic chair, clutching her handbag. She wore an anxious look, and she rose to her feet as Dervla approached.

'Have you come to take me home, miss?' she asked.

'I'm sorry,' said Dervla. 'I haven't.'

The old lady started to cry. 'They promised me I could go home,' she said. 'But nobody's come. I shouldn't be here, you know. This place is full of mad people. And they're not looking after me properly. This isn't even my own cardigan I'm wearing.' She reached out a bony hand and clutched Dervla's sleeve. 'Please find my son and tell him to come for me. Please.'

'I'll try,' said Dervla, taking her hand.

'Do you promise?'

'Yes.'

'Thank you. I'll just sit and wait here then, shall I, until he comes.'

The old lady sat down again upon her chair, and recommenced her vigil.

'Don't mind Eunice,' said an officious-looking woman, bustling into the foyer. 'She sits there all day, every day, bothering people and waiting for no one. Are you Dervla Vaughan?'

'No,' said Dervla, backing away. 'I'm not. I'm sorry. I've come to the wrong place. Excuse me.' She reached for the door handle and pulled, but nothing happened.

'All right. Just let me release the lock,' said the woman. She leaned over the reception desk and unlocked the door, and as Dervla passed through she heard Eunice say in a small, desperate voice, 'Please don't forget to tell him. Tell him I'll be waiting here by the door.'

She sits there all day, every day, waiting for no one . . . And, Dervla conjectured, that's what Eunice would be doing all day, every day, for the rest of her life. *Old age ain't no place for sissies . . .* Oh, shit. Maybe old age was no place for survivors, either.

Chapter Twenty-Six

Bethany was standing on the mark that the assistant director had given her – an X chalked onto the flagstoned courtyard. On 'Action', she was to cross the yard carrying a hatbox that belonged to the character played by Elena Sweetman, and climb after her into a carriage. She was feeling nervous. What if she stumbled? What if she dropped the hatbox, and they had to go for another take? Time meant money on a film set. What would she say to Miss Sweetman, once she was in the carriage? Miss Sweetman was Hollywood royalty, and would probably have no truck with a mere extra like her.

But at least she didn't have to do a scene with Nasty Harris, who was living up to her nickname and had earned herself a reputation as Christian Bale in petticoats. Cast and crew had watched in gobsmacked silence yesterday as she'd laid into a make-up assistant who had dared to approach her while she was 'in character'. Considering the character Nasty played was the spoilt Anglo-Irish daughter of the wicked landlord, Bethany figured that this was a fairly easy mistake for the make-up girl to have made.

'Nervous?'

A man had come up behind her. Bethany recognized him as the executive producer of the film – an important man. She gave him a deferential smile. 'A little,' she admitted.

'No worries. I've been watching you on screen. You're a natural.'

'I am?'

'Yes. You have a lovely, luminescent quality. Have you thought about taking up acting professionally?'

'Well, yes, actually. I'm hoping for a place in the Gaiety School in Dublin.'

Corban O'Hara produced a leather card case from his pocket. 'Here's my card,' he said, handing her one. 'Don't hesitate to get in touch if you want help. A personal reference from me can do no harm.'

'Oh! Thank you so much, Mr O'Hara.'

'Corban. And you're Bethany, right?'

'Yes.'

'It's a beautiful name.'

The assistant director approached. 'There's been a delay, I'm afraid. You can relax, Bethany. Good morning, Mr O'Hara.'

'Good morning, Jake. I was just telling Bethany here how great she looks in the rushes. We might think about giving her a line or two to say.'

'Seriously?' Bethany was awestruck.

'Why not? It would look good on your CV, wouldn't it? To be credited with a speaking role in *The O'Hara Affair*. I'll have a word with the director.'

And Corban O'Hara winked at her and strolled away.

'What a nice man!' said Bethany.

'Aren't you suspicious of men who wink?' Jake was looking down at her with an amused expression.

'I've never really thought about it.'

'Think about it now.' He winked at her, and Bethany laughed. 'You clearly have a trusting nature. Did I see you the other day, walking the beach at Díseart?'

366

'Yes, that could have been me. How did you find the beach? Not many people know about it.'

'Shane Byrne let me in on the secret. Do you live around there?'

'My parents have a holiday cottage in Díseart, so I'm staying here until the film's finished. I live in Dublin.'

'So once we're wrapped, you'll be heading back east?'

'Yes.' Bethany found herself looking from Jake's eyes to his mouth. She looked back at his eyes at once, feeling shy. 'What about you?'

'I'm from Dublin too.'

'Dublin too, or Dublin 2?'

'Both. I've a flat in the city centre.'

'Cool!'

'Yeah, I guess it is pretty cool. I'm lucky enough to have a roof garden.'

'Even cooler.' She resisted the temptation to let her eyes slide to his mouth again. 'I'd love to live in the city centre. My parents are miles out in Dalkey and I'm going to have to commute every day, if – *when* I start college in September.'

Bethany had deliberately substituted 'when' for 'if'. It was part of her new positive-thinking strategy, and if Corban O'Hara's interest in her was anything to go by, it seemed to be paying off.

'What are you studying?'

'Drama, at the Gaiety. Well – fingers crossed.'

'So you're planning on being an actress?'

'Yes.'

Jake heaved a sigh. 'Another one bites the dust,' he said.

'Hey!' she said indignantly. 'Don't be so negative! Didn't Corban O'Hara just give me his card?'

'You and a thousand other hopefuls,' said Jake. 'Here. Take mine instead. I might be of real use to you. I'll be working

367

on a film for Lawless Productions next, filming in Dublin. And the casting director's a friend of mine.'

Bethany gave him an oblique look. 'I bet that's what you say to all the girls,' she heard herself saying. Ohmigod! She was *flirting*!

'Ah ha. So you *do* have a mistrustful side, after all.'

'My mummy told me never to take sweets from strangers.'

'And mine told me never to look a gift horse in the mouth,' he said, with a wicked smile. 'Are you going to take my card or not?'

Bethany took it, just as Jake's walkie-talkie crackled into life. He gave it a reproachful look, then segued back into authoritarian mode.

'Back to work, boys and girls,' he called out. Then he turned back to Bethany. 'Good luck, sweetheart,' he said. And winked.

Corban was due that evening. But Fleur wasn't going to let him in. She wasn't going to pick up the phone to him, she wasn't going to respond to any emails or text messages, or any blandishments he might send in the shape of flowers or champagne – *ouf*! Since she was still nursing her Chablis hangover, the very thought of champagne made her feel ill. Instead, she was going to spend her evening having fun with Hero Evanier.

She entered Corban's password and waited for Hero to rezz. Here he came . . . Oh! How cool he was, working that Johnny Depp rock star look! But – hmm. Maybe it was time he had a makeover. He was *way* too tall, and he needed to put on some weight. Fleur adjusted his height downward, and fattened him up a bit. Well, she actually fattened him up a lot. Then she gave him a small, squashed head, big sticky-out ears, bug eyes and a Cyrano de Bergerac nose.

Love handles? You bet! Bulging ones. Facial hair? Yes! A handlebar moustache. Shorter arms suited him, and bandy legs, and dainty hands and feet. Well, you know what they say about men with small feet?

Fleur played around with his clothing, too. She gave Hero short pants, mid-calf-length socks, and a puffy, diaphanous skirt. She added a big gold medallion to compensate for his small feet, and glittering earrings to draw light and radiance to his face, and then she changed his password from 'theoharaaffair' to the much more appropriate one of 'fleursrevenge'. Now, she thought with satisfaction, poor Monsieur Evanier would be trapped forever like a fly in amber as the ugliest avatar ever to frequent Second Life.

What's that smell? asked someone when Hero landed in Sweethearts nightclub, where the crème de la crème met up. **Who let the dog out?** said somebody else. Eyebrows were raised, elegant shoulders shrugged, and patrician noses pointed skywards. All the most beautiful residents of Second Life seemed to have congregated here tonight, and Hero stomped around randomly on his little feet, trying to make friends with them. He walked up to a slim blonde in a drop-dead-gorgeous frock. She disappeared without trace. He greeted a group of dudes with a **Yo, bros!** They ignored him. He sat down beside a Beyoncé lookalike, who curled her lip at him before taking to her sparkly heels.

Where, oh where was Hero's charm and charisma? But wait . . .

Where r u babe? asked a coquettish someone called Bo Peep.

I'm over here, typed Fleur.

But where? I want to see u.

I'm over by the bar.

Well, dude. Wanna buy me a drink?

Sure.

I'm coming to get you! Dainty Bo Peep rounded the corner of the bar, chocolate-box pretty in her shepherdess ensemble. **Hey!** she said.

Hello! typed Fleur.

OMG. What happened to you? You are so . . . Yes?

Ugly and small. Bo Peep gave him a repulsed look. **Bye, loser,** she said, and shimmied away.

Hmm. This Hero was clearly not the one Bo Peep was used to meeting up with in Sweethearts. Fleur wondered how many female avatars had been seduced by Hero Evanier on Second Life, how many he had invited to his cottage or dallied with on nudist beaches or fucked in orgy palaces. She knew now that Corban was an arch manipulator. He'd manipulated her and Bethany and Anastasia Harris and who knew how many other malleable women, and it felt good now to manipulate him here in Second Life. As for real life? That pleasure was yet to come.

In Sweethearts, Hero jumped. He laughed. He blew random kisses. He salsa danced. He plonked himself down in front of a drum kit and played worse than Animal in *The Muppets*. He stumbled around on his little bandy legs, crashing into people and landing on top of them, until someone approached and cautioned him. Oops! Skulking off, he sat by himself in a corner. Fleur didn't want to go too far – she wanted Hero's image tarnished, but she didn't want him banned from Second Life altogether. She had other plans for him.

At eight o'clock, she would send him to Shakespeare Island.

Bethany had been looking forward to eight o'clock p.m. since eight o'clock that morning. It had been a fabulous day, and she was desperate to share it with Hero. She was dying to tell him that she'd been promised a couple of lines in *The O'Hara Affair*; that she hadn't stumbled or dropped the hatbox; that not one, but two influential people had given her their cards; and that Elena Sweetman had been as sweet as her name and had told Bethany that she was wonderfully photogenic, and had given her a kiss on the cheek.

At around ten minutes before the appointed hour, Bethany took Poppet off to Shakespeare Island. Hero had not yet arrived. She made her avatar comfortable on their usual divan in the library, then decided to spend the intervening minutes until her date showed up by checking out Facebook.

Oh! Jake Malone had invited her to be his friend, adding a ;-) She accepted, then checked out his profile. Hmm. They shared a lot of the same interests. Films, theatre, books. His photo album was full of arty/amusing pictures, including one of a party on his roof garden. Lots of people had written witty comments on his wall. He had three hundred and eighty-six friends. Even Shane Byrne and Elena Sweetman were on there! Jake was too popular for her, Bethany decided. She was scared to write on his wall, scared that she might say something stupid and look like a loser.

But hurray! Flirty O'Farrell was online! Bethany sent her an IM saying, **Just off to meet my boyfriend in Second Life!**

The message she got back read: You're spending too much time there! And how do you know that your Hero isn't some pervy old git?

But Hero couldn't be a pervy old git. He spoke directly to Bethany's soul.

Back to the library on Shakespeare Island she went. Oh. Oh! Hero was sitting next to her – his nametag told her so, but he wasn't his beautiful self. He was misshapen, hideously ugly, and he was wearing a puffy see-through skirt, with short pants underneath. Poppet jumped up.

Hero! Is this a joke? she asked.

I'm afraid not, came the reply. **I'm showing you my true colours, Poppet. I know it's harsh, but this is your wake-up call. Life is real, life is earnest.**

Hero? It is you?

Yes.

Why have you changed?

I told you. These are my true colours. In the real world I am a sad middle-aged man who likes to pretend that I can recapture my youth by seducing young girls in Second Life.

Hero? You're joking, right?

No, Poppet. Go to my profile. You'll find a picture of me there.

Bethany clicked, and clicked again. There, on Hero's real-life profile, was a photograph of a fifty-something man. He was heavy-set, with a six o'clock shadow, and hooded eyes. It was Corban O'Hara.

No! she typed. **Stop it, Hero. You're scaring me.**

Poppet. I am teaching you a lesson. It may be an unpalatable one, but it's a lesson you need to learn. Look before you leap. And never judge a book by its cover.

Hero!

Never judge a book by its cover.

Hero? What are you playing at? Is this some stupid—

You heard me, Poppet. Never judge a book by its cover.

He was gone.

Bewildered, Bethany stared at her screen, waiting for Hero to come back as her prince valiant. After several moments of no show, she went to 'People' and searched. He wasn't online. What had happened? Why had he changed his avatar? And why had he put a picture of Corban O'Hara on his real-life profile? This was too, too weird.

Her IM blinked at her. Flirty.

No one ever told me I was pretty when I was a little girl. All little girls should be told they're pretty, even when they aren't: Marilyn Monroe.

Bethany couldn't engage. **Flirty – something strange just happened in SL,** she blurted.

What? Didn't your BF show up?

Yes, he did. But he had changed. He was awful and ugly. And he didn't sound like himself.

Tell me all about it.

So Bethany told Flirty everything that had happened on Shakespeare Island – everything, that is, bar the picture of Corban O'Hara that had featured on Hero's profile page. For some reason, that had been the most unsettling thing about the whole bizarre encounter, and she didn't want to share it.

Do you think it was his way of dumping you? asked Flirty, when Bethany had finished her tale of woe.

I guess maybe it was.

Are you upset?

Bethany realized that she was. Very upset. **Yes,** she said. She was almost too embarrassed to admit to Flirty how upsetting her 'date' with Hero had been. What a loser she was! To be upset because she'd been dumped by a virtual boyfriend in a virtual world!

I'm sorry to hear that, honey. Are you still in Diseart?

Yes.

Is it a lovely evening there?

Yes.

Go for a walk, sweetie-pie. It will clear your head.

Flirty was right. She should go for a walk, for a run – a swim, even. She needed to feel the evening sun on her face, the wind in her hair, the sand under her feet.

I'll do that, she told Flirty.

Take your phone. What's your number?

Bethany typed it in and sent it.

I'll text you mine. If you feel like talking, just give me a call.

You're very good to me.

I've become very fond of you. You take care.

I will.

Bethany logged off, resisting the temptation to go in search of her Hero. Flirty had been right. She'd been spending far too much time in fantasy land: it was time she got herself a real life. What was she doing, dancing on a beach in a virtual world when she could be doing it for real, just yards away? But, she thought, reaching for her phone, the sad fact was that in real life she had no one to dance with. She missed Hero already.

She tucked a towel and her swimming costume into her backpack, slid her feet into flip-flops, and opened the front door. Beyond the garden gate the sea was diamantine. There was a tang of salt in the air, a dolphin-shaped cloud was sailing in an expanse of cerulean sky, a curlew was calling plaintively. As she raised her face to the evening sun, the wind pulled her hair across her cheeks. *This* was life! This was real life. She didn't need a stupid Hero to make it good for her. Did she?

Shutting the front door behind her, Bethany hit the beach.

Chapter Twenty-Seven

Fleur logged off, feeling a little shaky. Had she done the right thing? She didn't want to make Bethany miserable, but she simply could not have allowed the girl's virtual relationship with that so-called 'Hero' Evanier to go any further. It would almost certainly have led to real harm: what Fleur had done was an exercise in damage limitation.

She wondered if Corban had tried to log in to Second Life yet; and how he'd react when he found he couldn't. She wondered if he had noticed that his home movie had gone missing, and what he'd make of that. She had not yet heard from him, but she knew he'd been in town because his car was no longer parked outside his apartment. She guessed he'd been working late on set, schmoozing with the glitterati.

She turned on the radio and turned it off again. She flipped through the pages of French *Vogue*, then let it drop to the floor. She reached for one of the smooth stones that she kept in a glass bowl on the table, and tossed it from hand to hand. Oh! How she longed for company. She wished she could bring forward her date with Jake Malone: she would love to get revenge on her erstwhile lover by openly flirting with a beautiful young man over a glass of wine, right here on her deck where the entire village could see – but really, what good would that do? She wasn't in the mood for flirting:

she needed to talk woman to woman. And Río was just down the road.

Grabbing her bag and phone, Fleur was just about to let herself out of her duplex when the door bell sounded. She froze. Corban? But, on checking the security cam, she saw that it was Dervla.

'Come up, come up!' she said, pressing the release.

Dervla climbed the stairs, looking drained. 'Can I have a glass of wine?' was the first thing she said.

Instantly, Fleur segued into counsellor mode. 'Of course, *chérie*. Red or white?'

'Preferably a bottle of each.' Dervla kissed Fleur on the cheek. 'Sorry. Whatever's open.'

'As always, there's a bottle on the deck,' smiled Fleur. 'You know, sometimes I feel like Captain Cat in *Under Milk Wood*, observing the goings-on of the village from his eyrie.'

'But wasn't he blind?'

'That's no excuse, when you have a first-class vantage point. Take a seat, and tell me what's troubling you. But first –' Fleur grabbed another glass from the cabinet '– tell me how you got away from your role as gaoler.'

Dervla collapsed on a patio chair, and put her head in her hands. 'I begged Finn to take over,' she said. 'Daphne gets on so well with him that I said I'd pay him double if he gave me a couple of hours off this evening. That's how badly I needed to get out of that house.'

'Are things worse than ever?'

'Yes. I got a phone call from Nemia today. Her mother's had a stroke. She won't be coming back.'

'*Merde!*' Fleur sucked in her breath. This *was* bad news. 'But surely it will be easy enough to find a replacement?'

Dervla shook her head. 'I made some phone calls today. It's actually *not* easy, Fleur. Carers are reluctant to live in a remote part of the country – we were really lucky that Nemia was dedicated enough to come all the way from London with Daphne. And there are all kinds of terms and conditions and clauses when you go through an agency. There may even have to be interviews to see if we're suitable candidates—'

'Hang on, dear one – shouldn't *you* be vetting *them*?'

'You'd think it would be that way, wouldn't you?' said Dervla, with a mirthless laugh. 'But agencies are so fussy now. Hell, they can afford to be. I'm not the only person in the country going demented caring for someone with dementia. There are thousands of us out there, desperate for help.'

Fleur unstoppered the bottle, and poured wine. 'What about hiring somebody local?'

'I did put an ad up in Ryan's when Nemia was due to go off on holiday, but the only person who replied was a boy with piercings who was into Radiohead.'

'OK. What about the homes you said you were going to visit?'

Dervla drooped. 'Oh, Fleur. You'd put a dog out of its misery rather than abandon it somewhere like that.'

'They're that bad?'

'No – they're not *bad*. It's not that they're unhygienic or anything like that: at least the one I saw wasn't.'

'I thought you had arranged to look at more than one?'

'I didn't get much past the first one – La Paloma. I wimped out, Fleur. I just found the whole exercise so dispiriting.'

'Here. Have wine.' Fleur handed Dervla a glass.

'Thanks.' Dervla swigged, then set her wineglass on the table. 'The thing is, La Paloma was lovely, and the staff were just gorgeous. But all the old people sit around in these big chairs, just kind of *lolling*. That's the only word I can find for it. They don't inhabit their bodies any more. They're all vacant, as if their souls have left the building and the lights have all been turned off, but there are ghosts living there still. And I know that I don't like Daphne much, but if she goes into one of those places, her lights will be put out and she'll haunt her own body for another ten, maybe twenty years, because she'll be kept alive by the miracle that is medical science, regardless of whether or not she wants to go on living.' Dervla took another swig of wine.

'D'you know what living with Daphne is like? It's like living with a dementor from Harry Potter. She's sucking away my soul. Look – she's even driven me to drink.' Dervla drained her glass, then reached for the bottle.

Fleur watched as Dervla filled her glass beyond what was an acceptable limit. 'OK,' she said. 'You clearly are not cut out for caring.'

'Who is?'

'Lots of people are. Caring is a vocation. It's something some really talented people are put on this planet to do. Mother Teresa was a shining example. But it's not your vocation, Dervla, and you can't beat yourself up about that.'

'But I'm being paid to look after Daphne! It's my job!'

'And you're doing it to the best of your ability. If someone handed me a violin and said, "I'll pay you to play that", I could take a stab at it, but it doesn't mean I'd be any good. You've bitten off more than you can chew, Dervla.'

'But I feel like such a wimp! I was the toughest gal in the auctioneering game, once upon a time. Look at me now, brought to my knees by a little old lady.'

Fleur raised an eyebrow. 'Maybe you should stand up to her more.'

'What do you mean?'

'Well, you say she treats you like a servant. Maybe if you

378

were less biddable she'd respect you more. Maybe, if you were more authoritative—'

'You don't understand, Fleur. I can't be authoritative. I have no shots to call. I am her employee. I *am* her servant.'

'That doesn't mean you shouldn't be treated with some respect.'

Dervla laughed. 'That's a bit like saying, "terms and conditions apply". Hel*lo*, Fleur! When it comes to dementia, there are no terms and conditions. Base cunning and guerrilla tactics are all that will get me through the next week.'

'You need a walk,' said Fleur, getting to her feet. 'Come on, up you get.'

'Beach or bog road?' asked Dervla listlessly.

'Beach. In situations like this, a blast of ozone is mandatory. We'll go down to Díseart.'

At this hour of the evening, the beach at Díseart was magical. The air seemed to shimmer with the intense golden glow of the low-slung sun, and the light bouncing off the islands made them gleam like cabochon emeralds. Feeling weightless in the water, Bethany found herself singing as she rolled over onto her back and followed the flight path of a seagull overhead. It felt good to be swimming in the sea instead of the pool she frequented in Dublin. Salt water was so much more buoyant: you could float forever. But actually, she realized, she couldn't stay in much longer. The water was not warm. She remembered how, as a child, she would immerse herself so long in the sea that she would be blue with cold when she emerged, and how she'd run back to the cottage where her mother would have hot chocolate waiting for her. She wished there was someone there now, waiting with hot chocolate and a towel warm from the airing cupboard to wrap her in.

Kicking her legs vigorously, she swam back to shore, to the scalloped shallows. She stood up and shook her head, sending droplets spinning like diamonds, then reached up to wring the rest of the water from her hair. She took a couple of steps through the thigh-high water, then stopped dead.

Where she had left her towel and her clothes, a man was standing, watching her.

Dervla clamped a hand over her mouth. 'I am so sorry!' she said. 'I've been so engrossed in my own problems that I didn't stop to think that you might have some of your own to share.'

Fleur and Dervla were walking along the boreen that led to the beach at Díseart. Since they'd left Fleur's place, they'd been lobbing between them the pros and cons of home versus residential care, without coming to any real conclusions. Dervla was in a real dilemma, thought Fleur. The tribulations of her own love life seemed petty in comparison, but she'd aired her grievances now, and it was good to hear Dervla call Corban a bastard, and worse.

'So he's been having an affair with Nasty Harris all along?' asked Dervla.

'So it would appear,' said Fleur. 'And it wouldn't surprise me if she weren't the only one.'

'Really? Do you think he's a sex addict, Fleur?'

'I think he's a fuckwit – literally. I think he's into mind fucking. He's like a serial collector of women.' Fleur shuddered. 'The most horrible part is to picture him in his penthouse watching me on my deck when I was on the phone to him, imagining he was in London. I bet he really got off on that.'

'What are you going to do?'

380

'I'm going to start seeing someone else.' Fleur affected a smug expression, but inside she was still feeling a little raw. 'Remember Jake Malone – the assistant director who showed us around the set the other day? He's asked me out. I'm meeting him for a drink next week.'

'Oh, Fleur! What fun!'

'Living well is the best revenge,' she quipped. 'Scott Fitzgerald said that. Sadly, he died an alcoholic in LA, writing unfilmable scripts for MGM and virtually destitute.'

'Did *anybody* in that Hollywood era live happily ever after?'

'Yes. Lauren Bacall did. And she's still going strong. *Merde*,' added Fleur as they rounded the bend of the boreen onto the beach. 'Somebody got here first.'

At the far end of the strand, a couple was sitting on the sand.

'They must be locals,' said Dervla. 'This beach is one of the best-kept secrets in Coolnamara. What I love is being able to walk it, knowing that mine will be the only footprints on it until the next tide washes them away.'

'Or until your footprints are joined by an otter's.' Fleur stooped to pick up a pebble. It was jade green, perfectly round, with a line of amber running through it. 'Look! How pretty is this! I'm going to add it to my collection. Ooh! And this one too.'

'You're going to have to buy another bowl to put them in. You've enough in that collection to pave a patio.'

'You can never have too many pretty pebbles. Ha. Maybe I should stand sentinel on my deck and throw them at Corban bloody O'Hara any time he passes.'

'Are you going to let him know you have his porny DVD?'

Fleur considered, then shook her head. 'No. I'll let him stew. Maybe he'll think that Audrey took it.'

'Are you sad, Fleur?'

'I'm more angry than sad. And I feel so stupid to have been manipulated by him, I really do. In all my relationships in the past, Dervla, I have called the shots. I suppose it's the result of my marriage going so wrong. Wanting to be in control of things. That's why I've always dated younger men. Corban was the first older man I'd been with since I followed my ex-husband to Ireland.'

'Do you ever hear from Tom?'

'No.' Fleur smiled a little nostalgically. Her ill-advised marriage had been enormous fun while it had lasted – turbulent and torrid and tender. 'I wonder if he's still with his Mountie in Canada. Maybe I should track him down on Facebook.' Abruptly, Fleur stopped in her tracks.

'What's wrong?' asked Dervla.

'The couple at the end of the beach. It's Jake Malone and Bethany O'Brien. Oh! Fucking men! Can't live with them, can't live without them.' Fleur hurled her pebbles into the sea. 'Now look what he's made me do! I really liked those pebbles.'

'There are lots more where they came from,' soothed Dervla.

Fleur made a *moue*. 'It is a truth universally acknowledged that there are more pebbles in the world than there are men you can trust.' Turning, she stomped back in the direction from which they'd come. 'I'm sorry, Dervla. I can't walk past them. They say you're getting old when you start looking at young people the way you might look at exotic flowers, and that pair resemble particularly luscious orchids.'

'No worries.' Dervla glanced at her watch. 'I should really get going, anyway. I promised Finn I'd be back by half-past nine, to put Daphne to bed.'

'How lucky is she, to have someone to put her to bed! If I ever get to that age, I'll have nobody.'

382

'You have your gorgeous niece, who is devoted to you.'

'I'm hardly going to expect Daisy to put me to bed and change my nappies. Oh, God, Dervla! It's so difficult to grow old – I hate, hate, *hate* it. Especially when one was beautiful once.'

'You're still beautiful, Fleur O'Farrell,' protested Dervla.

Fleur shook her head. 'You're not beautiful if you don't feel it from the inside. And I have that feeling less and less frequently these days.' She stooped automatically to pick up another pebble, then tossed it aside. It wasn't pretty enough for inclusion in her collection. 'I guess that's why I am fascinated by young people. Hooking up with them makes me feel as if I'm on an energy transfusion.'

'Tsk tsk. You have to embrace your inner goddess, my dear.'

'Except my inner goddess is probably Hecate.'

'Who was she?'

'The crone goddess worshipped by witches.'

'Oh, Fleur! Don't let him do this to you! This is all Corban's fault!'

'Sorry.' Fleur knew she was being truculent, but she couldn't help it. Seeing Jake and Bethany sitting together laughing on the sand had made her feel redundant and wretched. But Dervla was right. 'Are *you* on Facebook?' she asked, changing the subject.

'Yes. It was practically mandatory to be on Facebook in my estate agent days. I don't go there so often now.'

'Maybe I'll hunt you down when I get home.'

'Do that. It's funny – I was going to look for Corban and add him. I won't be doing that now.'

'Maybe we should just poke him to death.'

'Now there's a thought.'

Fleur wondered whether Corban's Facebook password was

the ubiquitous 'theoharaaffair', and concluded that that was unlikely. He had set up his Facebook account long before the film had gone into production. Shame. It would have been fun to mess about with his Facebook profile the way she had with his Second Life persona, and let the universe know what an ugly person Mr O'Hara really was.

'Look!' said Dervla, pointing at another pebble on the beach. 'There's a likely candidate.'

Fleur pounced on the pebble and pocketed it. 'More ammo,' she said.

Chapter Twenty-Eight

Bethany's hair was nearly dry. The air was still balmy, even though it was dusk. She ran a comb through her tangled mane and shook it out.

'You look like somebody in a shampoo ad,' said Jake, with a smile.

'Get away!'

'I worked on a shampoo commercial once. Those girls' hair's photoshopped to fuck. Fancy going to O'Toole's for a drink?'

Oh, yes, yes – she did!

'Um. OK. Cool. But I can hardly roll up in a damp swim-suit. Just let me go change.' Jumping to her feet, Bethany grabbed her backpack and ran to the cottage where she divested herself of the towel she had wrapped around herself earlier, sarong-style. What to wear, what to wear, what to wear? A delphinium blue cotton frock, flip-flops, a misting of Stila scent, a transparent slick of Vaseline on lips and eyebrows. An ankle bracelet. Why not?

When she came back out, shrugging into the sleeves of her prettiest cardigan, Jake was lounging against the garden gate looking like a *ragazzo*. 'OK,' he said. 'Now you don't look like someone in a shampoo commercial. You look like someone in an ad for fabric conditioner.'

'Fabric conditioner?'

'All clean and fresh and smelling of flowers. Mister O'Hara was right. You have a great face for camera, Bethany.'

'But I don't want to do ads! I want to be a proper actress.'

'Don't knock ads. There's a lot of money to be made from them.'

'Money isn't everything.'

'Not until you don't have any. I know actors who once turned up their noses at commercial work who would now kill for a gig.'

Bethany resisted the impulse to reach for his arm as they began to negotiate the uneven terrain.

'Tell me about the actors you've worked with,' she said. 'Have you met anyone famous?'

'Don't be fooled by the fame game, Bethany. Kids these days don't know what they're letting themselves in for when they woo the cult of celebrity. There's nothing very glamorous about being famous – it's hard graft. Imagine trying to stroll down to O'Toole's for a quiet pint if you're Kate Winslet or Colin Farrell looking anything other than one hundred per cent gorgeous.'

'I'm not afraid of hard work.'

'If you can get it. I know a casting director whose kids use the backs of actors' CVs as drawing paper.'

And as they walked along the boreen that would take them to the main road, Jake told Bethany cautionary tale after cautionary tale about the film industry until, by the time they reached O'Toole's, Bethany was wondering if she really wanted to be an actress after all.

Dervla pulled up outside Daphne's cottage, steeling herself to go in. Maybe she could just flee – head for the hills and leave Finn to it? But then she'd be investigated by the social services and arrested for dereliction of care. Besides, she could hardly land her nephew with the chore of putting Daphne to bed. She switched off the engine. Mozart's sixth came to an abrupt end, to be replaced by the strains of 'Summer Holiday' wafting through the open window of the sitting room. Finn and Daphne were dancing to Cliff Richard. Well, Finn was doing a vigorous twist; Daphne was clutching the back of a chair and swaying gently from side to side, a beatific smile on her face, a white rose tucked behind her ear.

Dervla hurried through the front door and into the sitting room.

'What's going on?' she yelled, over the din.

'We're having a party!' Finn yelled back, as Dervla picked up the remote and cut the music.

Daphne stepped backwards and fell into her armchair with an 'Oof!' Then she glared at Dervla. 'Spoilsport,' she said, reaching for a glass and swigging back the contents. 'More gin, young Finn!' she said. 'I'm a poet and I know it.'

Dervla turned aghast eyes on Finn. 'You haven't been giving her gin?!' she said.

'She asked for it. She said you always have gin and tonic in the evening.'

'You're a tonic, young Finn. Finn and tonic.'

'How many has she had?' asked Dervla.

'Two.'

'There once was a man called Michael Finnegan,' sang Daphne, then hiccuped.

'Just two? Are you sure?'

'He had whiskers on his chinnegan. Hic.'

'Yes,' said Finn.

'They fell out and then grew in again.'

'You must have poured her bloody large measures,' Dervla rebuked him.

'Poor old Michael *finny finny Finnegan*,' finished Daphne, triumphantly.

'I'm not that irresponsible, Dervla.'

Dervla drew Finn into the kitchen, where the gin bottle was unstoppered on a work surface. It had been full before Dervla left the cottage this evening: now it was nearly half empty.

'Oh shite,' said Finn. 'She must have been helping herself while I was on the phone. I honestly didn't give her that much.'

From the sitting room came the sound of Daphne singing along to Cliff Richard.

'She's in flying form,' remarked Finn. 'We had a really good time. She showed me around the patio, and we sat singing on her swing seat for ages. We picked flowers, too – look.' Finn indicated a jug on the windowsill in which half a dozen white roses had been arranged.

'Pretty!' remarked Dervla, abstractedly.

'She arranged them herself. She said she'd had plenty of practice as a girl when her beaux used to bring her flowers. I told her I'd bring her a dozen red ones next time I came.'

Dervla gave a wan smile. 'You smooth-talker, you! I don't suppose you'd think about taking on the job full time?'

'I could sure do with the cash, but – Jesus! What kind of life would that be? Stuck in a cottage in the country with a batty old woman!'

That's my life, thought Dervla. Who would ever have thought it?

'I'm going to have to get her into bed now,' she said with a sigh. 'I've a feeling she won't go quietly.' Dervla reached for the Gordons and poured herself a large one. 'If you can't beat 'em . . .' she said.

'How much longer do you have to do this?'

'Christian's due back on Friday.'

'So you've another week to go. I'll help out, Dervla, any time I'm not involved in filming.'

'How does it feel,' Dervla asked, droppng ice cubes into her drink, 'to prance around on horseback wearing women's clothes?'

'I could get used to it,' said Finn with an arch smile.

'What a weird way to earn a living.'

'Piggy on the railway, picking up stones,' sang Daphne, from the sitting room. 'I want a gin and tonic!'

'Right back atcha, Piggy!' said Finn. 'I'd better go, Dervla. I promised Dad I'd meet him in O'Toole's.'

'It must be fun, working on the same project as your mum and dad.'

'Well, we haven't had a row yet. Ma even volunteered to cook for Dad tonight.'

'What's she doing?'

'Some Nigella Lawson thingy. She's even been practising!' Finn bent and kissed his aunt's cheek. 'Good luck, Aunty dear, and good night.'

'Good night, darling.'

Dervla leaned back against the kitchen island and took a swig of her drink. From the kitchen she could hear Finn's farewell to Daphne.

'I'm off now, Mrs Vaughan,' he said. 'Thank you for having me.'

'You're welcome, young man. Come back and visit me again soon. And ask someone to bring me a drink on your way out, will you please?'

'I'm not sure you should be having another drink, Mrs Vaughan. It's late. Dervla will be in soon, to help put you to bed.'

'I'm perfectly capable of putting myself to bed, thank you. Good night. Sleep tight.'

'And don't let the bugs bite,' said Finn. Then Dervla heard the front door close behind him.

The house fell suddenly silent – Dervla felt awfully lonely. She knew she should go into the sitting room and persuade her mother-in-law to go to bed, but she didn't have the energy. She'd stay on here for five minutes, finish her drink. Then she'd cross the last hurdle of the day: get Daphne into bed, and get an early night herself. She'd taken to making sure that her bedroom door was locked at night, because she found the prospect of Daphne coming into her bedroom so unnerving.

The ice tinkled in her glass, and then she heard a sound from the sitting room. Daphne was moving around. She came out into the corridor, and Dervla stiffened, thinking that she might be heading for the kitchen to replenish her glass, but instead she heard the old lady make her way slowly but steadily along the corridor towards her bedroom. She was going quietly, without kicking up her usual stink about not wanting to go to bed. The gin must have made her sleepy. Dervla heard her go into the bathroom and have a tinkle, and she thought: Thank God! Maybe she will last the night without needing to go again. She really didn't want to make the effort of persuading Daphne to get into incontinence pants this evening.

Dervla took another couple of hits of her drink, then followed Daphne into her bedroom, where she was drawing the curtains.

'Oh!' Daphne said, when she turned and saw Dervla. 'You gave me a fright!'

'It's all right, Daphne,' said Dervla. 'I'm Dervla, who is married to your son Christian, and I'm staying here with you.'

'Oh, yes.' Daphne teetered towards her dressing table, and

started rummaging among the items there. To Dervla's astonishment, she picked up her lipstick, and slicked some on.

'Daphne? Why are you putting on lipstick?'

'Aren't we going out?'

'No. It's late – it's ten o'clock at night.'

'Ten o'clock? But that's early! I always dance till dawn.'

'Wouldn't you rather have a nice story?' suggested Dervla.

'A story? I haven't had a story read to me since I was a child! Are you my mother?'

'No,' said Dervla.

Daphne sat down on the edge of the bed. 'I must telephone my mother. She worries about me if I don't come home.'

'You can telephone her in the morning,' Dervla assured her. 'It's too late to phone her now. She'll be asleep.' She took hold of the sleeve of Daphne's cardigan, and pulled it gently off first one arm, then the other. Then she plumped up the pillows, and persuaded Daphne back against them before taking hold of her legs and levering them up onto the mattress. She took off Daphne's slippers, and gave her her ARICEPT, and drew the duvet up over the old lady's sunken chest. Then she reached for the volume from which she'd been reading Daphne's bedtime stories. She'd given up on Roald Dahl – his stuff was too dark – and had opted for *The Fairy Stories of Oscar Wilde* instead.

'"The Selfish Giant",' said Dervla, opening the book.

'The what giant?'

'The *selfish* giant. It's the one about the giant who wouldn't let the children play in his garden.'

'Oh. All right. Go on.'

Oh, God. Dervla hoped that Daphne wasn't going to ask her to repeat herself every few words. She made sure to keep her decibel level up and her enunciation crisp, so that there could be no complaints.

391

By the end of the story, Daphne had tears in her eyes, and so did Dervla.

"'And the child smiled on the Giant',' said Dervla, "'and said to him, 'You let me play once in your garden, today you shall come with me to my garden, which is Paradise.' And when the children ran in that afternoon, they found the Giant lying dead under the tree, all covered with white blossoms.'"

'Oh!' cried Daphne. 'That's very sad.'

'Yes,' said Dervla, closing the book and setting it on the table. 'It is a sad story. But it's a very beautiful one. A nice way to go, come to think of it, in a garden covered in blossom.'

She pulled the covers up around Daphne's neck, and kissed her on the forehead. At the door, she turned and said, as she always did, 'Good night, Daphne. Sleep tight and sweet dreams.'

And then she went into the kitchen and topped up her glass. She'd take one of Christian's sleeping pills tonight, she decided. She deserved to sleep like a log.

Chapter Twenty-Nine

Fleur had arrived home after her aborted walk in Díseart with Dervla to find both her landline and her mobile phone full of messages. They were all from Corban. 'Hey, beautiful. I've been thinking of you for two weeks now. I'll call around later with your present. Can't wait to see you, gorgeous.' Click. 'Hi, sweetheart. Do you know what the story is with your cleaning person? She doesn't seem to have come in.' Click. 'Fleur? Are you there? I wish you'd pick up. I think your cleaning person may have helped herself to some of my personal effects.' Click. 'Fleur. This is deeply serious. I think your cleaning person has been fiddling around with my computer. I wish you'd pick up. Fleur? *Fleur?*' Click.

Your cleaning person. He hadn't even bothered to remember Audrey's name. But then, that's what people were to Corban. Commodities, not sentient beings. *Merde!* Let him stew. She never wanted to see him again. The man with whom she had believed herself to be in love was a construct, not the real thing.

She started up her laptop, then went upstairs to change. Once upon a time she'd have got into something slinky for Corban and spent the entire evening trying to hold her tummy in. Tonight she got into baggy sweat pants and a T-shirt, scraped her hair back from her face, secured it with a scrunchy, then scrubbed her face with an exfoliating cleanser. She slathered on a vitamin E face mask, tucked her feet into gel-lined moisturizing socks, went into the kitchen and made herself a cup of cocoa. Then she lit a scented candle, sat down at her computer, and thought about logging on to Second Life. Her lip curled. She didn't think so.

Instead, she logged on to Facebook. She'd chosen as her latest Facebook avatar an image of the young Audrey Hepburn circa *Roman Holiday*. *Merde!* What was she doing, masquerading as a twenty-something cutie with her finger on the pulse? She should do herself a favour, and 'fess up. She should enter her real birthdate into Facebook, her real profession, her real worries and concerns, and communicate with the real world without hiding behind a twenty-one-year-old alias called Flirty, or avatars disguised as glamour queens and *gamines*. It was time for Fleur to grow up. Youth was the preserve of – well – the young, and she should leave them to it.

But, hell – she suspected that growing up took energy, and she was too tired to do it tonight. Scrolling down through her list of friends, she found herself looking at the image of her bright and beautiful niece. She entered Daisy's password and clicked. Daisy had hundreds of friends, but they were not all bright and beautiful. They were an eclectic bunch. Daisy had old friends and young, friends who were members of MENSA, and friends who had special needs. She had friends of all creeds and colours, all shapes and sizes, and all sexual persuasions. Daisy embraced the world.

Fleur went to her own home page, opened a box, and started to type in a message. She didn't know when Daisy would be visiting the next hill station in KwaZulu Natal where she could pick it up, but she had an overwhelming impulse to reach out to the niece who was the daughter she'd never had.

However, she hadn't got beyond *Daisy-Belle! I miss you!* when the doorbell rang. She barely needed to check the security cam to know that it was Corban. He rang again. And again. And again. He kept his finger on the doorbell until Fleur wanted to scream at him to shut up and go away. But she wasn't going to let him win this time. She went back to her laptop, put on headphones and played 'Diamonds are a Girl's Best Friend' very loudly. Marilyn Monroe had never sung a truer word.

In Díseart, Jake had walked Bethany to her front door, kissed her on the cheek, and said good night. They'd had a fine time in O'Toole's. They hadn't been able to talk much because there'd been a music session on, but after a couple of drinks they'd left with that feeling of exhilaration that live Irish music always stirs in the soul.

Bethany felt like dancing still: she was restless, wide awake. She wished she'd invited Jake in for coffee, but she didn't want to look too keen on a first date. Was that what it had been? A date? Maybe not, exactly. But it seemed he had sought her out. What else could have brought him to Díseart?

Oh – stupid, stupid girl! *What else could have brought him to Díseart?* she parroted in a parody of her own voice. Only the view, the sea air, the fact that it was a perfect evening for a stroll along one of the loveliest strands in all of Coolnamara? Of all the attractions in Díseart, Bethany O'Brien would rate well low on the list.

She had a quick shower to wash the sea salt from her skin, got into the T-shirt and boxers she always wore to bed, made herself a cup of green tea, then sat down in front of her laptop. Second Life? No. No vicarious living for her. Bethany had had a flavour of real life today, and it had tasted good.

She went to 'Favourites', and clicked on Facebook. Hey!

She had four more requests for friendship, and Elena Sweetman had added her! There was lots of YouTube stuff to check out, and a status update from . . . Jake!

'What's on my mind? "Erin Shore" . . .'

'Erin Shore' had been the last piece of music played in the pub this evening! Bethany hugged herself. Her fingers hovered over the keyboard for a time, itching to type in a comment, but since she could think of no suitable riposte, she went instead to Windows Live Messenger to see who else was online. Yay! Flirty was signed in. Bethany clicked.

Hey, Flirty! she said. **How are you? I've had such a fab evening!**

Glad to hear it! came the response. What did you get up to?

I went for a swim and then I went for a drink with the cute AD on the film. There was a session on in O'Toole's.

I know. I could hear it from my deck.

What the—? Had Bethany read this right?

What do you mean? she typed.

There was a pause, and then an 'embarrassed face' icon appeared in the chat box.

I have a confession to make, Bethany. I am not 21 and my name is not Flirty. My real name is Fleur, and I own the shop just down the road from O'Toole's in Lissamore.

You mean you're Fleur of Fleurissima? If Bethany had been speaking rather than typing, she'd have stammered.

Yes. Another blushing emoticon appeared. I feel very embarrassed about this.

No worries! replied Bethany, feeling the need to say something – *anything* – while she got her head around this.

But why don't you want people to know who you are really? I would have thought that you'd be proud to be you.

I like to keep up with the younger demographic, and I've found Facebook and MSN a great place to do it. I didn't think any young people would want to talk to me if I gave my real age.

Bethany hesitated, then smiled and typed, **What's to be sorry for? Sure, don't loads of people hide behind different identities online. Some of them might be weirdos** – and she'd learned *that* to her cost this evening – **but you've always been so kind and nice to me and full of good advice.**

You really mean that?

Yes. I think it's quite a clever thing to do, actually. In your line of work you need to know what's going on and there's no better way of keeping up to spin than Facebook. Bethany sniggered. How weird it felt to be giving Flirty advice, instead of it being the other way round! **Apparently Anastasia Harris goes on all the time under an alias to find out what people are saying about her.**

Bethany pressed 'Send', then drained her cup of tea. What a weird, weird, small, small world it was! And as she waited for her new friend Fleur to respond, she heard a car draw up outside the gate of her cottage.

Apparently Anastasia Harris goes on all the time under an alias to find out what people are saying about her, Fleur read, and smiled. If that pornographic home movie ever made it on to YouTube, she bet Anastasia Harris would have another think about wanting to know what people were saying about her.

I hope she hasn't found out what her nick-name is, Fleur typed, in response to Bethany's last comment.

There was no response.

Bethany? Fleur took another sip of cocoa. *Hello, Bethany – are you there?*

Her phone rang. She ignored it. It would be that bastard bastarding Corban again. He'd given up ringing her door-bell at last, and Fleur had watched through the kitchen window as he'd lumbered away and got into his car. That man should not be driving, she'd thought, as he'd taken off at speed. He was quite clearly drunk – which was most unlike Corban. Fleur had never seen him drunk before – he was always far too focused on staying in control. The disappeared DVD must have rattled him badly. Or else he was missing her so desperately already that he was drowning his sorrows and preparing to drive off the pier – ha ha ha. Knocking back the rest of the cocoa in her mug, Fleur rinsed it, stacked it in the dishwasher, then went upstairs to fetch her tooth-brush. When she came back to the kitchen, the following was waiting for her in her inbox.

I NEED TO TALK URGENT CAN U FONE PLS

Fleur picked up her phone. The number of the missed call displayed on her screen told her that it had not been from Corban. It had been from Bethany. Without hesitation, she pressed 'Reply'.

It rang for some moments before Bethany picked up. 'Hello?' she said, in a very small voice.

'Bethany? It's Fleur.'

'Oh – thank God! I thought it might have been him.'

'Who?'

'The producer of the film – Corban O'Hara.'

'*What?* Why?'

'He's outside my house,' she whispered.

Fleur put a hand on the table for support. 'Bethany! What's going on?'

'I – I heard a car stop, and then someone came up the path and rang the doorbell. I looked out the top window and it was him. And then he rang again a couple of times, but I didn't want to let him in. I mean, maybe there's a perfectly reasonable explanation for it, but I'd feel uncomfortable answering the door in my night clothes, and it's late, and I'm awful scared, Flirty.'

'Is he still at the door?'

'No. He's down on the beach. He's walking around in circles like a – like a bear or something. Oh, please, Flirty – can you help? I don't want to phone the guards because I don't want to make a fuss—'

'Why not?'

'He – he's an important guy and it might harm my acting career if I get him into trouble. Maybe he'll think I'm asleep or something, and go away.'

'Is there a light on in the cottage?'

'Yes. I didn't want to turn it off because that would mean he'd know there was definitely someone at home.'

'Bethany – sit tight. Do not move. Do not go to the door. I'll be there in five minutes. Wait for me.'

Fleur grabbed her car keys, snuffed out the candle and let herself out, incandescent with rage. What did that bastard think he was playing at, harassing girls young enough to be his daughter? He'd truly overstepped the mark this time – all that power he wielded had made him lose the plot. How many women did Mr O'Hara need to seduce and manipulate before he was satisfied? *She* – Fleur Thérèse Odette de Saint-Euverte, compliant mistress and elegant arm candy – was no longer one of his harem, that was for sure. And maybe, she thought – just maybe – that was what was maddening him most? That – by refusing to take his calls nor allowing him access all areas as she normally did – she had gained the upper hand?

Her car was parked opposite O'Toole's. As she inserted the key, Shane and Finn came rollicking through the door, laughing, clearly having enjoyed a few pints. Fleur suddenly realized that it could be a massive act of folly to go down to Díseart alone. Someone had once told her that Díseart was the Irish for 'desert or isolated place'. And – oh! Bethany was alone and in danger there.

'You two!' said Fleur, in her most commanding voice. 'Come with me!'

Shane and Finn turned astonished eyes on her. Fleur knew she must look like a madwoman, in her gel socks and with her face gooey with vitamin E cream, but she didn't care.

'What's up?' asked Finn, cautiously.

'Get in the car and I'll tell you.' Her tone brooked no dissent.

Shane and Finn exchanged looks, and got meekly into the car, Finn having to practically fold himself double on the narrow back seat.

'Where are we going?'

'Díseart.'

'Díseart? Why Díseart?' asked Shane.

'Because there's a girl there who is under threat from Corban bastard O'Hara.'

Fleur put the car into gear with an aggression that made Shane wince. As she drove, she filled her passengers in on exactly what Corban had done. They knew already about his duplicity – about his affair with Anastasia Harris – but the fresh details of his debauchery shocked them to the core.

'So you think he's been targeting this girl?' asked Shane.

'Yes. But he has – um – how do you say it? He has lost the run of himself.'

'I always mistrusted that gobshite,' said Shane. 'He's a fucking sociopath. I've been looking for ages for an excuse to tell him to shove his film up his hole and hit him a good dig.'

'You are not going to hit him a dig. I am.'

'Fleur! That'd be like pitting a miniature poodle against a Rottweiler.'

Fleur gave Shane a supercilious look. 'Don't you know how I keep in shape, *chéri*? I kick-box.'

'Well, Fleur O'Farrell – you rock!'

'*Merde!*' said Fleur with feeling. 'I forgot my phone. Has one of you a camera phone? I'd like this to be on record.'

'Yes,' said Finn. 'I have.'

'And please don't either of you intervene unless I ask you to. I want to have the pleasure of knocking Mr O'Hara's lights out all to myself.'

A minute or so later, they came to the end of the boreen. All was quiet, apart from the sussuration of wavelets on the shore. Corban's car was parked outside Bethany's cottage: Fleur pulled up beside it. There was no sign of him on the beach, in the garden, or in the field beyond.

Getting out of the car, Fleur marched up the garden path. She was invincible – Jeanne d'Arc flanked by her generals, and she was firing on all cylinders.

'Bethany!' she called, pressing the doorbell. 'Are you there?'

There was no answer.

'Bethany!' Fleur raised a fist to bang on the door, then realized that it was open a fraction. The lock had been forced. She pushed.

Inside the cottage, Corban was lolling on a sofa, one leg dangling over the arm, the other stretched out before him.

'Well, *bonsoir*, beloved,' he slurred. 'What a coincidence. I came looking for Bethany too, but it would appear that there's no one home. Little Red Riding Hood must have run back to mummy.' Unhooking his leg from the arm of the sofa, Corban rose unsteadily to his feet. It was clear that he wasn't aware of Shane and Finn standing just outside the front door. He gave an unpleasant laugh. 'What's this?' he said, peering at her face. 'Fleur *sans maquillage. Ooh la la*! Looks like you're past your sell-by date, sugar. Best before . . . hmm . . . five, ten years ago, maybe.'

Fleur regarded him levelly. Then, very calmly, she shifted her balance, raised her right leg, and aimed a leisurely kick at Corban's shoulder. He reeled backwards.

'What the fuck!' he cried, clutching the arm of the sofa.

Fleur laughed out loud at the expression on his face. He looked like the school bully surprised by the class wimp; Goliath toppled by David.

Raising a hand, he rubbed his left shoulder. Then he turned a dazed look back at her and narrowed his eyes. 'You stupid bitch,' he growled. 'Oh, you stupid little bitch. You are so going to regret that, Mademoiselle O'Farrell.'

'I don't think so,' said Fleur, with hauteur. 'I'm not sure that wasn't one of the most enjoyable moments of my life.'

Corban took a step towards her, murder in his eyes. This time, Fleur smashed a foot into his chest, and he fell heavily onto the sofa.

'Did you get that on camera, Finn?' she asked, glancing over her shoulder.

'Sure did.' Finn ambled into the room, checking out the images on his screen. 'Wow. That's some sequence. Lucy Liu, eat your heart out. You could be a Charlie's Angels stunt double, Fleur.'

'Who the fuck are you?' demanded Corban.

'He's my cameraman,' Fleur told him. 'I'm filming a

402

documentary on the making of *The O'Hara Affair*. I've already got some extremely interesting footage.'

Finn was joined by Shane, who took the phone, looked at it and smiled. 'You look like a prize loser, O'Hara,' he said. 'You look like the tosser I've always suspected you to be.'

Corban's face had turned an ugly shade of puce. 'What are you doing here, you arse-wipe actor?'

Shane handed the phone back to Finn. 'I'm here because I wanted to see you get what you deserve. And it was well worth watching. You're a nasty piece of work, Mr O'Hara. I don't like men who prey on little girls.'

A creak on a floorboard from above made them look up. Bethany was crouching on the landing, pale-faced and vulnerable in scanty sleepwear. 'Thank you,' she said.

Lumbering to his feet, Corban fixed Shane with a threatening look. 'You don't want to mess with me, pal,' he warned. 'I could pull the plug on this movie in the morning.'

'But you won't pull the plug,' said Fleur, with equanimity. 'Because you won't want my documentary to be made public. Are you still filming, Finn?'

'Yes, ma'am.'

'And the additional footage I have at home could be of even more interest to the general public,' she continued. 'Except *that* is X-rated stuff.'

A closed look came over Corban's face.

'I took the DVD from your apartment, Corban,' Fleur told him. 'I've burned several more copies, and they're in a vault in the bank. If you cut finance to this movie, I will make sure that not only will Finn's video be made available to the disappointed distributors – your own escapades on celluloid will be too.'

'Fleur, don't be so fucking—'

'Shut up, Corban. There's more, so listen carefully. I do

not want you to come back to Lissamore. I want you to put your penthouse on the market. I do not want you to attend the wrap party of *The O'Hara Affair*. If you do, my documentary will have its premiere in the community hall in Lissamore that same night. And then it will go up on YouTube.' Fleur shifted her balance, looking at him with intent, and Corban flinched. 'I want you to go now,' she said. 'And you are to *walk* back to the village, because if you get into the car I shall call the guards and have you charged not only with drunk-driving, but with breaking and entering.' She indicated the forced lock with a brief nod. 'Go now, Corban. *Vas t'en*. Run along like a good boy.'

Corban looked balefully around at the room. Then, mustering whatever dignity a debauched drunk can manage, he blundered through the door of Bethany's cottage, and staggered into the night.

There was silence in the room. Then Shane started to clap his hands. 'Fleur O'Farrell!' he said. 'You are the stuff of legend!'

Finn and Bethany joined in the applause, as Fleur collapsed on the sofa. 'Oh – *merci à Dieu!*' she said. 'I need a drink after that.'

'There's brandy,' said Bethany. Getting to her feet, she descended the stairs and crossed the room to a cupboard.

'Let me do it,' said Shane. 'You go sit down.'

Bethany sat on the sofa beside Fleur, and tucked her feet up under her.

Fleur took her hand. 'Are you all right?' she asked.

Bethany nodded. 'I'm just a bit shaken.'

'I'm not surprised,' said Fleur. 'You poor little kitten. Tell me *chérie* – do you want to press charges?'

'I don't know. I –' Bethany considered, then shook her head '– no. I don't want to press charges. A friend of mine reported a minor assault once, and she was put through the mill by barristers. She said that in the end the courtroom experience was worse than the attack.'

'Well, rest assured that *Monsieur* won't be bothering you again, *ma petite*.'

Shane handed Fleur a glass, and offered another to Bethany. 'No thanks,' she said. 'You have it. I hate brandy.'

'Can I get you something else?'

'Green tea would be good. There's a box of teabags by the kettle in the kitchen.'

'Mind if I help myself to a brandy, too?' asked Finn.

'Sure,' said Bethany. Then she made a 'yikes' face. 'Shit. My dad will think I've been partying.'

'No worries. I'll replace it,' said Shane, disappearing into the kitchen.

'And I'll organize someone to fix the door,' said Fleur. 'Are your parents coming down for the long weekend?'

'Yes. They never miss the regatta.'

'OK. So you're sorted for company this weekend. And you're staying with me tonight.'

'Oh, can I, Fleur? Thank you – thank you so much.'

Fleur squeezed her hand. 'You can stay as long as you like – why not stay until the film wraps?'

'That's real kind of you, but I'm going to ask Mummy to stay on here. I didn't realize until now how much I missed her.'

Fleur smiled. This babe who looked drop-dead gorgeous in scanties still needed her mother . . .

'It must have been dead lonely for you staying here all by yourself,' remarked Finn.

'Not really. I love this place so much I haven't ever been spooked.'

Until tonight, thought Fleur, grimly. Corban O'Hara may

have the Midas touch when it came to making money, but he besmirched everything else he laid his hands on.

'What did you do, darling, when he forced the door?' she asked.

'I hid in the airing cupboard.'

'*Mon Dieu!* Flogging is too good for that man. Were you there for long?'

'No. Just a couple of minutes. I heard him fall through the door, and then nothing till you arrived.'

'Let's definitely scupper his boat,' Finn piped up.

'What?'

'Dad and me are going to scupper his boat,' he repeated. 'We could do it, no problem. Couldn't we, Dad?'

'Sure,' said Shane from the kitchen. 'If you get hold of the gear.'

'What gear?' said Bethany, puzzled.

'Scuba kit. We'll go down some night when there's a gale forecast and cut through his moorings. It'll look like an accident, and even if he suspects it ain't, there's not a lot he's going to want to do about it.'

Fleur clapped her hands. 'My godson, *le héros!*' she said. 'What sweet revenge!'

'I'm sorry to have put you to all this trouble,' said Bethany. 'I mean, it's not as if he did any real harm.'

Fleur saw that the girl was looking a little confused. All she knew was that a trio comprising a mad-looking French woman and two half-cut men, one of them a Hollywood A-lister, had come barging into her cottage, beaten a man up, ordered him to get out of town, and were now planning to scupper his yacht. That was pretty harsh punishment to mete out to a drunk whose seeming only crime had been to break into a cottage and collapse upon a couch. No wonder she was confused! She must think that the civilian law enforcement ethos in the sleepy hamlet of Lissamore was akin to that in *Kill Bill*.

'Trust me,' said Fleur, putting an arm around Bethany's shoulders. 'You don't know the half of it.'

And as she took a welcome hit of brandy, Fleur hoped that that was all that Bethany would ever know about the toxic incident that had been the O'Hara affair. She hoped neither of them would have the misfortune to have an encounter – virtual or otherwise – with Corban O'Hara ever again in their lives.

Chapter Thirty

When Dervla awoke, sunshine was streaming through the bedroom window. She'd forgotten to shut the curtains last night before getting into bed. She lay still for some time, thinking. Her sleep had been profound, dreamless, and uninterrupted by any rattling of the door handle. She felt rested for the first time in weeks. That sleeping pill had certainly done the job.

She wished Christian were here. She'd love a cuddle whilst enjoying a lie-in, a laugh with her husband. When was the last time she'd laughed for pure joy? The only adverbs to describe the way she laughed now were 'mirthlessly' or 'darkly' or 'sourly'. Christian had emailed her a joke last night that had made her laugh 'grimly'. It went: 'Did you hear about the eighty-three-year-old woman who talked herself out of a speeding ticket by telling the officer that she had to get there before she forgot where she was going?'

She got out of bed, slid into her kimono, and went to the loo. In the kitchen, she switched on the kettle and the radio, and set about making Daphne's breakfast.

'Irish people now live longer than the EU average,' announced the newsreader on RTE 1. 'The HSE says this poses its own challenges for the health services in dealing with chronic illnesses that would previously have reduced life expectancy—'

Challenges! Why not call a spade a spade and use the word 'problems'?

Dervla changed the channel to Lyric FM, and Mozart's clarinet concerto came cascading through the speakers. She chopped strawberries and she buttered toast and filled the little cream jug and made sure there were no dusty bits in the Crunchy Nut Cornflakes. Then she took a white rose from the jug on the windowsill and set it by the toast rack, before carrying the breakfast tray through to Daphne's room.

The bed was empty. Dervla set the tray down on the table and went into the bathroom. There was no sign of her mother-in-law there, nor any sign that she had used the loo. She wasn't in the sitting room, and she hadn't strayed into Dervla's room by mistake. Oh, God! Could she have escaped through the front door? But Dervla distinctly remembered having locked it last night, after she'd put Kitty to bed in the kitchen of the big house. She went to double-check, just in case. Yes. The mortise had been turned twice, the Yale secured, and the safety chain hooked in place. The kitchen door was locked too. That only left . . . the sliding doors in Daphne's bedroom – the ones that were usually locked. But last night – last night Finn and Daphne had been out there, picking flowers and swinging on the garden seat . . .

Dervla raced back to the room. The curtains were still closed, but lifting a little in the breeze. The room smelled not of old lady, but of jasmine. That could only mean one thing.

Feeling like an ice sculpture, Dervla crossed to the window and pulled the curtains. Beyond the open glass doors, two white peacocks were strutting on the grass, which was stippled with daisies. Daphne was sitting on the swing seat, her face turned to the sun. She was wearing her nightgown, and there was jasmine blossom on her lap and in her hair. As Dervla approached, she saw that Daphne's smiling mouth still bore the traces of the lipstick she'd put on the night before.

'Daphne?' said Dervla. 'Are you all right?'

There was no reply. Dervla didn't need to touch her mother-in-law to know that she was dead.

Christian flew home immediately. His sister Josephine came from Australia, and his daughter Megan from the UK, while his ex-wife Valentina flew in from Tuscany. Nemia returned from Malta to pay her respects and pack her bags before heading off to care for her mother in London.

On the evening before the funeral, all six of them went for dinner in O'Toole's.

'What a fabulous send-off,' said Nemia. 'Dancing to Cliff Richard with a beautiful boy and swigging back gin and tonic.'

'And being read *The Selfish Giant*,' said Josephine. 'The most beautiful, uplifting account of death ever written. I can't thank you enough, Dervla.'

Dervla felt guilty. She could hardly tell Josephine the kind of black thoughts that she'd been harbouring about her mother-in-law during the days leading up to her death. But Nemia was right: Daphne had had a damned fine death. She was glad that the old lady had had her teeth in, and had not been wearing nappies. She was glad that she'd been wearing lipstick, and her favourite pale pink nightdress, and that she'd had a bath that day, and that she'd been spritzed with *Je Reviens*. She liked to think that the last things on earth Daphne might have seen were a pair of pristine white peacocks, that her last breath had been scented with jasmine, that the last sounds she'd heard were the strains of the clarinet concerto from the kitchen.

'I know it's not kosher to ask,' said Megan. 'But how much was granny worth?'

'Not much,' said Christian, gloomily. 'There's her collection of japonaiserie, but that's about it.'

'But I thought money had been invested from the sale of her flat in London?'

'It was invested by her broker in Northern Rock.'

Megan's face was a picture of disgust. 'Northern Rock? What a fucking plonker!' she said. 'So it's all gone?'

'More or less. The broker did her no favours over the past decade. We'd have been able to carry on caring for her for another couple of years, and then we'd have had to apply for state aid.'

This was news to Dervla. Sweet divine Jesus! She'd been checking out residential care that cost in the region of €1,500 per week, when all the time Daphne's finances were leakier than a sieve! She felt a little dizzy, suddenly.

'State care would never have been an option for Mummy,' said Josephine, categorically. 'We'd simply have had to club together and cover the cost ourselves.'

'Yes,' said Christian. 'We'd have had to find the money somehow.'

'Find the money somehow?' said Megan, looking even more disgusted. 'Hel*lo!* Megan calling planet Dad? Where does your daughter come in the pecking order? I am an impoverished student whose parent contributes a measly thousand a month to her education. How can you justify paying that kind of *stupid* money to keep a batty old woman in the lap of luxury when I am living in a crappy bedsit and can barely afford to pay for my course books! Do you know how much a textbook on applied psychology cost me? Thirty-five fucking pounds!'

'Megan! That's enough!' said Valentina sharply. 'This isn't about you.'

'It shouldn't be about money, either,' said Nemia. 'Where

412

I come from, we take care of our old people because we respect them.'

Maybe, thought Dervla. But I bet your old people are healthier than ours, and younger. I bet most of your old people die from 'premature' natural causes, and I bet most of them have happier deaths, surrounded by family and friends – not alone in a care home or lying on a trolley in A&E.

But she kept her lip zipped.

Across the table, she saw that Valentina was watching her. 'Are you all right?' she asked.

'I'm actually feeling a little under the weather,' said Dervla. 'I could do with some fresh air.'

Valentina rose to her feet. 'So could I. Come on. We'll go sit on the sea wall for a while.'

They descended the stairs of the restaurant and crossed the road. To the west, the sky was a cyclorama, displaying dramatic plumes of crimson and purple cloud. A seagull perched on the wall gave them a resentful look and took off as they sat down.

'I must say, I'm glad of the chance to have got you on your own. I'm so grateful for your hospitality,' said Valentina.

Dervla had accommodated most of Christian's extended family in Daphne's cottage. Valentina was sleeping in Daphne's old room, Nemia was ensconced in the room that had once been hers, and Megan had been put up on a futon that Dervla had borrowed from Fleur.

'You're very welcome.'

'Fabulous sunset.'

'Yes.'

There was a pause, and then Valentina said, 'How did you find looking after our mother-in-law?'

'I found it . . . very difficult.'

'I'm not surprised.'

'Did you know Daphne well?'

'Yes and no. In the early days she was wonderful, I'm sorry you didn't know her then. She helped us out financially when we were first married, and she spoilt Megan rotten. But then, after Christian and I divorced, I didn't see her for some years. I found the change quite shocking. That's why – when Christian told me you were taking over the caring – I felt some concern for you. I wasn't sure you could handle her.'

'I had to handle her, Valentina. I was being paid to handle her.'

'She thought I was the maid the last time I visited her in London.'

Dervla laughed. 'I can relate to that! She made me feel like Dobby the house-elf – she even used to whistle for me when she wanted me to do something for her. And she threw a spoon at me once because her cornflakes tasted of dust.'

'She threw a spoon?! How did you resist the impulse to throw it right back at her?'

'It's like I said. I was being paid to look after her, and you don't throw missiles at your employer. I have a fiercely strong work ethic, Valentina, and if I undertake to do something, I damned well make sure that I do it to the very best of my ability.'

Valentina gave Dervla a quizzical look. 'If you *weren't* being paid, do you think the same high standard would apply?'

'Oh, God! That is such a tough question! I honestly don't know. I mean, there were times when I wanted to turn around and say, "Get your own fucking breakfast, you spoilt cow!" Or, "Wipe your own fucking arse, you smelly old bitch!" – excuse my French – and then take to my heels and leave her to it. But you don't, do you? You just don't.'

'You *wiped* her?'

'Of course. Someone had to do it. It made me laugh when

414

she told me that she was "perfectly capable of looking after myself thank you very much". And it made me wonder – if I did walk out on her – what would Daphne have *done*? I mean, what happens to old people who have *no one* to care for them? You know those boreens you pass all over Coolnamara, that lead to derelict-looking cottages, miles from anywhere? Lots of them aren't derelict, you know. Lots of them have people living there still – some old farmer, or some old farmer's widow. Or a couple, maybe, one looking after the other, trying to get by, the blind leading the blind – literally. And nobody fucking *cares*! And if medical science intervenes and they get their new hip or knee or miracle cure or whatever – what then? They're sent back home and expected to get by on a paltry handful of euros a week.'

Valentina was looking at Dervla with interest.

'I'm sorry for the rant,' apologized Dervla. 'It's just that I've been thinking more and more about this since I had to take care of Daphne, and I'm convinced it's going to be the next huge political issue. Who's going to take responsibility for our ageing demographic? The so-called "community"? I don't think so. Not so long ago in Mayo, an old woman's body was found decomposing in a bedroom. She'd been dead for a year.'

'Oh! Had she been living on her own?'

'No. She'd been living with her brother and sister.'

'Dear Jesus!' Valentina's expression of horror changed to one of gravity. 'Why don't you run for election?' she said.

Dervla laughed. 'How funny! Christian's always saying that to me when I go off on a rant.'

'Well, this is clearly something you feel very passionately about, so why not do something about it?'

Dervla looked dubious. 'I've never considered a career in politics.'

'Why not? You're intelligent, you're articulate, and –'

Valentina raised an amused eyebrow '– I imagine you've the requisite machiavellian streak.'

Dervla returned the smile. 'I'm not sure whether that's a compliment or an insult.'

'Name me one successful estate agent who hasn't used at least some of Machiavelli's principles.'

'You're right,' conceded Dervla. 'Plus I learned a lot of base cunning in my dealings with Daphne. I could have been a role model for Gollum in *Lord of the Rings*.'

Dervla suddenly remembered a story from a book she had loved as a child, about a little old lady called Granny Farthing, whose mind was like a garden, all full of lovely thoughts. And the fairies took those thoughts and planted them in Granny's garden, so that everyone might see what pretty flowers Granny Farthing could grow. Once upon a time Dervla had imagined that that was what happened in your 'twilight' years – you turned into a storybook little old lady. Storybook little old ladies are meant to be sweet and rosy-cheeked and loveable. Storybook little old ladies are meant to smell of lavender, and wear their silvery hair in a bun, and do things like knit tea cosies and pass on words of wisdom and tales of yore, and smile upon their grand-children. They never say 'fuck', they never fart, they never pick their noses, they never wet the bed.

How would she and Christian end up? Dervla wondered. What would the future hold for them when – if – they survived to Daphne's age? Would they be shouting at each other and throwing spoons? Would they find it common-place to come across giraffes in the garden? Would they be listening to some 'animator' playing the guitar in a day room painted in shades of soothing peach and dove grey?

Oh! *Oh!* She gave a shudder. It didn't bear thinking about.

'Goose walk over your grave?' asked Valentina.

'Something like that.'

The sun had sunk beyond the horizon, leaving a legacy of mandarin sky. Dervla and Valentina regarded it in silence for a long moment, and then Valentina said, 'You're good together, you know – you and Christian.'

'Thank you. I'm very glad we found each other.'

'I'm glad too. I'm fond of my ex-husband.'

'What's your new one like?'

Valentina laughed. 'Gio? He's fat and fond of his pasta and wine. But we have a good life.'

'Sometimes I think I'd like to grow fat on wine and pasta and retire somewhere like the Tuscan hills.'

'You're far too young to retire, Dervla!' Valentina reproached her. 'Besides, the Old Rectory is beautiful.'

'It is. But we can't afford to live in it.'

'Why don't you live in the cottage now it's empty, and let the big house?'

'Now there's a thought,' mused Dervla. 'It would make sense for us to down-size, and we'd get a lot more rent for the big house than we would for the cottage. I'll talk it over with Christian later.'

But later that evening it slipped her mind to mention it, because Christian's mind was on matters amatory.

After he'd fallen asleep, Dervla made her way up to her turret room, where her laptop awaited her. She wanted to note down some thoughts that had been clamouring for her attention since her chat with Valentina earlier that day. She flexed her fingers, and typed the following:

- Youth culture versus respect for the old. In some parts of the world, the greatest compliment is to call someone an 'old' man.

417

- Older people's dependency on the social infrastructure is the result of compulsory retirement, poverty, and diminished status in the community. This dependency = lack of respect = ageism.
- Women live longer, ergo older women suffer most from ageism.
- Life expectancy is increasing, but so too is *active* life expectancy. People are enjoying good health longer than their ancestors thanks to advances in medical science. But people are also being 'kept' alive longer due to medical science.
- Our carers – slaves to a system that needs urgent overhauling.

By the time Dervla had finished, she'd notched up another dozen or so bullet points. She could have gone on, but it was after one o'clock in the morning, and she needed to be on the ball for Daphne's funeral. She'd just have to delay writing to her political rep until after Christian's family had gone back to their respective homes.

Moving to the window, she looked out over the sleeping countryside. She was wide awake – raring to go and fighting fit. Dervla Vaughan, née Kinsella, was back in the arena.

Chapter Thirty-One

Fleur had treated herself to a long bath with L'Occitane oils, a glass of chilled Sancerre and a Penny Vincenzi novel, accompanied by Dean Martin on the stereo and a long chat with Río on the phone, during which Corban O'Hara's name had not once been uttered without the prefix 'bastard'. She had slathered her face in vitamin E cream and put on her robe and her gel-lined moisturizing socks, and was looking forward to comfort food. Macaroni cheese, or mash, or a stuffed baked potato.

She was standing in the kitchen regarding the contents of her fridge when her door bell rang. She froze. Corban? Hardly. She hadn't seen him since the night he'd blundered bear-like into the dark at Díseart. That night, she had taken Bethany home and made cocoa for her, and they'd stayed up late chatting, and it had felt like having her beloved Daisy back – although Bethany and Daisy were very different creatures.

Bethany had found an issue of one of Daisy's old *Cosmopolitan* magazines in the spare room, and she and Fleur had discussed the issues aired on the problem pages and criticized the gear on the fashion pages and read each other's horoscopes from last year, to see if any of the predictions had come true, and oh! it had been fun to have Bethany as a friend in real life and not just in a virtual world. They had done one of those silly quizzes to rate your self-esteem, and Bethany's score had been higher than Fleur's! (Fleur *had* cheated a little . . .) Maybe it was Bethany at the door now? She hoped so.

Fleur padded in her gel socks to the door. The security camera told her it wasn't Bethany who'd rung the doorbell. It had been Jake Malone. *Jake?* And suddenly Fleur remembered the date they'd made last week – the drink she'd rashly invited him up for, about which she had completely forgotten.

Jake was looking into the security camera, smiling directly at her. And then he raised his hand to show that he was carrying a bottle. It was raining and he had no hood or umbrella. Shit. She couldn't not let him in. She pressed the buzzer. She didn't care that her face looked like an oil slick. She was, after all, now officially an old bag who had vowed that she would never again in her life have to worry about making herself look good for a man. She knew she'd have to make an effort at work, of course – it went without saying that Fleur of Fleurissima should look a million dollars – but here, in her own private space, she no longer gave a damn about how she looked. Oh! Except for the gel moisturizing socks. They were a hideous shade of pink, and they made a squelchy sound when she walked. She quickly whipped them off and stuffed them in the pocket of her bathrobe.

'I'm sorry,' she said, as Jake climbed the stairs. 'I'd completely forgotten that I'd invited you around this evening.'

'*I* hadn't,' he said, giving her a look of mock indignation. 'I've been looking forward to this evening all day.' He gave her a brief kiss first on one cheek, then the other.

Fleur remained vacillating in the doorway. 'Um. I've just got out of the bath and there's nothing to eat except store cupboard staples.'

'Store cupboard staples? What are they?'

'Oh – I forgot. You're a boy. Store cupboard staples are – you know, like basics.'

'Oh. They sound like some kind of snack.'

Fleur laughed. 'I could do a macaroni cheese.'

'Sounds good to me.'

'Come on into the kitchen, then. Normally at this time of the evening I'd be sitting on the deck, but it is clear that our summer is over. Do you need a drier for your hair?'

Jake gave her a scornful look. 'Do I look like a man who blow-dries his hair?'

Since the night of the showdown at Díseart, the weather had changed. They had had only one cloud-free day since, which had been the day of Daphne Vaughan's funeral, when the sun had shone as brightly as the yellow lilies that bedecked her coffin. Christian's daughter, Megan, had been the only inconsolable person at the event, and Dervla had told Fleur afterwards that the reason the girl had been so distraught was because she'd been expecting a legacy that had not materialized.

Fleur led the way into the kitchen, where Jake set his bottle on the counter. 'I'm afraid Vaughan's was clean out of pink fizz,' he told her.

Why am I not surprised? thought Fleur.

'Well, thank you. That's a very acceptable Bordeaux,' she said, reaching for the corkscrew and tossing it to him.

Jake caught it adroitly, then sniffed the air as Fleur wafted past him to fetch glasses. 'Wow. You smell gorgeous, Ms O'Farrell.'

'Thanks to L'Occitane,' said Fleur. 'I was having some "Me" time.'

'That girly thing of reading a book in the bath with a glass of wine and the telephone?'

'Got it in one.'

'Nice.'

Fleur set wineglasses on the table, watching as Jake stripped the foil away from the neck of the bottle. Through the speakers, Dean Martin was crooning about *amore*, and Fleur found herself thinking that Jake actually bore a strong resemblance to the young Dean Martin – buff and Italianate.

'I'll cook, if you like,' he said, as he poured wine into their glasses. 'I do a mean macaroni cheese.'

Fleur raised an impressed eyebrow. Not once in their relationshp had Corban ever volunteered to cook for her. 'I'll take you up on that,' she said, sitting down at the kitchen table.

Oh! *Cosmopolitan* was lying open on the surface. The photograph on display was of a half-naked, extremely nubile Lily Cole. Fleur wished she could close the magazine – it made her agonizingly aware of her own advanced age – but she knew that by closing it she would simply draw attention to the mag and make herself look like a prude. So Lily continued to gaze provocatively up at Fleur and Jake like the elephant in the room. Well, more like the vixen in the room.

'*Santé*,' said Jake, handing Fleur a glass.

'Bottoms up,' responded Fleur. *What?* What had she just said? Fleur couldn't remember ever having said 'bottoms up' before in her life. She supposed it was because she couldn't get the mental image of Lily Cole's extremely pert bottom out of her head. She took a swift swig of wine to cover her embarrassment.

'Where will I find the pasta?' asked Jake.

'In a jar on the shelf.' Fleur pointed. 'You'll find flour there too, and all the rest is in the fridge.'

She watched as Jake assembled the ingredients. He'd make a terrific television chef: lean and limber and oh! so easy on the eye. She almost wished she hadn't taken her vow of celibacy. Never again, she thought, would she feel the pressure of a man's hand upon her breast, never again feel a finger slide inside her knowing the best was yet to come, never again feel that frantic flare of lust, that urgent surge, that rosy afterglow . . .

'You're looking very thoughtful, Fleur,' said Jake. 'Penny for them?'

'Sorry?'

'A penny for your thoughts.'

'Oh – that must be one of your obscure English phrases. What does it mean?'

Jake explained, and as he explained, Fleur found her eyes going to his mouth. How mobile it was! How fluently his lips articulated the words! Fleur of course knew very well what 'a penny for your thoughts' meant, but she wasn't about to divulge to Jake Malone that she'd been fantasizing about having sex with him.

As Jake stirred the saucepan, Fleur took the opportunity of leafing idly through the fashion pages of *Cosmopolitan* during the lulls in their small talk. Page after page of beautiful young creatures gazed up at her from between the covers, and she felt like reaching for a pen and scribbling them out. Page after page of anti-ageing and age-defying products screamed at her, and hey! – how did Evangeline Lilly *know* Fleur was worth it? She scowled at lovely Evangeline, and glowered at Penélope Cruz who was batting her L'Oréal eyelashes at her on the next page.

'Now it's cross you're looking,' observed Jake.

Fleur closed the magazine. 'Oh – I just remembered that I forgot to do something,' she improvised.

Attract Hot Guys Like Crazy! the strapline exhorted her. *Foreplay Your Guy's Way!*

Thirty Things to Do with a Naked Man!

No, *no*! Why had she closed the damned mag? Lily Cole's derrière was far less embarrassing than the cover copy. And then Fleur realized that Jake would think that she – a woman teetering on the brink of middle age – subscribed to *Cosmo*. It would be a bit like finding out that Gordon Brown read *Loaded*.

'And now you look horrified,' said Jake with a laugh. 'You're like the Irish weather – four seasons in one day.'

'I just remembered that the thing I forgot to do was really urgent,' said Fleur, jumping to her feet and leaving the kitchen with the offending magazine tucked under her arm. She sprinted upstairs and slung it through her bedroom door, then went into the bathroom and ran water into the basin for thirty seconds.

'What was so urgent?' asked Jake, when she came back into the kitchen.

'I needed to water a plant on my balcony.'

Jake looked unconvinced. 'It was *that* thirsty?'

'Yes. It was a – a Narcisse Blanc. They need lots of water.'

Fleur looked away from him, towards the deck, where the rain was now teeming down. *Merde*. She couldn't have invented a more implausible excuse. Jake probably thought that her real reason for leaving the room was because she needed the loo. And if she needed it that urgently, he would conclude that she had old-lady bladder control problems. And if she'd actually forgotten that she needed the loo urgently, that could only mean that she was suffering from early onset Alzheimer's. He'd be wondering how he'd fetched up here, serving meals on wheels to a batty middle-aged French woman who read sex tips in *Cosmopolitan*. And then she saw that her hideous gel socks had fallen out of her pocket and were lying in the middle of the kitchen floor. *Merde*, and again *merde!* He'd never want to take her to bed now.

Hel*lo*, Fleur? Sorry? What did you just think? She had taken a vow of celibacy. She didn't *want* Jake Malone to take her to bed. But actually she did, *she did*! She did, more than anything. Because she had a feeling it would be the last time in her life she would ever have sex.

Stupid Fleur! How could she have forgotten that Jake was due to call around this evening? Why hadn't she made an effort, and slipped into something a little sexier than her towelling bath robe? Why hadn't she applied a little *maquillage*, spritzed herself with scent, shopped for aphrodisiacs and champagne and had them ready to go in the fridge? There was *nothing* sexy about this evening's scenario. Macaroni cheese had to be the most homely dish ever invented. Why hadn't she suggested slurpy tagliatelle or spaghetti or fettuccine? Even Dean Martin's mood music had come to an end, now.

Oh! What was she thinking? Jake was not hers for the taking – even if he wanted to be taken. Jake belonged to Bethany – or at least, Fleur hoped that he might one day belong to Bethany. But he wasn't Bethany's . . . yet. And in the meantime, maybe Bethany wouldn't mind if Fleur – poor, ageing, loveless Fleur – had just a tiny teeny taste of him?

Fleur suddenly *yearned* for sex, as one might yearn for an object shrouded in nostalgia. Because – let's face it – for Fleur, an object shrouded in nostalgia was what the sexual act would soon become. Oh! How wonderful to go out with a bang! How glorious to have one last flesh fest with a fit young man and not worry about how she looked, or whether the outfit she was wearing was sexy enough. How sad that the last time in her life she had made love she'd been wearing a tacky peep-hole bra with matching crotchless panties and suspenders and a pair of killer heels because Corban had indicated that that was his preference *du jour*. He'd wanted a whore that evening – he hadn't wanted Fleur.

'You're looking sad, now,' observed Jake.

'That's because I am sad. I – I'm thinking of my little dog that died.' *Please, please forgive me for the fib, Babette*, she prayed inwardly. *But I could scarcely tell him the truth . . .*

And then visions of Babette rose before Fleur's mind's eye: Babette sitting on the sea wall, squinting into the sunset; Babette flirting with the local dogs before tossing her head and prancing coquettishly away; Babette looking up at her mistress after the vet had given her the lethal injection, eyes full of love as Fleur rocked her into her final sleep, apologizing for wetting her doggie's fur with the copious tears that had come spilling from her own eyes . . .

And then Fleur was sobbing, sobbing uncontrollably with her hands clutched over her head and her elbows on the table, and Jake was hunkered down beside her, saying, 'there, there,' and 'hush, hush,' and his soothing only served to make Fleur cry harder. And then Jake pulled her head against his shoulder, and she smelled citrus top notes, aromatic middle notes, and woody base notes. Oh! she thought. *Acqua di Parma*! The sexiest aftershave in the world. And then she remembered how Babette had used to smell of La Pooch cologne after she'd been to the canine beauty parlour, and she sobbed even harder. And then Jake was stroking her hair and wiping the tears from her eyes with his thumbs, and then a thumb accidentally brushed her mouth and she found herself inviting it between her lips, and she was tasting her own tears, and they actually tasted really nice, so she curled her tongue around the thumb and sucked a little. And then she felt a finger trace the curve of her ear, and caress the lobe and explore the dip beneath before travelling further along her throat to the scoop of her collarbone, where it lingered, waiting for permission.

Fleur bit down gently on Jake's thumb. He slid it from

between her lips and rubbed her mouth, and she was glad that she was wearing no lipstick.

'Yes,' she said, granting the permission he sought, feeling like royalty. And when he parted the folds of her robe with reverent hands she didn't feel like royalty any more: she felt like a goddess. Not Hecate the crone goddess; not Aphrodite, the goddess of youth and love and beauty. She felt like Persephone, delivered from the underworld. She felt alive and succulent and worthy of worship as she loosened the sash on her robe and allowed Jake access. And then they were on the floor and he was between her legs telling her how beautiful she was, how gorgeous, how divine – just like a goddess! And, thought Fleur, she really was a goddess, because here she was in heaven, soaring through a galaxy of stars, outshining the Pleiades and consorting with Adonis.

'Uh-oh. I'm afraid the saucepan's ruined.' Jake turned the ring off underneath the pan, from which drifted a smell of burned butter.

'You were worth it,' said Fleur, with a catlike smile, sliding her arms back into her robe. As she eased herself into a stretch, some words of her favourite French writer, Collette, came to mind. *I love my past, I love my present. I am not ashamed of what I've had, and I'm not sad because I no longer have it . . .*

Did Fleur no longer have it? If Jake's performance had been anything to go by, she clearly still had *something* – a certain *je ne sais quoi*. There was life in the old girl yet, and she felt rather proud of herself.

'Shall I start again?' Jake asked.

'So *soon*?'

'I meant the sauce.' He crossed the room, took her in his arms, and kissed her. 'I've wanted to do that since the day

I came into your shop. You have the loveliest, most kissable, Frenchest mouth I've ever seen.'

'Thank you. And you are the most dynamic man I've ever had,' said Fleur, reaching down a hand and cupping his crotch, thinking that, actually, maybe he *could* start again. Should she encourage him? No. She shouldn't be greedy. She'd promised herself she'd go out with a bang, and that's exactly what she had done. She'd had the best no-frills sex of her life right here on her kitchen floor, and if they decided now to go to the bedroom or the bathroom there would be nothing spontaneous about the act. Besides, she'd had her teeny tiny taste of him, and it was now time for her to send him off in pursuit of Bethany.

She'd cook for him, then bid him adieu.

'Let me take over,' she said, moving to the stove. 'I don't want any more burned saucepans.'

She took another pan from the cupboard and set about making a roux. 'Did I see you on the beach at Díseart the other evening?' she remarked, casually.

He had the good grace to look a little guilty. 'Yes,' he said.

'I was worried for a while about Bethany O'Brien staying down there on her own. I really admire her. I'm not sure that I'd have had the guts for that kind of solitude when I was her age.'

'She loves it. She's been going there since she was a child. I suppose when you've been visiting a place all your life it can hold no fear for you.' He poured more wine. 'It must get lonely here for you, in the winter. Bethany tells me Lissamore is like a ghost town then.'

'It is, but I rather love it. In winter in Coolnamara you get the most astonishing weather – big blue beautiful skies and crystalline air. There's nothing like wrapping yourself up to go walking on the beach, and then come back to a blazing fire. I usually treat myself to a holiday somewhere exotic after Christmas. I'm thinking of Belize this year.'

It would, Fleur realized, be the first time she'd taken a holiday on her own. Last year she had gone to Barbados with Corban, and in previous years she had usually been accompanied by her dish of the day. It would be nice to go off on her own for a change, footloose and fancy free. It would be nice not to have to take someone else's agenda into account when deciding which sights to see or where to eat or what time to get up in the morning. It would be nice to spend some time enjoying the pleasure of her own company.

'I spent time in Belize,' said Jake. 'Best beer in the world.'

Fleur smiled. Beer! *Quel garcon!*

'Oh – I heard from Daisy today,' he added. 'She wrote on my Facebook wall.'

'Oh, good! There will be a treat in store for me when I log on later.'

And Jake and Fleur continued to chat idly as she prepared the pasta. They talked about holidays they'd had, and they talked about Jake's ambition to direct his own film one day, and they talked about whether or not Fleur should get herself another dog, and when they sat down to eat Jake said, 'Wow! This is even better than my mother makes!' and Fleur smiled and said that the secret was to add grated mozzarella and Gruyère to the cheddar. And when Jake suggested that they open another bottle of wine, Fleur said no.

His face fell. 'Why not?' he asked.

'Because if we have another bottle of wine, we might end up on the kitchen floor again,' said Fleur, 'and I don't think that's a good idea.'

'You don't?'

Fleur shook her head. 'Don't get me wrong. I don't regret

for an instant what happened. But it was a one-off, Jake, and it's not going to happen again.'

His downcast expression gave him the look of a small boy deprived of sweets, and made Fleur want to laugh.

'Now. It is time for you to go,' she told him. 'I have an early start in the morning and I want to check out Facebook before I go to bed to see if my beautiful niece has sent me a message.'

'What'll you put as your status?' he asked.

Fleur thought about it, then gave him a minxy smile. 'Extremely satisfied,' she said.

'I'm glad to know it.' He smiled back, before leaning across the table and kissing her lightly on the lips, and then they both got to their feet.

'Oh, look,' said Fleur. 'The rain's stopped. Let me just nip out onto the deck and fetch that photograph I was telling you about.'

As Fleur took the photograph down from its pride of place on Babette's shrine, she saw Bethany leaving Ryan's corner shop. She was peeling the wrapper from an ice cream, and heading towards the place on the sea wall where she liked to sit. Fleur went back into the kitchen.

'Here's my Babette! Isn't she gorgeous,' she said, waving the picture under Jake's nose.

'Yes.' Jake tried to take the photograph from Fleur so that he could examine it more closely, but she set it face down on the kitchen table. 'Now! Off you go,' she said, briskly leading the way to the front door.

'Um. OK.'

As he followed her, looking a little baffled, Jake reached for the smallest of a series of hand-carved Russian nesting dolls that stood on the console table in the hall. 'A matryoshka doll!' he said. 'I remember my sister had—'

'Did she? Keep it,' Fleur said, ushering him out.

'But I can't—'

'Keep it as a souvenir of your – erm – sister,' she commanded, holding the door open for him.

'Oh. Well, thanks,' said Jake, sliding the tiny doll into his pocket.

On the threshold, he tried to draw her into an embrace, but Fleur just allowed him a perfunctory kiss on the lips. 'Be off with you!' she scolded. 'I've a list of things to do before I go to bed.'

'Oh. I thought you were just going to have a leisurely perusal of Facebook.'

'No. I've to water the plants on the deck and have a bath.'

'But I thought you'd just had—'

'*Au revoir, chéri.*' And Fleur shut the door on Jake's surprised face.

Back in the kitchen, she opened another bottle of red and poured herself a glass. Then she strolled back onto the deck, where her plants were all dripping and glistening with rain. There was a smell of moist earth in the air, and a rainbow told her a pot of gold was hidden somewhere near Díseart. She re-instated Babette on her shrine, then turned to survey her view.

Down near the harbour, Jake had joined Bethany on the sea wall: she was swinging her legs, he was sitting astride it. He was laughing at something she'd said, and she had let her hair down from its scrunchy, and was shaking it back over her shoulders. She held out the ice cream to him so that he could have a taste, and then Jake put his hand in his pocket, withdrew it and handed something to Bethany. The squeak of delight she gave made Fleur smile: she just hoped that Bethany hadn't spotted the matryoshka dolls the night she had stayed over.

But when Bethany leaned over to give Jake a spontaneous kiss on the cheek, Fleur's guess was that she hadn't.

Chapter Thirty-Two

Dervla and Christian were clearing out Daphne's house.

'What'll we do with this thing?' asked Dervla, looking disconsolately at Daphne's electric bath chair, which they'd just dismantled.

'Sell it on eBay.'

'A second-hand bath chair!' Dervla turned aghast eyes on Christian.

'That was a joke,' he said. 'We'll have to get a skip. There's loads of stuff here that can't even be recycled.'

'You're right. Look at this.' Dervla turned back to the medicine chest she'd been about to sort out, and swept the entire contents into a bin bag. These were followed by loofahs, sponges, flannels, baby wipes, nail scissors and disposable gloves.

'What do you think we'll be like, Christian, when we get to Daphne's age?' mused Dervla. 'I always thought that we'd wear Boden clothes and go on Saga cruises and play golf, but now I'm not so sure.'

'Why? You think we might end up in nappies too?'

'Nappies might be preferable to Bottom Buddies.'

'What are Bottom Buddies?'

Dervla explained.

'Jesus!' said Christian. 'Just think of the kind of rows we'd have if we got confused. "That's my Bottom Buddy!" "No – that's *my* Bottom Buddy. Yours is the green one, mine is the purple." "No, yours is the purple *tooth*brush, not the purple Buddy."'

'And any time we went away, we'd have to pack our Buddies,' said Dervla. 'Could you imagine security saying: "What is this suspicious object?" "Oh – it's just my Bottom Buddy." "Well, I'm afraid you can't take it in your hand luggage. It could be classified as a dangerous weapon."'

'"But it's a long-haul flight!"' put in Christian. '"What'll I do between here and New Zealand?"'

Dervla started to laugh until the tears ran down her cheeks. 'Oh, God! Do you think we'll die before we get old, Christian?'

'We'll be grand,' he told her. 'We'll keep our brains active by eating lots of fish and doing Sudoku. And we'll exercise on the Wii Fit.'

'And Kitty will look after us, like Nana in *Peter Pan*.'

'And it's probably just as well that we're going to downsize here, because you won't be able to manage the stairs to your turret room.'

'I could put a stairlift in,' suggested Dervla.

'I don't think they make them for spiral staircases.'

'They'll have the technology by then.'

'But they still won't make them in case the old person gets dizzy going up and down the spiral staircase and falls off and sues.'

Dervla fired a rubber bath mat into the bin bag.

'Oh!' she said. 'Let's stop. I need fresh air.'

'And I know just the place to get it,' said Christian.

'The beach? Or the bog road?'

'Neither,' said Christian. 'Let's go to Coolnamara Castle and walk around the lake, and then have dinner.'

'But it's expensive!'

434

'I don't care,' said Christian. 'We deserve a treat. And anyway, it's on Daphne. I found an envelope full of petty cash in the drawer of her bureau. We might even run to a bottle of champagne and an overnight stay in a lake-view room.'

'Oh, Christian!' Dervla flung her arms around her husband's neck. 'I would love that more than anything! It's so long since we had a treat! And I can dress up!'

Dervla dressed with care. She chose a timeless Betty Jackson LBD and heels that had cost her a fortune a decade ago and had now come back into fashion. Her underpinnings were chosen with equal care – lingerie that Christian had bought her for her last birthday. She slid on own-brand stockings, and decided that they were easily as sexy as the Wolfords for which she had used to fork out silly money. And before they left, she made sure that she'd packed her walking boots and socks and a raincoat.

They walked for miles through the woodlands surrounding Coolnamara Castle, around lakes and over bridges and beside rivers. And as they walked, they discussed their future together. Moving into the cottage made sense. Dervla outlined the practicalities behind renting out the Old Rectory. It would be a gamble. It was unsustainable as a holiday rental, and too remote for a family to live there. It was, however, perfect for a residential home.

'You mean for old people?' said Christian, apprehensively.

'Yes.'

'But you had such a hard time looking after my mother.'

'I won't be doing the hands-on caring,' said Dervla. 'I know quite well that that's not my vocation. But I'm thinking pragmatically. How lucky were we – in retrospect – that we weren't able to afford to furnish the place. We can start from scratch. If we set up a business that caters for the elderly – the most booming demographic in Europe – we're bound to get a loan. And if not, I'll sell my apartment in Galway for whatever I can get and be done with it. We'll install all the latest high-tech equipment—'

'Bottom Buddies?'

'They go without saying. And we'll have no problem hiring staff, and we'll get a great chef, who won't just cook cabbage and sausages and mashed potato and old people pap. You see, Christian, my idea is that there are hundreds of people out there who don't want to be stuck in residential care plagued by animators or non-stop *Sky News* or singsongs. I'm convinced that there's a market for old people who may not be physically capable of doing much, but who are still mentally alert enough to want to watch art house films instead of *Teletubbies* or *Judge Judy*, or read the broadsheets instead of *Now!* magazine, or listen to Proust or PD James on audio book.'

'You could be right. In one of the homes I went into, an old lady was looking crossways at an article in some magazine with the headline "I Slept with My Brother, then Shot Him". And Lyric FM was playing – but it wasn't soothing, classical stuff. It was the movie theme programme, and the movie theme in question was *The Terminator*.'

'You see! There's so little thought put into what old people really want. I mean, how many of them are going to want to eat crap and drink orange squash and listen to movie theme tunes? They should have their own stuff downloaded onto iPods so they can listen to Chuck Berry or the Beatles or Beethoven or whatever they want. We could provide chess sets in the drawing room, and backgammon and Scrabble and Wii. We could have wine tasting evenings – you could do those – or poetry readings or music appreciation classes.'

'The people I saw in the homes I visited didn't look as if they could appreciate anything very much,' Christian pointed out.

'But that's exactly why they turn into zombies! They don't get enough stimulation! Think about it. We could have Wifi, so that the residents can keep up to spin with friends and family on Facebook, or talk to their grandchildren in Australia via Skype and webcam. And we have our garden! Maybe the more physically able could have their own plots to tend. Maybe we could keep chickens and goats. Maybe we could allow pets!'

'You've been thinking about this a lot, haven't you?'

'Yes, I have. I'm going to approach the matron in La Paloma and ask her if she'd be interested in being head-hunted. I know there's a market out there for top-end care, and both you and I are business people who know a good idea when we see one. It's bloody awful that both our businesses have been bashed by the recession, but the mark of a truly clever business person is the ability to forecast coming trends. And quality care for the elderly is the next big one.'

Christian looked thoughtful. 'You could be right. We could certainly manage the business side of things.'

'It's a great idea – I know it is,' said Dervla, as they came to the end of their walk. 'I get this kind of fizzy feeling in my bones when I know I'm onto something good.' Christian zapped the locks on the car, and Dervla doffed her raincoat and exchanged her walking boots for her heels. 'We'll talk it over later during dinner, shall we?'

'I'll have other things on my mind during dinner.'

'Oh yeah?' said Dervla, chucking her binoculars into the boot. 'What things?'

'Taking my wife to bed, of course,' said Christian.

* * *

They ordered dinner in the bar, over drinks. Dervla went for watercress soup and duck breast with rosemary polenta, while Christian opted for pan-fried wild mushrooms to start, followed by beef fillet with *foie gras* butter. He was texting his business partner when a call came through.

'I'm sorry, love,' he told Dervla. 'This one's urgent. One of the wine-tasting tourists has missed the flight from Montpellier. I'll take it outside.'

Christian got to his feet and left the bar just as a man Dervla recognized came through the door. He was Mike Coughlan, a man who had successfully run as an independent candidate in the local elections some years before, but who had since retired from politics. He took a seat at the table next to Dervla, and nodded at her.

'Lovely evening,' he said.

'Yes. We could be in for an Indian summer.'

'Do I know you from somewhere?' he asked. 'You're something in property, am I right?'

'I used to be,' smiled Dervla. 'But I'm out of the property game now.'

'*Well* out, in the current climate. The name's Mike Coughlan,' he said, extending a hand.

'Dervla Vaughan.'

'So what are you up to now, Dervla?'

'I'm between jobs. Making plans for the future. And as a matter of fact, Mr Coughlan—'

'Mike.'

'Mike – you might be able to help me. May I ask you a question?'

'Fire ahead.'

'How does one go about getting into politics?'

'Well, it really depends on how proactive you want to be. Have you a party in mind?'

'I used to support the Greens until they got into bed with Fianna Fáil. Now I'm a floating voter, I guess.'

'In that case I suggest you have a look at party websites and determine which endorses your own ethics. Join up, and start going to their local meetings. At election time it's a good idea to canvas on their behalf, drop leaflets, doorstep – that kind of thing. And apply to become a tally man. That way you can keep up to spin on PR and STVs – that kind of thing.'

Dervla was thankful that she'd read *The Bluffer's Guide to Politics*. STVs, she recalled, stood for single transferable votes.

'Don't underestimate the art of schmoozing,' continued Mike. 'And backtrack on your morals and principles if you think it'll help drum up support.'

'But that's – *un*principled!' protested Dervla.

'That's why I got out of the game. You could take the independent route, but that's expensive.'

'Oh.' Dervla drooped a little.

'You need a tough skin to be involved in politics,' Mike warned. 'You'll shake hands with people and want to wash your hands right after. You'll set yourself up as a target for some of the most vindictive sniping you'll ever experience in your life. You'll weep into your pillow at night, and leave the house with a mile-wide smile the next morning to show the world you're invincible. You'll kiss some of the ugliest babies you've ever seen.'

Dervla laughed. 'So who in their right mind goes into politics in the first place?'

'No one,' said Mike Coughlan.

'Madam?' said the maître d', approaching. 'Would you care to come through to the dining room now?'

'Thank you,' said Dervla, rising to her feet. 'And thank you, Mike, for your advice.'

'My pleasure,' said Mike. 'Here's my card. Feel free to contact me if you need help.'

'Thank you,' said Dervla again, before turning to follow the maître d'.

Oo-er, she thought, as they passed through the foyer. She wouldn't mind kissing ugly babies, but Dervla had spent enough sleepless nights in her life crying into her pillow. Life was too short to be shedding more tears. Besides, she was definitely in her *right* mind. She didn't have the lunatic credentials to be a politician. Anyway, she'd have her hands full if she and Christian really were going to go ahead with their plans for setting up a retirement home with a difference.

She sat down at the window table they'd requested. The view was spectacular – airy mountains, rushy glens – and the sun was just beginning to dip over a gold and indigo horizon. In the lake below, a salmon flashed silver as it leaped from the water.

On the other side of the room, a family was celebrating something – a birthday, or an anniversary. There was lots of laughter, lots of wine being poured and glasses chinked. There appeared to be three generations at the table: children ranging in age from babies to teens, parents and grandparents, all in rollicking form. But wait – maybe there was a member of a fourth generation there, too. At a far corner, sandwiched between a burly, red-faced man and a middle-aged blonde spilling out of a too-tight dress was a tiny shrivelled lady of about ninety. She looked confused, as if she had no idea where she was or how she had got there, and she kept looking around with anxious, blinking eyes, like a capuchin monkey. Nobody spoke to her, and she spoke to nobody. And as the first course arrived, the blonde got to her feet and tied a bib around the old lady's neck, all the while listening to and laughing at a joke with which the red-faced man was regaling the table.

Dervla looked away.

'You're looking very pensive,' Christian said, joining her at the table. 'I'm sorry about the phone call. That took some sorting out. The bloke was half-cut.'

'He'd been swallowing instead of spitting?'

Christian nodded. 'Most of them do, if the truth be told. They can't resist the temptation on wine tastings.'

'Madam? Watercress soup with sweet onions.'

'Sir? Pan-fried wild mushrooms with parmesan and thyme butter.'

The two waiters set down the dishes, and retreated. Then the sommelier arrived, and – upon Christian's pronounce- ment that the wine was excellent – he too retreated, leaving Christian and Dervla smiling at each other.

'This is blissful,' said Dervla. 'Thank you for suggesting it.'

Christian raised his glass. 'To Daphne,' he said.

'To Daphne,' Dervla echoed, mirroring the gesture.

And as she drank, beyond the window the salmon leaped again.

After dinner, they took coffee in the drawing room. Before it was poured, Dervla excused herself to visit the loo. In the ladies, two of the teenage girls who were members of the big family party were retouching their make-up and chatting.

Dervla eavesdropped on their conversation through the door of her cubicle.

'I *begged* Dad not to bring Nana,' one of the girls was saying. 'I knew she'd ruin the whole evening, sitting there, staring into space like something out of *Night of the Living Dead*.'

441

'She dribbled soup all over herself – did you see?' said the other girl. 'And now we're going to have to go home the long way around and dump her back in that stinking old folk's place. And we're going to have to kiss her – ew! I *hate* kissing Nana. It gives me the heebie-jeebies. I always want to wipe my mouth afterwards.'

'I know. But we can't very well not kiss her on her ninetieth birthday. Especially since she's forking out for the party.'

'Let's order another sneaky glass of champagne from the bar and stick it on the tab.'

'Excellent idea! Mmm. What's that perfume?'

'It's Kylie's new one.'

'Spray some of it on Nana, will you, before she gets into the car – otherwise I'll have to hold my nose for the entire journey.'

The two girls giggled, and then Dervla heard the door of the ladies shut behind them.

She emerged from the cubicle and washed her hands, regarding herself solemnly in the mirror.

When she got back to the drawing room, Christian looked up at her. 'You're wearing that pensive look again,' he remarked.

'That's because I've been thinking about our future – again,' she told him.

'Oh? What else are we going to have in our old folk's home? Fairground rides? Paintball? Pole dancing?'

'Christian. I happen to think my idea is genius.'

'So do I. But it's not going to be easy.'

She smiled at him over the rim of her glass. 'Just as well I'm a gal who loves a challenge.'

'What particular challenge have you in mind now? Aside from finding out where to get your hands on large-print publications of *Finnegan's Wake* and audio books on quantum physics?'

'You know I was once short-listed for female entrepreneur of the year?'

'How could I forget it?' he said with an indulgent smile.

'And you know that entrepreneurs are renowned for their skills in diversifying, team building and multi-tasking?'

'I'm knackered even thinking about it. But I've a feeling you've found yourself yet another fish to fry.'

'Fishy business is right,' she agreed.

'You're going to become a Mafiosa?'

'Warm, but not smokin'.'

'OK. I give up.'

'The elderly need a voice.'

'That's some non sequitur.'

'They need someone to speak on their behalf.'

'But of course. And that person might be?'

'Me. I'm going into politics,' said Dervla.

Chapter Thirty-Three

Some weeks later, the day of the wrap party dawned.

'What are you wearing?' Río asked Fleur over the phone.

'I haven't been invited.'

'Shane's invited you,' Río told her.

'Well, thank you, dear one!'

Fleur put the phone down and smiled. A party! It was a long time since she'd been to a party – in fact, now she thought about it, the last big party she'd attended had been that costume ball where she had first met Corban Bastard O'Hara. She'd be curious to go this evening, to see if he had the nerve to show up. She smiled at the memory of the expression on his face when she'd shoved her foot into his chest that evening in Díseart, and told him to stay out of town. Maybe she should ask Finn to isolate that image on his camera phone and print it out for her. She could frame it, and hang it on the wall in her loo.

What would she wear to the party? A replica of the iconic halter-necked dress designed by Trevilla for Marilyn in *The Seven Year Itch* had just come into the shop, but Fleur was too self-conscious about her upper arms to risk it. However, there was a darling little tea dress with fluted sleeves floating around in her wardrobe upstairs. She'd only worn it twice – and it also had the advantage of being comfortable. Fleur was fed up with wearing sucky-in knickers that seemed to do nothing but leave cheese-cutter marks around her waist and thighs. She'd even toyed with the idea of sending away for one of those old-lady comfy-style bras that she had seen advertised in the *Guardian*'s Saturday magazine.

She looked up as the bell to the shop tinkled, and Bethany O'Brien came in.

'Hello, baby girl!' she said. 'What can I do for you this fine morning?'

'Hi, Fleur. I'm actually here to buy something. D'you mind if I browse?'

'But of course I don't mind! Browse away, and I shall come to your aid as soon as I've finished this invoice. How are you, *chérie*, and what is it you are looking for?'

'I'm fine, thanks. I'm actually looking for a dress for the wrap party this evening.'

Fleur was astonished. 'You mean all those hundreds of extras are invited to the wrap party? That's going to be one hell of an entertainment bill for Mr Bas— Mr O'Hara.'

'Well, no, the extras haven't been invited,' said Bethany, looking apologetic. 'I was lucky. I got a personal invitation from one of the ADs.'

'Oh? Which one?'

'The one I told you about on Facebook – Jake Malone.'

Aha! thought Fleur. So Jake *had* become more than just a Facebook friend for Bethany. She, Fleur, hadn't been on Facebook in ages; nor had she been on Second Life. She'd been more creative with her spare time: she'd taken up knitting. *Alors* – if Meryl Streep and Elena Sweetman found it relaxing, why shouldn't Fleur? It was time she had a few more middle-aged moments in her life. 'Oh, Jake Malone! Of course I remember!' she told Bethany. 'The one you said took you to a session in O'Toole's?'

446

'Yes. That's him.'

'You like him, yes?'

Bethany pinkened and nodded, and Fleur said. '*Bonne chance, chérie!*' before returning her attention to her invoices. As she checked the figures, she looked up from time to time to see what class of frock Bethany was drawn to. She was, Fleur could tell, checking out ones that were a little too old for her, or a little too glitzy. And then, upon clocking the price tags, she'd hastily hang the garments back on the rail.

She definitely needed some help here. Fleur took off her reading glasses and said, 'All done!' – when in fact she had several more invoices to attend to. But this morning, Bethany was her priority.

'Hmm,' she said, as the girl helped herself to a silk tulle confection in burnt sienna. It was a little like something you'd buy in aDiva couture in Second Life. 'I'm not quite sure that's your colour.'

'What about this?' asked Bethany, reaching for a baby-pink frilled silk gown, the skirt of which was slit to the crotch.

'No, no,' said Fleur. 'That's too Anastasia Harris. You need something simpler.' Taking Bethany's hand, she led her across the shop floor to where a sleeveless white broderie anglaise frock with a scalloped hem was displayed. It was young, it was fresh, it was virginal. 'Try this,' she suggested.

Bethany looked dubious. 'It's not very – well – sexy, is it?'

'Trust me,' said Fleur. 'It's perfect for you. Just let me make sure the zipper is working. Sometimes they get caught, you know, and then they're a bitch to get into.'

Fleur examined the zip, and as she did, she detached the price tag. '*Voilà!* Go try it on.'

'Thank you.' Bethany took the dress from her and slipped into the changing cubicle, and Fleur returned to her finances.

Moments later, Bethany emerged from behind the curtain.

Fleur looked up, then blew Bethany an extravagant kiss. 'I was right,' she said. 'It *is* perfect.'

Bethany looked like something out of a story book. She was barefoot, barelegged. Her hair tumbled artlessly over her shoulders, and diminutive, pointilliste dots of golden skin were visible through the eyelet embroidery.

Fleur put her head on one side, and considered. 'Quite, quite perfect! There is just one thing amiss,' she said. 'You must not wear a bra with this dress.'

'But it's a white bra I have on!' protested Bethany.

Fleur shook her head. 'No matter. Better a flesh-coloured bra than white under a semi-diaphanous garment – but flesh-coloured bras are *so* unsexy! White panties you can get away with, sure – but no bra with this dress. Don't you know how lucky you are not to need a bra, darling? Look at yourself.'

Bethany did. She regarded her reflection in that way teenage girls do, questioningly, uncertainly, as if trying to work out who she was, as if hoping to forge an identity for herself. And then she smiled. 'You're right,' she said to Fleur. 'It *is* perfect. But can I afford it? There's no price tag.'

'That's because there is no price,' lied Fleur. 'Designers often send me samples for free, to induce me to stock them. You can have it for nothing.'

'I don't believe you!' said Bethany.

Fleur shrugged. 'Take a look around. Can you see another one like it? It's a one-off. You're lucky you are so slender. Samples only ever come in size eight.'

'But – I can't accept this, Fleur!'

'If you don't, I shall have to keep it for my niece Daisy and give it to her when she comes back from Africa. And by then it will be too wintry to wear a dress like this.'

Bethany bit her lip. 'Are you sure? Are you absolutely sure?'

'Yes, sweetheart, I am absolutely sure. You picked a good day to come into my shop, didn't you?'

'I did. Oh, I did!' And Bethany dance-stepped up to Fleur and flung her arms around her. 'Thank you so, so much! I was scared I'd have to blow a big chunk of my earnings on an outfit for tonight, and I so want to look good.'

'And you will, that's for sure. Now. How about shoes?'

That dubious look came over Bethany's face again. 'I don't really have anything dressy,' she said. 'Would I get away with flip-flops?'

'Flip-flops are perfect! What colour?'

'I have some blue ones?'

'No,' said Fleur categorically. 'Blue will not work. I have a pair of ecru leather ones upstairs. I can lend them to you – we're about the same size. And I have a mother-of-pearl necklace, which would go perfectly.'

'I honestly don't know how to thank you, Fleur,' said Bethany. 'You're like the fairy godmother in *Cinderella*.'

Fleur waved an imaginary magic wand. Then, 'Shoo, shoo!' she said. 'Here comes Anastasia Harris, to whom I must devote all of my attention! She must be in need of a gown for this evening.'

'Oh! I'll scarper, so, and leave you to her. Thanks a million, Fleur – you've been legend!'

'Come back in half an hour, and I'll have your accessories ready for you.'

'Thanks so much! And –' this in an undertone '– good luck with Nasty!'

As the smiling extra shimmied out of the shop and the starlet made her entrance with her bodyguard, Fleur already knew which gown Nasty Harris would be wearing this evening. It would be the baby pink frilled silk, the one with the skirt slit to the crotch. And it would cost her a cool €890.

Bethany's would have been better value, Fleur thought, as she welcomed Ms Harris into her humble premises. The price tag on that one had been only €340.

Fleur was showered and shampooed and had applied a little *maquillage*: MAC's Pink Nouveau to her lips, a dusting of LeClerc's Orchidée to her face (it was perfect for evening; a luminous lavender pink – which sounded awful, but looked fabulous). She spritzed herself with *Vent Vert* – having changed allegiance from *Narcisse Blanc*, hating the fact that Corban had liked it – twisted her hair into a chignon, and set off for the wrap party.

Parking her little Karmann Ghia between a Lexus and a Maserati (Recession? What recession?), she sashayed into the marquee that had been set up in the grounds of Arnoldscourt House. Fleur knew the value of making an entrance, and she was pleased to see that she could still make an impact. Men looked at her with interest and women checked out her style, hoping maybe that they could steal some of it. But Fleur's style was innate, unique and inimitable, and she knew it.

The marquee was draped and swagged in bog-standard ivory tat. The dining chairs even had those horrid stretch covers on that – when taken off – looked like some kind of old-lady underpinning. Fleur gave a sigh of irritation. The production company had a genius on their hands: Río could have transformed the place into a pleasure dome worthy of Coleridge if she'd been given the remit.

However, the partygoers crowding into the palatial marquee were truly beautiful. All the guys and gals involved in the making of *The O'Hara Affair* had come forth tonight in hummingbird silks and raven-sleek suits. They glistened, they gleamed, they shimmered, they sparkled. And yes – Fleur was delighted to see – Elena Sweetman outshone them all in her plain silk sheath, courtesy of Fleurissima.

Fleur wandered between tables, taking everything in. She scanned the crowd to see if Mr Bastard O'Hara might have had the nerve to attend, and was glad to see that there was no sign of him anywhere. His baby love was there, though, with her husband, Jay David. Mr David was built like Arnold Schwarzenegger, and Fleur wondered what his reaction might be if he knew that one of the film's executive producers had been screwing his wife. If she, Fleur, had been able to immobilize Corban with her amateur kick-boxing skills, how might her ex fare when faced with the wrath of the actor who was famous for playing superheroes? But then she remembered what Shane had told her – that his last wife had kept 'walking into doors', and she knew that the DVD she'd purloined would never make it onto YouTube.

Fleur wondered what on earth had induced the starlet to go to bed with Corban. Had it been the promise of another leading role? Maybe. After the footage of her on-set tantrum had been aired on the internet, Nasty Harris's future as the new Julia Roberts had been seriously jeopardized. Perhaps she'd deemed it advantageous to sleep with someone who was in a position to help put her career back on track? Fleur had heard through the grapevine that Corban's next project was to be a screen adaptation of *Zuleika Dobson* – and the role of the eponymous heroine would score a to-die-for rating on any Hollywood wannabe's wish list. Or maybe Corban had simply charmed her, the way he seemed to charm everybody? Shane had called him a sociopath, and Fleur had read somewhere that sociopaths were game players, skilled at winning people over, and expert manipulators. She'd witnessed Corban in action dozens of times. He'd even charmed Dervla – and Dervla was no pushover. As for pretty little Anastasia Harris? She had been just another conquest for him to add to the list of people he'd suckered – including foolish, foolish Fleur O'Farrell.

Nasty and Jay, both of them with scowls on their faces, were sitting behind a velvet rope that segregated them from the hoi polloi. Silly girl, thought Fleur. She should be out there in the thick of things, working the room, instead of trying to maintain her unsustainable princess status. Her PR person had issued an apology to the press, and implied that Ms Harris was undergoing therapy for anger management: however, to judge by the expression she was wearing, the anger management wasn't working.

Unsurprisingly, really, since she'd been dissed by Perez Hilton, appeared in *Heat* magazine's Hoop of Horror, and TMZ was breaking news about her low-life drug dealer brother. It looked as if Nasty Harris's fifteen minutes were up.

At another table, locals who had worked on the film were filling half-empty pints of Guinness with champagne to make Black Velvets. Lissamore would suffer from a massive collective hangover tomorrow, Fleur conjectured. Still, the lean season would soon be upon them, so it made sense to party like it was 1999.

There was Paddy Lonergan, who had worked as an assistant to the voice coach on the film, and who was already selling pilfered *O'Hara Affair* memorabilia on eBay. There was Noreen Conroy, who had cleaned Elena Sweetman's trailer, and collected all the tissues that bore lipstick kisses. Ms Sweetman had very obligingly agreed to sign them so that Noreen could frame them and auction them at a Cancer Research coffee morning. There was Vinnie McGinley, who had advised the set designer on the building of dry-stone walls, and who was – according to Sean the Post – working undercover for the *National Enquirer*.

And, joy! There was Río, and there was Dervla, along with Shane and Finn, all sitting together at a big round table. As she drifted across the floor to join them, she apologized to a man whose face had been brushed by the end of her trailing chiffon scarf. 'No apology necessary,' he told her with a smile.

'How do you do it?' asked Dervla, as Fleur sat down.

'Do what? Ooh! Goodie bags!' A silk beribboned bag was waiting by each place setting.

'You have a kind of aura about you that makes people look twice.'

Fleur laughed. 'It's like Dolores del Río once said. "So long as a woman has twinkles in her eyes, no man notices whether she has wrinkles under them."' She reached for a bread roll from the basket, and spread it generously with butter. 'Is Christian not with you, Dervla?'

'He's actually working. The caterers underestimated how much wine would be consumed, so he's in Bacchante, filling an order.'

'Imagine underestimating the amount of booze that film people put away,' scoffed Shane. 'Actors are the biggest liggers on the planet. I remember a PR event for the Galway Arts Festival once, where none of the actors wanted to be photographed because it meant they'd have to be dragged away from the buffet table. You know, there are just four words that can make an actor the happiest man on the planet.'

'And they are?' prompted Fleur.

'Free food and drink,' said Shane.

'But you're rich now, Dad!' protested Finn.

'That doesn't mean I don't embrace my inner out-of-work actor. I steal stuff from hotels all the time. Have a gander at what's in the goodie bags, Fleur.'

Fleur pounced, and riffled among the contents of the glossy bag. First up was a T-shirt with *The O'Hara Affair* emblazoned upon it in a blood-red font. 'Well, that's one T-shirt I won't be wearing,' she said, waspishly.

'Give it to me then,' said Shane, reaching for it. 'Girls love it when I give them souvenir T-shirts, and I love signing them.'

'I suppose you sign across their tits,' said Río, crossly.

'Of course. They love it nearly as much as I do.'

Next up were signed photographs of the principal stars of the movie.

'Give me the one of Shane, please,' said Río, 'so that I can draw spots and facial hair and squinty eyes on it.'

'It's more juvenile every day you're getting, Río Kinsella,' Shane told her.

Río gave him an arch look. 'A van with four actors in it goes over a cliff,' she challenged. 'Where's the tragedy in this?'

Shane heaved a sigh. 'OK, where's the tragedy?'

'You can fit a lot more than four actors in a van,' replied Río, tartly.

'Ma! Pa! Cut it out,' Finn rebuked them.

'What's this?' said Fleur, holding up a small statuette of an emaciated man in rags.

'I suppose it's to commemorate the famine,' said Shane. 'It's in massively poor taste, considering we're all sitting here stuffing our faces and swigging back wine.'

'How many actors does it take to wallpaper a room? asked Río.

Shane shot her a look of exasperated enquiry.

'Only three,' came the response, 'if you slice them very thin.'

'Hello, sweetheart,' said Shane, turning to a passing waitress. 'Could you bring us some more wine here, please?'

'Certainly, Mr Byrne.' The waitress dimpled at him, then shimmied away.

'Ma Branagan's Barmbrack,' announced Fleur, who was continuing to root through her goodie bag. 'Handmade Irish chocolates, miniature Baileys – you can have that, Finn – Mother McGuire's shortbread biscuits, Carrageen Candy, Shamrock Soda Tasties.'

'It looks like it's far from a famine we Irish were raised,' remarked Shane. 'Can I have your Carrageen Candy, Fleur? I love it, and you can't get it in LA.'

'Certainly,' said Fleur, sliding the bag across the table to him. 'You can have all my stuff, apart from the chocolates. How come you're not hobnobbing with the stars, Shane?'

'Fuck the stars. Sure, don't I hobnob with them every day? I'd rather hobnob with my family and friends.'

On a podium in the middle of the marquee, a girl in Irish costume started playing a lament on a fiddle.

'Riverdance has a lot to answer for,' observed Río, draining her wineglass. 'Before you know it, there'll be a musical about the Irish famine, and Michael Flatley'll have to go on a crash diet.'

'Will there be dancing later?' asked Dervla.

'There will.'

'Shame I've forgotten all my moves.'

'Hop on left foot, point right toe.' Fleur demonstrated on the tabletop with her fingers.

'I'd forgotten you did Irish dancing as well as kick-boxing,' said Dervla.

'You've taken up kick-boxing, Fleur?' said Río. 'Nobody ever tells me anything.'

'She's very good at it,' said Finn and Shane simultaneously.

'How do you know?'

'She – erm – did a demonstration for us in Fleurissima one day,' improvised Shane.

'That must have drawn quite a crowd,' remarked Río.

'Yeah. I should have filmed it and put it up on YouTube,' said Finn. '"Fashionista Kick-boxes in Jimmy Choo Stilettos and Tight Skirt."'

Across the room, Fleur saw Jake and Bethany arrive. Bethany looked a little shy as her date took her by the hand and led her to their table, and she watched as Jake held out her chair for her. He had manners! How sexy was that! Then he bent to say something in Bethany's ear before taking the seat next to her, and Fleur felt a little nostalgic for the lost last love of her life. But no, no! Nostalgia was unnecessary. She was just happy – truly happy – that Bethany seemed to have sorted her life out.

And then she saw that the animal wrangler – who was at the same table as Jake and Bethany – was sending her interested signals. Fleur arched an eyebrow a fraction, bit her lip and pushed a stray tendril of hair back into her chignon, then lowered demure eyes to her place setting. The waitress was just about to pour wine into her glass, but Fleur put her hand over it. 'No wine for me, thank you,' she said.

'No wine?' exclaimed Río, sliding her glass in the direction of the waitress. 'Woah – what's the matter with you, Ms O'Farrell? Are you pregnant?'

What the hell. She was going to have to come clean sooner or later.

'Yes,' said Fleur.

Later, after the dancing had started, Dervla took the seat next to Fleur. 'You're really thrilled about this baby, aren't you?'

Fleur nodded. 'It's what I've always wanted.'

'And you're adamant about not telling the father?'

'Absolutely. It would just succeed in messing up his life big time.'

'It's Corban, of course.'

'No,' Fleur told her, 'as a matter of fact, it's not. And I'm not prepared to divulge any more than that.'

'So you're going to do this all on your own?'

'I'll get by,' Fleur said with a serene smile, 'with a little help from my friends.'

Reaching for Dervla's hand, she held it against her belly. On the dance floor, Shane and Río were swaying together to the rhythm of 'She Moves Through the Fair'.

'I hope those two come to their senses soon,' remarked Fleur.

'I hope they do, too,' said Dervla. 'Just look at that body language.'

'Río's been in denial all her life.'

'What's Ma been in denial about?' Finn had plonked himself down beside them.

'None of your business, godson,' Fleur told him. 'This is private girl talk.'

'Yeah! Let me join in! I've always wanted to know what girls talk about in private.'

Fleur gave him an arch look. 'We talk about things that are of no interest to smelly boys. We talk about kittens and roses and frilly underwear.'

'Frilly underwear's of interest to me,' said Finn, happily. 'I could spend hours in your shop riffling through the ruffly stuff.'

'I don't have a problem with that, as long as you have no intention of buying it for your own use.' Fleur returned her attention to the dance floor.

There, lost in the music, a blissed-out look in her eyes, a girl was dancing on her own, barefoot. Dressed in a short denim skirt that boasted ragged tulle petticoats and with a bandanna wrapped around her head, she was beautiful in an unconventional, *jolie-laide* way, and she was very, very sexy.

'Who's that?' asked Fleur.

Finn looked in the direction Fleur had indicated. 'Oh, that Gallagher girl! She worked as a scenic artist on the film. She scares me. There's something feral about her.'

'She *scares* you? But she's lovely!' protested Dervla.

Finn shrugged. 'She doesn't seem to like people much. I think she prefers animals. She spent most of her coffee breaks talking to the horses.'

'What's her first name?'

'Catriona. Cat for short.'

'Here's a challenge for you, Finn!' Dervla drew a couple of bank notes out of her evening purse. 'I'll bet you twenty euros that you don't have the nerve to ask her up for a dance.'

Finn gave Dervla an incredulous look. 'Are you out of your mind, auntie dearest? Twenty euros for an auld dance? Nothing scares me *that* much.'

Dervla and Fleur exchanged amused glances as Finn got to his feet and pocketed the cash.

And as he made his way across the dance floor, the Gallagher girl seemed to sense that Finn was coming, because she turned to him in slow motion, put her hands on her hips, and smiled.

Epilogue

Fleur was reclining on her chaise longue, her laptop on a tray in front of her. She knew her days of reclining *con* laptop were numbered since – as WikiAnswers had warned her – the further her pregnancy advanced, the less expanse of lap she would have. One of the first questions Fleur had Googled when she'd discovered she was pregnant was how safe it was to use her MacBook Air. The answers were all reassuring.

She was just under seven months pregnant now, and loving it. It was wonderful to have an excuse to laze like a big cat, and she adored the fact that she was allowed to. She spent her days reading, eating comfort food, knitting, and watching vintage movies. Now that she was to be a mother, Barbara Stanwyck in *Stella Dallas* made her weep harder than ever.

She'd decided to close the shop completely for the winter, apart from the fortnight before Christmas when it would have been cruel not to allow her patrons access to last-minute purchases. Río was going to take over when the season started up after Patrick's Day, and Fleur would come back to work only when she felt ready. It might take some time, for she was under no illusions that her situation wasn't the easiest. She would have less energy than your average first-time mum, and she had no partner to help her. But Fleur simply thought, *Je m'en fou.* She was now in proud possession of her heart's desire

– a baby girl (she'd been told she was carrying a girl), and that was all that mattered to her. She didn't even care that in a few months' time her pristine chaise longue would doubtless become a nappy-changing station, or that there'd be puke stains on her peignoir and on her lace-trimmed Irish linen sheets. In fact, she rather fancied her white walls would be a perfect canvas for her precocious infant's first finger paintings.

The Eircom home page shimmered onto her screen. Among the recent headlines was the following: *The O'Hara Affair Premieres in Dublin*.

'With searchlights blazing into the cold night sky and a battery of digital cameras capturing every moment,' Fleur read, 'the most expensive film ever to be made in Ireland premiered at Dublin's Savoy cinema last night – with a good dose of Hollywood razzmatazz to add va va voom. When Galway garsoon-made-good Shane Byrne, and his co-star Elena Sweetman, emerged fashionably late from their chauffeur-driven limo, the crowd went wild. Ms Sweetman was wearing vintage Sorelle Fontana: a strapless cerulean satin gown with bead-encrusted bodice, accessorized by a sapphire and diamond necklace and matching earrings.' Channelling Ava Gardner in *The Barefoot Contessa*, Fleur surmised, with a smile. 'Next up was Hollywood's favourite ingénue –' (Ha! thought Fleur) '– Anastasia Harris, who stars as Shane's daughter in the film. Anastasia – accompanied by her new husband, veteran star of the *DevilCop* series, Jay David – was looking ravishing in barely-there Roberto Cavalli, and swathed in ropes of pearls. Then came the turn of up-and-coming Irish actor Doncha Hennessy – who plays the eponymous hero of *The O'Hara Affair*. Doncha was accompanied by his girlfriend, Ida O'Doherty, who is the newest – and possibly most glamorous – cast member of Ireland's favourite soap opera, *Fair City*. Ida was wearing a dress which, she told reporters, had been made specially for the occasion by her brother, Central London fashion design student, Gerard Doherty. Awwww!!! Don't we just love our home-grown talent!

'After the showing of the film (watch this space for a review!), cast and crew danced and drank champagne until the early hours at a glittering party in Dublin Castle. Other guests included Gabriel Byrne, Colin Farrell, Ciarán Hinds, Liam Neeson and Bono.'

Fleur wondered if Río had danced until the early hours. She'd been invited along with Finn, and – being Río – she would have dumped the invite in the bin without a second thought if Finn hadn't blackmailed her into going. He'd told her that if she didn't attend, then neither would he – and think of the headlines this would provoke! *Shane's Son Boycotts Premier! Lovechild Finn-ishes with Shane! The Byrne Affair: Río Ashamed to Show!* It had been this final chimera that had proven to be the red rag to Río's bull. She had driven up to Dublin in her beat-up hackney with Finn in the passenger seat and an overnight bag in the boot that contained a hired tux (Finn had never worn one before), a pair of eBay Louboutins, and an emerald-green Vivienne Westwood drape dress on loan from Fleur.

Had Bethany made it to the premiere? Fleur wondered. She'd been keeping tabs on her young friend, but these days Bethany didn't seem to be spending much time on Facebook. Fleur knew that her application to the Gaiety School had been successful, and that shortly before Christmas she had moved into Jake's city-centre apartment– where they'd hosted a New Year's Eve party on the roof garden. Fleur had been very pleased to have received an invitation from Bethany, but had turned it down, citing the icy roads as an excuse. She rarely received personal messages from her former protégée any more, and she was glad of this because it meant that Bethany had found her feet at last, and was moving on.

After the event, Fleur had looked at all the Facebook photos of laughing young people, dressed in seasonal winter woollies and drinking hot toddies, but the one she loved most was of Bethany and Jake smiling to camera with their arms wrapped around each other. Bethany was wearing a festive red tinsel bow in her hair, and the caption read: **Jake giftwraps his Christmas present.**

Now that Fleur ventured out less frequently (it was bitterly cold in Coolnamara this winter), she was becoming more dependent on the internet for gossip. She missed her chats *en français* with Peggy in Ryan's, but Facebook notifications kept her up to speed. As for Second Life? With robust real life kick-boxing and turning somersaults inside her, Fleur had no need of a vacuous vicarious existence.

From her online surfing, she had learned that the Bolgers' place – the house that Río had christened 'Coral Mansion' – had finally been sold at a vastly reduced price to an unknown buyer. Speculation was rife as to who the new owner might be. Some said it was a hugely successful chick lit writer, others that it was a disgraced archbishop. Some said it was a former Taoiseach, others that it was a boy band member. Even Dervla – despite all her connections in the property business – did not know who had bought the house.

Dervla had finished her book, and hadn't been surprised to see that it had barely crept into the first top fifty Irish non-fiction titles before disappearing without a trace after charting for just one week. It would appear that people were still waiting for property values to rise before they sought advice about selling their homes. But – Dervla had told Fleur – she really didn't care: she was just so damned relieved to see the back of the bloody thing and move on. She and Christian had moved into the cottage and were working hard on converting the Old Rectory into a state-of-the-art retirement home.

They'd managed to get a bank loan and a decent tender from a construction company, but Dervla had still been obliged to sell her Galway apartment, and Christian had leased out his shop. He was happy to do this: it gave him more time to work hands-on on the Old Rectory while Dervla pursued her fledgling career in politics. She couldn't afford yet to run as an independent, but she was testing her wings in what she hoped would prove to be a brave new world: 'Enfranchizing Old Farts', as Christian – politically incorrect as ever – put it.

As well as messing about on the internet, Fleur had invested in a pair of binoculars so that she could while away time on her deck. Towards the end of last summer, she had been pleased to see a 'For Sale' sign go up outside Corban's penthouse, and late last autumn she'd been even more pleased to see it replaced by a 'Sale Agreed' sign. The *Lolita* had mysteriously disappeared one night after a force ten gale, and had been washed up on Inishclare, but when Fleur had asked Finn if he was responsible, he had widened his eyes at her and said: 'Godmother! Would you – who are after all responsible for my spiritual upbringing – countenance such behaviour? Naughty Fleur! Shame on you for even thinking such wicked thoughts.'

Fleur flexed her fingers, then fired off an email to Río, asking her if she'd met Bono last night. Then she typed in her password and accessed her Facebook home page. She hadn't updated her status for months, and none of her Facebook friends – apart from Daisy – even knew she was pregnant. But before she could dream up a status update, her phone alerted her to a text.

Hey, Flirty! she read. **On my way now with cake & NO wine** ☺ **XXX**

Fleur smiled, and rose to her feet to put the kettle on. Minutes later, Daisy was bounding up the stairs. She'd put on weight, her skin was bronzed, her riotous hair had been bleached by sea and sun and was inches longer. She looked astonishing, as if she'd been kissed all over by King Midas.

Gathering Fleur into her arms with infinite care, she said: 'No bear hugs for you, Flirty, even though I'd love to hug the living daylights out of you. From now on I must be careful to treat my aunt like a porcelain doll.' Holding her at arms' length, Daisy's eyes went to Fleur's bump. 'Oh! *Oh!* She's in there! *Ma cousine!*' She knelt down and kissed her aunt's rounded belly. Can I be her godmother as well as her cousin?'

'But of course,' said Fleur.

'What are you going to call her?'

'Well, her surname will revert to de Saint-Euverte. I'm not calling her after that Mountie-loving ex-husband of mine.'

'And not after her daddy, neither?' asked Daisy cautiously.

'Her daddy is a Pooka with no name.'

'Fair enough,' conceded Daisy. 'What about her Christian name?'

'That's easy. I'm calling her after you.'

'But how can there be two Daisy de Saint-Euvertes in the same family?'

'There won't be. I'm giving her the name of the French flower.'

'Marguerite?'

Fleur nodded.

Daisy pressed her cheek against Fleur's belly. 'Hello, darling little Marguerite de Saint-Euverte! How do you like being named after your big cousin?' She listened for a moment or two, and then she turned smiling eyes to Fleur. 'She likes it,' she declared.

'How do you know?' asked Fleur.

'I can hear her giggling,' said Daisy.

THE END.

464

Points for Discussion on The O'Hara Affair

Are you a subscriber to Second Life or a similar virtual world? Can you analyse its appeal? Do you think it is a harmless way of relaxing, or do you consider it a useful networking tool? Might it be a novel way of keeping in touch with old friends, or making new ones? Might you be worried that you could become obsessed by it? Do you think that we are becoming increasingly like the space travellers in Wall-E who spent all their times on their backsides in front of their computer screens? Are you concerned about any children you may have who seem to spend more time in virtual worlds than in the real world?

On p. 414, Valentina asks Dervla: 'If you *weren't* being paid, do you think the same high standard [of caring for her mother-in-law] would apply?' If you found yourself in the position of having to care perforce without remuneration for someone who was not a blood relative, do you think that you might find yourself becoming embittered and resentful? Do you think these negative feelings would impact on the standard of care delivered?

Dervla makes the observation that in some parts of the world, it is a great compliment is to call someone an 'old' man. Why has it become an expression of derision and contempt in our society? Do you think that our pursuit of eternal youth and our obsession with youth culture is responsible for our fear of old age?

Older people's dependency on the social infrastructure is the result of compulsory retirement, poverty, and diminished stature in the community. This dependency = lack of respect = ageism. Women tend to live longer than men, ergo older women suffer most from ageism. Have you put much, if any thought into how you might confront the problems of aging? Or do you secretly hope that – to paraphrase the words of Roger Daltrey – you die before you get too old to cope?

Life expectancy is increasing, but so too is *active* life expectancy. People are enjoying good health longer than their ancestors thanks to advances in medical science. But people are also being 'kept' alive longer due to medical science. Philosopher Mary Warnock lamented the fact that swine flu would not prove to be the new 'old man's friend' (a euphemism for pneumonia), since most swine flu fatalities occur within a younger demographic. Do you agree with the sentiment that pneumonia is the 'old man's friend'? Do you think that it is right to continue to administer medicines (such as antibiotics) and vaccines (such as the flu jab) to people who are clearly exhausted by life and who have no say as to whether or not their suffering should be prolonged?

The pros and cons of voluntary euthanasia continue to be argued in bioethical debates. Statistics indicate that more and more people are in support of the right to a dignified death for the terminally ill. What are your views on this? Do you think it is possible to draw up a bill that would realistically address the concerns of those who believe that such a law would be open to abuse?

Read on for an exclusive extract of
Kate Thompson's next novel –
That Gallagher Girl – to be published
by AVON in 2011.

Prologue

On the morning of her seventeenth birthday, Cat Gallagher learned how to break into a house. It was fourth on the list of ten things she wanted to accomplish before she was twenty-one. The first three things she had already achieved. She had learned how to ride bareback, how to play a winning hand at poker, and how to paint with a seagull's feather. She had also learned how to conquer fear – although that particular lesson wasn't itemised on Cat's list of things to learn, for she had always been fearless.

The house in question was a showcase that had never been lived in. It was the product of a former economy, a ghost house boasting brickwork so symmetrical and a roof so streamlined it appeared incongruous next to the unfinished structures that surrounded it, their foundations mapping what was to have been an exclusive development of half-a-dozen luxury dwellings. Those houses would never be finished now. The show house stood alone and resplendent on a building site that was being reclaimed by bindweed, buddleia and feral cats.

Cat and her half-brother Raoul were sitting on a low wall, sharing a bottle of wine. It had a posh French name and a picture of a French château on the label, but Cat hadn't paid for it. She'd stolen it from her dad's collection of vintage

Burgundy, along with a second bottle from his collection of vintage Bordeaux. 'Cheers,' said Raoul, touching his paper cup to hers. 'Happy birthday, Cat.'

'Cheers.'

'I hope you didn't expect a present.'

'Are you mad? I'm as broke as you are,' said Cat. 'Anyway, isn't teaching me the art of breaking and entering more valuable than any old gift wrapped crap? Passing on skills is the new birthday present.'

Raoul was ten years older than Cat. He was a student of architecture at Galway University, and had always indulged her. He had been responsible for teaching her to row a boat and fix a bike chain and skip stones, and now he was mentoring her in the art of housebreaking. Her father, Hugo, had never mentored her in anything much, apart from how to tell the difference between a Burgundy and a Bordeaux.

Cat and Raoul both took after their father in looks. It was said that the Gallaghers had descended from shipwrecked survivors of the Armada, and that they had Spanish blood. Both Cat and Raoul were dark-haired and olive-skinned, with patrician noses and cheekbones like razor shells. Cat's vaguely piratical appearance was enhanced today by the fact that she sported a bandana, and a small gold hoop in one ear. Her eyes were heavily rimmed with black kohl, but that was her only concession to cosmetics. Cat had never used lipstick in her life, nor had she ever painted her nails nor GHD'd her mane of black hair.

'I wonder what Hugo would say if he knew you were teaching me how to break into houses,' Cat remarked as Raoul upended the bottle into their paper cups and stuck it in his duffle bag.

'Being a champagne socialist, he'd applaud the fact that

I'm encouraging you in the art of redistributing wealth.'

'I told you, Raoul – I'm not doing this to steal stuff. I just need to know how to get into places.'

'Why, exactly?'

'I have a feeling in my bones that it's going to be useful some time.'

'When you become a fugitive from justice, you mean?'

'When I become a fugitive from our father, more like.'

'You'll let me know, won't you, when you decide to run away? I'll worry if you don't keep in touch.'

'You'll be the only person I'll let know,' she told him, kissing his cheek. 'You'll be the only person who'll worry.'

Cat drained her cup, then got up from the wall and stumbled sideways as her foot clipped the edge of a pothole and the earth crumbled beneath her boot. 'Yikes! Look at the size of that pothole. I wouldn't like to be negotiating this place at night.'

'Better get used to it. Good cat burglars – excuse the pun – need extra sensory night vision.'

'Let me say it again – I ain't in the business of burgling, Raoul.'

'Never say never.' Raoul took Cat's cup and drained his own before stowing them and the bottle in his duffle bag. 'Let's go recce,' he said.

Together they made their way along the path that led to the front door of the unoccupied house. It was fashioned from solid oak, and had an impenetrable air. 'Open, Sesame!' cried Cat. 'Bring on the breaking and entering master class, Raoul.'

Raoul gave the façade of the house the once-over. 'Okay. Your first challenge is to find out if a joint is wired for alarm. You're safe with a place like this, because the security system has never been activated. You'd be amazed, as well, at how few holiday home owners on the west coast bother to set alarms while they're away.'

'Why don't they bother?'

'Too much hassle if they're activated by stormy weather. There are only so many times you can prevail upon your local neighbouring farmer to reset your alarm. A lot of those boxes are dummies, by the way.'

'So which houses are the most likely candidates?'

'Ones that haven't been lived in for a while.'

'How can you tell if they haven't been lived in?'

'Jemmy the mail box and have a look at the postmarks on the envelopes. The dates will tell you. If you find bills it's a bonus, because they're unlikely to have been paid. Unpaid Eircom Phone Watch bills mean that the joint's no longer being monitored.'

'Isn't there a battery back-up on those systems?'

'If the bills haven't been paid, the Phone Watch people are under no obligation to let the home owner know that their batteries need replacing.'

Cat moved along the side of the house, and set her palms against a picture window, pressing her face close so that she could peer through. With the sun bouncing off the glass, it proved difficult, but she could make out an expanse of timber floor and walls painted in a tasteful shade of cappuccino. 'Why are people so careless about protecting their properties, Raoul?'

'It's a sign of the times. A decade ago people were reckless when they bought their second homes. All that money being thrown at them by the banks made them buy into an unsustainable lifestyle, and now they can't sell it on.' Raoul shaded his eyes with a hand, and squinted up at the roof, where a seagull was eyeing him suspiciously. 'The water tax and the tax on second homes was a disaster for the property market on the west coast. The owners resent every penny they're obliged to spend on a place they can't afford to maintain, so they just don't bother their arses. They're not going to throw good money after bad – look at the state of this place.' He indicated the garden with an expansive gesture. 'Once upon a time the lawn would have been mowed every month to keep up the show house façade. It hasn't been done for a year, by the look of it.'

Cat turned and surveyed the quarter acre of garden. The grass was thigh high, the flower beds thick with weeds. Dandelions were pushing their way up through the golden gravel that covered the path to the front door, and judging by the wasp activity immediately overhead, a nest was being constructed in the eaves.

'Keep an eye out for unkempt gardens and For Sale signs,' Raoul told her. 'The properties that have been on the market for more than a year are the ones you want to target.'

'How can I tell how long they've been on the market?'

'Go to Daft.ie and see how much the price has dropped. The bigger the bargain, the more desperate the seller, and the further down the listing, the more obvious it is that nobody's been interested enough to view. These are generally the babies that have been languishing with no TLC.' Raoul gave her a shrewd look. 'Now, tell me. How do you think you're going to get in here?'

'Not through the front door, that's for sure.'

'Top marks. And not through this sheet of plate glass, neither. Let's have a look around the back.'

They made their way to the rear of the house, where the door to a utility room was located. A look through a small window to the left of the door told Cat that there was access to the kitchen from there. Pulling a pair of latex gloves from her pocket, she slid them on. 'Do I smash it?' she asked Raoul.

'Tch tch, Cat! How inelegant. Think again.'

'Cut the pane with a glass cutter?'

'No, darling. You'd need suction pads, you could cut yourself, and you don't want to leave samples of your DNA splashed around. Take a closer look.'

Cat ran a finger over the edge of the window. It was beaded with varnished teak, in which plugs of matching hardwood were dotted at regular intervals.

'What's underneath those?' she asked. 'They're camouflaging something, aren't they?'

'You could be right, Kitty Cat,' said Raoul. 'What do you think they might be camouflaging?'

Cat turned and gave him a speculative look. 'Nails?'

'Have a gander.'

Raoul reached into his duffle bag and handed her a narrow-bladed chisel. Inserting it into the fissure between the plug and the main body of the wood, Cat found purchase and prised out the fragment of teak. Underneath was the slotted crosshead of a screw. Setting to, she methodically removed each knot of wood, then set down the chisel. 'I guess I need a screwdriver now,' she said, pushing a strand of hair behind her ear. 'But a regular one won't do the job. The screws are too close to the glass.'

'That,' said Raoul, 'is why I have one of these.' Reaching into his duffle bag again, he produced a Z-shaped tool and handed it to Cat.

'A right-angled screwdriver?'

'Go to the top of the class. I'm not going to help you, by the way. You're going to have to learn how to do this on your own.'

'Why did they fit the screws on the outside of the window?' she asked, taking the screwdriver from Raoul and inserting the bit in the crosshead of the first screw. 'It would make a lot more sense to fit them inside.'

476

'You're inviting serious problems if you fit them on the inside. The rain streams in.'

Cat smiled. 'This is so simple, it's stupid.' She started to unscrew the beading from the glass panel, frowning a little in concentration as she manipulated the bit. Once she got to the final couple of screws, she held the window in place by leaning a shoulder against it. Then she prised away the strip of wood, dropped the screwdriver, and went to lift the glass from its frame.

'Wait,' said Raoul. 'You'll need proper gloves for this. Here.'

Taking care not to let the glass fall, Cat slipped her hands into first the right, then the left glove, and turned back to her task. 'Voilà!' she said, as the double-glazed panel came away. 'Access all areas!' With great care, she leaned the pane against the exterior wall before setting her palms on the sill and hoisting herself up.

'Wait!' said Raoul. 'Take your boots off. You don't want to leave footprints.'

Cat undid the laces on her boots, pulled them off and dropped them on the muddy ground below the window. Then she twisted around, slid her legs through the empty frame, and eeled herself into the house.

'How easy was that!' she crowed, and her words came back to her, bouncing off the smooth plaster walls of the house that would never be sold, never be lived in. 'Come and have a look, Raoul.'

He followed her through.

Both utility room and kitchen were equipped with state-of-the-art white goods. The kitchen floor was marble, the work surfaces polished granite. The adjacent sitting-room boasted a gas fire and a panelled alcove in which to house a plasma screen. Beyond the sitting room, beyond doors that accessed study, den and conservatory, carpeted stairs led from

477

the light-filled lobby to bedrooms and bathrooms above. The walk-in wardrobe in the master bedroom was bigger than Cat's room in Hugo's house.

She wondered what it must be like to live in a house like this. Would you live a life here, or a lifestyle? Would you curl your feet up on a suede upholstered sofa while aiming a remote at your entertainment suite? Would you microwave a ready meal from a top end outlet while uncorking a chilled bottle of Sauvignon Blanc? Would you cuff an infant lovingly when he or she trotted mud onto your marble tiles before reaching for your eco-friendly floor wipes?

Hugo's house was so very different. Hugo's house stood all alone in the middle of a forest, and was like something out of a Grimms' fairytale. It was dark and tumbledown with a cruck frame and exposed beams and a roof that slumped in the middle. Having settled comfortably into its foundations over the course of three hundred years, Hugo's house listed to starboard, and had crooked windows and wonky stairs and worn flagstones. Hugo refused to compromise the character of his house by introducing twenty-first century fixtures and fittings: his fridge was clad in elm planks, he cooked on an ancient Rayburn. There was no television, no broadband and no power shower. People described Hugo's house as 'quaint'. But they didn't have to live there. Cat had never been able to call Hugo's house home.

She had returned there when she was thirteen, after her mother – Hugo's third wife – had died of uterine cancer. Paloma had left Hugo and the crooked house six years previously, taking Cat with her to Dublin, where they had lived until Paloma's untimely death. Back on the west coast, the teenage Cat, bereaved and isolated, found it impossible to make friends. Her Dublin accent singled her out as being different – that and the fact that her eccentric father was living with his fourth (some said fifth) wife.

Cat hated school. Hugo had tried the boarding option, but she just kept absconding, and running away to Raoul's bedsit in Galway. When she was expelled from boarding school, she mitched from the local school so often that Hugo made a pledge to the authorities to home-school his daughter. But Cat shrugged off his half-hearted attempts. How could you have faith in a teacher who sloshed brandy into his morning coffee and smoked roll-ups while he recited Shakespeare and Seamus Heaney in maudlin tones? The answer was - you didn't. You gave him the finger, and went off in search of ponies to ride, or cloudscapes to paint, or – which activity she was presently engaged in – houses to break into.

And neither the authorities nor her father seemed to give a shit.

Cat strolled across the pristine oatmeal carpet of the show home's master bedroom to a big dormer window that looked out over the building site. How many houses might there be all over Ireland languishing unfinished, waiting for someone to occupy them? She reckoned she could have her pick of thousands. To the east – inland – ribbon developments straggled Dublin-ward along the sides of the roads. To the south, the landscape was dotted with unoccupied holiday homes. To the west, an expanse of ocean glittered diamantine.

'Look, Raoul!' she said, turning to him as he followed her through the door. 'You can see the cemetery on Inishcaillín from here.'

Inishcaillín was where Cat's mother, Paloma, had been buried. It was on the summit of a drowned drumlin, and Cat would occasionally take a boat out to spend a day on the island, talking to her mother, undisturbed by anyone since the island was uninhabited now. Paloma's grave was surrounded by dozens of graves of victims of the Irish famine, all with their headstones facing west towards the Atlantic, that they might see in the setting sun the ghosts of all those loved ones who had fled Ireland for America. It was a desolate place, whipped by raging gales that came in from the ocean, but it had been a place that Paloma had loved like no other, and that was why Cat had insisted she be buried there. When she was a little girl, she and her mother had used to take picnics over to the island, and swim in the more sheltered of the easterly coves. They'd explored the abandoned village, too, making up stories about the people who used to live there, and had once even pitched a tent and stayed overnight in one of the roofless cottages.

'Do you miss her still?' asked Raoul.

Cat turned to him. 'Of course I do. But I hate her too, in a way, for leaving me alone with that bastard and his whore.' She saw Raoul raise an eyebrow. 'What's up?' she asked. 'You know how I feel about them.'

'Cat, Cat, you drama queen,' he chided. 'Sometimes you talk like something out of Shakespeare.'

'That bastard and his ho, then,' she returned, pettishly. 'Let's open the other bottle. I feel like getting drunk.'

Cat had never been able to call her stepmother anything other than whore. Although Sophie had been Mrs Gallagher for nearly ten years now, Cat refused to acknowledge her. When she had moved in with Hugo four years ago she had steadfastly resisted all Sophie's attempts to befriend her. Stepmother and stepdaughter barely bothered with each other now.

Raoul took the second bottle of wine from his duffle bag, and started to strip away the foil from the neck. 'You're seventeen now, Cat,' he pointed out. 'Legally speaking, you could leave home, with our father's permission.'

'Sure, he'd give it in a heartbeat.' Cat leaned against the wall, and slid down until she was sitting on the carpet.

'Well, then?'

'Don't think I haven't thought about it. But where would I go - and *don't* tell me I can move in with you because there's no way I'm gonna cramp your style with the ladies.' Raoul inserted the corkscrew and pulled the cork, and Cat smiled up at him. 'I'll never forget how pissed-off your girl-friends used to look every time I escaped from the boarding school of doom and landed on your doorstep.'

Raoul laughed. 'It was a little bizarre. Remember the night you sleepwalked your way into bed with me and - what was her name? It was some hippy-dippy thing.'

'Windsong. I could never keep my face straight when I talked to her. Windsong *hated* me.'

Raoul poured wine, then handed Cat a cup, and sat down beside her. 'So let's have a serious think about this. You can't move in with me, and you can't afford to rent anywhere.'

'You're right. There's no way I could afford to live on my allowance. And I can't live without it. It's a catch twenty-two. I may hate our dad, but he doles out the dosh.'

'And he's not going to cut you off, kid. If you do move out, get him to lodge money to your bank account.'

'I don't have a savings account. And I can't open a current account until I'm eighteen.'

'Get him to send you postal orders.'

Cat gave him a sceptical look. 'To where? Cat Gallagher – no fixed abode?'

'It's dead simple. I used to do it all the time when I was travelling. You set up a Poste Restante in the local post office, and pick up your mail there.'

Cat made a face. 'Maybe I should get a job.'

'Maybe you should.'

'Ha! Let's face it, Raoul – I'm unemployable.'

'Don't be defeatist, sweetheart. And, hang on – I think . . . I *think* . . .'

'Share. I hate enigmatic pauses.' Cat took a hit of her wine.

'I think I might be having a very good idea.' Raoul gave her a speculative look. 'How would you feel about living on a houseboat, Kitty Cat?'

'A houseboat! How cool! Tell me about it.'

'I have a friend who has one in Coolnamara. He could do with someone to caretake it for him.'

'Are you serious?'

'Yes. His wife's in a wheelchair, and they can't live on a boat any more. Can't sell it, either. And he doesn't want it to rot away on the water.'

'Where is it?'

'It's on a stretch of canal near Lissamore, the one that goes from nowhere to nowhere.'

'Nowhere to nowhere?'

'It was one of those pointless famine relief projects, designed to give the starving locals the wherewithal to buy a few grains of Indian corn back in the 1840's. As far as I know, it was never used for anything. But my mate Aidan had his houseboat transported and plonked down in a safe berth. He hasn't visited it for over a year now, and he'd love it to be given some TLC. He couldn't pay you, but I'm pretty sure he'd let you live there rent free.'

'Oh, Raoul! I'd love to live on a houseboat!'

'I'll see what I can do.' Raoul picked up the wine bottle. 'Here. Have some more Château Whatever.'

* * *

Raoul was as good as his word. He put in a call to his mate Aidan, and sorted Cat out with her brand new home from the place she couldn't call home. And by the time they'd finished the bottle and left the house the way they'd come in and hit the main road, Cat was feeling buoyant and full of hope.

'Bye bye, Raoul,' she said, as the twice-weekly bus to Galway appeared over the brow of the hill, and drew up by the turn-off to Hugo's house. 'You are my fairy half-brother.'

'Less of the fairy, thanks. I'll be in touch.'

Cat hugged Raoul the way she never hugged anybody else, and watched him board the bus.

'Here,' he said, taking something out of his duffle bag, and tossing it to her. 'You may need this.' He gave her a final salute, and then the bus door slid shut and he was gone.

In her hand, Cat was clutching the screwdriver she'd used to gain access to the show house. She smiled, and turned toward the path that would take her to the house in the forest, the house that she hoped to leave soon. As she passed through the gate and rounded the first bend, a voice from behind her hissed: 'Cat! Cat! Here, Kitty Cat!'

She swung round as they emerged from the trees. There were three of them. They were wearing stocking masks and stupid grins. Someone said, 'A little bird told me it was your birthday, Kitty Cat. Come here to us now, like a good girl, and let us give you your birthday present.'

Without pausing for thought, Cat aimed the first kick.

MIRANDA DICKINSON

Fairytale of New York

Are happy-ever-afters made in Manhattan?

Florist Rosie Duncan's life couldn't be better, she has a flourishing business on New York's Upper West Side and fantastic friends. Moving to Manhattan feels like the best decision she ever made. Even though at the time, it was her escape route from heartbreak . . . .

For the past six years Rosie has kept her heart under lock and key, despite the protests of her closest friends – the charming, commitment-phobic Ed, unlucky in love Marnie and the one-woman tornado that is Celia.

Then a blossoming friendship with publishing hot-shot Nate begins to shake Rosie's resolve at the same time as her brother arrives in the Big Apple, hiding a secret.

But a chance meeting brings Rosie face to face with her past, unravelling the mystery behind her arrival in New York. Rosie is forced to confront questions she has long been trying to ignore, including is Nate her Prince Charming? And will she ever get her very own happy-ever-after?

A sparkling, romantic comedy about a girl who finds herself in the city where dreams can come true – or so she thinks . . .

ISBN: 978-1-84756-165-7

Out now

ERIN KAYE

The Art of Friendship

Chance brought Kirsty, Clare, Janice and Patsy together fifteen years ago. But friendship has bound them. Until now . . .

Over the years, in the small Irish town of Ballyfergus, the four women have shared tears of joy and sorrow, triumphs and tragedy and countless glasses of wine. Men have come and gone, children been born and left home. Life has taken them down paths they never expected, but through it all their relationship has endured.

But all that's about to change. This year their friendship will be tested as never before as:

Widowed Kirsty falls in love with someone she shouldn't.
Patsy struggles to cope with her beloved husband's redundancy and a shocking revelation from her daughter.
Janice is forced to address ghosts from her past.
Clare takes control of her life, only to discover that her new-found independence comes at a high price.

Can the sisterhood survive the strains placed upon it and come through it unscathed? Find out in this warm, emotive tale from an Irish bestseller, perfect for fans of Cathy Kelly and Maeve Binchy.

ISBN: 978-0-00-734036-1
Out spring 2010

KATE THOMPSON

The Kinsella Sisters

Free spirit Rio Kinsella finds herself settled in the picture-postcard village of Lissamore on Ireland's West Coast. It's where she took her first step, had her first kiss and conceived her beloved son Finn. But now Finn's spread his wings and flown the nest, what's to keep her here? An old flame and a new prospect may provide the answer . . .

City girl Dervla is poles apart from her bohemian sister. A businesswoman with a quick mind, a hard heart and a nose for a good deal, she has no time for love. But is there anywhere she can really call home? And will the arrival of a new client throw her glossy magazine life-style into disarray?

Torn apart by a long-standing feud, the Kinsella sisters are reunited upon the death of their wayward father. But on clearing the family home, they discover a secret so intriguing it could change their lives forever . . .

Welcome to blissfully unpredictable Lissamore. It's guaranteed you'll never want to leave . . .

ISBN: 978-1-84756-099-5

Out now

LAURA ELLIOT

Stolen Child

Two families are torn apart by an act that will shape their futures forever . . .

When Carla Kelly and Robert Gardner marry, they seem destined for happiness. But tragedy strikes when their four-day-old baby, Isobel, is stolen. Distraught, they must cope with the media frenzy that follows at the same time as searching for their precious child.

Isobel's whereabouts remains a mystery for sixteen years. As hope of finding her fades, their marriage disintegrates. Robert moves to Australia and Carla, who had been a successful model, becomes a recluse.

Meanwhile, miles away in a small country town, Joy Nolan, unaware of her true identity, is the adored only child of Susan and David Nolan.

Home schooled and shunned away from the community, Joy is a troubled teenager. As Susan's health begins to deteriorate, will Joy ever learn the truth or will she be left without a mother? And will Carla ever be able to give up the hunt for her child?

ISBN: 978-1-84756-144-2
Out spring 2010